STOLEN KISSES

"I'm not a child, Joshua," Stacey said. "I know what I'm doing."

"I don't think so," he replied, stroking her silky golden hair with his fingertips.

She gazed at the sight of his handsome, rugged face bathed in the moonlight. "Did you like kissing me?"

"Stacey, don't . . ." his voice carried a note of warning.

She knew he didn't want her to push him further. Her lips brushed his. When he didn't respond, her kisses grew fiercer, driven by a hunger she had yet to understand. She wanted to feel Joshua's searing possessive kisses once again, before he rode out of her life forever. She didn't care about tomorrow. She only wanted today. . . .

HISTORICAL ROMANCE IN THE MAKING!

SAVAGE ECSTASY (824, $3.50)
by Janelle Taylor
It was like lightning striking, the first time the Indian brave Gray Eagle looked into the eyes of the beautiful young settler Alisha. And from the moment he saw her, he knew that he must possess her—and make her his slave!

DEFIANT ECSTASY (931, $3.50)
by Janelle Taylor
When Gray Eagle returned to Fort Pierre's gates with his hundred warriors behind him, Alisha's heart skipped a beat: would Gray Eagle destroy her—or make his destiny her own?

FORBIDDEN ECSTASY (1014, $3.50)
by Janelle Taylor
Gray Eagle had promised Alisha his heart forever—nothing could keep him from her. But when Alisha woke to find her red-skinned lover gone, she felt abandoned and alone. Lost between two worlds, desperate and fearful of betrayal, Alisha hungered for the return of her FORBIDDEN ECSTASY.

RAPTURE'S BOUNTY (1002, $3.50)
by Wanda Owen
It was a rapturous dream come true: two lovers sailing alone in the endless sea. But the peaks of passion sink to the depths of despair when Elise is kidnapped by a ruthless pirate who forces her to succumb—to his every need!

PORTRAIT OF DESIRE (1003, $3.50)
by Cassie Edwards
As Nicholas's brush stroked the lines of Jennifer's full, sensuous mouth and the curves of her soft, feminine shape, he came to feel that he was touching every part of her that he painted. Soon, lips sought lips, heart sought heart, and they came together in a wild storm of passion. . . .

Available wherever paperbacks are sold, or order direct from the Publisher. Send cover price plus 50¢ per copy for mailing and handling to Zebra Books, 475 Park Avenue South, New York, N.Y. 10016. DO NOT SEND CASH.

ECSTASY'S FURY

BY LINDA BENJAMIN

ZEBRA BOOKS
KENSINGTON PUBLISHING CORP.

ZEBRA BOOKS

are published by

KENSINGTON PUBLISHING CORP.
475 Park Avenue South
New York, N.Y. 10016

Printed in the United States of America

VIRGINIA
The Wilderness
May 6, 1864

CHAPTER ONE

"This is madness!" Stacey Hamilton stared in horror at the carnage surrounding her. "Madness!"

She closed her eyes to shut out the sight of acre upon acre of broken, bleeding bodies. But even crushing her hands against her ears could not shut out the agonized screams of the wounded, nor the stench of rotting flesh that hung cloyingly in the air. She sank to her knees, sobbing. The Battle of the Wilderness was in its second day.

"Stacey! Stacey, for God's sake, are you all right? You're not hit, are you?" A tall spare man cut a zig zag path around a half dozen lifeless bodies to reach her hunched, slender form.

The anxiety in her father's voice brought her abruptly back to reality.

"No, no, papa," she assured him quickly, struggling to her feet, absently brushing back a stray tendril of sun-colored hair. "I'm fine. Really." She grimaced at the blood that stained the lower half of her skirt. The ground was saturated with it.

Colonel Ben Hamilton hugged his only child hard against him. "You scared me half to death. When I saw you slumped over like that . . ." His voice grew stern, "Stacey, if you're going to stay with me at the field hospital—you stay in the main tent. Do you understand? The litter bearers will bring the casualties to us. You don't have to go looking for them."

She drew in a deep breath. "I was worried someone might still be alive farther out in the field. Look at them, pa." She waved an arm helplessly at the body-strewn clearing. "There must be a thousand of them, a thousand dead boys!" Her voice trembled again. "Like this one." She indicated the body lying at her feet.

She knelt again on the blood soaked grass. "He can't be more than fifteen years old," she raged, "but he'll never be sixteen." She began sobbing quietly again.

Colonel Hamilton reached down and gently pulled his daughter to her feet. Numbly, she allowed him to lead her back to the main tent of the Union field hospital one hundred yards away.

Inside, the tent surged with activity. Doctors cut, probed, sewed, and bandaged the conscious, the semi-conscious, and the blessed few unconscious. As soon as one patient was lifted off one of the seven operating tables, another was settled in his place.

"I'll get the next one," Ben Hamilton told the doctor at the table nearest him. The man acknowledged Hamilton's promise with a nod of his head, but did not take his eyes from his patient.

The colonel sat Stacey down on a rickety cane back chair and poured her a cup of brandy. He had to curl her fingers around the cup, and when she made no effort to drink it, he held the cup to her lips and forced her to take a swallow.

She sputtered, her nose wrinkling at the vile taste.

"Oh, that's awful." Reading the concern in her father's eyes, she stood up and patted his arm. "I'm fine now, papa. Honestly. Just a momentary lapse."

"I want you to get some sleep," her father said.

She started to protest, but he had that stern look she knew so well. "All right," she sighed. "If you're sure you don't need me for anything."

"I'm sure. You haven't slept in over twenty hours."

"But . . ."

"Sleep."

She stepped outside the tent, stretching her aching shoulder muscles. Her long corn silk hair fell loosely about her oval face. Her emerald green eyes, normally sparkling with life, reflected only a staggering weariness. Though just seventeen, today she felt unutterably old. Her body sagged to the trampled grass near a tent pole. She scraped together a few scraps of clean hay for a make-shift pillow and lay down. She was asleep the instant she closed her eyes.

Colonel Hamilton regarded his daughter thoughtfully, his heart aching with pride. Was it only thirty-odd days ago that she'd shown up near Alexandria in a private's uniform? He'd wanted to wring her neck.

"I'm staying, father," she'd said with suppressed vehemence. "I've read your letters, I've seen the newspapers, I've been in the hospitals, and I couldn't bear it any longer. I had to come." She'd paused, gathering up her courage. "I've been thinking about it a long time now, and I've decided. I want to be a doctor."

She'd said it as though it was the most natural choice of profession in the world for the beautiful society-bred daughter of one of Albany's most prominent families. "If Elizabeth Blackwell can do it," she said, "then, by God, so can I." Elizabeth Blackwell had been the first woman ever graduated from an American medical school nearly fifteen years earlier. "And where better to learn than at the side of one of the finest surgeons in the country, my own father."

He'd argued, cajoled, raged, swore, begged, and ultimately capitulated to her demand to stay with him. He hadn't been sorry. Her medical perception was uncanny. She had absorbed more in a month than many doctors did in a lifetime.

He remembered her as a young child always clambering after him on his rounds, hungering after scraps of his knowledge. He realized now that he'd often answered her questions just to shut her up. He shook his head, rubbing the back of his neck with his hand. She had been the most loquacious child. . . .

But if any woman could buck the odds and the flat-out prejudice to become a woman doctor, it was Stacey. As a father, he longed to shield her from the hurt that was inevitable in her quest; as a doctor he recognized her almost instinctive talent and was determined to nurture it.

She slept barely two hours. It wasn't the artillery fire that woke her, it was the lack of it. She noticed her father sitting on a wooden crate next to her.

"They've stopped murdering each other for a few minutes," she noted, getting stiffly to her feet. Even as she spoke, the firing began again.

She stared out at the Wilderness. What an apt name for it, she thought. An endless maze of scrub oak, pine, sweet gum, and cedar in the back country of Virginia. The front line of timber stood sentry-like for mile upon mile, scarcely five hundred yards from where she stood. Looking into those woods was like trying to look through a wall. She shook her head, as the sounds of battle escalated. The Union's superior numbers and extensive artillery were rendered virtually worthless by that impenetrable maze. The War Between the States, here at least, had been reduced to man against man against environment.

She'd talked to wounded soldiers, Yankee and Confederate alike, who told her of companions being burned alive when musket blasts set fire to the dry underbrush that was everywhere. The image of bodies dangling from prickly vines and chinquapin bushes flashed through her mind. With bitter irony she remembered the soldier who had died in her arms under a huge dogwood tree, heavy with spring blooms. The horror of this place would be with her all of her days.

"More wounded," she sighed, watching soldiers half-carrying, half-dragging injured comrades toward the tent. "I'll wash up and help you, pa."

"I'd prefer it, if you'd ride back to the supply train and bring back more of everything they've got," he said. Before she could protest, he added, "I know you'd rather I send someone else . . ."

"But I'm the most dispensable," she finished.

"No, you're not," he said flatly. "You're a better doctor already than several of my surgeons, but I think they'd balk at being sent for supplies."

"I'll go," she said. She patted her pocket. "It'll give me a chance to mail this letter I wrote to mother."

Ben Hamilton barked an order to a corporal to

carry the first of the newly arrived wounded into the tent. He paused before going back inside, giving his daughter a sidelong glance. "I hope you aren't telling her that I'm letting you stay with me behind the main lines. She'd kill me."

Stacey laughed, something she'd done rarely these past weeks. "Actually I told her I'm in Boston with Uncle Sam and Aunt Jenny. I'm even mailing the letter to Sam so that he can post it from Boston."

Ben Hamilton chuckled. Sam wasn't immune to Stacey's powers of persuasion either. He'd always had a high regard for his wife's brother. The man was a fine surgeon himself.

"You could have stayed in Boston and learned just as much medicine from Sam as from me," her father said. "And without having to dodge stray bullets."

"He asked me," she admitted, "but he's leaving for the New Mexico Territory in a couple of months because of Aunt Jenny's health." She shook her head sadly. "She really has the consumption bad, pa."

"Sam will do everything he can for her."

"I know. They even asked me to join them on their trip west, but I wanted to be with you."

"If anything happens to you, Stace . . ."

"I can take care of myself, pa."

"So I'm finding out," he said dryly.

"We need you in here, doctor," a voice called from inside the tent.

Hamilton jerked his head toward the voice. "Right there," he said. To Stacey he said, "Are you sure Sam will be party to your subterfuge?"

"Sam knows mother," she said, as though that settled everything. "Beatrice Curtis Hamilton is hopelessly predictable." At her father's scowl she hurried on, "Meaning that she would heartily disapprove of my being here."

"I can't say as I could fault her for that," her father said.

"But that's not all, pa," Stacey moaned, "she is also dead set on my marrying that horrid Benson boy."

"Gregory?"

"Himself."

"What's wrong with him? I seem to recall him to be a well-mannered young man."

"Oh, papa," Stacey cried, exasperated. "I should certainly hope that there is more to marriage than good manners. Not only that, but Gregory actually bought his way out of conscription." Her voice carried the disgust she felt. "You're much older, but you didn't shirk your duty. And, as appalling as all of this mayhem is, we must put the Union back together."

Ben Hamilton smiled indulgently at the fervor of the young. "I'm more interested in putting these boys' bodies back together."

"I'll get after those supplies right away," she said. "You're not completely out of anything, are you?"

"We'll manage until you get back."

He stepped back inside the tent and immediately hurried over to a writhing corporal lying unattended on the first table. Stacey had been right earlier. It was madness. The boy would lose both of his legs.

Stacey fingered the dried blood on the skirt she was wearing. Odd, how it didn't seem to horrify her any more. If she was going to ride a horse, though, she intended to be comfortable. Hurrying inside the tent, she snatched up the wrapped parcel she carried with her everywhere. She unfastened her skirt and wriggled out of it, then pulled her blouse over her head. Clad only in her chemise, she ripped open the parcel and shook out her freshly laundered private's uniform.

"Stacey, for heaven's sake," her father snapped, glancing up from the operating table and noting her state of undress. "Even though these men are wounded, they're still men, and they've been without a woman a long time. And the litter bearers are not wounded."

She flushed as his meaning came clear to her. "I'm sorry, pa. I didn't think." Swiftly she donned the uniform, stuffing her long blonde hair under the cap on her head. She transferred her mother's letter to her trouser pocket.

"That's better," her father growled. "Now you be careful out there."

"Yes, sir."

She hurried out of the tent, tucking in her shirttail as she went. Spying an unattended horse, she gathered up the trailing reins and scrambled onto its back. No doubt the officer who owned the animal would be outraged, but she wasn't about to walk the three miles for supplies.

She kicked the horse into an easy canter. She'd gone nearly two miles, when she noticed the silence. She reined the horse to a halt. It wasn't the sporadic lull of battle. It was heavy, ominous. She gigged the horse into a gallop.

She swore later she could feel the heat of the artillery shell as it whistled past her head. It exploded forty feet to her left, sending shards of metal and dirt flying in all directions.

The horse screamed in terror and pain, as a fragment struck its hindquarters. The animal bolted into a dead run.

Stacey was an expert horsewoman, but she was no match for the terrified gelding. She sawed back on the reins, shouting whoa, but the horse's pace did not slacken. She stared in horror as the distance between her and the solid mass of trees ahead disappeared under the ground-devouring strides of the runaway horse. The animal would tear headlong into the brush-choked forest. Any low hanging branch could break her neck. Leaping off the horse at this speed merely offered an alternative form of suicide.

Using every ounce of strength she possessed, she hauled back on one side of the reins, trying desperately to turn the horse's head. It was hopeless. The gelding was too strong, too scared. She did the only thing she could do. The trees were less than thirty yards away. She pressed forward, clinging low to the horse's neck, closed her eyes and prayed.

The horse began to slow. For a moment she was reverentially aware of the power of prayer, then she opened her eyes to see that a strong, tanned hand had seized the reins, veering the horse brutally to the right. The horseman held on as both Stacey's mount and his swept past the line of trees, hanging to a parallel course as branches clawed out on her left, the nearest just inches away.

They plunged on for another half mile, the closeness of thundering hooves drowning out the sound of battle, before Stacey's mount finally relinquished the bit from sheer exhaustion. Only then did the horseman release his grip on her reins. Stacey brought the animal to a trembling halt. The other rider eased past her a few yards, then turned his horse and loped back.

"You'd better get youself less horse, private," a hard voice grated. "If you can't handle an animal, don't ride it.'

She rankled at the man's imperious tone, but bit back the retort that was on her lips when she looked up and encountered her rescuer's steady gaze for the first time. He wore the blue uniform of a Union Cavalry officer, the gold bars on his shoulders giving him the rank of captain. He was roguishly handsome with well-chiseled features and dark hair that curled slightly at the nape of his neck. But it was the look of flinty hardness in his wolf-gray eyes that left Stacey uncharacteristically tongue-tied.

The captain removed his hat, impatiently running a hand through this thick hair. "Have you lost your tongue, boy? Where's your unit?" His eyes narrowed suspiciously. "And what is an infantry private doing on a horse?"

Stacey gaped at the infantry insignia on the buttons of her borrowed uniform. She knew, too, that the lighter blue trim running up the outer seam of her trousers would have been yellow for a cavalryman, as it, in fact, was on the captain's trousers. Obviously, he had not yet noticed she was female. She had her cap perched low over her eyes, the blue bandana around her neck hiding her slender throat. Her face must be a grimy mess from the wild ride, and her gloves hid her distinctly feminine hands. What would he do when he found out?

"Are you going to answer me, private?" he

demanded, his bay horse prancing nervously forward, as if it wanted to continue the race. The man patted the animal's neck and swung down from the saddle. He let the reins trail, ground tying the horse. In two strides he was standing next to her right stirrup.

"Get off the horse, soldier," he growled. "Unless I'm mistaken, I've got a deserter on my hands."

"You most certainly have not!"

His head jerked up, his eyes staring at her. "What the hell? . . . ." He seized her around the waist and dragged her from the saddle. He yanked the cap off her head, sending her long blonde hair cascading down around her shoulders.

He gripped her upper arms savagely, his gray eyes almost black with anger. For a wild moment she thought he meant to harm her, but he only pushed her toward a narrow opening in the trees. Artillery fire rumbled to the east.

"Get in there," he said.

He gathered up the reins of both horses and pulled the animals in after them.

Stacey stumbled over the heavy undergrowth, but he made no move to help her. She forged ahead for several more yards, brushing aside low hanging branches. She halted before an impassable mass of chinquapin bushes, whirling to face him.

"You have no right," she sputtered.

"On the contrary," he interrupted easily, seizing her right wrist, "I'm a captain, you're a private. I have every right." She saw that he was mocking her. "So, let's hear your story. And, it had better be good."

She took an involuntary step backward at the menace in his eyes, but was held fast by his iron grip on her arm. Why was he so angry with her? "You will unhand me at once," she commanded, though her voice shook. She had stood up to artillery fire, blood up to her ankles, soldiers dying in her arms, but this cavalry officer with his piercing gray eyes and his rigid jaw had her quaking in her boots.

"You will answer me, girl. What are you doing in the middle of a war?"

"I'm here with my father," she retorted, some of her courage returning. She guessed his anger stemmed mostly out of fear for her safety.

"On a picnic no doubt."

"Hardly! My father is Colonel Hamilton."

"Ben Hamilton?"

She nodded. Incredibly, she saw a glint of amusement come into his eyes. "So you're Stacey," he observed dryly, as if he had at sometime been regaled of her outrageous exploits and dismissed them as utter fantasy.

"I'm Eustacia Hamilton," she acknowledged, stiffening. "And I'll thank you to let me go this instant."

To her surprise he did so. Side-stepping an uprooted oak tree, he ambled over to a huge cedar. He slanted a look back over his shoulder. "I thought you were something a couple of my troops made up to relieve the horrors of war." He turned toward her, his eyes raking over her body with ill-concealed scorn. "I can see they've more than slightly exaggerated your feminine attributes."

Her cheeks burned. How dare he? But for the first time she was painfully aware of how shapeless and drab the uniform made her look. Its anonymity had been its major asset when she had begun her journey to join her father. No one had suspected her sex, especially since she had bound her breasts tightly with a wrap-around bandage. But they were not bound today and she thought that their fullness should have been obvious to him. Her pride was stung because apparently they were not.

"My feminine attributes or lack of them are absolutely none of your concern," she snapped. "Now if you're quite finished, I'll be on my way." She collected the reins to her horse.

He made no move to stop her. "You know," he drawled softly, "where I come from, it's customary to at least thank a person for saving one's life."

She closed her eyes, fighting down the unreasonable irritation this man provoked in her. He was right. He had saved her life. And she had behaved badly. She turned to face him.

"I do thank you, Captain. . . ?"

"Steele. Joshua Steele." He clicked his heels together and inclined his head toward her. "Lately under Major-General Winfield Scott Hancock, but now, unfortunately," he patted the leather pouch attached to his belt, "summoned to Washington for some secret skullduggery."

She smiled at his deliberately pompous introduction and was rewarded with a smile in return. It transformed his hard, chiseled face, giving him an almost boyish appearance, though she guessed his age at nearly thirty.

"Not dangerous skullduggery, I hope," she said.

But he ignored her question and countered with one of his own. "Is it really true that an infantry colonel commandeered you on your way to join your father and ordered you to take a dispatch to General Grant, and that neither of those illustrious military men saw through your disguise?"

Stacey cringed at the memory. She had nearly died when she'd entered Grant's tent. He was in the process of getting dressed and was clad in only the lower half of his long johns. She had thrust the dispatch in his hands, saluted, and fled. Whatever had been in the dispatch had evidently been important enough that the burly commander didn't take time to reflect on the fleeing private's decidedly unmilitary behavior.

"Just another exaggerated exploit," she managed to choke out.

His gaze became thoughtful, his expression unreadable. "Where exactly were you going at such breakneck speed just now, Miss Hamilton?"

"I was headed for the supply wagons," she said, pulling off her gloves and stuffing them under her belt. "My father is in need of several medicines and bandages." She knew she should be about her task, too, but for some reason she refused to examine the fact that she did not want to leave this man's company just yet.

Captain Steele was shaking his head. "You're a very lucky girl. I had just checked in at supply myself. That's where I picked up this dispatch. If these orders hadn't been there, I would have been heading in the opposite direction to rejoin my command. And you would be adorning one of these trees."

She shivered. "I am very grateful, Captain Steele. I didn't mean to seem that I was not."

Steele sank down against the cedar tree, stretching

his long legs in front of him. "Spare a couple of minutes for a lonely soldier, long denied the pleasure of female companionship?" He spread his left hand palm upward, indicating that he wanted her to sit beside him.

She hesitated. "I thought my feminine attributes had been greatly exaggerated," she teased, as she tried vainly to primp up the hopelessly shapeless uniform.

He laughed, and she was warmed by the sound of it.

"I may have spoken too hastily," he admitted, his eyes devouring what curves were visible, as she planted her hands on her hips.

She thought she should have been outraged by his bold scrutiny; instead she felt unaccountably pleased. She crunched across the dense undergrowth and sat down beside him. Nervously, she picked up a twig and twirled it between her thumb and forefinger. Not enough light reached the ground in the Wilderness, and after the trees leafed out much of the ground cover died. It was easy to see why so many fires broke out.

"What makes a child, a girl child no less, want to join her father in a war zone?"

The twig snapped. "I'm not a child," she protested. "I'm seventeen."

"My mistake," he said dryly. Then more seriously, "Why are you here, Stacey?"

She liked the sound of her name on his lips. Such full, passionate lips. She blushed hotly. "It'd been more than three years since I'd seen my father," she hedged.

"That's not a good enough reason to descend into hell."

She sensed his abhorrence at the killing and felt a kinship with him. Perhaps he could understand her desire to be a doctor—to save lives.

"I've pestered my father about medicine for as long as I can remember," she began. "Naturally, when the wounded started coming home, I volunteered to work in the hospital in Albany. That's where I grew up. Well, my mother was impossible. She'd never heard of anything so unladylike in her life. Nursing to her is on a par with a servant. The Hamiltons do not serve, they are served." She smiled ruefully. "Mother had an extremely sheltered unbringing, so it's not totally her fault. When I'd sneak out to work at the hospital, she would alternate between attacks of the vapors and threatening to send me abroad."

"So you ran away from home?"

"Sort of," she admitted. "I told her I was going to visit relatives in Boston. And I did for awhile, but only long enough to convince my Uncle Sam to go along with my plan to help me to get to my father. Heaven knows what mother would do, if she knew where I am now."

"You could have stayed at the hospital in Albany, or in Boston for that matter. Why didn't you?"

His interest was genuine, and she felt childishly pleased talking to him. "Because the doctors in Albany and Boston weren't much more cooperative than my mother. They had the traditional male attitude toward women in medicine." She said it without rancor, more as though she felt sorry for their ignorance. "So I resolved then and there that if my dream was to be realized, I would need my father's help."

"Your dream?"

"To be a doctor."

She shot him a quick glance, but there was no shock, no contempt, no disgust in his eyes—only a mild surprise. He shifted his position, bringing up one knee and resting his arm on top of it. The war seemed a thousand miles away.

"Ben Hamilton's one of the best," he acknowledged. "If you have half his skill, you'll be a better doctor than most men ever achieve."

"You've met my father?"

"Unfortunately, no. But his reputation among the troops is awesome."

Stacey smiled. "He is good, so very good. He believes in the discoveries of Semmelweiss and Pasteur—about the need for cleanliness during surgery. It's all so fascinating." She paused. "But so often he fights a losing battle. Even his subordinates frequently flaunt his rules. When he's not looking, they . . ." Her voice had grown fierce. "I'm sorry."

"Fot what? Loving your father? I like the way those green eyes of yours flash when you're angry."

She was suddenly conscious of his nearness, his sheer maleness. She'd never been in such a situation before. Trying to calm herself, she asked, "And what about you? Were you always a soldier?"

He laughed. "Actually I'd just finished panning for gold in the Colorado Territory when the war broke out. I believe in the Union, so I came back."

"Did you find gold?"

"No, something infinitely better." He spoke slower, his voice fused with passion. "I found a mountain lake, where just before dawn the silence is absolute. And the beauty: my God, Stacey, there are no words for it."

She didn't need words, she could see it in his eyes "You're going back after the war?"

His eyes clouded, as if just for a moment it occurred to him that he might never see it again. Then he grinned. "I'll go back. It's mine now. I own it. As much as any man can ever own something like that. I've got a couple of Indian friends and an old mountain coot looking after things until I get back."

"I've always wanted to go west," she said, "but my mother said it's for heathens."

"If this war is an example of God-fearing people in action, I'll take heathens any time."

She shuddered at the unbidden memory of blood-soaked fields. "Amen," she whispered.

She couldn't say how he managed it, but suddenly his arms were around her. He pulled her against him, crushing her against his hard chest. His lips claimed her lips, gently at first, then, when he found no resistance, harder, more demanding.

She moaned deep in her throat as emotions new to her vied for command of her senses. She felt as though she were floating. Gregory Benson had kissed her once, but it had been nothing at all like this.

His hands entwined themselves in her hair as he kissed her cheeks, her chin, her neck. When his lips found hers again, she opened her mouth to gasp and felt his tongue invade her mouth, sending shivers of excitement coursing through her body. She was being enveloped by a sweetness she had never dreamed existed.

"Joshua." She breathed his name, her arms instinctively going around his neck.

When his hand slid under her uniform blouse and

cupped her breast, she thought she would faint from the shattering pleasure. His knowing fingers teased her nipple beneath the thin fabric of her chemise. She arched against him, feeling her breast swell with desire. Her body burned for a fulfillment she did not understand.

He loosened her bandana and slipped it off of her neck. He undid the first two buttons of her blouse, nuzzling his face against her throat, letting his tongue trail to the valley between her breasts. As the insatiably curious daughter of a doctor, she recognized his arousal for what it was when his body pressed against her thigh. Even so, it startled her, for up to this moment she had had only her imagination to conjure up what took place between a man and a woman. The reality far surpassed her fantasies.

He was whispering sweet, sweet words in her ear. Reality was slipping away. She wanted to give him anything he asked and more, if only he would bring an end to this nameless torment.

From somewhere behind her her horse snorted impatiently. She opened her eyes. The trees, the sky, the din of musket fire no longer so far away—all snapped back into place. She began struggling, and he did not protest when she pushed herself away from him.

Embarrassed, she quickly re-arranged her uniform. She dared a glance at Steele. His breathing was ragged, his gray eyes dark with desire. He sucked in a deep breath and released it before he spoke, "I honestly didn't mean for that to get out of hand."

She believed him. And that she had so obviously aroused him in spite of her inexperience was a source of considerable pleasure to her. She took a few steadying breaths, still marvelling at the pounding of her heart. Surely he must hear it too?

"I'd better be getting those supplies," she said.

He stood up and helped her to her feet. He held the reins of her horse, but before he let her mount he cupped her chin in his large hand and said, "You may not believe this, Stacey, but I've never enjoyed a kiss more. If you can kiss like that at seventeen, heaven help the man you marry. He'll never be able to let you out of his bed."

She stifled an impulse to protest the bluntness of his remarks. But in truth, she was not at all angry. She was suddenly, achingly sad. The thought of never seeing this man again—this man she had met scarcely twenty minutes ago—assailed her like a physical pain.

Tears stung her eyes. He did not take his hand away from her chin, but shifted it slightly to stroke her cheek with his thumb. She closed her eyes, allowing a single tear to escape down the side of her face.

"The world's not so big, green eyes," he soothed, as though comforting a child. "Maybe we'll meet again one day."

His lips brushed hers. He meant it to be a good-bye gesture, a thank you for solace in the midst of chaos. Instead, as before, the kiss sent liquid fire raging through his veins, and he again plundered her mouth with his own.

They were both a little unsteady when they parted. She reached up and gently stroked the side of his face. He gripped her hand in his, kissing her palm before setting her away from him.

"My God, I envy that future husband of yours," he

muttered hoarsely. The rumble of war edging ever closer drowned out his softly spoken words.

"What did you say?" Stacey asked.

"Nothing, I . . ."

A bullet slammed into the tree directly behind them, bare inches above Stacey's head.

CHAPTER TWO

Joshua drove Stacey hard to the right, forcing her to the ground behind a fallen tree.

"Don't move!" he hissed, keeping his body between hers and the direction from which the bullet had come. In the same motion he unhooked the flap of the holster on his hip and dragged out his long-barreled Army Colt.

The rotting hulk of the uprooted oak tree provided cover only as long as they lay flattened behind it. When Steele dared peer over it, trying to get a fix on their attacker's location, his head proved too tempting a target. A bullet gouged a fist-sized hole in the decaying carcass of the tree, spraying splinters in all directions.

Steele cursed feelingly when one of the splinters traced a painful path across his right cheek. He ducked behind the log once again, wiping brusquely at the blood on his face.

"You're hurt!" Stacey cried.

He ignored the observation, saying, "From the sounds of that musket fire to the east our lone johnny reb may soon be joined by his fellow troopers."

"Maybe they were just stray bullets," Stacey offered hopefully.

"One, I might believe," Steele said. "But both of them came too painfully close to this blue uniform of mine to be an accident."

"What are we going to do?" Stacey couldn't keep a trace of fear out of her voice. Less than five yards separated them from their horses, yet they weren't close enough to risk a run for it. Running wasn't even a possibility in this tangle of trailing vines and scrub timber. At least their adversary had to contend with the same disadvantages.

"I'm going to get you out of here," Steele said.

She guessed he tried to put more confidence in his voice than he actually felt.

"Maybe those are Union troops heading this way," she said.

"In this jungle it may not matter," Joshua mused, glancing around them. "There's nowhere you can stand and see twenty yards in any direction. The smoke from twenty thousand muskets won't help them any. They might as well be fighting blind."

Stacey could see the truth in his words for herself. The bulk of the fighting was perhaps no more than a thousand yards to their left, yet for all she could actually see the two armies might as well have been battling on the moon. It was a war of sound. A war with an enemy who could not be seen, but whose bullet could end your life just as quickly by fluke as by design.

They lay still behind the fallen tree for several minutes, minutes that seemed like hours to Stacey. Yet even in this perilous situation, she could not totally dismiss the pounding of her heart to the presence of their unseen foe. This man beside her,

Captain Joshua Steele, had awakened feelings entirely new to her experience. She remembered with blushing clarity how his kisses had created a blissful weakness in her limbs. And there was another emotion as well, a nameless ache in the pit of her stomach and lower, which had flamed inside her when his lips had burned into her breasts.

She watched him covertly, as he shifted his body sideways, seeking a better vantage point from which to defend their position. What were his thoughts now? Had the kiss meant as much to him as it had to her? Or was she merely being a foolish young girl, creating fantasies that would probably make this man of obvious experience laugh out loud at her adolescent silliness?

His strong features betrayed no fear, only a kind of tense wariness coupled with a suppressed excitement, as if he enjoyed this part of combat at least—a contest of wills, a battle of wits between predator and prey. If there was any sign of strain in him, she knew, it was because of his sense of responsibility for her safety.

When more minutes dragged by with no further shots fired in their direction, Steele decided to risk another look. He crawled forward on his belly until he reached the gnarled mass of twisted roots at the end of the fallen tree. Here he could crouch comfortably without exposing himself as a target.

"Be careful," Stacey breathed to herself. She thought of the wounded soldiers she had seen these past few months—both on the battlefield and in the hospitals. All of them in their way had been important to her. Even so, the sheer volume of death and mutilation had forced her to erect a kind of emotional barrier around herself, which prevented her, for the most part, from feeling each man's pain personally. If she hadn't, she feared she would go mad. Suddenly, somehow, this man was different. She couldn't have said why, but she knew she couldn't bear the thought of Joshua's being hurt.

Steele surveyed the scene in front of him. He detected no signs of movement in the morass of vegetation. He supposed the soldier could have fallen back to try to rejoin his unit, but for some reason he didn't think so.

He suddenly had an uneasy feeling about the whole affair. The main fighting force was nearly three-quarters of a mile to the east. Some stragglers were inevitable in this jungle, but he doubted a single soldier could be this far afield by accident. Surely, the man could gauge the direction of the main assault. Then why wasn't he closer to it? Or at least heading toward it? Steele had the disquieting feeling that the soldier had not been heading into the Wilderness, but out of it. Was the man truly lost? Or was he a deserter?

A deserter could prove a much more dangerous enemy than any regular Confederate foot soldier. The man would be prepared to shoot anything that moved, regardless of the color of a man's uniform. In fact, if the man was a runaway, he could just as well be from Grant's Army of the Potomac, shooting scared at an officer he feared barred his path to freedom.

"Do you see anything?" Stacey whispered.

Joshua did not turn around, but held up his left hand indicating he wanted her to keep silent. He flexed the fingers of his right hand, getting a more comfortable grip on the heavy Colt. The racket of thousands of guns being fired to the east could easily muffle the sounds of a single man's footsteps, even on ground smothered with dry underbrush and matted duff.

His ears strained the thicket surrounding them. Had the soldier merely pinned them down long enough to make good his escape? Or did he intend to make certain there were no witnesses to his cowardice?

"I'm going to try to make it to the horses," Steele said at last.

"No!" Stacey blurted involuntarily. "I mean, what if he's still out there. He'll kill you!"

"We can't spend the day here," Steele answered reasonably. "That assualt is steadily moving this way. Either we fight it out with one man, or we'll have twenty thousand soldiers taking his place in the next few hours."

Stacey shuddered. If she had hoped the two earlier bullets had been strays, she recognized the deadly inevitability of thousands of bullets screaming through this section of the woods before the day was over. She prayed her father hadn't yet become concerned by her absence. The battle's newly wounded would give him enough to worry about.

"All right," Stacey said, trying to stay calm. "But, please, Joshua, be careful."

It may have been the added softness of her voice when she said his name, but whatever it was he shot her a curious glance. A smile tugged at one corner of his mouth. "Don't worry, green eyes," he said, "I fully intend to get both of us out of this alive."

Stacey kept her eyes on the ground. She lay on her

stomach, absently crumbling a dead leaf with her fingers. "If it weren't for me, you wouldn't be in this predicament."

She heard him twist around in his crouched position. She felt his eyes regarding her, but still she did not look up. Her heart beat faster. How could this man—this stranger—create such havoc with her feelings?

What if he guessed the direction of her shameful thoughts? How her body even now in the face of very real danger longed to feel his burning touch once again? No, this could not be happening to her!

His fingers gently touched the tip of her chin. He tilted her head back. His gray eyes were soft, warm. The tears she had held at bay so long spilled freely down her cheeks.

"Oh, Joshua, I'm so sorry," she cried, scrambling to her knees.

He tried belatedly to restrain her, to prevent her from rising, but she knew suddenly that his need would match her own. To be held again in those strong, protective arms was all that mattered in the world right now. She pressed herself hard against his chest, revelling in the musky male scent of him, as she nuzzled against his neck.

He sucked in his breath, bringing his left hand up to cradle her head. In his right he still held the cocked .44.

"Kiss me, Joshua," she murmured.

"Stacey, this is insane," he said thickly. "It's too dangerous. I have to get to the horses and get us out of here." Even so, his lips brushed against her forehead. He marvelled again at the ease with which this fiery girl-woman could arouse him.

"The soldier is gone," she persisted. "Or he would have shot at us again by now. The armies won't be here for awhile. Please, Joshua, this war is what's insane. Being with you is the first time I've been able to think about anything but death for months." Later she would wonder at her boldness, berating herself for behaving in such a shameless manner. Now nothing else mattered. Her mouth found his, the sweet mingling of their lips sending a joyous weakness through every fiber of her being.

A warning bell sounded in Steele's mind, but he ignored it. The soldier probably was gone. He uncocked the Colt and lay it on the ground beside him. He would still be on his guard, he told himself, as he wrapped his arms around her. His lips possessed her with an urgency that sent a fever through his blood. What was it about this green-eyed vixen that seemed to rob him of his common sense? Surrounded by war, he sought the blissful haven of her embrace.

Stacey had never known such rapturous delight. As Joshua's hands began a slow, torturous exploration of her body, a whimpering moan escaped her lips. A mindless euphoria settled over her. This was reality. The war did not exist. He unbuttoned the first two buttons of her shirt, pushing the material roughly off her right shoulder. His kisses trailed along her throat, across her bare shoulder and back toward the trembling, chemise-covered softness of her breasts.

"Now ain't that a purty sight?" a leering voice laughed.

Joshua grabbed for his gun and whirled, shoving Stacey violently away from him. But he never brought the gun to bear. He was staring into the bore of a

Springfield rifle, bayonet in place on its muzzle. He lowered the gun to his side, self-disgust rivaling a growing inner fury. This would never have happened, he knew, if he hadn't allowed himself to be distracted by Stacey. His inexcusable carelessness had now put her life in deadly jeopardy.

"Drop it!" the man ordered.

Steele let go of the weapon.

"You're a Yankee private," Stacey said wonderingly. She fumbled with the buttons of her shirt, as she climbed unsteadily to her feet. She stared at the soldier, who kept his gun pointed at Joshua.

The man was hatless. His dark blue uniform shirt was stained and ragged looking. The overly-large trousers he wore hung loosely on his bony frame. His black, scraggly beard did little to disguise the hard angles of his face.

"Why did you shoot at us?" she demanded. "We're on the same side."

"Private Hector Caulfield ain't on nobody's side, missy," the soldier sneered. "Not no more." He grinned, revealing a mouth only half full of near black teeth.

"He's a deserter," Steele said quietly.

Stacey gasped, expecting the man to deny the accusation with righteous indignation. When he did not she realized the chilling truth of Joshua's remark. Why else would Caulfield have tried to ambush a superior officer?

"You tried to kill us!" Stacey accused.

"Actually, missy, I was jes' hopin' you'd cut 'n run. I wanted me one o' them mounts yonder." He indicated their horses with a wave of his hand. "Figure I'd make a lot better time that way. 'Course," he paused meaningfully, "that was afore I know'd one of you was a woman." He cast an insolent gaze along the soft curves of Stacey's body.

Unconsciously, she pulled the open neck of her shirt closer together.

"I suggest you let the girl go," Steele said.

The ring of authority mixed with cold anger in Joshua's voice amazed Stacey, in light of the fact that Caulfield still held his gun levelled at Steele's stomach.

"You take me fer a fool, cap'n?" the man snorted. "She'd jes' run fer help."

"There's no one she could bring back here before our business together would be finished, Caulfield," Joshua said.

Stacey guessed Joshua meant that the man would have plenty of time to kill him. Her knees almost buckled. This was all her fault! All of it! If she hadn't lost control of her horse . . . But even so, they had been safe enough. Joshua had been on his guard until she had so disgracefully thrown herself at him. What in the world had possessed her? She had never even thought of being so bold with a man. Yet the intoxicating effect of Joshua's kisses had been her undoing. Before the sun set it might even get them both killed.

CHAPTER THREE

"Caulfield, take the horses and get the hell out of here," Steele snapped.

"Why, cap'n," the private sneered, "I do believe you're gettin' riled. Could be you got an idea what I'm plannin' fer your lady friend?"

Stacey's skin crawled. Joshua's hands balled into fists, though they remained stiffly at his sides. His gray eyes narrowed with barely controlled rage.

"I should jes' gut shoot ya," Caulfield said, "like I did my lieutenant back on the line. But I don't want you to miss all the fun."

"You shot your commanding officer?" Stacey cried.

Caulfield shrugged. "I told him I quit. Didn't want to soldier no more. He didn't like the idea. Wasn't much else I could do."

"You murdered a man and speak of it as though you had a perfect right . . ."

"Shut up, missy," Caulfield warned. "I don't take no lip from no woman. That bastard lieutenant woulda had me court-martialed and hanged."

Stacey would not be silent. "You agreed to be a part of this war when you put on that uniform."

Caulfield laughed. It was not a pleasant sound. "Some dandy in Ohio gimme fifty greenbacks to take

37

his place in the conscription. I didn't mind soldierin' at first, but fightin' in this briar patch is pure crazy."

"You can't just quit the army," Stacey went on stubbornly.

"That's what Lieutenant Williams tried to tell me. So I put my pistol in his belly and told him I was leavin' anyways. Damn fool said I was under arrest, started hollerin' for the sergeant. So I killed him."

Stacey could scarcely believe the matter-of-fact way Caulfield spoke of cold-blooded murder. "Someone must have seen you," she said. "They'll catch you and arrest you for murder and desertion."

"Ain't nobody gonna catch ol' Hector Caulfield, missy. Hell, I been dodgin' the law since I was ten years old. Why'd you think I joined the Army in the first place? Wasn't only the fifty greenbacks I'll tell ya."

The rumble of musket fire to the east seemed to have levelled off. Neither army had gotten any closer to them in the last half hour. Stacey trembled. There was little hope that the battle would interrupt Caulfield's plans for them.

The deserter stepped closer to Stacey, though his eyes remained on Steele. "Missy," he said, "I want you to go and fetch the piggin' strings that're holdin' the cap'n's bedroll to his saddle."

Stacey didn't move.

Enraged, the private lurched forward, seized her upper arm and shoved her toward the two horses five yards away. Stacey stumbled, but recovered in time to keep from falling. Caulfield kept Steele in his line of sight at all times, "Move one inch," he warned, "and I'll kill her."

When they were within a few feet of the horses, Caulfield released her. "Next time I tell you to do something, I won't be so polite."

"Touch her again, you son-of-a-bitch, and it'll be the last thing you ever do," Steele grated.

Caulfield glared at the Union officer. "I don't think so, cap'n."

"Take the horses and go, Caulfield," Steele repeated. "Neither of us could possibly follow."

"You can be sure of that, cap'n," said Caulfield. "Neither one of you is going to be followin' nobody." He chuckled malevolently.

Stacey's fingers trembled as she untied the rawhide strings that secured Joshua's bedroll to his saddle. Even when artillery shells had exploded within ten yards of the hospital tent where she had been working with her father, she hadn't been as frightened as she was now. Hector Caulfield was an evil of a different sort. The shells were impersonal. But Caulfield could murder another human being while looking him straight in the face.

"Hurry up, girl," the deserter growled, when Stacey had taken too long at her task.

Stacey loosed the last thong and stepped back toward Caulfield. She stopped several paces away from him and held out the pieces of rawhide in his direction.

"Oh, no, missy," Caulfield said. "I ain't goin' near that hombre cap'n of yours. He's a mean one. You kin see it in them wolf eyes. He'd like to gut me where I stand." Caulfield cackled, amused in some bizarre way by the look of raw hate in Steele's eyes. "You tie him, missy. And do a good job, 'cause I'll be checkin' it afterwards. God help you if it ain't tight."

Shaking from head to foot, Stacey walked over to Joshua. "I'm so sorry," she whispered.

Wordlessly, he clasped his hands together and held them out in front of him. His eyes never left Caulfield.

Stacey started to wrap the rawhide strings around Joshua's wrists.

"Oh, no, you don't," Caulfield interrupted. "You tie them hands behind his back, missy. I don't want him havin' no chance to use them fists as a club."

Steele jerked his hands apart and handed the rawhide back to Stacey. The tenseness in his lean, hard body was palpable. She ached for some kind of reassurance from him. His silence was unnerving. Yet realistically she knew there was nothing he could say. Nothing he could do.

Steele put his hand behind his back. Caulfield stepped nearer to watch Stacey bind them together. She tried to make it snug, knowing the man would not be fooled by anything less, but at the same time she didn't want to cut into Joshua's circulation.

"Tighter!" Caulfield seethed, coming up beside her. He was too intent on Stacey's actions to notice that Steele had shifted his balance slightly, waiting for any opening the deserter might give him.

"Any tighter and it would cut into his wrists," Stacey said.

Caulfield backhanded her across the face. Stacey cried out in surprise and pain.

Joshua launched himself at Caulfield, catching the private squarely in the chest with his shoulder. Caulfield fell heavily, the air exploding from his lungs.

"Stacey, get his rifle!" Steele shouted, scrambling to

his feet. With his hands lashed behind his back, he attempted to boot Caulfield in the jaw.

The private saw it coming and at the last instant avoided the brunt of the blow by rolling quickly to his right. He rolled back, catching the awkwardly balanced Steele by his upraised boot. He twisted the leg violently. Steele fell hard, unable to brace himself because of his bound hands.

Caulfield was on his feet like a cat, dragging his pistol from its holster. He aimed it at Steele, who had not yet gained his feet.

"No!" Stacey screamed. "Drop it! Now!"

Caulfield whirled, glaring at Stacey. She held his rifle leveled at his mid-section.

"I said drop it," she repeated.

Caulfield dropped the pistol.

"Now untie him."

"Would you really shoot me, missy?" Caulfield asked, taking a step toward her. Scarcely three yards separated them.

She steadied the heavy weapon against her body with her left hand and cocked it with her right. "I said untie him."

Caulfield made no move to do so.

"If he takes another step, shoot him," Joshua warned, climbing to his feet.

"I bet you never shot nothin' in your life, missy," Caulfield said. "Not even a jackrabbit." He took another step toward her.

Stacey swallowed hard. Her finger was on the trigger, but Caulfield was right. She had never aimed a gun at a living thing. The only time she'd ever even shot one was seven years ago on a dare by a male

41

classmate. She'd put a hole in the ceiling of her father's study. It was the only time her father had ever physically punished her. The fear in his eyes when he'd bolted into the room and seen the gun in her hands had haunted her long after the pain from the spanking subsided. She'd had no inclination to touch a gun since. That her life might now depend on the one in her hands sickened her. How could she kill a human being? She wanted to be a doctor, to save lives.

She didn't dare let Caulfield see how right he was. She brought the weapon up to her shoulder. "I don't think even I could miss at this distance, private," she said.

Caulfield hesitated.

Joshua edged over to Stacey. "Take the bayonet off the end of the musket and cut this rawhide." His eyes never left the deserter.

Stacey lowered the weapon enough to disengage the bayonet. She gripped the knife-like instrument solidly in her left hand, but let Joshua work the thongs across it, rather than risk a glance downward. She balanced the gun along her hip with her other hand.

"I really don't think you're going to shoot me, missy," Caulfield said. The captain was almost free. If he didn't try for freedom now, he never could. He dove for the pistol he had thrown to the ground.

Stacey gasped in surprise. She dropped the bayonet, swinging the rifle instinctively to follow Caulfield's motion.

Steele jerked his hands free with a final mighty effort. He was too late.

In that frozen instant of time Stacey would know for the rest of her days that if she had pulled the trigger on Caulfield's rifle, she could have prevented all that followed. But she hesitated at the thought of killing, when Caulfield did not. The gun bucked in Caulfield's hand.

As Joshua lunged toward the deserter, it was as though he struck a wall. His head snapped back. He fell heavily without a sound and lay motionless, blood streaming from the left side of his head to form a murky pool in the dead vegetation.

"Joshua!"

Stacey screamed his name over and over again, not noticing when Caulfield yanked his rifle from her grasp. It wasn't until he slapped her face, that reality re-asserted itself. Her medical instincts took over. She avoided Caulfield's grasping hand and rushed to kneel beside Joshua.

He was so still and there was so much blood. All she wanted to do was cry. But she couldn't afford that luxury. She untied the yellow bandana around Steele's neck, wishing to heaven she had something cleaner. She daubed at the wound, reminding herself that it was a head injury and even a minor cut could bleed profusely.

Before she could finish her examination, Caulfield gripped her left arm and dragged her painfully to her feet.

"Please, he's hurt," she cried. She looked into Caulfield's cold, lizard eyes and suppressed an involuntary shudder.

"He ain't hurt, missy," Caulfield said. "He's dead. Or he will be real soon. He's bleedin' like a throat-sliced steer."

The deserter grinned at her with teeth so decayed

and breath so foul, that it was all Stacey could do to keep from retching.

"I'm a doctor. I could save his life," she pleaded.

"You ain't no doctor, girlie," Caulfield snarled. "What do you think I am? Stupid? And even if you was a doctor, you still wouldn't be doin' no doctorin' on the cap'n. I got other plans for me and you."

He reached up and dug his fingers cruelly into the shirt-covered flesh of her left breast. Stacey jerked back violently, nearly falling over a tangle of vines. "No," she whispered. "In the name of God, no!"

"Now don't go gettin' uppity," Caulfield said, suddenly angry. "I seen you an' the cap'n kissin' and touchin' and all afore I drew down on him. That's what give me the idea not to take the horses right off. I wanted me a taste of what the cap'n was gettin'."

Stacey took a backward step, a nearly hysterical sob tearing from her throat. Her senses reeled. She would rather die than have this pig of a man touch her again. She stared at Joshua, willing him to wake up, to save her from this nightmare. But he remained still and ominously silent, not uttering so much as a moan. Dear God, what if he were dead!

"Come on now, missy," Caulfield said, "it ain't gonna be so bad." He pulled her against him.

Stacey screamed, pounding at him with her fists, scratching, kicking. Caulfield lost his balance. In trying to steady himself he let go of her. In that instant Stacey turned and ran blindly in the opposite direction. Branches whipped at her, twigs caught her hair, roots and creepers tore at her clothes, but still she plunged forward. She ran until she thought her lungs would burst.

Tears streamed down her face. Her heart ached when she thought of Joshua lying in his own blood somewhere behind her. *What if he's still alive?* her mind screamed at her. He could die before any medical aid reached him. He was wounded because of her. If she had shot Caulfield . . . if she hadn't kissed Joshua . . . Oh, God, she was so frightened, so terribly frightened!

She stopped, fighting to catch her breath. She listened. There was no sound of Caulfield's pursuit. The battle to the east was edging closer again, now barely a half mile off. Perhaps Caulfield had noticed it, too, and decided against coming after her. Maybe he'd taken their horses and fled.

She dared a glance behind her. Only the jumble of scrub timber and vines met her gaze. She had come little more than fifty yards, yet the jungle growth made sighting the spot where Joshua lay impossible. Where was Caulfield? Had Joshua regained consciousness and killed him? Her hopes soared for an instant. She quashed them at once, realizing that if Joshua had killed Caulfield, he would now be calling for her to return.

She couldn't just leave Joshua lying back there. She had to know if he was still alive. Damn, where was Caulfield?

"Come on back, missy." She heard the man's unmistakable voice. "I know you're out there. So why don't you just save us both a lot of misery and come on back here like a good little girl."

Stacey hugged her arms tight against her body. Caulfield had to be insane if he thought she was going back to him. Why on earth would he even think she might. . . ?

Cold terror struck her heart. There was only one reason she would go back. And Caulfield knew that reason. Joshua!

She retraced her steps, driving branches and vines aside in her haste. When she caught sight of them, her heart jumped.

Caulfield sat on the ground next to Steele, his bayonet pressed so hard against Joshua's throat that Stacey watched it begin to draw blood.

"Please, God," she choked. "No!" The blood told her two things. That Joshua was still alive, and that he was still deeply unconscious. Despair washed over her.

"I knew you'd see it my way, missy," Caulfield said. "You just come right on over here and sit down beside me, and maybe, just maybe, I won't slit your cap'n's throat."

CHAPTER FOUR

Stacey's heart hammered in her chest. Her knees threatened to give way with each step she took. She ignored the snapping twigs and insidious creepers, stepping toward Caulfield as though she were sleepwalking.

Tears stung her eyes. "Please, oh, please, private, just take our horses and go."

Caulfield exerted more pressure on the bayonet he held against Steele's throat. Blood trickled down the blade.

"Don't! You'll kill him!" she sobbed.

"That's the general idea, missy," Caulfield said. "But, don't worry, I'm not gonna do it now. If the cap'n keeps bleedin' like he is, I won't have to bother." Caulfield tilted Joshua's head toward her, so that she could see the left side of his face. It was covered with blood.

"Why are you doing this?" Stacey cried. "All you have to do is take the horses and leave. If you stay much longer, other soldiers are bound to stumble in here."

"We've got plenty of time for what I have in mind, missy," the private smirked. "Plenty of time. So don't you worry about ol' Hector. To tell you the truth, I ain't a man hankerin' to take many chances with my skin. But you give a man a powerful reason to stay on a few extry minutes."

He gazed leeringly at the rise and fall of her breasts. "Sit down here, missy," he said, patting the ground beside him.

When she didn't move, he raised the bayonet several inches above Joshua's throat. He left no doubt in her mind that he would plunge the knife into Joshua's neck if she didn't obey him at once. She sank to her knees beside him.

"Why can't you just leave us alone?" She whimpered.

He chuckled. "Why missy, a purty lady like yourself should know the reason for that." He grabbed a fistful of her hair and leaned toward her.

Stacey willed herself not to move. She had to keep Caulfield's attention away from Joshua. If only there were some way to reason with the man. Distract him. Anything to keep Joshua and herself alive until the war came down on top of them all, and Caulfield would be forced to flee for his life.

"The battle is moving closer," she said, "unless you want them to hang you for murder, you'd better go now."

"I'm real touched that you care so much, missy," he snorted. "But like I said, a couple minutes ain't gonna make no difference one way or the other." He ran a hand along her arm, across her shoulder and down her shirtfront. Dropping the bayonet, he yanked the shirt open, ripping off the buttons as he did so. He licked his lips at the sight of the thin chemise covering her full, firm breasts.

Stacey resisted the urge to scream and scream and never stop. This couldn't be happening to her. It had to be some kind of horrid nightmare. Scarcely two hours ago she had left her father to gather supplies for the wounded. Now she faced the very real possibility of being raped and murdered at the hands of a madman. Part of the pain she felt was for her father. Someone was bound to discover her body. What a torment of guilt her death would put her father through. He had never wanted her to stay with him on the front lines. But she had won him over, as she had since she was a little girl. He could never refuse her anything.

No! She couldn't let Caulfield win. Not without a fight to her last breath. Not only did Joshua's life depend on her, for Caulfield would kill him when he'd finished with her, of that she had no doubt; but in a very real sense her father's life depended on her survival as well. If she could just get Caulfield's mind on something else, anything, just long enough for more soldiers to arrive she might have a chance. She took a deep breath.

"If you're so afraid of the Wilderness," she said,"Then why are you staying in it one minute longer than you have to?"

He looked at her. "Hector Caulfield ain't afeared of nothin'," he snapped.

So, the man had a sore spot when it came to questioning his courage. She continued, "But you said you were running away from this 'briar patch', as you called it. That would certainly seem to suggest fear to me." She was playing a dangerous game, she knew. She wanted Caulfield distracted and angry, but not so angry that he might kill her in a fit of rage. To her vast relief Caulfield stood up and stalked away from her for several yards. When he turned, his beady eyes regarded her with open disgust.

"Ain't you got eyes, girlie?" he cried. "Look around you. Fightin' in this brush is pure crazy. Why it can get a man just as dead by fire as by bullets. And I just wasn't aimin' to fry for nobody."

Stacey knew the truth of his words, still she pressed him. "That's ridiculous," she said.

"Is it?" he shouted, tramping over to stand by the uprooted oak. "I was with Hancock's artillery. I was standin' next to a bugle boy who started screamin' like a banshee. We looked down and this here skeleton was grinnin' back at us."

Caulfield was caught up in the horror of his recollection and did not notice Joshua's left hand move ever so slightly. Stacey, who had scarcely taken her eyes off Steele for a second, did notice. She immediately climbed to her feet, placing her body between Joshua and Caulfield. The deserter would kill Joshua in an instant if he thought he was regaining consciousness.

"I've seen skeletons on the battlefield," Stacey said derisively, though the memory of it chilled her to her soul. "So what?" She had to keep Caulfield talking. If possible, she had to get him away from here. Any time now Joshua might cry out when the pain of his wound reached his conscious mind.

"So what?" Caulfield raged. "Missy, that skeleton used to be a soldier boy jes' like me. Only he was in the first fightin' here, or maybe Chancellorsville last year. And there he lay, back broke by a bullet. You could tell it lookin' at the bones. And his bony hands was coverin' what used to be his eyes. You know why, missy?"

Hugging her sides, Stacey dared a step closer to Caulfield. "No, I don't," she said quietly. She walked past him, terrified that at any second he would reach out and grab her. When he did not, she nearly collapsed with relief. He did what she had hoped he would do, he turned to follow her movements. That left his back to Joshua. She said a silent, fervent prayer of thanks.

"Well, I'll tell you why," Caulfield said. " 'Cause whilst that soldier boy was laying there, not able to move because of his broke back, he was starin' at the flames of a fire that was creepin' up on 'im. He screamed for help. You know'd he did. He couldn't move. But the fire could. And it did. He covered his eyes to keep from seein' it, missy. And he burned alive. Jes' like a lot of soldier boys are doin' farther into these woods right now. Purty soon they'll be close enough to hear 'em screamin'."

Stacey closed her mind against the images his words provoked. She could well understand Caulfield's fear, but that didn't excuse cold-blooded murder.

"But why did you have to kill your lieutenant?" she asked, daring a quick glance at Joshua. He was still unconscious, but he was moving his head from side to side as though trying to wake up. Please, God, don't let Caulfield turn around! she prayed. "Couldn't you just have tied him up or something?"

Strangely, Caulfield laughed. "I did that once. Hit a man instead of killin' him." He pulled his shirttail out of his pants and unbuttoned his shirt. He pulled it open and shifted his body so that she could see his right side. A good long scar, white with age, snaked its way down from near his shoulder blade all the way to his hip. "That's what I got for my trouble."

His eyes narrowed. "I think you've had me talkin' long enough, missy. We got business together you and me."

Stacey took an involuntary step backward. "Please, private, there's no reason to do this. You want to live. Well, so do I. Please, I beg you. Take the horses and go. You'll be safe. I won't say a word about you to anyone. I swear."

"No, missy, I know you won't say a word to nobody."

The glint in his eyes was unmistakable. In a terror-filled voice she shrieked at him, "Just go! Damn you! Get out of here! Your freedom is what you want, isn't it?"

"Oh, it's what I want all right," Caulfield agreed. "But it's not all I want." He edged closer to her. "I figure I got time enough to have me a purty woman afore we get any soldier boy company."

A primitive urge to survive made Stacey bolt away from him. His words stopped her in her tracks.

"You run, missy, and I'll slit your cap'n's throat. I swear I will."

Stacey stood perfectly still, staring at the trees all around her. They seemed to beckon her, offering her a haven from this maniac. But she couldn't run and leave Joshua to his death. Nor could she allow this animal to have his way with her. Maybe she could lure him away from here. Get them both lost in the Wilderness. No Caulfield had already said he would not follow her. Just as he had not before. He had known she would come back because of Joshua. He was scarcely five feet behind her now. She could hear his boots crunching against the undergrowth as he stepped toward her.

"Oh, God," she sobbed, "please, don't touch me. I beg you. Please."

"Don't go actin' the scairt virgin on me, girl," Caulfield growled. "Like I tol' you, I seen you kissin' and feelin' on the captain. You weren't givin' him no objections."

How could she tell this monster that Joshua's kisses had made her whole body come to life as nothing ever had before? Caulfield would care nothing of that. He was a man who cared for nothing and no one, but himself.

She forced herself to turn and face him. If she ran, it would cost Joshua his life.

Caulfield read the terror in her eyes. If anything, it made him more anxious to have her. He quickly closed the distance between them.

He halted directly in front of her. She had to tilt her head back to look up at his grimy, beard-stubbled face. Again a wave of nausea washed over her at the scent of the man's fetid breath. His whole body reeked as though it had not known water since the last rains of spring. She brought her hand to her mouth in an effort to keep from gagging. Caulfield snarled at the gesture.

"You don't like the smell, missy," he said. "Well, don't you worry, I'll be sheddin' these clothes quick enough."

That was all she could take. Stacey bent over,

holding her stomach. Caulfield swung his right arm and caught her with a hard backhand across her cheek. She slumped forward, but quickly struggled to her feet. The pain somehow caused the nausea to vanish. She was determined to fight Caulfield to the last ounce of her strength.

The deserter advanced on her. With a malevolent grin he gripped her arm and brought his mouth down on hers. Stacey spat at him, twisting and screaming, screaming until she had no breath left with which to scream.

Steele had seen the change in Caulfield's expression, while Stacey was slicing through the rawhide thongs that bound his hands. He knew the deserter was going to make a last desperate bid for freedom. As the private dove for his pistol, Steele yanked free of his bonds and lunged for him. But even as he did so, he knew he would be too late.

Though Stacey had a rifle aimed at Caulfield, she never pulled the trigger. Steele did not hear the shot that slammed into the side of his head. An instant of blinding pain preceded him into oblivion.

From what seemed a long way off he heard someone screaming. It took him several seconds to focus on the sound, using it to force himself awake. His head throbbed brutally. He resisted the urge to feel the wound with his hand. He lay still, waiting for his groggy mind to remember where he was and what was happening before he moved. The scream came again.

Stacey!

And Caulfield!

He opened his eyes. For a long minute the world

around him was nothing but a foggy blur. He heard the scuffle to his left. He shook his head in an effort to clear his vision. The resulting pain almost caused him to black out. Gritting his teeth, he struggled to a sitting position. Again he had to fight the unconsciousness that threatened to overwhelm him.

His muscles seemed to respond in slow motion to his brain's commands. He knew Stacey was in terrible danger, and yet he could not seem to get to his feet. Each time he tried, he sank back on his haunches. He willed his eyes to focus on the struggle to his left.

White hot rage ripped through him. Caulfield held Stacey pinioned against a tree, his body pressed hard against hers, his slimy mouth covering her mouth. She flailed at him with her fists, but because of her position the blows merely glanced off Caulfield's body.

Steele lurched to his feet, folding his head to steady himself. The bleeding had stopped, but the bullet had gouged a trail above his left temple. He could tell from his shirt and the ground around him that he had lost a good deal of blood. He spied Caulfield's bayonet on the dead leaves in front of him. His fingers curled around it. With the stealth of a wild animal he crept toward Caulfield.

Stacey was fighting with the last vestige of her strength, and still she could not break free of Caulfield's iron grip. He tore at her chemise, and she sobbed with terror and humiliation as his fingers closed over her bare flesh.

"Stop it! Stop it!" she screamed. Out of the corner of her eye she caught the movement. Joshua! He was advancing on Caulfield. He held a bayonet in his hand. She pushed herself beyond the pain, her heart pounding. Caulfield mustn't become aware of Joshua's approach. She went limp.

Caulfield stared at her quizzically for a few seconds, then sneered, "Now that's better, missy. Startin' to like it, ain't you? I know'd you would. Maybe I'll even take you with me." His mouth closed over her breast.

With a roar of animal rage Steele jerked Caulfield by the shirt collar and dragged him off Stacey's bruised and battered body. His eyes were black with fury.

Startled, Caulfield still managed to swing around and land a glancing blow to the left side of Steele's head. Joshua's mind reeled, but he did not go down. Caulfield started to drag his pistol from his holster.

Stacey threw herself at Caulfield's gun arm. It gave Steele the seconds he needed. He drove into the man, sending them both sprawling into the brush.

Caulfield snarled and spat like a trapped weasel, struggling fiercely to shove his gun into Steele's stomach. Steele could barely think through the stabbing pain in his head. He gripped the bayonet with an instinct born in the will to survive and rammed it into Caulfield's gut. The tip exited through his spine. The deserter grunted in pain, slumped and lay still.

Steele collapsed forward onto Caulfield's body.

Stacey was at his side in an instant. "Joshua! Joshua, are you all right?" she cried. She tried to lift him off Caulfield, but he was too heavy for her. "Oh, God, don't be dead," she sobbed, "please, don't be dead."

He groaned, pushing himself up with his arms. "I can't be dead," he said tiredly. "It can't hurt this much to be dead." He gave her a weak grin.

She helped him over to a log, where he sat down. Her own legs proved too shaky to support her. She sank to her knees beside him, pulling her shirt tightly closed in front of her. She tried unsuccessfully to still the trembling, racking sobs that suddenly overwhelmed her.

Joshua pulled her against him, smoothing her hair, speaking soothingly to her. "Did he hurt you?" he asked.

She couldn't stop crying. The thought of what Caulfield would have done to her, if Joshua hadn't come to when he did, sent a new wave of near-hysteria through her slender body.

"It's all right, Stacey," Joshua murmured. "He's dead. He'll never hurt anyone again."

Stacey's trembling lessened, but she did not loosen her grip on Steele's shirt. It was several minutes before her heart beat returned to a more normal rate. She raised her head from his chest, brushing away the tears on her cheeks. She noticed the dried blood on his uniform jacket.

"Oh, my God," she cried. "Why didn't you say something? Your wound! I've got to see to it!"

"It hasn't killed me yet," he said. "I don't suppose it's going to."

"Just never mind." She took a deep breath and steadied herself. "Do you have a clean bandana, or shirt, or anything I could use as a bandage?" She was determined to be her medically professional self once again.

"In my saddlebags."

"I'll need some water, too."

"I have a canteen on my horse."

57

She climbed to her feet and walked over to the horses. She avoided looking at Caulfield's body. When she'd found the bandana and canteen, she returned to Steele's side. Several minutes passed while she cleaned up the wound, doing her best to spare him any additional pain.

"You have a nice touch," he said softly.

She felt her body flush at the obvious double meaning of his words. "You'd better have a doctor take a look at this," she managed, as she wrapped the makeshift bandage around his head. "Maybe you could ride back with me and let my father see to it."

"I have orders sending me to Washington, remember?"

Yes, she remembered, but she didn't want to think about that right now. She didn't want to think about never seeing Joshua Steele again. She tied off the bandage and sat down beside him. "That should hold you for awhile," she said.

"Thank you." Gingerly, he touched the bandage above the wound. "Not bad. Maybe you will be a doctor."

"You doubt it?" Her voice carried the hurt she felt.

He shrugged. "It's just that I've never met a woman doctor."

"You've probably never seen the Pacific Ocean either," she snapped. "Does that mean you doubt its existence?"

He grinned. "Ah, but I have seen the Pacific . . ."

She frowned furiously, until she saw the teasing glint in his eyes. "You're insufferable," she said.

"I've been known to be at times," he admitted, still smiling. The smile vanished as the sounds of the battle

58

to the east escalated. "We'd better get out of here."

"Not yet," she said quickly, hardly daring to admit why. She just couldn't let him ride out of her life. Not yet. She'd been through too much today. She was still terribly shaken by what Caulfield had done to her, and by thoughts of what he had tried to do.

"Stacey," Joshua said, "the war is going to be upon us within the hour. Knowing this jungle, there might already be a fire or two headed this way."

"Just a little while longer," she pleaded.

He sighed. "All right."

"But not here."

He frowned, not understanding. Then he noticed that her gaze had settled on Caulfield's body. He allowed her to help him to his feet. They pushed through several yards of brush, settling into the middle of a thicket. The three foot by six foot opening afforded them a comfortable bed of dead pine needles. Steele leaned back against a tree. Eagerly, Stacey snuggled into his arms.

"I'm so sorry I couldn't shoot him," she whispered, after several minutes of companionable silence.

"Forget it. It's done."

But she couldn't forget it. Not ever. Caulfield's bullet could just as easily have killed Joshua as grazed him. "I just couldn't shoot him, Joshua." Her voice broke. "I couldn't."

"It's all right, Stacey."

"No, it's not all right!" she cried, her tears moistening his shirt. "You could be dead now. It's only a miracle that you're not."

He kissed the top of her head. "It's all right," he soothed again.

She wrapped her arms tightly around him. "He was such an awful man. When he touched me, I thought I would die."

She felt him stiffen. "Don't think of it," he said.

"I feel so dirty, so ashamed."

"You have nothing to be ashamed of," he snapped. "Nothing happened. He was forcing himself on you."

She looked into his eyes. "You're angry with me."

"I'm not angry with you, Stacey." He sighed heavily. "I'm angry with myself. If I'd been more alert, Caulfield never would have taken us prisoner in the first place."

"But that was my fault, too," she said miserably.

"You're a girl. I'm a grown man. I knew better."

"I'm not a child, Joshua," she said. "I knew what I was doing."

"I don't think so," he said, stroking her silky hair with his hand.

"Did you like kissing me?"

"Stacey, don't . . ."

His voice carried a note of warning. She knew he didn't want her to push him further. But the slimy feel of Hector Caulfield would not go away. She wanted to purge herself of his touch. She wanted to feel Joshua's searing, possessive kisses once again, before he rode out of her life forever. She didn't care about tomorrow. She only wanted today.

Her lips brushed his. Her fears of the day's events left her open, vulnerable, aching to be held and comforted. When he did not respond, her kisses grew fiercer, driven by a hunger she had yet to understand. She pressed her body against his, feeling the thudding of his heart beneath the softness of her breasts.

Mindful of his wound, her hands gently caressed his hair, the back of his neck. Instinctively, she molded her body to his. She felt the involuntary shudder that swept through him and knew she was succeeding in reaching him. He would kiss her now, and she would wish that he would never stop.

CHAPTER FIVE

Steele gripped her upper arms and pushed her abruptly away from him. "For God's sake, Stacey," he rasped, "there are men fighting and dying five hundred yards east of here."

Stacey stiffened as if he'd slapped her. "Don't you think I know that! I've worked in a field hospital for over a month now. I know only too well what those two armies are doing to one another." Her voice softened, "Maybe that's why, for just a few minutes, I want to forget all of it."

His eyes locked on hers. "Just what do you want of me, Stacey?"

She met his gaze with equal determination. "I want you to kiss me," she said, as boldly as she could manage against the hammering of her heart. "To make me forget Caulfield, forget a war."

He knew he should put an end to this right now. She was so young. She didn't fully realize the potential consequences of what she asked. Yet he heard himself saying, "Is that all you want me to do? Kiss you?"

"Of course," she whispered, but that nameless ache in the very center of her being was beginning again.

He cradled the side of her head in his large hand. "Then kiss you I will," he said. He drew her to him.

His lips burned against her mouth, bruising, possessing.

With remarkable tenderness his tongue teased its way between her lips. Stacey moaned deep in her throat, unprepared for the violent emotions that swept through her. His kisses suddenly weren't enough. She wanted, needed more.

"Stacey, don't," he said thickly, as her fingers tugged at the buttons of his shirt. "Don't."

But she was beyond caring about tomorrow, only today, this minute, mattered. She laid his shirt open and burrowed her fingers into the soft, dark mat of hair on his chest.

"Stacey, this isn't right," he said. "It's only because you were so frightened earlier. Stacey, I don't want to hurt you." But even as he spoke the words, his hands were caressing her, exploring the curving softness of her body.

He eased her out of her shirt, then gently pushed aside the torn chemise. He teased the nipples of her firm, young breasts, revelling at the way they stiffened at his touch. She was too young, he should stop this now before it couldn't be stopped. But the taste of her fiery innocence bewitched him. He had been with many other women more practiced in the art of arousing a man, but none of them had prepared him for what was happening to him now.

Somewhere in his mind he realized that she was probably confusing the feeling of comfort and security that he gave her with a deeper emotion. But he was losing the battle with his more rational nature. It had been a long time since he'd been with a woman. And this woman—this girl-woman—was driving him to the point of madness. He wanted her, and she wanted him. That was his reality now.

He undressed her slowly, with deliberate ease. He would make certain she needed it as much as he did. When he moved away from her for a moment in order to shed his own clothes, she whimpered with longing.

"Be patient, green eyes," he said softly. "It's almost time."

Stacey watched with shy pleasure as he undressed. Strangely, she felt no embarrassment at her own nakedness. Her flesh still tingled with the memory of his touch. She gasped at the sight of his manhood and saw a smile crook one corner of his mouth.

"A doctor who doesn't know the secrets of a man's body?" he teased gently, caressingly, as he lay down beside her.

"I want to know the secrets, Joshua," she breathed. "I want to know all the secrets of your body—and mine." Obeying an instinct older than time, she turned her body toward his.

Steele's conscience took one final jab at him. As he gathered her in his arms, he whispered against her hair, "We can stop this now, Stacey. We can get dressed and pretend it never happened."

Stacey swallowed hard. This was wrong. Surely, she knew it was wrong. The rumble of war crept closer. She could hear muffled shouts every so often now. Part of her wanted to go to the wounded, but practicality told her the litter bearers were doing all that could be done. She would be back with her father soon enough, back to the ugly realities of the dead and dying. She would have her moment of forgetfulness, she would know the ultimate touch of this man. They might both be dead tomorrow. She would live for today.

She moved against him, blending her body with his, curving herself into the welcoming contours of his flesh. She heard him stifle a groan, felt him reach for her, and she was lost.

"Oh, God, Stacey. Please. Please."

She couldn't tell it if was a plea for her to let him, or a plea to make him stop. She only knew that she didn't want him to stop. His hands were fevered, setting fire to her body. She writhed against him with an ancient primitive need.

His mouth invaded her mouth. His hands touched all of her gently, patiently, allowing her to explore each plateau of her feelings before he took her higher, higher.

"Joshua, please, " she cried, "I need . . . I need something. I don't know."

"You will, my sweet. You will."

She was floating, spiraling along in a world of pure sensation. "Please, Joshua . . ."

His own need pushed him hard, urging him to take her. But he wanted her to be ready, more than ready. He would torment himself to please her. He covered her with his body, his arousal complete, his hunger for her driving him to the edge of his sanity. "There will be a little pain at first," he whispered, each word an effort. He didn't want to think, he only wanted to feel.

"Take me, Joshua," she pleaded. "I want you. I need you. Oh, God, Joshua, please."

She felt him touch her, felt him hesitate. Then his hips thrust forward, and his mouth kissed away her cry of pain. In an instant the pain was gone, and she was swallowed up by a sweet euphoria. Instinctively, she matched his movements with her own, until she was enveloped by a rapturous ecstasy. She screamed his name as he transported her to paradise.

He stared at her for long minutes afterwards, savoring the shifting emotions in her emerald eyes. From deep pleasure to rapture to delight to the one he was looking at now—astonishment.

"I never knew," she said, in awe of what had just happened to her. "I never knew anything could be so wonderful."

"So you like the secrets of a man's body," he said, kissing her palm, "and your own." He twirled a long strand of sun-colored hair around his fingers.

"Mmmmmm," she smiled. "The man's body is especially interesting."

"It surprised you that much?"

"Not at all," she said, "I found it quite fascinating, in fact."

"I would like to think that's a woman talking," he said dryly, "but I think somehow the doctor has arrived."

She giggled and snuggled closer to him, delighting in the special rapport that had sprung up between them. The war racketed closer. She felt him tense.

He sat up, grabbing up her clothes. "Get dressed. We'd best get out of here."

She sensed his sudden withdrawal. Sitting up, she took her clothes from him. Embarrassed all at once, she held her torn blouse against her breasts.

Steele caught the gesture. A muscle worked in his jaw. Already she was regretting what had happened. He had been a fool not to put a stop to it. He turned his back, allowing her to dress, while he pulled on his uniform. His head still ached viciously, but he doubted it would cause him any further trouble.

The silence between them stretched to awkward lengths. There was so much Stacey wanted to say to him, but she couldn't seem to find the words. The acrid smell of gunsmoke reached her nostrils.

"They're damned close now," Steele muttered. "We'd better go."

"I can see some of the trees burning!" Stacey cried. "Maybe there are wounded men. We could get them out."

"Stay here," Steele said. He left her to tromp toward the fighting.

Stacey stood watching after him, not yet able to sort out her feelings about what had just taken place between them. When he had been gone for several minutes, she began to worry that his head wound might have caused him to pass out. He appeared out of the thickening smoke like a spectre.

"You can't see your hand in front of your face in there," he coughed out. "Bullets are flying in all directions. The litter bearers will have to come in from the other side. The wind is driving the fire this way. Come on, we've got to get out of here." He coughed again, nearly doubling over. He stumbled over the underbrush. Stacey came under his arm and helped him toward his horse.

Ten yards behind them, obscured by the billowing smoke and a thick clump of chinquapin bushes, Hector Caulfield opened his eyes. He tried to call out, but no words came from his throat. He tried to move and found that he could not. The smoke stung his eyes. Smoke? A fire! He could see the tops of trees burning, then the lower branches would fire, until the entire tree was a flaming torch. He could feel the heat of it now. Flaming bits of bark singed his clothes. He winced when one settled on his cheek. His lungs ached with the effort to breathe the smoke-clogged air. Flames sparked the underbrush five yards to his left. If he didn't get out of the way . . . Move! Run! his mind screamed at his unresponsive body. When the first flames touched his flesh, his mouth fell open at the searing pain. But even then he could not scream. He put his hands over his eyes against the relentless fire. Then Hector Caulfield quietly burned to death.

Stacey was finding it harder to breathe. Joshua supported her now, more than she supported him. Her eyes watered, her throat hurt, as they lurched toward the horses. Her mount flattened his ears against his head, his eyes rolling wildly, when she tried to grab his bridle. Joshua's horse reared against the reins that secured him to a tree branch. The smell of smoke and fire had both animals terrified. She tried again to get hold of her gelding's head, but he shied away from her.

"Let me get the horses," Steele shouted, the din of battle no longer making normal conversation possible. "You get the hell out of these woods."

He pushed her ahead of him. She stopped. "I'm staying with you," she yelled back at him.

He swore angrily, but did not press the issue. There wasn't time. The horses were rapidly becoming unmanageable. Unless he got them out now, they would bolt free and leave him and Stacey stranded afoot. He collected the reins of both animals. The shrill neighs of the panic-stricken horses pierced the air, rising above the sound of gunfire. Steele had to use all of his strength to lead them out of the Wilderness. Only when they were several yards out into the clearing did the horses begin to settle down. Stacey took the reins of her gelding from Joshua, patting the animal's neck and speaking soothingly.

Wearily Steele leaned against his saddle, the combination of smoke and loss of blood making him weak. He closed his eyes. He felt Stacey hand on his shoulder. "We're not safe out here in the open," he said. He turned to look at her. "It's best we be on our way."

She stared at him for a long time, burning his image into her brain—the bloody bandage around his head, the soot blackened face, the haggard look in his gray eyes. He'd been through hell today, all because of her. How could she ever thank him for that? The memory of the fierce, but gentle way he had made love to her seared through her mind. How could she bear never to see him again?

She wanted to say something, anything that would hold him there, prevent him from leaving, as she knew he must. They each had duties, responsibilities, his to the War Department, hers to saving lives.

"Joshua . . ." she began, then stopped. There was so much she wanted to say, but no time in which to say it. The war would not be halted merely because she wished it so. Perhaps he would come for her after the war was over. . . . His next words destroyed her dream.

"Stacey, I'm sorry for what happened." He reached up as if to touch her face, then suddenly dropped the hand to his side. "I can't offer any excuses for what I did. I can only tell you how much I regret . . ."

"Stop it!" she screamed, stepping back from him as though his nearness caused her physical pain. "How dare you apologize? How dare you?" Until this moment she had not regretted any part of what had passed between them. But his apology somehow changed all that. She felt her face grow hot with embarrassment. That he saw her shame made it all the more unbearable.

She clutched the reins of her horse, staring at the ground. Tears scalded her cheeks. Sorry! He was sorry he had made love to her! Sorry she was a foolish young girl, who had turned a man's sexual need into something more than it really was. She heard the creak of saddle leather, as he mounted his horse, but she kept her eyes riveted on the ground.

His voice came to her again, this time with a strange quality she couldn't read. "Take care what horse you ride from now on, green eyes," he said. "I might not be there to save that pretty little neck of yours next time."

She said nothing. She did not look up.

Joshua sighed heavily. "Good-bye, Stacey." With that he kicked his horse in the sides and rode away toward the north. He did not look back.

Stacey knew that he did not look back, because she did not take her eyes from the path he rode until he was long out of sight.

NEW MEXICO TERRITORY
1871

CHAPTER SIX

Spring Canyon, New Mexico Territory, boasted a population of nearly eighteen hundred men, women, and children in June 1871, with outlying ranches and stage stops inflating the number to well over two thousand. In the two years since her arrival Stacey Hamilton had come to regard the small community as more of a home than the over-large Albany, New York, had ever been.

She eyed herself critically in the full-length mirror on the door of her bedroom closet. Her lovely sun-colored hair was delicately done up atop her head to enhance the sparkling green of her eyes. She wrinkled her nose at the hair style. Why she had let Mrs. Harrison talk her into it, she couldn't now understand. She remembered each prick of each pin with renewed pain.

"Mr. Randolph will just love it," Mrs. Harrison had said. Mr. Randolph didn't have to wear it, Stacey grimaced.

If she had been lovely at seventeen, she was stunningly beautiful now. The simple lime green taffeta dress she wore accented her slender figure to perfection.

She would have to hurry if she was to be on time for

her luncheon date with Martin Randolph. Martin detested tardiness, and considering the announcement she was going to make during lunch, she wanted to make every effort to please him beforehand.

As she turned to leave the room the gilt-framed photograph on her vanity caught her eye. She paused to give her parents an affectionate smile. Picking up the picture, she trailed a slender finger over the beloved images. Her parents had had the picture taken a week after the firing on Fort Sumter. It was as if her father had known. . . .

Ben Hamilton stood next to his wife, his right hand on her left shoulder. He looked so stern, so severe, so unlike the warm, caring father she had loved with all her heart. She swallowed the tears that stung her eyes. Had he really been dead nearly seven years? Felled by a stray bullet near tree-studded Cedar Creek in Virginia in October 1864. She couldn't suppress a brief twinge of the bitterness she had once felt so fiercely over the senselessness of his death.

It hadn't been the bullet that killed him. It had been the blind ignorance of a fellow doctor, who refused to believe that harm could come from things that couldn't be seen. A dirty scalpel, a filthy bandage, and her father had died in agony. Blood poisoning.

"It would never have happened, mother," she said softly, speaking to the lovely, delicate looking woman in the photograph, "if I had been there with him."

For the first three months after Stacey had joined her father, her uncle, Sam Curtis, had been her intermediary, mailing Stacey's letters to her mother from his home in Boston. But Sam had left Boston in

July, travelling to Spring Canyon in hopes of adding a few years to the life of his desperately ill wife. Stacey had been forced to send her letters directly home. Not writing at all would have made her mother even more suspicious.

Maude Hobson, her mother's lifelong personal maid, was well aware of Stacey's battlefield nursing activities and had taken up the job as go-between for her letters. Beatrice Hamilton was never supposed to see the postmarks. But somehow she had intercepted one of the letters before Maude could dispose of the envelope. When she'd found out about her daughter's presence in the middle of a war, she'd all but had a stroke. Maude had posted a letter to Stacey, begging her to come home for the sake of her mother's health. The letter had reached her in September near Fisher Hill in Strasburg, Virginia.

Stacey had shown Maude's letter to her father, and though, he, too, sensed Bea's theatrics, he had urged her to go. Ben Hamilton had seized on the opportunity to get his daughter out of constant danger.

Part of the reason, Stacey realized at the time, was because her father had never fully accepted her reason for her disheveled appearance when she had returned from getting medical supplies that day in the Wilderness. A fall from her horse had not been a plausible enough excuse for the bruises on her face and her torn uniform shirt, though she never wavered from her story. Her father had had enough to worry about.

Her mother's recovery had been just short of miraculous when Stacey returned home. But it was short-lived. Word reached them a month later about the death of Colonel Ben Hamilton. This time her mother's deteriorating health had not been an act. It was a shock from which she never fully recovered.

Stacey yanked herself out of her somber reverie. If she wasn't careful, she would start thinking about wolf-gray eyes, and then the tears would really come.

Martin would not appreciate a melancholy luncheon companion. If she hurried, she would just make it to Jensen's Cafe on time.

Her pace quickened along Spring Canyon's dusty main street, when she spied Martin checking his watch in front of the restaurant. He was looking especially dapper today, his dark broadcloth jacket tailored perfectly to his medium frame. When he caught sight of her, he doffed his hat, revealing wavy brownish hair, cropped short. His blue eyes twinkled as he flashed her a brilliant smile. He was, she admitted, devilishly handsome.

"Right on time," he beamed, opening the cafe door for her.

"I do try to be prompt, Martin," she said, breathing an inward sigh of relief.

Inside the cafe Stacey and Randolph smiled polite greetings to several other diners as they made their way to an unoccupied table near one of the cafe's two windows. Randolph eased Stacey's chair out for her and she sat down. She grimaced slightly at the scattered crumbs that speckled the top of the blue checked tablecloth, remnants of the table's previous occupants. Without being too obvious she used her napkin to gather them up, then placed the napkin unobtrusively on the window sill to her immediate right. The main dining area of the cafe was overcrowded as usual. Isaiah Jensen had arranged sixteen tables in a room that would have comfortably accommodated ten.

Stacey forced a wan smile, when she noticed Claire Jensen approaching their table. She knew Claire was overworked and so she would not mention the appetite-suppressing appearance of the tablecloth. But she really was not in the mood for one of Claire's performances right now.

Dressed in a gingham dress that nearly matched the cafe's table coverings, Claire sidled up to Martin Randolph's seat and flashed him her most enchanting smile. "Oh, Mr. Randolph, it's so nice to see you again."

Her dark hair was drawn back in a bun at the nape of her neck, but her warm brown eyes, pert nose, and perfect teeth softened the severity of the hair style. She was, Stacey acknowledged, a very pretty girl. If only she didn't have to be such a patently obvious flirt . . .

"The special today is steak and eggs," Claire went on, as she poured Randolph a cup of steaming hot coffee. "And you can be sure I'll have papa fix yours up just right, Mr. Randoph."

"I'm sure you will, Claire," Randolph said, his eyes falling first on the girl's slim waist, then trailing upward over her full, curving breasts to settle on her face. "You can bring us two orders, one for Miss Hamilton and one for me."

Randolph's mention of her name forced Claire to acknowledge Stacey's presence for the first time. "Oh, hello, Stacey," she said too sweetly. "You know you really should take better care of yourself. You look like you haven't been sleeping too well. Too much of that doctoring nonsense maybe."

"I sleep just fine, thank you, Claire," Stacey managed, choosing to ignore the girl's reference to her medical career. It was a touchy enough subject with Martin already. She didn't need the two of them lecturing her.

Claire ignored a customer who asked for the second time that his coffee cup be re-filled. "Will I be seeing you at the dance tonight, Mr. Randolph?"

"Stacey and I will be there," Randolph said.

"Maybe I'll save you a dance," Claire beamed.

"You do that," Randolph sighed, casting an exasperated look at Stacey. Couldn't this girl take a hint?

"Claire! We've got orders to be filled in here!" a harsh voice called, from the rear of the cafe. "And why haven't you refilled Mr. Anderson's coffee cup? Get to work, girl!"

"Yes, papa," Claire called hurrying toward the kitchen.

Isaiah Jensen's portly frame took up most of the doorway between the dining area and the kitchen. Claire kept a wary eye on him, as she skirted around him to pick up a tray piled high with food-filled plates.

"She looks like she expected him to hit her," Stacey said.

"Maybe he should," Randolph muttered.

"Martin!"

"The girl's an outrageous flirt," he said. "No decent girl would behave that way."

"I didn't get the impression you disliked her so

much," Stacey chided. "In fact, there was a moment there when you couldn't seem to take your eyes off her."

Randolph smiled. "Jealous?"

"Of course not," she said. At his frown she hastened to add, "I mean it seemed you weren't exactly discouraging her flirting with you. She's had a hard life, Martin."

"I can't believe you're defending her."

Stacey was a little surprised herself. Claire could be such a vexatious person at times. But Stacey also understood the roots of the girl's behavior. Sam had told her Claire's mother died six years ago, when Claire was barely twelve. Isaiah had driven his wife with the same slavish indifference he now heaped upon his daughter. The girl had been waiting tables in this cafe since she was eight years old, and never once had her father hired anyone to help her. Little wonder Claire's main goal in life was to snare a husband. She'd long ago decided it was the only way she could escape her father.

"I guess I feel a little sorry for her," Stacey said.

"Sorry for her?" Randolph snorted. "She's got more than one man in this town drooling over her. She'll be married before she's nineteen."

"I've heard her father scares off any prospective suitors," Stacey said, fingering her coffee cup. "He doesn't want to lose his slave."

Claire arrived with their orders and set them on the table. "I'm sorry for the delay," she said, already turning to leave.

Stacey caught her wrist. "Are you all right, Claire?" she asked.

The girl cast a furtive glance toward the door leading to the kitchen. Her father was nowhere in sight. "Actually, Stacey," she said, "I've been having those stomach pains again." She lowered her eyes. "Excuse me, Mr. Randolph, I don't mean to be indelicate in front of you."

"It's quite all right, Claire," Randolph assured her.

Claire batted her eyelashes at him. "I just knew you'd understand."

Stacey listened as Claire recounted her symptoms, even though she'd heard the same story countless previous times. Being sick was the only way Claire could ever get a few minutes off from her job. Her father couldn't afford to have her ill. But, Stacey knew, Claire would also use the occasion of her supposed medical problem to flirt with any male patients who happened to be in the waiting room at Sam's house. She smiled inwardly at Claire's single-minded resolve. In the on-going battle for freedom between the girl and her father, the odds had to be with Claire. The girl would simply never give up.

"Just come by the office any time, Claire," Stacey said.

"Oh, thank you, I will," the girl said. "I'll tell my father he has to let me go for a few minutes this afternoon." She seemed to visibly relax. Her coy smile was back on her lips as she re-filled Martin's coffee cup. She then hurried to take the orders of several newly arrived customers.

Stacey spent the next several minutes absently toying with her food, moving it from one side of the plate to the other with her fork. She really wasn't very hungry, or maybe it was what she had been avoiding saying to Martin that was making her lose her appetite. She hadn't seen him for two days, but he had finally cornered her this morning at home and insisted on having lunch. She slanted her emerald green eyes across the table for a covert glance at her escort. Martin could be so inflexible sometimes. Her hair style only added to her sense of constriction. Never again, she mused.

"All right, Stacey," Randolph said, setting down his coffee cup. "Let's have it."

"I don't know what you mean, Martin," she stammered.

"You've picked at that same piece of meat for five minutes," he explained, "and you've been very studiously ignoring me the last two days."

Stacey frowned. Why did he have to be so perceptive of her moods all at once? Or maybe it really didn't take much perception for him to notice that he hadn't seen his intended bride in over forty-eight hours. Spring Canyon wasn't big enough to account for such an occurrence.

"It's nothing really," she sighed, aware that the good humor he had displayed since meeting her for lunch would soon vanish.

He was studying her thoughtfully, his clear blue eyes obviously approving of Mrs. Harrison's handiwork on her hair. The new dress wasn't hurting his opinion either, as the soft material clung to her slender figure revealing the firm, rounded contours of her breasts. Her full sensuous lips pressed into a grim line that on Stacey only managed to look prettily obstinate. She set her fork down beside her plate. There was no more to be gained by side-stepping the inevitable.

"Martin," she said, "Sam is going to be needing more medical supplies, and he's asked me to go to Denver to pick them up."

Randolph halted his fork with its impaled piece of meat inches away from his mouth. His jaw clenched. Lowering his arm slowly, he placed the fork on his nearly empty plate.

"You are not taking a stagecoach to Denver by yourself, Eustacia," he stated flatly.

The heavy-handed tone of his voice infuriated her. How dare he presume to order her about? She was a twenty-four year old single woman, quite capable of making her own decisions. Heaven knew she'd had to make quite a few of them these past seven years. She strongly resented Martin's attempts to make them for her. Only her high regard for him kept her notable temper in check. She knew how much he detested making a scene. He was president of the Spring Canyon bank and the opinion of the community meant a great deal to him.

"Martin," she said, struggling to keep her voice even, "I was not asking your permission about going to Denver. I was simply telling you that I am going. I'm leaving Monday morning and that's all there is to it."

Randolph's blue eyes twitched angrily. He glanced about the cafe, noting with relief that no one seemed to be paying attention to their conversation. He relaxed a little. If he escalated the argument now, Stacey would retaliate in kind, and no doubt, end up by storming out of the cafe. He didn't need that kind of gossip.

He kept his voice deliberately soft. "My concern is for your safety, darling. You know that. I just don't like the idea of my girl traipsing around this godforsaken country unescorted. It just isn't proper behavior for a lady. And you know I can't go with you."

He stabbed a piece of meat with his fork and shoved it into his mouth. His temper was goading him hard. Stacey had to be the most stubborn female he had ever met, far too independent for her own good. Yet she was also the most beautiful woman he had ever seen, and she could be delightful company. The thought of introducing her as his wife sent a shiver of pleasure through him. She could only be an asset in his quest for the territorial governorship.

She sighed heavily. "Martin, I know you worry about me, and I think that's very sweet. But I'm perfectly capable of taking care of myself. For heaven's sake, two years ago I made the trip to Spring Canyon on my own all the way from New York. I think I should be able to manage Denver. Please, give me a little credit for self-sufficiency."

She smiled at him, hoping to cajole him into seeing her point of view. She liked Martin, liked him a lot. He was usually very gracious toward her, and his striking good looks made his attentions to her the envy of every unattached woman in Spring Canyon; even, she knew, some of the married ones. Most of the time she enjoyed his company very much. So much so that they would probably get married one day. It was something they had only touched upon briefly, and though nothing formal had been announced, a tacit understanding nevertheless existed between them.

"If I don't go," she argued, "Sam and I might receive the wrong medicines. When we have them shipped that frequently happens. So this time, we've agreed that I should pick them up personally."

"Sam could go instead," Martin insisted, also trying to keep their discussion from becoming a full blown argument. "He's the doctor, so he's the one who should pick out the medicines."

It was the wrong thing to say. Martin watched as her lovely green eyes narrowed ominously. There would be no holding her temper now.

"You're not going to start that again, Martin," she snapped. "I won't let you. You know perfectly well that I intend to become a doctor myself, that as far as actual knowledge is concerned, I already am one! It was only the ill health of my mother that prevented me from attaining the certified proof of that fact in the form of a diploma!"

Randolph gritted his teeth in cold fury. If there was one subject he and Stacey violently disagreed on it was her unabashed determination to become a doctor. Of all the unladylike professions she could have chosen, he considered it next to worst. Somewhere just short of saloon tramp.

"Just because a couple of sexless females back east have become doctresses . . ."

Stacey frowned furiously at the word she considered a slur chosen by prejudiced male counterparts.

"Doesn't mean you have to become one," he went on. "A nurse would be more reasonable, though still not acceptable for a woman of your breeding. Everyone know the wonderful work Florence Nightingale and Clara Barton have done to elevate the station of that thankless job, but, a doctor, Stacey, there are just some things a woman cannot do. She is biologically incapable . . ."

"Martin, I suggest you don't say another word," Stacey said slowly, rising from her chair. She had given up on avoiding an argument. If he wanted a fight, she would be happy to oblige.

"How conveniently you forgot *Doctor* Mary Walker," she hissed, "who not only served the Union valiantly during the war, but was even awarded the Congressional Medal of Honor for her efforts by President Johnson. And while you're being so patronizing, *Mister* Randolph, don't bother to ever arrange for Mrs. Harrison to pin up my hair like this again." She began to yank out several of the meticulously placed pins. "You know how I detest getting all gussied up."

"I hardly call getting your hair fixed once in a coon's age getting all gussied up," Randolph retorted. He was furious and he was frustrated. He wanted Stacey as his wife one day, but for the life of him he couldn't understand why she insisted on running around like a tomboy so much of the time. Couple that with her notions of becoming a doctor and there were times when he felt like strangling her.

"Well, Martin," she said, glaring down at him, "I can see there's no point in continuing this conversation." Her voice had risen in spite of her attempt to keep it down, and several diners were gaping at them.

Randolph reached over, grabbing her wrist, forcing her to sit back down. He used more force than he realized.

"Martin, you're hurting me," she gasped in surprise.

"I'm sorry. Stacey," he said, releasing her. "I didn't

mean it." He couldn't really be sure about that. "I just don't want you going away angry." He really didn't want her to make a scene, but she would have thrown something at him, if he'd said that.

"Is something the matter with the meal?" Claire asked anxiously, hurrying over to their table.

"The food is fine," Randolph grated, not looking at her.

"I mean if the steak was overdone, I'll be happy to see that it's replaced," Claire continued. "Sometimes my father leaves them on the stove too long . . ."

"I said the food is fine," Randolph repeated. This time he did look up at her. "It's just that Miss Hamilton and I are having a slight difference of opinion."

"Oh," Claire said, brightening. "That's a shame."

Randolph knew an ally when he saw one. "Perhaps you could help me, Claire," he said.

"Oh, anything, Mr. Randolph."

Stacey was getting angrier by the second.

"Miss Hamilton has taken the notion that she is going to travel to Denver by stage to pick up medical supplies for her uncle."

"Alone?" Claire gasped. "Oh, Mr. Randolph, I've never heard of such a thing. Why my father, bless him, would never allow me to travel unescorted in this godforsaken country. Just think of all the outlaws and Indians and hooligans there might be on the trail. It's just not safe for a lady to be alone out here."

Stacey closed her eyes. She could have expected no less from Claire. When she opened them, she noted that Claire had somehow managed to put her hand in Martin's.

"Would you like me to talk to her?" the young waitress asked, as though Stacey were not even in the room. "Maybe she'd listen to another woman."

"I would really appreciate it, if you would," Randolph said.

Claire stepped over to Stacey's side of the table.

Before the girl could open her mouth Stacey said, "Don't, Claire."

"But, Stacey . . ."

"Just don't." She peered around the girl. "I believe that gentleman in the corner wants to order his lunch."

"I'm sorry, Mr. Randolph," Claire pouted. "She just . . ."

"It's all right, my dear," he interrupted. "You just run along now." He hadn't really held out much hope for Claire's success. All he hoped for now was that he and Stacey could leave the cafe quietly and together. He pulled out his handkerchief and patted his forehead. It wasn't from the heat either. He wasn't a man who liked attention drawn to himself, unless he planned it that way. He had made himself one of the most well-respected, well-liked men in this town and he wasn't going to let anyone ruin it for him, not even Stacey. As soon as they were married he would put an abrupt end to all of this nonsense about her becoming a doctor. For now, he would humor her.

"Can we start over again, Stacey?" he smiled. He still had a day and a half to foil her plans about Denver.

Stacey nodded reluctantly, not sure what her reaction had been to Martin's vise-like grip on her arm. He must have been angrier than she'd thought.

She rubbed the spot where his hand had gripped her. There would be a bruise there tomorrow. She shrugged inwardly. Martin was just being overly protective. Even Sam didn't relish the idea of her travelling on the stagecoach alone. But in her own mind she knew she was perfectly capable of making the trip.

"Shall we have dessert?" she prompted, giving Martin one of her most radiant smiles.

"Sounds good to me," he said, settling back in his chair. The other diners had gone back about their business. "You're still going to the dance with me tonight, aren't you?"

"Of course, Martin," she said. "Just because we have a difference of opinion about something doesn't mean we can't still be friends."

Martin eyed her. He intended to be a lot more than friends with Stacey Hamilton. Her full breasts and slender waist were the source of more than one night of fitful sleeping.

"Here's your apple pie," Claire announced, setting a huge slice of the still steaming pastry in front of Martin. Stacey's portion wasn't nearly so generous. "Did you talk her out of that foolish trip, Mr. Randolph?"

"No," he said, being careful not to let the anger he still felt creep into his voice. "I've accepted the fact that Miss Hamilton knows her own mind."

Claire arched her brows in surprise, then giggled, "Oh, you know how we women are, Mr. Randolph. She's just being stubborn. She'll come around, you'll see."

Stacey placed her fork back on the table, no longer

interested in eating her minute piece of pie. If Claire said one more word *about* her, instead of *to* her, she was going to scream. She breathed an audible sigh of relief, when Martin changed the subject.

"This pie is wonderful, Claire," he told her. "Perhaps we will have that dance tonight."

Claire giggled, giving Martin a playful pat on the shoulder. "You're my witness, Stacey," she said. "I'm going to hold you to that tonight, Mr. Randolph. You can be sure of it," She hurried back toward the kitchen.

Stacey gave Martin an indulgent smile. She might be stubborn, but he was the one acting like a pouting little boy. If he expected, even wanted, her to be jealous over Claire, she discovered that, oddly, she was not. She thought about that a moment, but decided she was just being open-minded. After all, she and Martin had made no official announcement. If he was free to dance with other women, then certainly, she would be free to dance with other men.

When they left the cafe, Martin gave her a peck on the cheek and promised to pick her up for the dance around six.

Stacey watched him disappear toward the bank. He could be so exasperating at times, so thoughtful at others. She fingered the gold necklace around her neck, a present on her birthday two months before. If only they could discuss her wanting to be a doctor without the subject becoming so emotionally charged on both sides. Maybe she would ask Sam to referee next time.

She smiled warmly, thinking of her uncle, as she stepped off the boardwalk heading back toward the

89

two-story white frame house she shared with him. Sam Curtis had been nothing short of a godsend in her life. He had been wonderful to her, inviting her to come to Spring Canyon after her mother's death two years ago. It had been a difficult decision, and Sam had not pressed her.

She pushed open the gate to the white picket fence in front of the house and hurried up the porch steps. "Sam!" she called, but was greeted only by disappointing silence. He hadn't returned from the emergency call he'd had to make at the Placerman ranch.

No patients were in the waiting room, so she decided to busy herself tidying up the office. But that took only fifteen minutes. She tried concentrating on her latest medical journal, but found she could not. Thoughts of the past were intruding heavily on her today. The words on the page blurred and disappeared as she gave in to them.

She had fallen out of touch with Sam during her mother's illness. He had written her once, asking her to join his practice, apparently assuming she had followed her dream of becoming a doctor. She couldn't face writing back and telling him that she had not. Sam couldn't know that his sister's mental health had deteriorated almost as badly as her physical health.

For a full five months after Ben Hamilton's death, mother and daughter had consoled each other during a time of mutual grief, but finally Stacey could contain herself no longer. Perhaps it was partly a means of being a living legacy to her father's memory, but whatever it was her desire to be a doctor had increased a hundredfold. Her mother had been in good spirits for several days, when she decided to broach the subject.

"No daughter of mine will ever be a doctor," Beatrice Hamilton had shrieked. "It's filthy, degrading work for a woman. Eustacia, if you love me, you will never do this horrid thing."

But Stacey had stood her ground, and when her mother suffered a stroke that night, Stacey accepted the blame totally. The stroke left her mother a semi-invalid. With Maude Hobson's unflagging support, Stacey spent the next five years caring for her. Even so, she spent every spare moment poring over medical journals, reading texts, and talking to doctors who would talk to her. She knew more about medicine than many medical college graduates with diplomas in hand.

As always, thinking of those years with her mother brought back unbidden memories of her passionate encounter with Captain Joshua Steele. No matter how often her mind sought to relegate what had happened between them to the rash, impulsive act of a frightened adolescent, her heart would not be swayed. Her body ached for a fulfillment it had known but once, at the hands of a gray-eyed, dark-haired Union officer. An officer who had bluntly apologized for his behavior afterwards, leaving Stacey to bear an added burden of shame, because she had not been sorry at all. She shivered as the memories pressed in on her again.

During the daily sameness of caring for her mother, she had thought of Joshua often, wondering what had become of him, what dangers he might be facing. At times she imagined him a much-decorated war hero, squiring beautiful ladies around Washington, never once thinking of the young girl in the shapeless private's uniform. Or maybe he was back on that Colorado ranch of his, with a lovely wife and a brood of children.

Once, on a flight of daring whimsy in 1867, she had contacted a friend of her father's in the War Department. She asked him to discreetly check into the whereabouts of Steele. Nearly two months passed before she received a reply. When the letter arrived, she bolted upstairs and locked her bedroom door. She ripped open the letter, its words ripping open her heart.

November 15, 1867

My Dear Miss Hamilton,

This is in response to your inquiry as to the whereabouts of Captain Joshua Steele. It has taken me some time, but I have managed to piece together the following. Some of these matters are extremely delicate to our national security, and it is only out of respect to your father's memory that I have relayed them to you. I trust you will destroy this letter at once.

Captain Steele was dispatched by the War Department in May 1864 as an undercover agent for our government. He was to aid the cause of Benito Juarez in his fight to overthrow the French and Maximilian. At the time the French were known sympathizers with the Confederacy, and our late beloved President Lincoln wanted them stopped at all costs.

After the war ended, President Johnson continued to aid Juarez, because France still violated the Monroe Doctrine with their continued military presence in Mexico. Capt. Steele was instrumental in aiding the juarista cause until February of this year.

Here details become sketchy, but some sort of treachery on the part of a supposed ally of Steele's led to the ambush of an arms shipment Steele was in charge of escorting. Steele was wounded in the exchange of gunfire, and it seems that six Mexicans with Steele were massacred *after* they surrendered. Steele was taken prisoner.

After Maximilian's downfall at Querataro in June, French prisoners of war were set free. Steele was not among them. A private investigation uncovered suspicious circumstances surrounding Steele's treatment after his capture. It was this department's unofficial belief, later confirmed by eyewitnesses, that he was murdered.

No reply to official inquiries has been received. . . .

Her hands shook, her eyes blurred. Murdered!

All of the times she had dreamed of the way he had held her, the way he kissed her, made love to her, he had been in terrible danger, and now he was dead. Dead.

"Joshua!" She cried for so many days and weeks afterwards, that even her ailing mother had noticed and despaired of her daughter ever smiling again.

But that was long ago, and this was now. Even Joshua had been dead four years. She wiped the tears brusquely away, slamming the medical journal shut in front of her. Why did she torture herself with these memories? Why did she dream of the light in his eyes when he spoke of his paradise in the Colorado Territory, the way his hands had awakened her body to the wonders of being a woman? He had been so full of life—but so had so many men, dead because of war.

The world's not so big, green eyes. Maybe we'll meet again one day.

"That's enough," she snapped to herself. She drew in a sharp breath and picked up the note Sam had left her the day before. She might not be an official doctor yet, but Sam certainly considered her one. Since Sam was out of town, it fell to her to make the rounds of medical calls to their "regulars", as Sam called them.

She could have graduated from any medical college in the country. Those which would accept women, that is; she grimaced. But it would have taken three more years of her life. After her mother's death, she wanted, needed a change. She ached to get away. Away from memories of war, her parents' deaths, and warm gray eyes. She had written Sam that she would take him up on his kind offer. She had not been sorry. The stark beauty of this largely unsettled land had been a balm to her wounded spirit.

She snapped the black medical bag shut and stepped out into the sunshine.

CHAPTER SEVEN

Stacey's first patient lived in a room above Murphy's Mercantile. Maude Fremont, a sprightly woman in her early seventies, answered Stacey's knock.

"Where's your uncle?" she demanded at once.

"He's out on a call at the Placerman Ranch," Stacey said calmly. "He asked me to come in his place."

The old woman could scarcely hide her disappointment. Stacey suppressed a smile. Maude had quite a crush on her fiftyish uncle, much to Sam's everlasting embarrassment.

"I'm not sure you'll know how to treat my vapors," Maude said.

"I realize I'm not as practiced as my uncle," Stacey conceded gently, "but he left me very specific instructions regarding your care, Maude."

"He did?" Her watery blue eyes brightened at the thought that Sam would think of her at all when she was not in his presence.

"Most certainly," Stacey assured her. "You're one of his dearest patients, you know."

Maude blushed happily. "Oh, that uncle of yours, Stacey. He's such a fine man, I mean, doctor. Why ever since my Edward died . . ."

Maude launched into her litany of trials and

tribulations, all of which Stacey had heard scores of times previously, but she did not interrupt. She only half listened this time though, her argument with Martin intruding on her thoughts. Was she being unreasonable to expect Martin to support her desire to become a doctor? Maude paused, and Stacey realized suddenly that she was expecting some sort of comment from her.

"Life can be unduly harsh out here in the west," Stacey said quickly, hoping it fit in with whatever Maude had just been saying.

Maude smiled and seemed to accept Stacey's sympathy. Stacey chastised herself and vowed to listen more earnestly in the future. Maude was such a nice lady, she deserved that much at least. Stacey left her a few moments later, with Maude promising faithfully to take the medicines Sam had prescribed for her.

She made two more calls, both of which went uneventfully. She eyed the list, grimacing when she saw who was next. Garth Greevy. The name sent a repulsive shiver through her body. The man was insufferable, even to Sam. Stacey already knew what his response would be when he saw who was standing in his doorway. He did not disappoint her.

"Ain't no damned female going to do no doctoring on me, girlie," he snarled, showing an uneven row of yellowed teeth.

Leaving was a thought she cherished. He was such a grimy, smelly little man. But if she intended to be a doctor, she had to get used to all kinds of patients, including the ones with an abusive attitude toward her sex.

"Please, Mr. Greevy," Stacey sighed. "All I have to

do is change the dressing on the wound in your leg, then I'll be happy to be on my way. You don't want it to get infected, do you? Then I'll have to chop it off!"

Her patience was wearing thin. She was tired of constantly being on the defensive when she visited patients. Sam could make a mistake, but she couldn't. If she was going to be a doctor, she had to be perfect. Even the patients who accepted her, did so grudgingly, out of deference to Sam. No one but Sam encouraged her openly. Garth Greevy was the last straw in a day full of unpleasantness. She did not back down from her threat of amputation.

The thought of losing his leg won out. Greevy relented, though he cursed and swore the entire time she changed the bandage.

The last patient on the list wasn't home when Stacey called. It was another placebo call like Maude's, so she didn't pursue it. Instead, she trudged back home. It was almost time for the dance. She wanted to be ready when Martin arrived.

She heard his first knock on the door at precisely six o'clock. Partly as a peace offering, and partly because she really did like to pretty herself up on occasion, but was loathe to admit it, lest anyone think she was weakening in her resolve to become a doctor, Stacey wore her most becoming dress. It was daringly feminine, a white muslin with a tiny pink rosebud print and a scooped neckline that offered a tantalizing preview of the valley between her breasts.

She primped in front of the mirror for several more seconds, making certain everything was just right. Her long blonde hair was done up in a becoming chignon at the nape of her neck. At the second, more insistent, knock on the door, she hurried down the stairs. Easing the door open, she gave Martin her most disarming smile.

His eyes reflected the pleasure he found in her appearance. He stepped inside and took one of her slender hands in his larger one. "Stacey, you look lovely."

She sensed that he was going to kiss her, and she did not object. He took her in his arms and held her tightly against him. His mouth was wet, almost insulting, as it closed over hers. She was instinctively revolted, but pushed the thought from her mind.

She had more than once chided herself for being overly prudish, recognizing her behavior for what it was, an instinctive gesture of self-defense. She did not want to open her heart to another man. She had done it once and been crushingly hurt. She wouldn't let it happen again.

Yet, realistically, she had come to understand how foolish she was being. She had the rest of her life ahead of her. Her nature was too passionate to allow withdrawal from physical warmth forever. At least she had to give herself a fair chance.

She allowed herself to relax in Martin's embrace. His kisses grew more ardent. His tongue forced its way into her mouth.

Stacey waited for the pleasant flush of sweet euphoria to envelop her. It did not. Nor did her heartbeat increase. Involuntarily, she remembered another invading kiss of long ago. Why was Martin's kiss so different? And why did she have to think yet again of Joshua? Would she never rid herself of her longing for a dead man?

Almost desperately she clung to Martin, permitting him liberties she would otherwise never have done. His hands found her breasts, kneading the tender flesh beneath the thin fabric of her dress. She arched against him, almost sobbing with frustration. What was wrong with her? Martin Randolph was an attractive, passionate man.

"Oh, Stacey, Stacey," Martin moaned. "You're so beautiful. Sam's not home. Let's not go to the dance. Let me take you upstairs to your bed. Please, Stacey, please."

If she had been thinking more rationally, she would never have considered his suggestion. She was not in love with Martin. At least not yet. And she was no longer an impetuous teen-ager being driven to escape the miseries of war through a wanton, reckless act. She was a grown woman, fully responsible for her own actions. But thoughts of the past had weighed heavily on her today. It was as though she hoped to banish her memories with another rash act.

She did not protest when Martin settled his arm around her waist and led her up the stairs to her room. He pushed the door open with his foot. She could sense the tenseness, the anticipation in him, and it set off warning signals to her more sensible nature. Yet she continued to ignore them.

Joshua is dead! she thought wildly. Bury him! If it takes another man's body to do it, then so be it.

Even as she gave coherence to the thought, reason began to return. When Martin again swept her into his arms, Stacey did not respond with the same calculated wantoness. This isn't right, she scolded herself fiercely. You're just using Martin! Using him to forget a ghost!

With one hand Martin sought to undo the fastenings of her dress. The other he slid beneath its scooped neckline. His fingers closed over the flesh of a firm, ripe breast. Reality snapped back into sharp focus for Stacey.

"Martin, no. Please!" she cried, her voice shaking with emotion. A deep stabbing shame assailed her.

"What are you trying to pull, Stacey?" he demanded, releasing her abruptly. "You all but invite me into your bed, and now you act the outraged virgin?"

"I'm sorry," she whispered. "I don't know what came over me." But in truth, she did. It was just that she could never tell Martin. Tell him her body yearned for the kiss and caress of a dead man? No, Martin didn't deserve that. This was all her fault. And now she had to pay the price.

"If you wear a dress like that and welcome a man's advances as you did, how do you expect me to react?" he shouted. She had never seen him so furious.

"You have every right to be angry, Martin," she said. "I can only say again that I'm sorry. Please, can't we just forget about it and go to the dance?"

"No, Stacey, we can't go to the dance just yet." He smiled, a strange look in his eyes. "You're just nervous, my dear. I should have realized." He slipped his arm around her waist once again.

"No, Martin, really," she pleaded, putting her hands on his chest and trying to shove him away from her. "Please!"

He pulled her roughly against him. "You shouldn't tease a man, Stacey. Now that I've started, I don't want to stop." He deliberately pressed himself against her thigh, so that she would have no doubt about his physical desire for her.

She felt his stiffness and shuddered. She had never meant for it to go this far. "No!" she cried. "Let me go!"

He kissed her brutally, angrily, without regard for her tender lips. His hands roamed hurtfully over her breasts.

"Let go of me, Martin!" she cried. "Let go of me this instant, or I'll scream this house down!"

To her surprise he did so. He let out a deep breath. "All right, Stacey," he said softly, too softly. "But mark my words, my sweet, don't ever play me for a fool again. Do you understand?" He took her arm. "Now we'll go."

She nodded weakly. She hadn't meant to play Martin for a fool or anything else, but she was too dazed by her own conflicting emotions at the moment to risk another argument. Maybe she should just stay home. But she dearly loved to dance. Why deprive herself of one of the few pleasures she allowed in her life? She followed Martin down the stairs and outside to his waiting buggy.

On the way to Jonas' livery, where the dance was to be held, they lapsed into an uncomfortable silence. Stacey was stung by Martin's lack of consideration for her feelings. She could accept that he had been carried away by his passions, but she could not forget the actual brutality behind his advances. There had been moments when she had dreamed of more passionate kisses from Martin, after so many sisterly pecks on the cheek. But she realized all too clearly now, she had been expecting the same passionate response Joshua Steele had once aroused in her. To her bitter disappointment she had not only been unmoved, but actually revolted by Martin's kiss.

She had allowed percious little time in her life for romance. Gregory Benson, the man her mother had once encouraged to come courting, had thankfully gotten married by the time Stacey returned home from the war. Her mother's illness prevented her from grooming any replacement suitors, much to Stacey's everlasting relief. She would have regarded them then as an interference to her medical studies. Martin Randolph's attentions six months ago had led to the most steady male companion she had ever had. What would he think of her, if he knew she compared his kisses to those of a man long dead?

Even the dance went badly. Normally the townspeople treated her with open warmth, when she wasn't "playing doctor." But tonight there was a definite chill in their reception. Seeing Claire Jensen's sly looks only confirmed her suspicions. Anyone who had not actually been in the cafe this afternoon, had by now no doubt been apprised of even the most minute detail of her argument with Martin. The smattering of phrases she overheard "too independent for her own good", "disgraceful conduct", "no decent woman", "if God had meant for women to be doctors" only added to the misery of her evening. At the cool stares she wondered bleakly if her goal of being a doctor was worth the price she was paying.

Martin had only danced with her twice. She glanced around to see him squiring Claire around the dance floor. The buxom 18-year-old looked to be in seventh heaven to be seen in the arms of the handsome bank president.

Stacey sighed. She felt no jealousy at the doe-eyed expression Claire cast at Martin. Claire looked that way at most men. She projected a kind of vulnerability that seemed to endear her to them. Not unlike a puppy, Stacey thought, smiling a little.

Claire was a woman in search of a husband. She was desperate to find a man who would take her away from the drudgery of working for her father. Martin was obviously basking in the attention of the lovely young woman. When the dance ended, he leaned closer to her and whispered something in her ear. The girl giggled, gasping with feigned embarrassment.

"Oh, Stacey," she cried, rushing over to her, "I don't know how you can let that man out of your sight for a minute."

"You didn't come by the house about your stomach," Stacey said, deliberately changing the subject.

"Papa just wouldn't hear of it," she pouted. "I guess I'll have to throw up or something next time to prove I'm really sick. You wouldn't have something that would make me do that, would you?"

Stacey rolled her eyes heavenward. "If you're really sick, you come by the office," she said. "Tell your father, I said so." She paused. "And since that probably wouldn't work, tell him Sam said so."

"Why, thank you, I'll do that," Claire said, scarcely listening. "But now you'll really have to excuse me. I must get back to Martin. He promised me the next dance."

What happened to "Mister" Randolph, Stacey thought sourly, then chided herself. Martin was simply using Claire. He wanted to punish Stacey for her shameful behavior earlier. She supposed she couldn't blame him, though she might have hoped for a more mature reaction.

"Oh, Martin, you mustn't," she heard Claire say in a voice meant to be overheard. "What would Stacey say?" The girl laughed giddily, as Martin whirled her around the dance floor once again.

Stacey suddenly felt stifled. She had to get some air. She hurried out of the gaily decorated barn. Outside a million stars dappled the clear black sky. She walked over to the livery corral, resting her chin on the top rail. She smiled, listening to the night sounds of restive horses, disturbed no doubt by the boisterous music of the town band. A blaze-faced sorrel pranced over and shoved his velvety muzzle against her cheek.

"Hi, Randy," she murmured at the horse, stroking him affectionately. "Where's Sheba?" She cast a glance across the corral, searching for Randy's latest mate. Sheba was due to foal in less than a month, and Nathan Jonas, the livery owner, had promised Stacey the foal in return for her medical services to his livestock. She considered it a more than fair exchange.

Sheba was nowhere to be seen, though. No doubt Nathan had moved her away from all the activity. She could be a bit skittish.

"Too bad people aren't as smart as horses," Stacey mused, patting the stallion's neck. "A horse doesn't care whether his doctor is male or female, just as long as the doctor knows doctoring."

She shook her head, gazing back at the brightly lit interior of the barn. She couldn't see Martin at the moment, but she had no doubt that he would be out later to escort her home. If he tried to kiss her again, she would do her best to enjoy it.

She heard rapidly approaching footsteps and turned around. George Arenson, bartender of the Double Eagle saloon, rushed over to her.

"Miss Stacey," he said urgently, "I was just at your place lookin' for Doc Sam, but he ain't there."

"Sam's on a call. What is it, George?" It had to be an emergency. The normally phlegmatic George was almost impossible to rile. That's why he was such a good bartender.

"It's Molly," George gasped.

Stacey's memory immediately identified Molly Webster, the youngest of the girls Rance Dawson used to entertain the cowboys in his saloon.

"The baby!" Stacey guessed at once. Molly was nine months pregnant.

"I already got Mrs. Ebert up there to see her, but Molly was asking for you."

"I'll run home and get my things and be right there. You tell Molly I'm coming."

"Thanks, Miss Stacey."

Stacey didn't take the time to tell Martin she was leaving. She started running the quarter-mile to the house. Quickly she gathered up the things she would need. The saloon was barely a block away. She raced toward it, medical bag in hand.

Rance Dawson barred her entry at the bat-wing doors of the Double Eagle. Stacey straightened her shoulders defiantly at the intimidating look in the burly saloon keeper's eyes. "Get out of my way, Mr. Dawson."

"You seem to forget that you're not welcome here, little lady doctor," Dawson sneered.

Stacey grimaced as she remembered the incident that had made Rance Dawson an enemy for life. Stacey had insisted that one of his best girls leave Dawson's establishment and go into a less strenuous line of "work." Dawson had never forgiven her.

"Molly asked for me, and I intend to see her," she snapped. She could feel her knees quaking, but she gave no outward sign of distress at his forbidding manner.

"Rance, please, let her come up," a shrill voice called from the stairs.

He glared at the woman, one of his other girls. Stacey did not know her name.

"Molly's in terrible pain. Please, Rance," the woman pleaded.

Stacey shoved Dawson's arm aside and started up the steps. He stormed after her, gripping her arm fiercely. "You do anything that gets another of my girls out of here and you're the one that's going to need a doctor."

Stacey returned his gaze coolly. At least she never had to worry about veiled threats from Rance Dawson. Everything was on the table with him. "I'll keep it in mind," was all she said, yanking her arm free. He did not stop her this time, as she hurried up the steps.

"She's inside," the saloon girl told Stacey, when she reached the hallway upstairs. She indicated Molly's room. "That old bat Mrs. Ebert is with her. She won't let nobody else come in."

Stacey patted the girl's arm. She was in obvious distress over her friend's condition. "Molly will be fine. She's a tough little girl. She'll be just fine. I'll let you

106

know if I need anything. And you never mind Mrs. Ebert."

The girl smiled her thanks. She wasn't used to being treated like a human being.

Stacey stepped into the sparsely furnished room and was immediately struck by its overwhelming stuffiness. The three windows were closed tightly.

"Mrs. Ebert," Stacey snapped, "get those windows open at once."

"The air is bad for a new baby," the matronly widow intoned. "I'll not have it, Miss Stacey."

"You'll do as I say, or you'll leave," Stacey retorted, allowing herself a brief, unwelcome slash of self-pity. Would it ever be easy? Did she have to fight them every single step of the way? She needed that trip to Denver for more reasons than medical supplies.

Striding over to the wall that faced the street, Stacey yanked one of the windows open. While Mrs. Ebert stood by and watched disapprovingly, she proceeded to open the other two windows as well.

The night air brought instant relief to the closed-in room. Once a tolerable temperature had been reached, Stacey closed one of the windows, but left the other two slightly open.

She stepped over to Molly's bedside. The girl's pinched narrow face was contorted in the throes of a contraction.

"Oh, Miss Stacey," she cried, "please, don't let my baby die."

Stacey touched the girl's fevered forehead. She was badly dehydrated from being in the sweltering room. Stacey's jaw clenched angrily. If God had intended babies to be born in ovens . . .

She pulled back the bedcovers and gave the girl a cursory examination. Her dilation was not yet complete. She could still be hours away from delivery.

"Mrs. Ebert, please go down to the saloon and get me some ice."

"Ice!" the woman cried, starting to protest.

"Now, Mrs. Ebert."

Muttering imprecations under her breath the heavy set woman left the room.

Stacey sat down on the bed, stroking the girl's overwarm forehead with a wet cloth.

"When the next pain comes," she told the frightened girl soothingly, "I want you to pant like a dog. It will help the pain be more bearable. Do you understand?"

Molly nodded, but her eyes were wide with terror. She had to be barely seventeen, Stacey thought sadly. What a horrible life she must have had to lead her to this.

"I want my baby, Miss Stacey," the girl sobbed. "I want you to promise me my baby will be all right."

"I'll do everything I can for you *and* your baby, you know that, Molly," Stacey said. She tugged the bedcovers off the bed and placed them in a pile on the room's only chair. She covered the girl with one thin blanket.

"Pull your knees up, Molly."

The girl did so, a contraction coming at the same time. She caught her breath and began to moan softly, holding her stomach.

"Pant, Molly," Stacey shouted, hoping to get through the girl's fierce concentration against the pain. Her tenseness was only making it worse.

"Breathe, Molly, breathe!" Stacey began to pant herself in the cadence she wanted Molly to follow. The girl began to imitate her, her face relaxing a little.

"That was better, wasn't it?" Stacey said, when the contraction had passed.

"Yes," Molly conceded. "It was."

They repeated the procedure with each contraction, now coming fifteen minutes apart. Between the contractions Stacey talked with Molly about anything that came into the girl's head.

Where was Mrs. Ebert with that ice? Stacey didn't want Molly drinking anything, but she could at least suck on some chips of ice.

The door to the room slammed open. Stacey jerked her head around, staring in disbelief.

"Martin, what on earth?" she began, but was cut off as Randolph stormed into the room, yanking her to her feet.

A contraction seized Molly. Randolph's presence so unnerved the girl that she forgot everything Stacey had taught her. The pain was agonizing. She screamed as it increased.

Mrs. Ebert walked into the room wearing a self-satisfied smile, watching as Martin Randolph dragged Stacey out of the room.

"That's it, Molly girl," Stacey heard the old woman say, "Just bear with it. You'll have to pay dearly for your sins before this night is out."

Stacey's heart lurched at the woman's vile, judgmental words. Of all the heartless . . . She whirled to face Martin.

"How dare you?" she hissed.

But he interrrupted her at once. "What are you doing here?"

"I should think that would be obvious."

"No woman of mine is going to be in the same room with a saloon tramp, let alone touch her vermin offspring."

"Martin, let's get a couple of things straight right now," she said. "I am a doctor, or damned close to being one, and that girl in there needs a doctor's care. If nothing else, think of me as a midwife. And secondly, I am not your woman. I belong to no one. We fought a war over slavery, remember?"

She turned to go back into the room, but his iron grip on her arm held her fast.

"You're not going back in there, Stacey. I forbid it!"

"Forbid? Forbid!" she shouted, losing the last slender hold she had on her temper. "And where do you get the right on God's green earth to forbid me to do anything, Martin Randolph? We're not married yet, and if this is any sample of what I can expect, well, I'll give you the opportunity here and now to retract your proposal."

Randolph's blue eyes glittered with suppressed rage, but he did not withdraw his request for her hand in marriage.

"I'm going back in that room, Martin, and nothing short of physical violence is going to stop me." She jerked her arm free of his restraining hand. She read the disgust in his eyes and was sorry for it, but Molly was her patient, and she came first.

"All right, Stacey," Randolph said. "I understand your moral obligation to the girl. I was only thinking of you . . . your reputation."

"My reputation or yours," she flung at him. "It certainly doesn't look good for the lady friend of

110

Spring Canyon's bank president to be caring for a saloon girl, does it?"

Randolph held his tongue, but Stacey saw the spark in his eyes and guessed that she had hit on the truth. He was more concerned about his image in the community than hers. Still she could see that he was relenting. Maybe Martin could be reasonable about her doctor career after all. She would just have to be patient.

"I'll see you before I leave for Denver tomorrow," she said quietly, then stepped back into Molly's room, closing the door.

Randolph stood staring at the closed door for several minutes. He was amazed at how close he had come to hitting her. But he was wise enough to know that she would never have forgiven him that. No, if he were going to teach her proper lessons in decorum, he would do well to wait until after they were married. Then the law would be on his side. With his fists clenched at his sides, he left the saloon.

After the glaring light of the hallway, it took Stacey a moment to again adjust her eyes to the dim lantern light of Molly's room. She was in time to see Mrs. Ebert closing the last window.

"Mrs. Ebert, if you can't help me with Molly according to my instructions, then get out!"

Mrs. Ebert bit off the retort she was about to make. She had never seen Stacey so angry. "I'll do as you say," she said, her voice giving away the fact that she continued to disapprove.

"Thank you, Mrs. Ebert," Stacey said wearily. "Now get the bedcovers back off her, too. Then I'll show you how I want you to help her with her breathing. I hope you brought back the ice, as well as Mr. Randolph."

The woman nodded, having the good grace to look at least a trifle embarrrassed.

Stacey's anger at the woman disappeared. She knew Mrs. Ebert had been the leading midwife in the area before her arrival. The widow woman still delivered a good percentage of the babies around town, even rivalling the number Sam delivered. But Stacey had made a few inroads into Mrs. Ebert's private domain, and the woman was naturally resentful.

Stacey took several deep breaths to calm herself and again sat down at Molly's side. There was little sense in upsetting the girl. She was scared enough already. Stacey chipped off some of the ice Mrs. Ebert had brought and eased some of it into the girl's mouth.

It wasn't Mrs. Ebert who was making her so angry anyway, Stacey admitted to herself. It was Martin's increasingly hostile attitude. She didn't have the time right now to examine her own feelings about that.

"Okay, Molly," she said, "let's see what we can do about getting this baby of yours born, shall we?"

But it was several more hours before Molly's baby was interested in making its debut. Molly was exhausted. Stacey was nearly so. But Mrs. Ebert seemed to thrive on the whole event. To Stacey's amazement the older woman continued to bustle around the room. It had to be nearly two in the afternoon.

"It's time, Stacey," Mrs. Ebert said all at once.

Stacey had stepped over to the window, but at Mrs. Ebert's words was instantly at Molly's bedside.

"Bear down, Molly. Bear down hard," she urged, as

she watched the baby's head, now intermittently visible between the girl's legs. Molly writhed in undiluted agony.

"Scream if you want to, Molly," Stacey encouraged. "I have no doubt that I would."

Stacey's presence at several births previous to this one still did not lessen the miracle of it for her. She watched the tiny head emerge, turning the small shoulders as the rest of the wiggling baby slipped out. Stacey scooped up the small bundle and deposited it on Molly's tummy.

"You've got yourself a daughter, Molly," Stacey beamed, rubbing the tiny infant's back, smiling at the healthy wail it emitted.

Mrs. Ebert helped Molly with the after-birth, as Stacey cut the cord and cleaned up the baby. Stacey had made scrupulously certain that Mrs. Ebert had washed her hands thoroughly before touching the baby or Molly.

Molly was crying and laughing at the same time.

"A girl? A little girl?" she sobbed. "My little angel. That's what I'm going to call her, Miss Stacey. Angel."

Mrs. Ebert was about to make a comment, but at the sharp look from Stacey, managed to keep her mouth shut. Stacey breathed a silent prayer of thanks.

Stacey stayed another hour, wrapping the infant in a soft clean blanket and nestling her next to her mother. Mrs. Ebert, who had been objecting to nearly everything Stacey did all night, had toward the end, finally begun giving her grudging compliments.

When Stacey was satisfied that Molly and the baby would sleep peacefully the remainder of the day, she stretched her arms tiredly and smiled at the older woman.

"I'm going home to get some sleep, Mrs. Ebert," she said, as she watched the slumbering pair. "I suggest you do the same."

Mrs. Ebert may have had to give Stacey credit for her medical skills at last, but that did not mean she was above a parting shot or two.

"I didn't want to cause a stir while the poor child was birthing," the widow woman said.

The heck you didn't, Stacey thought grimly, but she did not interrupt.

"But I have to agree with Mr. Randolph. It was not at all a ladylike thing for you to be here in this whore's bedroom. Only God knows who the father of that poor little bastard is."

"It's been a long night," Stacey sighed, unable and unwilling to renew their longstanding bickering at the moment. "As I said, I'm going to bed," She turned and left the woman standing by the door, her mouth still open, ready to do battle.

Stacey heard her muttering something about the ladies in the sewing circle hearing about this. She cast her eyes heavenward. What did she have to do to be accepted by these people? Every time she seemed to make a little headway, something always happened to slam her back down.

She thought again of the stage ride to Denver tomorrow and was grateful for the respite. She needed to get away from everything and everyone, if only for two weeks.

As she headed for the house, she prayed fervently that Sam had returned. It would be nice to encounter a friendly face for a change.

When she walked through the door, she was greeted only by silence. As tired as she was, she remembered an article in a medical journal that she wanted to read. It would only take a few minutes.

Dr. Sam Curtis was sound asleep when his horse and buggy pulled into Jonas' livery. Tobey, his bay gelding, knew the route to his home stall from just about anywhere. After a long day and night out at the Placerman ranch, Doc Curtis had simply dozed off, confident the horse would take him home.

When the motion of the carriage ceased, the doctor forced himself wearily awake. The Placerman foreman had proved to be a formidable patient. Setting his two broken legs had been the easy part, convincing him that he had to spend the next few weeks in bed had taken hours. Then a freak accident in the horse pen had injured old man Placerman himself. It was a good thing the man had two healthy sons to take over most of the chores.

Bone-tired and wanting nothing more than to collapse in his own bed, Curtis still took the time to unharness Tobey, rub him down, and give him a fresh ration of oats. He pulled out his pocket watch and squinted at it in the moonlight. Just about ten o'clock. Nathan Jonas, the livery owner, was probably asleep in his room in the back. Curtis moved about quietly. He didn't want to disturb another man's sleep, when he ached for sleep himself.

Sam Curtis was a wiry man in his mid-fifties with a shock of unruly gray-white hair and a perennial twinkle in his brown eyes. He hoped suddenly as he walked toward the house that Stacey was still awake.

He knew she would be leaving for Denver in the morning, and he thought about how empty the house was going to be without her friendly companionship.

He had come to depend on her more than he cared to admit, since the death of his wife over two years ago. He could've gone back and re-established his practice in Boston when Jenny died, but he found he couldn't leave this land of desolate beauty. And so he had invited his only living relative to join him here.

Stacey was the daughter he and Jenny had never had. He remembered how he and his wife had argued with her long into the night, when she had come to them in April of '64 and told them of her preposterous plan to join her father on the battlefield. He had been struck then by her candor and her forthright determination to be a doctor. During the war, he had received more than one letter from Ben praising Stacey's almost intuitive medical instincts.

Years later, when he'd received a nearly indecipherable letter from his sister, Beatrice, he'd quietly checked into Stacey's home situation. Though his niece hadn't been able to attend medical school, her medical acumen was astounding. Colleagues wrote him in awe of her surgical skill, at the same time swearing him to secrecy lest their peers discover their high regard for a woman doctor.

Yet with all of her knowledge, she had virtually nowhere to practice in the east. Without a diploma she was lost. The west was not so scrupulous. Here she could nurture her God-given talent by earning the trust of her patients. She'd had to handle the closed minds, the superstitious, and the foolish, but she was making progress all the time.

Walking toward the house, Sam brightened considerably to see the light glowing in his office. She was still awake. Studying medical journals no doubt.

He smiled when he stepped into his office and spied her. She was slumped over his desk. The lantern burned brightly on a nearby table. She had fallen asleep reading the latest *New England Journal of Medicine*. Gently he shook her shoulder.

"Oh, Sam," she yawned. "I must have fallen asleep."

"Uh huh. Hard day?"

"Molly Webster had her baby," she told him, rising to give him an affectionate hug. "It was wonderful. A little girl. She's so tiny, but perfect, absolutely perfect. Molly's deliriously happy. I just wish . . ."

"She had somewhere else to bring up the baby."

"Something like that."

"You look exhausted," he said. "Maybe you should postpone the trip to Denver."

"I'm fine," she said, straightening. "I'm going to Denver and that's all there is to it."

"What did I do?" he teased, noting the sharpness of her voice.

"I'm sorry, Sam," she sighed.

"Martin Randolph," Curtis stated simply.

"Oh, Sam, not only did that man say I could not go to Denver," she said, "but he had the unmitigated gall to drag me out of Molly's room while she was in labor. He said I had no business being in . . . Molly's room."

Curtis gave her a fatherly hug. "You know how dead set he is against your being a doctor. You couldn't have expected anything different. And I'm not too sure I like your gallivanting around the

117

contryside unescorted myself."

"Men!" she snorted in exasperation. "What am I? A china doll?" Then she sighed. Sam meant well and she knew he loved her. She rubbed her eyes tiredly. "I don't want to argue with you, Sam. It's been an ungodly long day. I should have been in bed hours ago. The stage leaves at seven."

"Is Martin seeing you off?"

"I'm afraid so. Though after the little scene in front of Molly's room, maybe he'll stay home."

"You need more fun in your life, Stacey," Sam chided, as he escorted her up the stairs to her room. "Everything can't be geared toward becoming a doctor."

"I don't have time for a lot of frivolity, Sam." She turned the knob on the door to her room. "And if Martin is any sample of what I can expect from a man who claims to want to marry me, I think I'll happily spend my days as a spinster." A pang shot through her, as for the third time that day she thought of Joshua Steele. Some day she had to put that ghost to rest once and for all.

Sam kissed his niece good night. As she closed the door to her room, he wondered if a man existed who could truly treasure his free-spirited niece. She deserved nothing less.

CHAPTER EIGHT

Joshua Steele reined his dun gelding to a halt. Mile after mile of undulating green peaks stretched before him. Peaks that held an eerie red cast in the light of the rising sun. The Sangre de Cristos. Blood of Christ. Sighting on Baldy Mountain, he continued along the rugged switchbacks leading up the slope. Juniper, spruce, and a sprinkling of aspen ranged to the limit of his vision and beyond. The dewy scent of pine seemed to permeate even the rocks. All around him an awesome beauty enhanced the image of a false paradise.

Steele's gray eyes detected a slight movement on the ground to his left. He turned his head in time to see a late-hunting owl spear an early-rising rabbit with its crushing talons. He kneed the dun forward, gray eyes missing nothing and mirroring nothing of the thoughts of the lone rider.

He rode effortlessly, his lean hipped, broad shouldered body at one with the movements of his horse. His sun darkened features and dark mustache added an extra grimness to the bitter set of his mouth. His swarthy good looks would have been considered handsome by many a member of the opposite sex, if they were not put off at once by the singular coldness in his wolf-gray eyes.

He was a man driven by one all-consuming purpose. An obsession. A need to personally crush the life out of the man who had betrayed him in Mexico four years ago. Merrick. Ross Merrick. The name was like a sickness in him, a wound that would not heal. He had spent nearly every waking moment since leaving Mexico in a relentless search for the man named Merrick, pausing only when his money had run out completely. At those times he had not been averse to hiring out his gun to survive. But even then Steele killed only when forced. He had only one exception. When he found Ross Merrick, he would murder him with his bare hands.

Merrick's trail had grown cold, then hot, then cold again, but Steele's smoldering drive for revenge had never once diminished. More than once the thought of the ranch, still his, in the Colorado Territory, had pulled hard on a need buried deep inside him, but he had shrugged it off and ridden on. He could never go back there, never allow the serenity of it to touch him, as long as Merrick still lived.

Lately too, he was disturbed by a sharp pain that seemed to have its origin in his left eye. The pain usually struck without warning and was becoming increasingly severe and longer in duration. At times his vision was affected without the accompanying pain. If it continued, he knew he would have little choice but to seek out a doctor. The frustration about the delay this might cause in his search was evident in his increasing restlessness. He spent less and less time in each town, pushing himself to exhaustion. If he determined Merrick was nowhere in the vicinity, he immediately rode on. Steele never considered what his quest was doing to him as a human being.

Two hours after sunset he reined the dun to a halt adjusting the brim of his well-worn Stetson. Like the cowhide vest, denim shirt and pants he wore, the hat had seen its better days. He looked the part of an entrenched saddle tramp, a long way from his privileged Pennsylvania unbringing. The Rocky Mountains were a long way from the high society of Philadelphia, too. But that was where he would go when Merrick was dead. He ached for the peace of his ranch. He would raise horses, cattle, maybe share it with a wife, children. Emerald eyes flashed through his mind. Furious, he threw off the thought. Merrick. He could think only of Merrick.

He climbed out of the saddle and set about making a meager camp for the night. After building a small fire, he hunkered down in front of it to heat up the last of a rabbit he had killed the day before. He gnawed on the tough meat, not even tasting it.

A few minutes later he swilled down the bitter dregs of his coffee. Leaning back against a huge boulder, he considered his position. He should have no trouble reaching Elizabethtown tomorrow. He stretched his long legs in front of him. He'd pushed himself too hard today. He was exhausted. The dream would come tonight, and he cringed at the thought.

Steele stared into the dying flames of his campfire. Merrick was in New Mexico. He could feel it in his bones. The bastard was close now. The West would have been like a magnet to a man like Merrick. He could bury his identity here in a land where law and order had yet to fully assert itself. Men didn't ask questions out here. You were accepted at face value, your past your own business and no one else's.

Here, too, Steele discovered, in the New Mexico of the 1870's was the perfect opportunity for vast amounts of wealth in land speculation. Merrick had the capital to invest from stolen gold shipments. And he had four years to build a respectable new life. Steele scratched his three day old beard thoughtfully. Sometimes it seemed more than a lifetime ago that he had first met Ross Merrick.

"Ah, welcome, Ross," General Ulysses Grant said, smiling at the blue-eyed, blond haired man who had just entered his office in Washington, D.C. "Come in. I want you to meet Captain Joshua Steele."

"Josh, this is Colonel Ross Merrick." Steele rose from the chair beside Grant's desk and extended his right hand. Merrick grasped it firmly.

"A pleasure, captain," Merrick said, his gaze falling briefly on the band-like bandage around Steele's head.

Steele indulged the man's curiosity by saying, "A flesh wound in the Wilderness. It won't cause any delay in the mission."

"Mission?" Merrick questioned.

"Ross hasn't been briefed on this assignment, yet, Captain," Grant interjected. "If you two gentlemen will have a seat, I'll fill you both in."

They listened intently while Grant detailed the plan that would send them to Mexico together. The hard-nosed general finished by saying, "President Lincoln is becoming more and more concerned with the activities of the French at the expense of our neighbor to the south. Not only are they violating the Monroe Doctrine, but the French have already been discovered secreting arms and money to the Confederacy. If Maximilian keeps the Mexican throne, the south can expect a blank check from Napoleon the Third in Europe."

Grant hooked one leg over a corner of his desk. "This Mexican thing may last far beyond our own war," he said. "If either of you wants out, I expect you to say so before you leave this room today." He flipped open the mahogany box that sat on the desk and extracted a long Cuban cigar. He bit off the end and grunted his thanks when Merrick struck a match for him, but he was looking at Steele. "You have a question, Captain?"

Steele nodded. "If I may ask, General, why were Colonel Merrick and I singled out for this assignment?"

"For Colonel Merrick's part he's a linguist," Grant explained. "Talk to him today and he sounds like a born and raised Washingtonian. Speak French and you'd swear he was raised on the streets of Paris. Spanish, Portuguese, Italian— he's fluent in each and every one, though for this mission only French and Spanish are a necessity. And Colonel Merrick has the true flair of the diplomat. People trust him."

Merrick laughed. "It also helps that I asked for an assigment—any assignment. I've been getting decidedly bored attending so-called diplomatic functions in Washington."

Steele fingered his bandaged head. "There's something to be said for a desk job, Colonel." To Grant he said, "I take it my past has caught up with me?"

"Guilty, Captain," Grant snorted. "You're one of my best field commanders, and I hate to lose you, but these orders come from President Lincoln himself. You've got the savvy we need down there. And, of course, you do speak Spanish?"

"Hace he tenido tres años." He grinned, translating for Grant, "Since I was three years old."

"The result of considerable childhood pampering by one Maria Huerta, a household maid, in your parent's home in Philadelphia," said Grant.

Steele grimaced. Whoever had done the checking into his background had been painstakingly thorough. And the general wasn't finished yet.

"When your mother died, you became something of a hellion, at least in the opinion of your father. He had you shunted off to Paris to attend the Univerisity at Sorbonne. You didn't care for the idea. Six months was all you managed, I believe."

Steele shifted uncomfortably in his chair.

"The official class record reads that you left school because of an illness in the family. However," Grant cocked an eyebrow at Steele, "it seems that unofficially there was the rumor of your dallying with the daughter of an Ancient Civilizations professor."

"You could have just asked me I spoke French," Steele said, his voice carrying just a trace of sarcasm. The general seemed to be deriving some kind of vicarious pleasure from the dossier of Steele's exploits.

Grant chuckled. As if to confirm Steele's thoughts, he said, "That wouldn't have been nearly as interesting, Captain." He perused the rest of the file in front of him, "You did manage to make peace with your father before his death, but left Philadelphia fo the West eight years ago. Only the War brought you back. Tell me, was the professor's daughter worth it?"

Steele's smile was self-mocking, "I suppose she was at the time." He thought of the petite mademoiselle, who had gotten him expelled from Sorbonne. He'd been young and foolish, and learned too late that she made a habit of getting her father's students expelled. Odd, how he couldn't quite picture her face any more. When he tried, emerald green eyes and hair the color of the sun superimposed themselves on the image.

Grant gave Steele a hearty slap on the back and extended his hand. Steele stood and accepted it. "I'll take it by the fact that you gentlemen are still here, that you accept this assignment, no matter how long it takes. You'll be leaving immediately." He shook Merrick's hand. "I wish you both Godspeed."

The next day Steele and Merrick departed for Mexico. The juarista cause had become their own.

They performed their tasks with exceptional skill, because three years later they were still in Mexico. The war between the states had ended, Lincoln was dead, but President Johnson continued the campaign to expel the French and Maximilian. Benito Juarez would get all the help he needed.

Steele and Merrick remained a part of that help. At least Steele did. Merrick proved to be more interested in his own pursuits right from the first. Often they didn't work together for months at a time. When they did, Steele would organize most of the mission, while Merrick remained in the background. Still, he did his job well enough so that Steele did not suspect the potential for treachery in the man until it was too late. It was one thing to think about being rich, as Merrick often did, but it was something else entirely to commit murder to achieve that end. The man was a chameleon, changing personalities to suit his environment. Steele accepted totally the blame for not foreseeing what Merrick was capable of. Because he had not, many good men were dead.

It was February of '67. The French were increasingly outnumbered as more and more Mexican peasants sided with the juaristas. But the imperialists were determined to fight to the end. At the supply port of Matamoros Steele arranged for a shipment of arms and gold to be escorted to Juarez's army.

Five wagons, each pulled by three teams of horses, wound their way through rocky countryside heading south. An armed guard sat perched beside each teamster on each wagon. Steele rode horseback alongside the plodding caravan. Ahead of the lead wagon rode four soldatos. The same number trailed the rear. Far to the front, two outriders rode point, scouting ahead several hundred yards. The journey to the delivery point was to take three days.

For three years now Steele had spoken, thought, and dreamed in Spanish. His swarthy features combined with the ragged serape that draped his shoulders and the floppy sombrero that sat on his head gave him the look of a pure-blooded Mexican. It was only when standing close and peering into those gray eyes, that he could be recognized as an Americano.

He was already on edge when the wagon train made camp the first night. He swallowed the last of his coffee and tossed the cup by the fire. The cook would collect it later. He pulled the Colt from his holster and hefted the weapon. The last three shipments he'd sent out had been ambushed, no matter how much secrecy he built into the plans. Merrick had been in on all three. They'd gone over each detail after the attacks, but neither could detect a flaw. There were no flaws, Steele realized. Save one. Merrick. He had betrayed them, gone over to the French. It was the only explanation. And this shipment was going to prove it, one way or the other. He hadn't told Merrick that he would be escorting this train himself. Though the day had gone without a hitch, he couldn't shake the feeling of uneasiness that had settled over him.

"You're worried, amigo," the mustachioed caballero said, as he squatted by the fire. "Why?"

Steele studied Rudy Montoya in the firelight. Not much more than twenty, the slightly built Mexican juarista was probably the best gunhand on the trip. He was cocky, fiercely patriotic, and filled with good humor. Steele had liked him instantly.

"It's nothing," Steele hedged, shoving the pistol back in his holster.

"You think the ambush will come tomorrow." It was a statement, not a question.

Steele's eyes narrowed. Rudy had an uncanny way of reading his mind. He sighed heavily. "If I were going to ambush this train, I'd do it tomorrow. It's the most rugged country on the route. The passable trail is extremely narrow, and it's the only way through."

Rudy nodded, settling himself next to Steele, but staring into the fire. "Many men will die tomorrow. But to free Mexico it must be so." He spoke of the matter-of-factness of death, as only one who had seen too much of it can. He gave Steele a sidelong glance. "I have often wondered, Joshua, why you take the cause of Juarez so seriously. After all, you are a gringo."

Steele grinned. From anyone else gringo might have been a slur, but from Rudy it was said with open camaraderie.

"It's my job," he said simply.

"You do your job with a great deal of fervor, amigo."

Steele shrugged. "Maximilian is a good man in the wrong place at the wrong time. The French are using him. Mexico belongs to the Mexicans, and while I don't hold with all that Juarez stands for, at least he was born here."

Rudy laughed. "I like you, gringo amigo." Then more seriously, he said, "What will you do when Juarez is president again?"

"Head for Colorado as fast as my horse will carry me," Steele said, "and try to remember how to speak English."

"You have a woman there?"

Steele's eyes clouded. How often had he thought of her these past three years? Green eyes that flashed fire, skin as soft as the finest silk, a passion that had astonished him in its intensity. Stacey. Where was she now? A well-married society woman of Albany, New York, no doubt. He unconsciously clenched his jaw at the thought of her sharing her bed with another man, husband or not.

He shook his head. He was behaving like an adolescent. Maybe his preoccupation with her was a way of assuaging his conscience. He had taken her virginity in the midst of a war, when she had been badly frightened and vulnerable. It should never have happened. But it had. And try as he might, in the arms of more than one faceless woman since, he could not forget the fiery girl-woman of the Wilderness.

"Ah, she must be a tigress," Rudy sighed wistfully.

"What?"

"Your woman. To make you feel such loneliness you must love her very much."

Steele only then realized how long he'd sat thinking of her. He rose, shoving Stacey from his thoughts. He gave Rudy a wry smile. "No, my friend, not love. Lust maybe. A chance encounter best forgotten."

"If you say so, Joshua," Rudy said, but for once he did not believe the tall Americano.

"It may be a long day tomorrow," Steele said. "You'd best turn in. So will I, after I check the guards."

Steele slept fitfully that night, drowning in the sweet rapture of Stacey Hamilton's arms.

The next morning the caravan picked its way cautiously along treacherous mountain roads. It was nearly noon when one of the point riders tore through the lead column of soldatos shouting. *"La montaña de rocas!"*

Rockslide. Steele's every sense was alert to a trap. Rockslides were common enough, but something about this one just didn't sit right. It was too convenient.

He spurred his horse into a gallop and followed the scout to the slide. The rocks couldn't have been more strategically placed if they had been brought in by hand one at a time. To the left of the mountain of boulders was a steep incline, unscalable by the wagons. To the right a sheer drop-off. Steele dismounted and kicked disgustedly at one of the smaller stones. They would have to move the slide rock by rock.

"I don't like it, senor," the scout said.

"Neither do I, Enrique," said Steele. "Did you see anything?"

"Nothing. But someone is watching. I feel it."

"So do I, but we don't have much choice in the matter. When the wagons get here, we'll unhitch a couple of the teams and start sending these rocks over the cliff."

"Si, senor."

"You and Salazar stay here," Steele said, referring to the second scout who had ridden in to join them. "I'll ride back and alert the others."

Steele mounted and spurred the horse back toward the wagons. He reined to a halt beside Alfredo Magaña, leader of the juarista band.

"It's a trap," Steele said. "And all we can do is ride into it. Tell your men to have their guns ready."

Magaña shouted an order to his men. Immediately each soldato yanked his rifle from his scabbard.

The juarista leader turned to Steele. "You think the French know about the guns and the gold, senor?"

"It would seem so," Steele muttered.

"I kept all of my men together all of the time," he said defensively, "ever since you announced the shipment two days ago. Rudy Montoya watched them. I do not see how anyone could know. We have taken every precaution, every back road. We left Matamoros in the middle of the night with individual wagons . . ."

"There's no use worrying about it now, Alfredo," Steele interrupted. "It's done."

Magaña swatted his horse's neck angrily, as the animal pranced nervously sideways. "In each of these wagons rides three hundred rifles and ten thousand rounds of ammunition," he said. "Enough to help my people win against the French dogs. And in the middle wagon rides fifty thousand dollars in gold to help our beloved presidente regain his rightful place as the leader of Mexico. The French cannot beat us, Senor Steele. They cannot!"

"They haven't won yet, Alfredo." The wagons were nearing the rockslide. "Keep your guard up."

Steele turned his horse and cantered back to the rear of the caravan. He could feel the hairs on the back of his neck rise. It would happen soon.

The first shot dropped one of the guards. The second felled one of the horses pulling the lead wagon. The five remaining horses screamed in terror at the smell of blood, rearing frantically against their harness, as the teamster struggled to keep them on the narrow road.

"Get off the wagons!" Steele shouted.

The shots had come from the top of the rise to their left. They were safe to the right because of the precipice, and to the front because of the rockslide. But their position was precarious at best. Their attackers had chosen the perfect spot for a long siege.

Steele dove behind the third wagon, his rifle in his hand. He fired several shots up the slope, providing cover for the soldatos and the scouts as they too bolted behind the wagons nearest them.

"It doesn't look too good, amigo," Rudy called to Josh from behind the second wagon.

"Cover me!" Steele shouted.

Rudy fired rapidly, while Steele made the dash to Rudy's wagon. "They've got a blind spot above the first wagon," Steele said, "because of the way the slide is sitting. If we could get up there . . ."

"I don't think so, senor."

Steele whirled. Magaña stood facing him, his gun levelled.

"What is this, Alfredo?" Rudy shouted.

"Drop your guns. Both of you," the juarista leader said.

"Filthy imperialist spy. *Hijo de puta!* Son of a bitch!" Rudy screamed. He lunged at Magaña before Steele could stop him. Magaña fired. Rudy slumped to the ground.

"Damn you to hell," Steele seethed. He knelt beside his friend. The wound didn't seem too serious. In fact, Rudy continued to hurl epithets at the imperialist infiltrator, even as Steele tried to get him to lie still.

Magaña chuckled. "Try to see my side of it, amigos," he said. "It just doesn't seem fair that Juarez should get all of that money, while Alfredo Magaña gets nothing."

"Hijo de puta!" Rudy raged again.

Magaña kicked him in the head.

Fury made Steele reckless. He launched himself at Magaña, who cried out in surprise and fear. Steele grappled him to the ground, wrestling his gun away. He backed off, cocking the weapon.

"No, senor, please," Magaña cried, holding up his hand as though to ward off Steele's bullet.

"Drop it, Josh," came the familiar voice.

Steele's shoulders slumped. He dropped the weapon. "I was wondering when you'd show up," he said, turning to glare at the man now holding a gun on him. Ross Merrick. He was flanked by a dozen French soldiers.

"Don't pretend you were expecting me, Josh," Merrick scolded. "You never knew. Never."

"Maybe I trusted you too long," Steele admitted. "But you got too greedy at the last, Ross. Too damned greedy. I knew. This time, I knew."

"Liar!"

A French officer stormed over to Merrick. "The rifle crates are loaded with bricks!" he shouted. "Worthless adobe bricks!"

Merrick's face contorted. "The gold!" he screamed. "Check the gold!" But he couldn't wait for the Frenchman to do as he ordered. He raced back to the third wagon himself and heaved two crates to the ground, spilling their useless contents. He tore up the exposed slats of the false bottom. More bricks!

"Steele!" he hissed.

He stalked back to where Joshua stood. Three men were holding him at bay with their rifles. Merrick backhanded Steele across the face. He stumbled backward, but didn't go down. "Where's the gold?" Merrick shouted. "Where?"

Steele said nothing.

"Bring the boy over here," Merrick snapped.

Two French soldiers had bound the wound in Rudy Montoya's shoulder. Now they picked him up and shoved him toward Merrick. The boy collapsed to his knees, weak from loss of blood.

"He needs a doctor," Steele gritted, taking a step toward his injured friend. One of the soldiers cocked his rifle. Steele stopped.

"Does he now?" Merrick mocked.

A nod from Merrick was a signal for one of the soldiers to settle his rifle barrel against Rudy's head. The boy's eyes widened briefly, but he made no plea for his life.

"I'll ask you just once more, Josh, old friend. Where's the gold?"

A muscle in Steele's jaw worked. "Why, Ross?" he demanded. "Why are you doing this?"

"Why else?" Merrick shrugged. "I like money. Lots of it."

"So much that you sold your honor for it?"

"Save your speeches for the peasants," Merrick said. "What's left of them."

Steele stared at the remains of the caravan. Magaña's traitors had made quick work of the men. Of the Mexican loyalists with the train only six caballeros survived, besides Rudy and himself. The rest lay slaughtered behind the wagons, most shot in the back.

"Where's the gold, damn you!" Merrick snarled.

"Tell them nothing, amigo," Rudy said, though his voice shook. "Nothing. Viva Juarez! Viva Mexico!"

The French soldier cocked his rifle.

"The mission's a decoy, Merrick," Steele snapped. "Can't you see that? I set you up. The gold, the rifles—they're most likely safe in Juarez's hands right now."

"You bastard!" Merrick shrieked. "You'll pay for this. Just watch how you'll pay!" To the soldier holding the rifle to Rudy Montoya's head, he barked, "Do it!"

The man pulled the trigger. Rudy's lifeless body pitched forward in the dirt.

"You filthy son of a bitch!" Steele roared. Heedless of the odds against him, he lunged at Merrick, catching him by the knees and driving him backwards. Joshua swore violently, pounding his fists into Merrick's face. It took five soldiers to pull him off. Even then, they had to beat him nearly senseless to subdue hm.

"I'll kill you, Merrick!" he swore. "My hand to God, I'll kill you!" He'd never known such single-minded hate in his life.

"I don't think so, Josh," Merrick gasped, staggering to his feet. "Where you're going, you don't do the killing. They do." He indicated the French soldiers. "But before you die, you'll tell me where that gold is. That's a promise I make to you."

He turned to the soldiers and spoke in rapid French. The words made Joshua's blood run cold. He watched helplessly as the six surviving juaristas were lined up in front of the rockslide.

Two soldiers shoved Steele toward them. The injuries from the beating he'd taken were beginning to tell. The soldiers had to brace him between them to keep him on his feet. His head sagged forward.

Merrick stomped over and gripped Steele's hair, jerking his head back. "No, no, Josh, boy, not yet," he said. "I don't want you to miss any of this. I want you to remember it well, so that when I ask you again where more gold is, you'll know better than to keep silent."

From somewhere over the rise a cannon was

135

brought up. Merrick backed away, leaving Joshua with the Frenchmen. Steele heard the barked command, "Fire!" The cannon shell exploded, obliterating the spot where the juaristas had been standing. Something slammed into the side of his head. He pitched forward, darkness swallowing him.

Joshua dumped the remainder of his coffee on his campfire, shrugging off the useless rehashing of what had already been. He could not alter what Merrick had done, but, as he had vowed to himself that day in Mexico, he could find Merrick and make him pay with his life for the misery he had brought to so many.

He looked up at the millions of stars dotting the night sky and inhaled deeply. The air was clear and crisp and cool. It should have soothed him, but it did not. Nothing did. Nothing had for a long time. Even the soft, scented mountain breezes could not reach the pain inside him. It was too deep. It had festered too long.

He spread the blankets that had been his bed for so many months. At least the eye had not bothered him today. Maybe whatever was wrong had cleared up by itself. He was tired, too tired. He had pushed himself hard today. He didn't want to sleep, but he could no longer stay awake. The past haunted his waking moments, and now it would haunt his dreams as well. He closed his eyes, praying that the dream would not come, knowing that it would. . . .

Two kerosene-drenched torches cast an unearthly light along the pitted walls of the mine. Joshua Steele stared with unblinking eyes at the flames leaping from one of the firebrands. He stood stripped to the waist, his arms arched above his head, his wrists secured by iron shackles bolted to the rock wall. His hands were balled into fists, the white knuckles mute testimony to a mind-numbing agony.

A half-circle of ill-clad Mexican soldiers watched without expression as Sergeant Miguel Garcia recoiled the blood-slickened bullwhip. Without effort his arm flexed. The black snake struck again, the sharp crack echoing eerily through the mine shaft. The tall prisoner shuddered but made no sound. A new trail of blood appeared across his back to mingle quickly with the torn flesh surrounding it.

Inured to this familiar violence the soldiers thought only of their own discomfort, wishing the prisoner would break as had so many before him. Their feet shifted uncomfortably, their boots making scraping noises on the rock floor. They were tired and cold. How much more could the prisoner endure? Surely, Steele realized he was only postponing the inevitable. In the end Garcia would win. He always won. The gringo was a fool. The whip snapped again.

To the left the only officer, a captain in an impeccably tailored French uniform, held himself apart from the others, conferring with a grinning blond haired American. The officer and the civilian seemed oblivious to the flogging.

Steele held his breath. The whip descended again. How many was it now? He had lost count after the twelfth. He exhaled deliberately, his full concentration now focused on keeping the oath he had made to himself. He would not give these Mexican and French imperialists the satisfaction of hearing him beg.

With each bite of the lash the promise grew harder to keep. He conceded, too, that it was his own stubborn pride that prolonged the punishment. If he asked the French captain to end it, he would. But Steele would not ask.

The soldiers despised Steele as a cunning and dangerous spy, because he dared work for the cause of Benito Juarez. Yet they admitted a grudging admiration for the willful gringo, who was proving a worthy match for their sadistic sergeant. Soldiers and prisoners alike cowered before Garcia. But not Steele. In the three months of his captivity he had been beaten in body, but not in will.

The Mexican sergeant seethed at his inability to break the Americano. His sunken black eyes glinted in the torch-light. This time he would succeed. This time the gringo would beg.

The blood-sodden leather slashed again. Joshua lurched violently. His body was drenched with sweat. He closed his eyes. The shackles cut cruelly into his wrists, as he pressed his face hard against the pitted rock, the eternal coolness of it providing his only relief. Ripples of agony cursed through every cell in his body.

To survive the torture of his flesh he fought to force his mind elsewhere. To a copse of trees and the eager, young body and sharp mind of a blonde-haired, green-eyed vixen. Eustacia Hamilton, only one of so many women he had known, yet somehow she had ensnared his being with a kiss. He remembered her warm sweet innocence, the way her body had arched instinctively toward his when he'd made love to her, the surrender in the bottomless depths of those emerald eyes. He could drown in those eyes.

And he willed himself to do so, even as his body tensed involuntarily awaiting the next blow. It did not come, but Joshua did not relax. Though he could not see him, he imagined the heavy-set sergeant pausing to guzzle down more tequila, gathering strength to continue. Even Captain Brissot did not interfere with Garcia's drinking.

In a semi-conscious stupor Steele did not hear the approaching footsteps. Something hard prodded him in the side. Scarcely able to maintain his footing, he did not turn to see what it was. A hand grabbed him by the hair, wrenching his head painfully around.

"Hello, Josh, boy. Are my friends treating you well?" A malevolent chuckle followed the words. The pale civilian then peered in disgust at the hand that had touched the prisoner. Steele's dark hair and heavy beard were matted and filthy after months of squalid confinement. The man looked in vain for a place to wipe the vermin from his hand. His voice hardened. "I asked you a question, boy."

Steele's pain-fogged brain could not immediately comprehend the words. The voice was familiar, but his mind refused to focus on it. He couldn't open his eyes.

"Now, Josh, boy, it's not polite to go to sleep when someone is talking to you," the blond man hissed, then nodded to the sergeant.

A bucket of water splashed over Steele. He blinked painfully to keep the brackish liquid out of his eyes.

"Now that's better, Josh, boy." The pale face drifted closer to Steele. "You know you can end all of this torment in a second. Just tell Captain Brissot here what he wants to know."

139

Steele stared into the smirking blue eyes. Rage replaced pain. Merrick. Ross Merrick. How dare the bastard show his face to him again? With an effort of iron will Steele straightened his legs until he could turn and face Merrick squarely, though his arms remained anchored above his head.

"I'll kill you. I swear to God, I'll kill you," Steele breathed, his voice scarcely more than a hoarse whisper, but for a brief instant the smile on Merrick's face vanished.

Merrick regained his composure at once, grinding his riding crop into Steele's mutilated back. If Steele noticed, it did not show in his gray eyes, which never left Merrick's face. Clearing his throat noisily Merrick backed away, his blue eyes twitching with a mixture of anger and fear.

"I'm afraid this one will never talk, mon capitan," Merrick said to the French commander. The officer's expression remained thoughtful. Merrick continued, "Perhaps we should just shoot him and be done with it. He's caused nothing but trouble since the day he was captured."

Merrick spoke in French, but Steele understood every word. His threat only fueled Steele's rage. He imagined his hands closing around the blond snake's traitorous throat, and for a moment the pain was forgotten.

"Let's not be hasty, Monsieur Merrick," said the Frenchman. Secretly he wished Steele would quit this show of stubborn superiority and speak. Nothing was going to be gained from any information he might have anyway. Merrick must realize that, too. Brissot wondered at the man's single-minded determination to destroy his fellow countryman. But he did not pursue the matter. Instead he said, "Sergeant Garcia's methods have never failed on a prisoner before. Perhaps a little different type of persuasion is all that is necessary."

Merrick considered the captain's words, an evil smile spreading across his handsome face. He whispered something to the commander. The Frenchman appeared reluctant, but Merrick would not be dissuaded. Finally, the captain nodded. He motioned to Garcia who stepped over to them. Merrick gave him a whispered order in Spanish that had the soldier snickering with glee. He hadn't been ready to give up on the big gringo just yet either. This was going to be a pleasure.

Steele heard the malignant laughter and wondered what Merrick had come up with this time. Over the past three months he had been beaten, starved, whipped, and at times forced to work twenty hours a day in the mines, though he only guessed at the hours, he hadn't seen the sun since the day he was captured.

Time and again he had been asked questions about American involvement with Juarez. He told them nothing, even though the information he possessed was dated and worthless. Yet Merrick persisted. Why? Steele considered that. Merrick must still think he had information on Mexican gold caches used to pay for arms shipments. Money was always the primary motivation behind everything Merrick did.

It didn't matter that the French were withdrawing throughout the Mexican countryside, that Maximilian would soon be left alone as their scapegoat, and that Juarez would take his rightful place as president

141

again. It only mattered that while Merrick's imperialist cronies were being ousted, the traitor could find himself a back door and leave Mexico a rich man.

Steele's thoughts were interrupted by the cold steel of Garcia's fifteen-inch hunting knife. The sergeant touched the edge of it to Steele's cheek, the blade reflecting the dancing light of the torches.

"Do you like the feel of the knife, gringo?" Garcia cackled, as he traced the tip of the blade down Steele's neck to his shoulder. The thick-set sergeant shifted his weight slightly and almost fell on the blood slickened floor. Cursing, he righted himself and angrily exerted more pressure on the knife, trailing it down Steele's back.

Steele struggled to shut his mind against the intolerable agony. His rage deepened at his own helplessness. He was a man used to being in charge of a situation. His feelings of impotence only added to his fury. Slowly, almost imperceptibly he tightened his hands around the bolted chains attached to the shackles on his wrists. If Garcia noticed, he paid it no mind.

"Now we do it to you, gringo, eh?" the sergeant hissed. "You don't want to talk. I think you will change your mind very quickly. Senor Merrick has suggested the perfect method to loosen your tongue."

The knife settled at Steele's waist. He set his jaw hard, expecting the blade to burrow deeper into his tortured flesh. Merrick had given up his hope of gleaning any information from him. Now the bastard just wanted him dead. Alive, Steele posed a continual threat. Not just a threat of treachery revealed, but the palpable threat of murderous rage should Steele be allowed to live.

Garcia was in no hurry. To prolong Steele's agony was to increase his own pleasure. He pressed the knife tip against the torn flesh of Steele's back. He watched the American's body twist in an instinctive move to escape the endless pain.

An anguished scream formed in Steele's mind, which when it reached his throat came out as a savage curse against his tormentors.

"Give me my hands for two seconds, Garcia! Two seconds! And I'll break your damned neck!" Steele gulped in several deep breaths to fight off the unconsciousness threatening to overwhelm him. If they were going to murder him they were going to have to look him in the eye to do it.

"Garcia, get on with it!" Merrick snapped suddenly, a nameless fear growing in the pit of his stomach. As long as Steele was alive, Merrick would never be safe. That he had betrayed him would have been reason enough to fear his ex-compatriot, but what had come afterwards, Merrick knew, had made of Steele an enemy who would stop at nothing in his quest for vengeance.

Garcia muttered an oath at having his fun interrupted, but he pulled the knife away from Steele's back. The blond fool! Steele was chained, beaten, and half-starved, and still the pale American feared him.

The sergeant grabbed the waistband of Steele's ragged levis, sliced at them with the knife, and with a hard yank pulled them away from the prisoner's body.

Steele trembled with rage. He stood there naked with an anger deeper than any he had ever known. What could be in Merrick's twisted mind now? He refused to consider the question. Whatever he might think, he knew Merrick's reality would be far worse.

Garcia laughed deep in his throat. This would finally bring the big gringo to his knees. In fact, it would destroy him. He inched the knife toward Steele's stomach, scant inches from the cave wall.

In a voice that was the personification of evil, he snarled, "I think you know what it is to geld the stallion, gringo."

Steele's whole body went rigid. He swallowed the raw terror that threatened to choke him. An insane fury blotted out any rational response. Garcia lunged. Steele used the leverage of the bolt to heave himself upwards, feet scrambling up the rock wall. With savage intent he balanced himself with one foot against the wall and rammed the other into the now off-balance Garcia. The sergeant let out a scream that was abruptly cut short. Steele never heard it. He kicked viciously at the slumped form on the mine floor, not feeling when a blow missed and his bare toes smashed into the pitted rock.

The bolt holding the shackles gave way. Falling, Steele still managed to maintain his balance. With maniacal strength he brought the two-foot length of chain down on the inert form of Garcia.

Stunned by what was happening, it took Captain Brissot several seconds to find his voice and order his disconcerted troops to bring the prisoner under control.

Steele swung the chains in a sweeping arc, holding everyone in the chamber at bay.

"Shoot him!" Steele heard Merrick scream at the disorganized soldiers, terror making his voice shrill.

Steele guessed he had only seconds before one of Brissot's men did just that. He intended to kill Merrick before that happened. Leaping with the agility of a wild animal, the pain blotted out by his overwhelming rage, Steele caught Merrick, by the throat and hung on.

He heard Merrick screaming for help. He heard Brissot say "Don't . . ." Then something exploded inside his head and he heard nothing else.

He woke to total darkness. For a bleak moment he wondered if he was blind. He couldn't decide. When he tried to move, waves of nausea washed over him. Rather than wonder if any bones were broken, he wondered grimly whether he had any that were not. His whole body was one throbbing ache. He struggled to sit up. His head connected solidly with a hard, uneven surface.

He lay down again, trying to think through the stabbing pain. His body seemed trapped in a strange fetal position. Probing painfully with his fingers he discovered that his arms were pinioned by shackles locked behind his back. His ankles were imprisoned by another chain that wound around his neck, forcing his knees to bend upward until they almost reached his chest. In no way could he straighten his body to its full length.

Like an ungodly serpent Steele tried to crawl forward. Again his head met a rock-hard obstruction. He tried to back up. Six excruciating inches later his feet touched metal bars. He squirmed to turn around and almost strangled himself in the chain. He was in some sort of hollowed out hole in the earth smaller than a coffin. From the feel and smell of the place it was no doubt part of the labyrinth of tunnels in the same Mexican lead mine.

Something crawled up his back. Tiny razor sharp teeth sank into his lacerated flesh. Steele cried out in pain and fear. It bit again. Violently he forced his back into the wall behind him. A tiny squeal of pain was abruptly cut off by a sickening scrunching noise. Steele's whole body trembled. Angrily he shook it off.

"I'll kill you, Merrick," he swore aloud. "I'll break your traitorous neck with my bare hands."

Over and over he repeated his oath of vengeance. He had to survive to kill Merrick. Yet it occurred to him suddenly that this could be his grave. They may have buried him alive, chained him here to starve to death.

For several moments Joshua forced his exhausted mind to examine ways of easing himself out of the chains that bound him. Nothing worked. He was hopelessly trapped. Still he refused to give up. He struggled against the chains until he lapsed into stuporous exhaustion.

He woke later and discovered that no matter how he moved he could not avoid lying on open sores. He could smell the infection in some of them. He laughed without humor. Perhaps this was indeed to be his grave. Centuries from now archaeologists might find his chained skeleton. He wondered what explanation they would invent for his demise.

A scraping noise diverted his attention from his morbid thoughts. A bolt was drawn back. The metal bars creaked open. A match flared briefly. So he wasn't blind at least.

"Still alive, gringo fool?" a surprisingly friendly voice

called. Perhaps he was awed by the American's will to live.

"Eat," came the gentle command.

A foul smelling slop was shoved near his face. The match died. The bars creaked shut. He heard the lock scrape into place once again. Because he couldn't use his hands, Steele was forced to eat like a dog. He prayed again that Merrick still lived. He wanted the pleasure of sending him to hell all to himself.

The food tin was withdrawn later, but Joshua did not hear it. A raging fever gripped him, alternating with teeth-chattering chills. The sores that covered his body grew angrier, the infection spreading. During lucid intervals he often found himself too weak to eat even the small bit of food and water pushed at him daily. Still naked, he had no protection from the wandering rats which infested the cavern. He occupied his mind by keeping a running count of how many he killed. All the gold in the world would not be too high a price to pay just to be able to stretch to his full length and sleep uninterrupted by nightmares, fever, chills, or rodents.

His only lock on sanity came during those rare rapturous delusions when Stacey Hamilton lay naked in his arms, surrendering herself utterly to his fevered lovemaking.

As days passed into weeks Steele found he no longer had the strength even to roll from one side to the other. Tiny teeth sank into his shoulder. Steele smashed at the animal with his emaciated body. He tried to shove it down toward the metal bars, but found he could no longer move at all. A frustrated sob was torn from his throat. In a tortured nightmare he remembered Garcia's last threat. It came to him that he didn't know . . . He prayed he would die.

"How could anyone treat another human being this way?"

The voice seemed to come from far away. Hands pulled at him. He fell heavily to another hard surface, but he felt no pain. A torch shone near his face. It was an effort to close his eyes to the blinding ache it produced.

"Is he alive?"

The chains rattled. A key was inserted into a lock. The shackles fell from his gaunt body. They tried to straighten his legs. He heard someone screaming. . . .

Throwing off the blankets, Steele sat bolt upright, biting off a second scream. He cradled his head on his knees, trembling violently. So many nights, so many nightmares, yet its effect on him had not diminished, but intensified.

The only thing that changes is his hate. With each succeeding nightmare it feeds upon itself, growing, reproducing, melding itself into an all-consuming sense of purpose. Nothing can deliver him from the pain, degradation, and betrayal he has endured but the slow, calculated death of Ross Merrick. The memory of sparkling emerald eyes is obliterated by an irrational lust for vengeance.

The gentle padre who had treated Steele's injuries after his rescue had tried without success to steer the hard, lean soldier from his vow, but Steele would not be dissuaded. It had taken four months to regain the strength of his body. Long months before that Merrick had already begun to bury his trail.

His only consolation was the shuddering sigh of relief that had coursed through him when he discovered that he was still a man.

When Steele left Mexico, he had reported first to Washington in January of '68, resigning his commission to the then Secretary of War, Ulysses S. Grant. Grant had been surprised to see him at first, for he had reports of Steele's death. He did not question his ex-captain's account of what had taken place in Mexico. But he knew Joshua had not told him everything. Even the battle-hardened Grant was taken aback by the bitter hatred in the tall man's eyes. If Ross Merrick still lived, he'd better have hidden his tracks well. Steele would show him no mercy.

Now, as dawn approached, Steele sat beneath an outcropping of rock in the Sangre de Cristo Mountains in the New Mexico Territory. Today he would reach Elizabethtown, and from there it was on to Spring Canyon.

Steele had recently met with a man named Danton Seaverman in Santa Fe. He'd learned from Seaverman about a businessman in Spring Canyon who'd been pressing to invest heavily in some of Seaverman's land speculations. From other things Seaverman had mentioned, the Spring Canyon bank president was a strong candidate to be Ross Merrick. Steele had followed plenty of bad leads in the past. This one could prove to be the same dead end. But he would leave not the slenderest clue unchecked in his search.

He shook off the after-affects of the nightmare. It was time to be on the trail again. Wearily, he climbed to his feet, saddled his horse, mounted, and nudged the gelding toward Elizabethtown.

CHAPTER NINE

Stacey eyed the stagecoach despairingly. She had arrived in Denver three days ago, taken care of buying the medical supplies she and Sam needed, done a little sightseeing, and was ready to make the return trip to Spring Canyon. Her bones protested the thought of another dusty, bone-jolting ride, but physical aches weren't her major concern.

Throughout the journey to Denver she had been forced to sit between a leering, overweight man and his wife. The man had squeezed Stacey's knee suggestively every time his wife had dozed off. Now she noticed with a sinking sensation that the same man intended making the trip back with her.

"My wife is going to stay on to visit her mother," the man smirked. "But I want to get started back to my business in Houston right away. I remember your saying you'd be leaving today, so I thought wouldn't it be pleasant if we could travel together again." He gave her an obscene grin.

Stacey's stomach lurched. The very smell of the man bordered on nauseous. She instinctively backed away but he edged forward to grab her arm and propel her toward the stage.

"Allow me to help you into the coach, Miss Hamilton."

Stacey recoiled. "Uh, my . . . uh," she stammered, "I . . . I forgot something in my hotel room. I'd better hurry and get it." She yanked her arm away from him and bolted up the street toward the hotel. She came to the two story structure and kept going.

The medicines were already securely on board the stage addressed to Sam in Spring Canyon. They would have to be all right. She wasn't going back to the stage station. She could stay over another day, but the man could do the same. She made up her mind. Quickening her pace, she headed for the livery.

"I want to hire a horse, please," she told the hostler.

That was four days ago. She hadn't regretted her decision. She'd seen no other living soul, since leaving Denver. The desolate beauty of the country nourished and replenished her. She had even had time to forgive Martin Randolph for his unconscionable actions in Molly Webster's room the night before she'd left home.

Martin had come to see her off at the stage station, and though he'd been overbearingly solicitous, it was all she could do to speak civilly to him. He told her that he would worry about her, but he knew she could take care of herself. She smiled now to think of it. He had obviously not wanted her to leave town thinking ill of him. Perhaps he was worried that she might meet some eligible gentleman in Denver.

She had told him that, of course, she forgave him, that she had understood his behavior, but in truth it was only now basked in the serenity of these mountains that she truly did understand and forgive him. Martin was a man vulnerable to the whims of public opinion. His community image was very important to him, and she had to respect that. She vowed she would be more sensitive to his feelings in the future. He had even given her a public good-bye kiss befre she had boarded the stage, and while it hadn't aroused a response in her, it hadn't been unpleasant either. Maybe she could get on with her life, after all.

Joshua was dead, and she was alive. Even if he lived he would not have come back for her. It was time she admitted that to herself. She was a woman now, not a foolish, dreamy-eyed young girl. Joshua had merely availed himself of a willing female. And even though it hurt to acknowledge that, she could nevertheless accept it now. She smiled at the bittersweet memory of Joshua Steele, then put him out of her mind. It was a gloriously beautiful day, and she intended to enjoy it. She even felt like being sociable again. She would stop in Elizabethtown before heading home.

She wanted to see John Beal again. It had been too long. Beal was the territorial marshal, and she remembered he frequently stopped off in E-town, the current county seat. Beal had been one of the first patients her uncle had treated after her arrival in Spring Canyon. He'd been wounded in some sort of fracas and had not objected to Stacey helping her uncle patch him up. He had her friendship for life. If he wasn't in town, she would have only lost a few hours and could continue to Spring Canyon from there.

She gigged the horse up the final rise leading to E-town. She smiled wryly as she looked down on the sprawling hamlet. She had seen mining towns before, but none with quite the character of Elizabethtown.

Nestled in the tree-studded Mareno Valley of the Sangre de Cristo Mountains, the whole feel of the place was temporary. Buildings constructed of unhewn logs, unpainted for the most part, stood in a haphazard arrangement as if someone had heaved a few hundred shacks into the air just to see how they would land. A smattering of tents dotted the rocky slopes. The town would probably disappear altogether one day, when the mines played out.

She stretched in the saddle, a little weary all at once of riding horseback. Maybe she would indulge herself in the luxury of a steaming hot tub bath while she was in town.

She kneed the horse down the slope, smiling at the sounds of saloon honky-tonks filling the air. It was barely past noon. Big stakes poker, monte and other games of chance rolled full steam inside the saloons. Struck-it-rich miners who didn't know how to hang onto the money they had slaved a lifetime to unearth, could lose their newfound fortunes in the blink of an eye, especially if the game was crooked. Sam had more than once warned her of the evils of gambling.

The word "Eats" garishly painted on the false front of a log hut caught her eye. She was suddenly ravenous. After four days of her own meager cooking, she would happily accept a meal cooked by anyone else. She reined the horse over to a hitching post and dismounted. After tying off the reins, she stepped inside the cafe.

"Stacey! Stacey Hamilton!"

She whirled at the sound of the familiar voice. "John!" she grinned, throwing he arms around the bow-legged lawman who tromped over to her from his table in the cafe.

"Is Sam with ya?" he asked, swallowing a mouthful of food. His brown eyes were warm with welcome.

"I'm alone."

His craggy brows knitted into a frown. "Alone? You came alone to Elizabethtown? Stacey Hamilton, does your uncle know where you are?"

"Oh, John, for heavens' sake," she said, "this conversation is much too stale. Really."

At his puzzled look she laughed. John couldn't know how many others had preceded him in having this protective little talk with her. "Let's just renew an old friendship, okay?" she prodded. "I'm awfully hungry."

"Join me, of course," the lawman urged. "You'll have to pardon my manners, they get a little rusty from non-use."

She sat down at his table and ordered two helpings of beef stew, mashed potatoes, and a huge slice of apple pie. While they ate, they talked of many things, though Stacey side-stepped any questions about her medical career. She'd had that conversation once too often lately too. She explained to John why she had decided to return to Spring Canyon on horseback instead of the stage.

"I'd have taught that reprobate a thing or two," John growled. "But you promise me, you'll wire Sam and tell him where you are. He's liable to be worried."

"I'm not due back for nearly a week," she assured him.

"Just the same . . ."

"All right, John, I'll telegraph him. I promise."

The lawman was insisting on paying for her lunch, when they heard the first shot.

"You stay here," he warned. "It sounds like it's coming from Montezuma's.

Beal drew his gun, peering cautiously out the cafe door. He wasn't anxious to get his head shot off by a careless move. The doors to the saloon down the street burst open. Two men poured out, guns blasting. One of them slammed into the dun horse being ridden by a man Beal had never seen before. The horse shied violently, nearly unseating its rider. Beal eased out the door and headed toward the commotion. He noticed that the horseman's Colt was already in his hand. The man had ridden into the middle of a gunfight, but he wasn't riding out.

One of the fleeing men took a shot at Joshua. He returned the fire with deadly accuracy. The man collapsed on the boardwalk in front of the saloon.

Three more men stormed out, cursing loudly, grabbing for hitch-tied horses. One of them felled the lawman with a quick shot. Steele fired at the shooter, but missed when his terrified horse shied again.

Steele leaped from the horse and ducked behind a water trough. Two of the gunmen, one looking like a full-blooded Apache, the other a stocky, mustachioed Mexican, managed to bring their horses under control long enough to mount. They spurred the animals savagely, heading out of town. Joshua didn't bother to shoot after them. His battle was with the trapped bandit now using the side of the saloon for shelter. He was the one who had shot the badge-toter.

From the open door of the cafe Stacey watched the entire scene with horrified fascination. The racket of gunfire brought back memories of war-time battle and endless death. She prayed no one would die here

155

today. When she saw John fall, she instinctively rushed toward him.

She forgot about the bullets in her concern for her friend. Beal was crawling toward the boardwalk in front of Montezuma's Saloon. Stacey raced up the street. A bullet kicked up dirt scarcely a foot to her right. She didn't stop. Suddenly, a hand gripped her waist. A brutal shove forced her into the muddy water behind the horse trough.

"Stay down," a hard voice grated.

Struggling to her knees, she glared at the man beside her. His profile was obscured by his hat. "How dare you!" she blustered. "I have to help John. He's been hurt!"

"And you'll be killed if you don't keep that apparently empty head of yours down."

Stacey's eyes widened in fury . . . and something else. What was it about that voice? She started to say something, but was silenced by the sound of bullets striking the trough above her head. She crouched lower.

From other sections of the street guns began roaring in cadence with Steele's. The corner of the saloon was being splintered to bits. E-town, peopled primarily by miners, gamblers, and assorted law dodgers, housed the kind of men who shot first and then asked what started it. In a town where there was little law enforcement more often than not, these hard men made their own rules. Rules brutally enforced.

"Okay, okay, I give up!" The angry voice came from alongside the saloon. Evidently the gunman had calculated the odds and decided if he kept shooting he wasn't going to keep breathing. Steele waited. The gunfire quieted. The wounded lawman grunted in pain, but managed to gain his feet.

"All right, you buzzard," Beal roared, "throw yer gun out now!"

A six-shooter landed in the dirt near Beal's feet.

"Come on out! Hands grabbin' sky!" To the town he bellowed, "I don't want to see no one shootin' this man, you hear me? I'll nail any man that tries fer murder!"

Stacey peered over the side of the water trough. She was trembling, but recovered enough to hurry over to Beal. She watched a hatless man of medium height with salt and pepper hair emerge from the side of the saloon with his hands in the air. The man was solidly built. Hate danced like a flame in his yellow eyes. His lips curled in a menacing snarl. A person would think he was the wronged party, instead of the other way around, Stacey marvelled. She noted, too, that the mans eyes never stopped moving, as if he fully expected to be shot down at any second. Beal's eyes were watchful too, even as Stacey tugged at his shirt to get at the bullet wound in his arm.

"You all right, Stacey?" he asked her quickly.

"Fine, John," she managed. "Thanks to this man," She turned, smiling, "I'd like to thank . . ." The words caught in her throat.

He was older, he had a mustache, but the chiseled features, the lean hard-muscled body and those compelling wolf-gray eyes were the same.

"Joshua?"

But it was impossible. She had the letter telling her that he was dead. Murdered. She stared at him. No one else could have those eyes.

"Joshua?" she said again, her voice shaking so much that even Beal noticed and shot her a curious glance.

Steele stared into the shimmering green eyes which had brought him back from the edge of madness time and time again. Ruthlessly, he rammed back the thought.

"Still incapable of taking care of yourself, I see," he snarled.

She took a step backward at the harshness of his voice. This couldn't be Joshua, but it was. He was alive! She stifled the sudden impulse to rush into his arms, fearing all at once that there would be no welcome for her there. Had she exaggerated the warmth, the life in those gray eyes seven years ago? This man who stood regarding her so cynically was a stranger. What could have changed him so? Or was this the real Joshua Steele? Her memory of him merely a young girl's fantasy wildly embellished by time?

She wanted to ask him a hundred questions at once, but the look in his eyes brooked no intrusion on his thoughts.

She was relieved at the distraction provided by an immense, bowlegged miner. The man sported a full red beard and balding pate, and he came sidling out of Montezuma's filled with righteous rage.

"I'll get us a rope so's we can hang this fella up right away, John," he shouted.

"There ain't gonna be no lynchin' in E'town today. Not while I'm here," the marshal growled. John was not a big man, but something about the way he carried himself convinced the burly miner that his necktie party was out. He stalked away, swearing loudly. The marshal did not let down his guard.

Stacey still felt stung by Joshua's curt dismissal of her. Before she thought him dead, she had fantasized an impassioned reunion one day. The reality left her somehow bereft. Couldn't he at least speak to her? He stood no more than two feet away, yet he would not even look at her. That he thought her stupid to have been in the street during a gun battle, she had to grudgingly admit, was not unreasonable. But he hadn't had to be so nasty about it.

She remembered with painful clarity his blunt apology for making love to her in the Wilderness. Perhaps he didn't like being reminded of a mistake from his past. The joy she felt at seeing him alive was tempered by his lack of it.

She regarded him covertly. His dusty, trail-grimy clothes and overall unkempt appearance would have made her dismiss him as a saddle tramp had they never met before. But this man had been an officer in the Union Army. Even with his disheveled appearance there was something almost arrogant about he way he carried himself.

Steele shoved his Colt back into its holster. The gun had seen a lot of use. But it was well-oiled. Obviously he took special care of it. Was that what he had become? A gunfighter?

Joshua eyed the two dead men in the street. One, the man he had shot, lay face down half on, half off the boardwalk in front of the saloon. The other body was perched against a hitching post, as if the man had just sat himself down for a rest. This man, like the marshal, had been shot by the man now in custody.

The lawman stuck his right hand out to the man who had saved Stacey's life, grimacing slightly as the movement aggravated the flesh wound in the upper part of his arm. He kept the gun in his left hand trained on the captured bandit.

"Name's John Beal," he said. "Obliged for the help, stranger."

"Joshua Steele." He shook the marshal's hand.

Another saloon patron came up to them. "This hombre and his polecat bunch was aimin' to clean out Monty-zumie's, marshal."

The outlaw paid no attention to the accusation. His eyes were riveted on one of the still forms in the street.

"We had ourselves a gee-haw game of stud poker goin'," the miner continued, "and this here beady-eyed one was in the game hisself. One of the boys caught 'im cold deckin' us. That's when him and his pistoleros decided to take the whole durn pot fer themselves. Musta been uperds o' five thousand dollars in paper and gold."

The marshal was listening, but Stacey's eyes were on the outlaw as he bent over the man Joshua had shot. Beal's gun followed the outlaw's every move, though the lawman did not appear to look at him.

With surprising care the bandit eased the dead man over onto his back. Stacey gasped. Steele grimiced. It was their first good look at the dead man. He couldn't have been much more than seventeen years old. Peach fuzz showed on his waxen face. Steele shook his head, looking at the marshal. The lawman read his thoughts. A waste.

The outlaw brushed the dirt from the dead boy's face. He spoke, his voice low and filled with venom.

"His name was Jeff Barnett. I want that put on the marker. I want it put there that he was killed like a man. And I want it put there that Jake Barnett, his brother, will kill the man who did it."

"You're Jake Barnett, I take it," observed Beal. He'd heard the name. He was making the mental connection with a couple of wanted dodgers he had in his saddle bags.

Barnett's eyes bored into Steele. Steele's gaze never wavered. He said nothing. Words would make no difference to a man like Barnett. He had made a deadly enemy. One who could seriously jeopardize his search for Merrick, were it not for the fact that he was about to be escorted to jail by the marshal.

"I'll see to it he's buried proper, mister," Beal said. "You just get yourself headed toward the calaboose up the street." Beal pointed with his gun. Barnett eased the boy's body back to the street, stood up, and walked ahead of them.

Stacey fell into step beside Joshua. She still could not believe it was really him. The letter from the War Department had told her he was dead. How could they have made such a mistake? There were so many questions she wanted to ask, yet feared to. He made no effort to speak to her as they walked. The only words he'd yet directed at her had been his cutting comment about her being incapable of taking care of herself. She couldn't bear to leave it at that. Besides, she still admitted he was somewhat justified in his sarcasm. It had been foolhardy at best to go to John's aid, while shots were still being fired.

Rather than risk drawing him into an argument she would surely lose, she said softly, "I would like to thank you, Joshua. You probably saved my life."

She watched a muscle in his jaw work. It was as

though it were an effort for him to speak to her. His demeanor was deceptively negligent, but she got the impression of a coiled spring.

"Do you often jump in front of blazing pistols, Miss Hamilton?" he mocked.

"Well, actually," she returned coolly, rankling at his continued insolence, "It was my first time this week. I've been trying to taper off lately."

For just an instant a smile tugged at the corner of his mouth, but it was gone so quickly she decided she must have imagined it. His voice was devoid of emotion when he said, "I'm glad to hear it."

Their arrival at the town jail put an end to the stilted conversation. The jail actually wasn't much more than a make-shift one. Beal pulled a ring of keys out of a desk drawer and locked Barnett in the back room.

"This place looks more like a storehouse for mining tools," Stacey commented.

"Regular jail burned down last week. Haven't got around to building a new one yet," Beal said.

"Bring your arm over here to this basin," Stacey told him. "I want to have a better look at that wound."

Beal stepped over to her, dragging his arm out of his shirtsleeve. Stacey surveyed the wound with professional detachment. She sensed Steele's eyes on her and wondered what he was thinking. "The bullet gouged out a chunk of flesh," she said, "but the bleeding's already stopped."

The marshal retrieved a bottle of whiskey from a small cupboard and handed it to her. She grinned and handed it back, letting him take a swig of the fiery liquid first. Then she poured some of it over the gash. He sucked in his breath at the sting it produced.

"I've heard of this Barnett fella," Beal told Joshua, while Stacey wrapped his arm in a clean cloth. "He's a cold blooded killer a dozen times over. Mean as they come. You better watch yourself, seein' as you're the one that done in his brother."

"I appreciate the warning, marshal," Steele said.

"Well, if you gentlemen will excuse me," Stacey interrupted, finishing up the bandage on Beal's arm. "I've got about a quarter inch of dried mud to remove from my person. I'll be back in about an hour."

She glanced at Joshua from the doorway, but he had his back turned and did not look at her. She hurried out of Beal's office.

It hadn't been the need for a bath that prompted her hasty exit. She didn't think she could bear Joshua's ignoring her for another second. Unbidden tears pricked her eyes, as she hurried up the street. She berated herself for allowing him to affect her this way. What did she expect? It had been seven years. She hadn't been the first woman in Joshua Steele's life, and no doubt she hadn't been the last. She was behaving like a petulant child, and she didn't like the feeling one bit.

Joshua had a life of his own. Judging by the looks of him, not an altogether pleasant one. But that was none of her business. She just wasn't going to think of him, or concern herself with him any more. She would have that hot bath, and she would forget she'd ever met Joshua Steele.

Back in Beal's office, the marshal turned to Steele.

"You've met Stacey before?"

"A long time ago," Steele hedged. "Does she live in E'town."

"Spring Canyon."

Steele's mind clicked. If Merrick actually lived in Spring Canyon, there was a strong possibility that Stacey knew him, maybe even regarded him as a friend. A wave of undiluted rage tore through him.

"Maybe if we're lucky Barnett won't last the night," Beal was saying, not noticing the tenseness in Steele.

The marshal's words brought Joshua up short. He forced Stacey from his mind.

"Them miners don't take to nobody tryin' to cheat 'em," Beal went on, "especially when they try to steal from 'em on top of it. They got their own rules. That jasper Barnett shot wouldn't win no popularity contest, but he was wronged and somebody will probably want to set things right."

"You saying you wouldn't do anything to stop it?" Steele's voice was mild, but his own regard for the law prodded him into making the lawman clarify himself.

"Sure, I'd try," Beal said. "But I'm not even in E'town that often any more. I ride a big territory. It's gotten so I don't even ask what happens between visits, if you get my meanin'. And I sure don't have no hankerin' to take this owlhoot with me with his gang in the hills."

"Couldn't you deputize a couple of men to keep an eye on him when you're not around?" he asked.

"I suppose I could to that. But I can't expect 'em to shoot their own friends over the likes of Barnett."

"Maybe you'd better think again about getting him out of here. I could ride along to the next town."

"Maybe," Beal said, though he was eyeing Josh strangely. He didn't know what to make of this tall man who handled a gun like he was born to it.

"Something bothering you, Beal?" Steele asked. He didn't like the scrutiny.

"Just wonderin' if I'd seen you somewhere before," the marshal mused.

"Not likely. And I'm not on any of your reward dodgers if that's what you have in mind."

Beal looked a little sheepish. "Sorry. Just that your appearance don't exactly make me think yer runnin' in a good streak of luck right now."

Steele grimaced. "I was about to do something about that before the shooting started. Got a place a man can have a decent meal and get himself cleaned up in this town?"

"Take your choice," Beal said. "There's two or three. Me, I like Rosie's Eats down the street. The Miner's Inn can take care of the cleanin' up part."

Steele said his thanks and headed out the door.

Stacey eased her body into the huge, round wooden tub. The steaming water felt heavenly to her weary bones. She'd already washed her hair in the basin, wrapping the long, wet tresses in a towel atop her head. All she wanted to do now was soak—maybe forever. The water just missed covering her full, firm breasts. She closed her eyes.

The door opened. She didn't open her eyes, assuming it was the maid with another bucket of hot water.

"Mmmmmm, just pour it in," she sighed. "This feels so wonderful." She placed her arms on the rim of the tub. A long minute passed and no water was added to her bath. She became conscious of the absolute silence in the room. She opened her eyes.

He was standing rigidly still, his eyes locked on hers. But she knew they had not been there all along. And even as she watched him, his gaze trailed to the water lapping at her breasts. Then he was looking at her face once again. The raw hunger mirrored in those wolf-gray eyes shocked her back to sensibility.

Yanking the towel from her hair, she pressed it fiercely against her chest, unmindful of the water. Damp strands of pale hair tumbled about her shoulders.

"How dare you?" she cried, suddenly terrified at her own momentary lapse of modesty. Even though there had been a time when they had lain naked in each other's arms, she sensed none of that long ago day's warmth in him now. She was mortified.

He said nothing, his expression again unreadable. He merely turned and walked out of the room.

The maid came chattering in a second later, carrying a heavy bucket of water. "I am so sorry, miss," she said, her pudgy face scarlet. "I told the gentleman the wrong room number. Oh, my dear, please, forgive me."

It was several seconds before Stacey could find her voice. "It's all right," she choked. "Please, just help me get dressed. I want to get out of here."

Steele wiped the remainder of the shaving soap from his face. He surveyed his barbering job in the cracked mirror. Fair. He at least looked human again. With a scissors he trimmed his dark mustache. His thick hair, which brushed against the collar of his shirt, would have to wait.

The more he tried not to think of it, the more the image of Stacey in that hot tub swam tantalizingly before him. He should have turned and left the room at once, but he couldn't tear his eyes away from her. Meeting her again today in the street had caught him off guard. He'd been hard on her to cover his own feelings, though he refused to examine what those feelings were. Seeing her lovely body sheltered only by shimmering water had left him transfixed. He couldn't move. Part of him had ached to go to her, to draw her into his arms and see if she could still kiss with the same fire of her adolescence. But another part of him had won out. The part that nurtured the twisted bitterness that would let nothing and no one interfere with his savage goal.

He would have preferred to leave E'town that minute and never see her again. But the fact that she lived in Spring Canyon meant that their paths would cross many more times in the next few days. More than ever, he was on his guard.

He stepped out of the inn and eyed the livery down the street. He'd left the dun to be rubbed down and given some oats. First he would fetch the horse, then head back to Beal's office. If the lawman wanted company to escort Barnett out of town, Steele was willing.

He stepped off the boardwalk. An agonizing pain shot through his left eye. He grabbed the support post of an overhang to keep from falling. When he tried to continue toward the barn, he discovered he could no longer see it clearly. Everything was out of focus. The pain grew stronger. He groped his way to the side of the building.

"Damn!" he rasped, pressing his hand against the eye. Staggering, he edged his way back into a cul de sac. He couldn't let himself be seen like this. He sank down next to a crate. A creeping uneasiness came over him. Whatever was wrong with the eye, it obviously was not clearing itself up.

Several minutes passed before Joshua was able to master his vision enough to make it back to the street. Recalling the town's layout in his mind, the vague shapes around him proved sufficient to guide him back to the marshal's office.

"Joshua, what's wrong?" Stacey cried, rushing to his side as he staggered into the room. She'd come back to John's office to continue their visit, and to try to recover from her devastatingly embarrassing encounter with Steele. Now the bathtub incident was forgotten, as she helped Beal get Joshua to a chair. "Joshua, can you hear me? What is it?"

"Nothing."

"Don't tell me nothing, Mr. Steele," she snapped. "I am not a imbecile. Something is hurting you. I want to know what it is."

"Leave me alone," he bit out the words one at a time.

"I will not leave you alone," she flared. "I wouldn't leave a dog hurting like this." He had hurt her time and again today and she wanted to hurt back. She could see by the rigid clenching of his jaw that maybe, just for an instant, she had succeeded in hitting a nerve.

"My left eye smarts a little," he hissed. Damn this

168

woman! She had to be the most willful female he'd ever met.

Stacey took his head firmly in her hands, feeling her pulse quicken, unable to prevent it. She prided herself on her professionalism, but this particular man's nearness was exerting a strange influence on her senses.

"I don't see a foreign object in the eye," she said.

"It's happened before," he said, irritation evident in his voice. Whether at her or the eye she couldn't tell.

"Joshua, I want you to see my uncle in Spring Canyon. He's a doctor."

"I was heading for Spring Canyon anyway," he conceded wearily. "Maybe I will."

She stepped away from him. The knowledge that his destination was Spring Canyon left her shaken. She had regarded their encounter as a bizarre coincidence. Now it seemed that they had been destined to meet again no matter what. *The world's not so big green eyes . . .*

She wanted him to see Sam, but at the same time she didn't know if she could bear being near him. He was so cold, so bitter. Did he hate her for what had happened between them so many years ago? Why else would he seem to single her out for his fits of temper?

A new spasm of pain seized him. He held himself rigid, closing his eyes and deliberately shutting her out. She supposed it stung his male pride to have her see him like this. Well, he hadn't been doing her pride any favors today either!

Beal helped Joshua over to a pallet spread out on the floor in one corner of the office. He stretched out. The pain would not allow sleep.

"You get yourself to Stacey's uncle, boy," the marshal said, his voice edged with concern. In spite of the natural way Joshua handled a gun, the lawman trusted and liked him. "Sam saved my bacon once. If anybody can figure this out, he can."

Stacey sat down in a chair next to where Joshua lay. She knew he was annoyed by her presence, but she wouldn't leave him like this.

"I've got some errands to run, Stacey," Beal said. "If you're going to stay with him. . . ?"

"You go ahead, John."

The lawman left the office.

Jake Barnett peered through the slit in the storage room door. He watched Steele. His brother's killer was in obvious pain. He smiled, though the scar on his lower lip gave the illusion of little more than a sneer. Steele's sickness would make it that much easier to kill him. For kill him he would. Steele had killed his brother. For that the man would die. The how or where wasn't decided, but that it would happen, of that Barnett had no doubt.

Stacey watched Joshua, too. His eyes were closed. He had his head turned toward the wall, but she knew he wasn't asleep. Though he was aware of her sitting beside him, he did not open his eyes.

She found herself fighting back tears. I will not cry, she told herself fiercely, silently. Yet looking at him, the tall, lean, hard-muscled reality of him sent shock waves through her whole system. They had made love once. They had shared a moment of mutual bliss, the only man ever to touch her so intimately, to take her to the heights of passion, only to shatter it all with one regret-filled phrase, "I'm sorry."

Even now, looking at him, listening to his strained breathing as he fought the pain in his eye, and remembering the sting of his harshly spoken words in the street today, she could not regret what had happened. In the time and place of its occurrence his making love to her had for a rapturous moment released her from the horrible realities of war.

Maybe when he felt better she could get him to talk about it. Then perhaps he wouldn't have to be so distant with her. Maybe it embarrassed him to be reminded of it, though she found it hard to imagine Joshua being embarrassed about anything. He was twelve years her senior. It was possible that he thought she held what happened against him somehow. She had to make him understand. Surely, they could be friends at least. She sighed with relief when his breathing grew more even, relaxed.

When Beal returned a couple of hours later, Stacey raised a finger to her lips. "He's asleep," she whispered.

Steele woke at the slight sounds.

"Sorry, we meant to leave you asleep," Beal said.

"It's all right." His head felt clear. Except for a dull ache, the pain was gone.

"Feeling better?" Stacey asked.

He only nodded.

"How often does this happen, Joshua?" she asked. She sensed his exasperation at her persistent questioning, but if she and Sam were to help him, she had to know all of his symptoms. To her relief he answered.

"Every few days or so. No particular pattern. Every time I hope it's the last. Just when I think maybe it is, it happens again."

She rubbed her chin with her hand, absently clicking off the latest medical journals she had read. Nothing stirred in her memory to match up with what Joshua had described. But she was confident she and Sam could find it.

"You be headin' out right away?" Beal questioned.

"I promised you help with Barnett. It can wait until . . ."

The marshal interrupted Steele with a wave of his hand. "Go on with you. I can handle that polecat one-handed. You let Stacey get you to Doc Curtis."

Steele scowled at the thought of traveling with Stacey. "A couple of days won't make any difference. You taking him out soon?"

"It'll be dark in three hours. Was figurin' on it then. You're welcome to come along. But I don't obligate you, son."

Steele settled his Stetson on his head. "I'll be back." But before he got out the door, he turned back to the lawman and asked the question burning in his mind. He never left a town without asking it at least once. He spoke matter-of-factly, but his eyes clouded with hate.

"I'm looking for a man, marshal," he said, "he's about five feet ten, a hundred sixty pounds, blondish hair, blue eyes, well educated." Steele paused, just giving Merrick's description sent a wave of sickness through him. Even after four years he wanted nothing more than to close his fingers around the bastard's throat and squeeze the life out of him. "He speaks French, Spanish, and English like a native." Steele knew the description was scarcely adequate, but he had little else. Merrick could even have altered his appearance somehow—grown a beard, gained weight.

When no recognition showed in John Beal's face, Steele added, "Sometimes when he's angry or afraid his eyes twitch."

Stacey had been busying herself cleaning up a spot of whiskey that had spilled when she'd bandaged the marshal's arm. She kept her face averted. It was preposterous to think that Joshua was looking for Martin Randolph. The hate in Steele was palpable. But she couldn't help noticing how close the physical description was, and she knew Martin spoke Spanish. French? Not that she'd ever heard. But Martin had always had that nervous tic in his eye when he was angry.

What could Martin have ever done to Joshua to warrant such loathing? No, there had to be some mistake. Martin couldn't possibly be the man Joshua was looking for. And she had no intention of mentioning any of these similarities to him. He would no doubt run into Martin himself when he stopped in Spring Canyon. She was certain it would be the first time the men had ever met.

Beal had pondered the description for a couple of minutes and was now shaking his head. "Sorry, Steele, don't ring no bells at all." But Beal now understood what caused the grimness in the big man. He pitied the blond, blue-eyed man when Steele finally did catch up with him.

"Obliged, marshal," Steele acknowledged. "I'll head on up to the livery and bring back my horse. I'm still riding out with you and Barnett."

"I might as well get started myself," Stacey said.

"Started?" Steele frowned.

173

"I'm heading back to Spring Canyon. With John leaving there's nothing to keep me here."

"That's a pretty stupid thing to be doing, considering Barnett's gang is in those hills."

"You know," she snapped, "I am getting pretty sick and tired of you calling me stupid. And I'll go anywhere I damn well please." She stormed out of the office, brushing past him. She couldn't make out his muttered oath.

Stacey reached the livery well ahead of him, and she did not turn around when she heard him stride in behind her. Why had their reunion turned out like this? What had made him so bitter, so cruel? He hadn't made the slightest reference to their previous meeting seven years ago. Refusing to cry, she threw the saddle on the back of her rented mare.

It would have been better to never have seen him again. She could have cherished the memory of their first passionate encounter the rest of her life. Now it was being tarnished by what he had become. Would she have preferred that the War Department's letter had been right? That he had been killed? She leaned against the horse's neck. No, she knew that wasn't true. She had been achingly glad to discover that he still lived.

Forcing herself to relax, she tightened the cinch under the mare's belly. She couldn't go on letting him affect her this way.

She waited until she heard him lead his horse from the stable. Only then did she pick up the mare's reins and turn to follow.

Shots racketed from up the street. Stacey dropped the reins and hurried to stand beside Joshua. His gun was in his hand. She saw several men running toward John's office. A nameless fear touched her.

Gun ready, Steele trotted up the street. Stacey fell in step behind him.

"This time stay out of the line of fire," he grated. She ignored him.

Several prospectors stood in the jail doorway, shaking their heads. Steele shouldered his way past them. The storage room door was wide open. Beal lay on the floor in front of his desk. His eyes were open. A large red stain crawled across his chest.

"John!" Stacey cried, rushing over to him.

Steele knelt beside him. The marshal's hand reached out and gripped Steele's shirt front. His hold was surprisingly strong considering the looks of the wound.

Tears streaked Stacey's cheeks as she looked up at Joshua. The lawman had only minutes left.

"It was that damned Indian and three others," he choked. "Busted Barnett out. I never had a chance." The marshal coughed blood. "Damn." He pulled himself closer to Steele as his voice grew weaker. "Josh, you watch yourself, boy. I heard Barnett say he was goin' after you. They'll kill ya." He was finding it harder to breathe. "You look after Stacey for me. Don't let her go home by herself."

Beal survived another spasm of choking coughs. But his eyes grew dimmer. "Promise . . . promise . . ." The marshal's grip slackened. His head slumped back. Beal was dead.

Steele eased the body the rest of the way to the floor. A fierce anger surged in him. Beal's gun was still in its holster. He had been shot in the back.

Stacey had her hand on Beal's shoulder, crying softly.

Joshua stood up. "Any of you men see which way Barnett and his bunch went?"

Three men indicated east. "I think I hit one of 'em," a man said.

Steele frowned. East. They would be ahead of him. Barnett had probably heard the conversation about Spring Canyon.

Men loitered about, talking. "It's a damn shame," said one. "John was a good one," said another. Nobody made any move, though, to go after his killers. That was the law's problem. They didn't want to leave their claims.

"We'll see to it he's buried good and proper," one of the men said.

Steele reached down and pulled Stacey to her feet, supporting her with his arm. He tried unsuccessfully to ignore the sweet, womanly scent of her, the softness. Angry at himself, he snapped at her.

"It's too dangerous for you to travel. Barnett will be gunning for me. I can't take a chance on your getting hurt."

She said only, "I'm leaving for Spring Canyon, Mr. Steele. I'll go with you, or without you, but I'm going."

"If you waited a few days . . ."

"No."

Steele's jaw clamped shut. She was impossible.

"Then we'd better leave now," he said, "before they have a chance to plan an ambush."

Listlessly, Stacey followed him back to the livery. Glancing behind her she saw several men carrying

John's body out of his office. She shivered, suddenly glad to know that Joshua would be with her.

Stacey mounted the sorrel mare. Steele climbed on the dun. In silence they headed east. Stacey's green eyes took in the rocky countryside. With its acres of forests it would provide dozens of opportunities for ambush. Even with Steele at her side, the trail to Spring Canyon suddenly looked twice as long.

CHAPTER TEN

Stacey eyed her traveling companion covertly as they rode out of town. She was still badly shaken over John Beal's death. Perhaps she should have waited a day or two before starting back to Spring Canyon. Barnett and his men might be laying an ambush for Joshua even now. She could be riding to their deaths.

His strong chiseled profile was silhouetted in the waning light. His dark features sparked an impression in her of a predatory beast on the prowl. He had not spoken since they'd left town, making her feel strangely alone. She was not used to being so soundly ignored. Her perception of him as cold and ruthless was continually softened by the memory of the sweet, sweet words he had whispered against her hair, as he made love to her in the Wilderness. Was that all they had been? Words?

He seemed genuinely ill-at-ease to be in her presence. Her few attempts to lure him into conversation had failed miserably. She finally gave up and rode along beside him in silence. He was on his guard, she knew that. His eyes never stopped moving. That his caution may have been extreme as a direct result of her presence was not lost on her. She was the albatross strung unwillingly around his neck.

Steele did not pause for supper, and Stacey's stomach growled a protest, though she said nothing. Silently, he handed her some beef jerky from his saddlebags, which she grudgingly accepted.

It was several hours after dark before he was ready to call a halt for the night. "The horses need the rest," he said, climbing out of the saddle.

The horses indeed, Stacey grimaced, rubbing her hip as she walked away from her tired mount. She was used to riding, but she was also used to taking rest breaks whenever it struck her fancy.

"Aren't you going to build a fire?" Stacey asked, when she realized he was making no attempt to do so.

"And invite Barnett to join us for a cup of coffee?" he mocked.

Stacey bristled. She bit back a sarcastic reply and stomped back to unsaddle and rub down her horse. Did he have to make some sort of caustic remark about everything she said? She finished tethering the horse almost by feel. Clouds had drifted over to blot out the stars. There was no moon. She groped her way back to the natural rock cul-de-sac Steele had chosen as their haven for the night.

Joshua was sitting in front of a fair-sized boulder, his legs stretched out in front of him. Stacey half-tripped over them. "I'm sorry," she muttered, straightening. "The dark is a little darker here than the dark over there."

He smiled in spite of himself at the humor in her voice. "Get some sleep," he growled.

"If I can find the ground."

"I'll stand the first watch. I'll wake you later to take your turn."

"Fine," she said, genuinely pleased that he would trust her as look-out. When she considered it more logically, she realized he had little choice in the matter. He couldn't stay awake twenty-four hours a day. Still, it made her feel less of a burden. She spread out her blankets and lay down.

Steele stood up and stepped over to the only available opening in the rocks that surrounded them. If Barnett came tonight, he would have to come in this direction. He heard Stacey straighten her blankets and lie down. He could scarcely make out her silhouette in the darkness. His breathing quickened. Her nearness fired a long buried need.

He remembered the terrified girl-woman, who had wrapped her arms around him in the Wilderness after Caulfield's attack. He should have put her away from him then, set her on her horse and been done with her. He'd rationalized what had followed, chalking it up to loneliness, battle fatigue. Later he'd recognized each rationalization for what it was—an excuse. He'd taken her because he wanted her. His body had responded to her dawning passion with an ardor that had astonished him.

In Mexico before Merrick's betrayal he had thought of her more than once, imagining her back in Albany, well-married and mothering a brood of children. He admitted some surprise at finding her in New Mexico, wondering briefly what had brought her here and why she had not married. She was a lovely woman, that much had not changed.

He cursed feelingly. Some accident of fate had brought them together again, but he was damned if he was going to let himself be distracted by her.

Merrick was his one and only goal. Angrily, he forced her from his mind.

He sat still for several minutes listening to the sounds of the night. They had been followed from E'town. He was sure of it. He hadn't seen their shadow, but he had been there just the same. He hadn't told Stacey, because he didn't want to alarm her. The boulders were adequate shelter for now. He doubted an attack would come in the dark. The outlaws might shoot each other by mistake.

Three hours later he was still listening, still watching. He rubbed his eyes. He knew he should wake her, but still he hesitated. What if the dream came? Wearily, he resigned himself to the possibility. He would be little help to her today if he didn't get some sleep. She lay on her right side, her pale hair caressing her cheek. He chalked up the stirring of his blood to a long unappeased hunger. He was a man. She was a woman. What woman made no difference. Gently, he shook her shoulder.

Stacey came sleepily awake. She sensed Joshua beside her. "Barnett?" she gasped.

"No," he said quickly, "it's just your turn to watch, if you're sure you'll be all right."

"I'll manage." Her voice was defensive at his imagined slur on her ability to even stay awake for a couple of hours.

He walked over to his blankets. "Wake me a half-hour before dawn."

She clambered over and perched herself on a small boulder. Shivering against the night chill, she pulled her blanket across her shoulders. She was grateful for the cold. Not that she would have told Joshua, but she

181

was still desperately tired. The cold would help her stay awake. The last thing she needed was to fall asleep and find his mocking face standing over her. Besides, she shuddered, it could even get them killed.

She stared into the night. For the second time Joshua Steele had entered her life, and as before he had her emotions in a turmoil. Even in sleep she had not been able to escape him. She had had the strangest dream tonight, made all the stranger because she could remember it with such vivid detail.

She had been lying naked in Joshua's arms. He was making love to her, his mouth trailing a path of fire across her eager body. When his body had joined with hers, she had cried out with the joy of it. But even as his body moved inside her, he had seemed detached, alert to some danger lurking in the tangle of branches that encircled them.

A spectre had loomed in the darkness. For a moment she had thought it was Hector Caulfield returning from the grave. She screamed in terror. Whatever it was, it meant to take Joshua away from her. Already he was looking toward it, not her. Her fingers gripped his arms, seeking to hold him closer. She pulled his head down, closing her mouth over his. But he jerked away as the spectre glided nearer.

"No, Joshua," she cried again and again. "Don't go! Don't leave me!"

The spectre had moved close enough so that she could see his features clearly. Jake Barnett. He cackled with delight, when Joshua pulled away from her. Each time she reached for him, he would slip through her fingers.

"I have to go, Stacey," he said. "I have to kill him."

His voice was cold and lifeless.

She pleaded with him to come back, but he followed Barnett into the forest. She called to him until her voice was gone. But he never looked back. Not once.

A cool breeze against her tear-stained cheeks brought Stacey abruptly back to reality. Brusquely, she wiped the tears away. She was being ridiculous. The dream had been unsettling enough, she didn't have to dwell on it now that she was awake. She returned her attention to guarding their position. It was almost daybreak. Too soon she and Joshua would be on the trail again, and she would have to deal with his continued aloofness. Perhaps she should have it out with him once and for all about that day in the Wilderness.

She heard him shift restlessly in his sleep. The cloud cover had drifted on, and she could see his outline clearly against the hard ground. He muttered something she couldn't understand. Suddenly worried that his eye might be bothering him, she padded over to him.

Garcia ripped the whip across his torn, agonized flesh. Again and again the blood-sucking black monster attacked his mutilated back. He twisted violently, desperately seeking to escape the unending hurt. Garcia's maniacal cackle seeped through his tortured brain. The knife, the rats, the chains, the black hole . . .

"Joshua! Joshua!" She shook him hard, but he pushed her away.

"Merrick. Kill Merrick."

"Joshua!"

He open his eyes to the flare of a match. He read the white-faced fear in her eyes. She was on her knees leaning over him, her hand on his quaking chest. Her long pale hair framed her oval face, a tendril kissing his cheek.

"Joshua?" His name was a question, her concern genuine. Her emerald green eyes searched his face. Those eyes, eyes that had saved him from madness. The match winked out.

He reached for her. His arms circled her neck. His mouth found and possessed hers. His hard, hungry kisses consumed her, blotted out her sense of reality. His lips burned into hers, lighting a fire in her own blood. Only once before had she ever experienced anything like this. She had not exaggerated her memory of him. Seven years fell away as nothing. His kisses left her weak, defenseless, clinging to him, needing, demanding more.

The sweet reality of his touch brought quick tears to her eyes. This was not a dream. Joshua was not dead. He was alive and he was holding her in his arms once again. She lay against his chest, revelling in the pounding of his heart. Only now did she realize how much she had wanted this moment.

He shifted his body so that they lay side by side. Her body molded itself to his. Her limbs felt blissfully weak. His fingers tugged at the buttons of her blouse. She bit her lip to hold back a whimper of pleasure, but she couldn't hold back the shuddering sigh that swept through her when his hands reached under her chemise and cupped a bare breast.

How could she let this happen? Hadn't she learned a harsh enough lesson at this man's hands seven years ago? She was no longer an impetuous seventeen-year-old girl drowning in a newborn tide of passion. She would have no one to blame but herself.

When his mouth closed over a full rounded breast, her senses snapped back. Even as her breast swelled with desire, her cheeks flamed with embarrassment. After what he had said to her, the cold, cruel way he had treated her, she couldn't let this happen. He was using her, using her now, as he must have used her then. He buried his hands in her hair, his mouth savaging hers once again. If she didn't stop him now, it would be too late.

"No," she whispered brokenly. "Please."

Steele's jaw clenched. Abruptly, he released her. His breathing was ragged, uneven. His aching frustration made his voice harsh. "I'm sorry. I had no right."

She stared at him in the darkness, unable to see whatever might be in those gray eyes. He was sorry. Sorry! Did he remember the last time he had apologized to her—after making love to her in the Wilderness? Oh, why did she have to meet this man again? Sitting up, she quickly rebuttoned her blouse. No, she was not going to let him hurt her again. She took a deep breath, forcing a calm she didn't feel.

"Was your eye bothering you?" she asked, trying to sound detached, professional.

"No."

She frowned. Then it was the dream. What kind of a dream could unnerve Joshua Steele? Awake, his sweating body shivered involuntarily in the night air.

Instinctively, it was the nurse in her she told herself later, she reached out to smooth his hair. It was a gesture meant to comfort, but she unwittingly re-kindled the fire his kisses had aroused. She longed for him to take her in his arms again. But after rejecting his advances, she didn't dare admit such a wanton thought.

"Are you all right?" she asked.

He jerked away from her. If she kept her hands on him like that, he wouldn't be responsible.

"Thank you for your concern, Miss Hamilton," he said stiffly. "But I assure you I am quite all right."

"That nightmare . . ."

"I said I'm all right," he snapped.

"Is Merrick the name of the man you described to John Beal?"

He muttered an oath and flung back his blankets. "It's almost light. We'd better get started."

No, she thought. They weren't going back on the trail. Not like this. Not until they had settled some things between them. She wasn't going to put up with another day of clipped comments.

He grabbed up his saddle blanket and headed for his horse.

"Joshua?"

He turned to look at her. "What now?"

"We need to talk."

"No. We don't." He threw the blanket over the animal's back and bent to pick up his saddle.

"I suppose it's none of my business . . ."

He settled the saddle on his horse. "You're right. It isn't."

Stacey straightened her shoulders and marched over to him. "Joshua, we must talk. I can't bear this tension between us."

He continued to ignore her, as he cinched down the saddle.

"I want to talk about that day in the Wilderness."

He had been about to mount his horse. His hand rested on the saddle horn. He sighed heavily. "I've been wondering how long it would take you to bring that up . . ."

"I'm not bringing it up for any reason you might think," she returned hotly.

He cocked an eyebrow at her. "No?"

"No! You think I'm going to accuse you of taking advantage of me. Or maybe you think I'm going to ask you to forgive the rash act of a foolish young girl . . ."

He winced, his jaw working, but he said nothing.

"Well, I'm not," she said. "It happened. It can't be undone. I don't blame you. I don't even blame myself any more. It's just that I thought . . . well, I thought that just possibly out of all of it, we might have established some kind of friendship."

He snorted derisively. "That's your idea of friendship?"

She felt the heat in her face. God, what had made him so cruel? "Joshua, please," she said, determined to finish what she had started, "I don't know what's happened to you since I saw you last. I think something or someone has hurt you terribly. You're not like this, I know you."

"You don't know anything about me, Stacey," he said, aware of how difficult he was making this for her. But she was already too close to the truth. How could he ever tell her about Mexico? It would be better if she hated him. "It's been seven years. A man changes, that's all. And just because a man beds a woman doesn't mean she knows him."

She didn't think words could hurt so much. "No, I suppose not," she whispered.

He heard the pain in her voice. He forced himself not to look at her. "We'd better go."

"Was it in Mexico?"

In one motion he was standing in front of her. His fingers dug cruelly into her upper arms. "What did you say?"

His gray eyes were narrowed to slits. Stacey trembled from head to foot at the cold menace in those eyes.

"Answer me, woman! What do you know about Mexico?" Did Merrick live in Spring Canyon? Did Stacey know him? Had he ever mentioned Mexico to her? "Answer me!"

"I received a letter . . . a letter from the War Department," she stammered. If her heart beat any faster, it would burst from her chest. She could feel the rage in him. "Joshua, please . . . you're hurting me."

He stared at his hands, as if he had only now become aware that he held her prisoner. He relaxed his grip, but did not release her. "What did this letter say?"

"It said you were dead."

He stared at her incredulously. "Why would the War Department notify you of my death?"

"Because I asked them."

His grip tightened again. "Asked them what?"

"I . . . I asked a friend of my father's to check on your whereabouts," she said, blushing furiously. Why had she begun this conversation? Her pride was

188

already in ruins where this man was concerned. Now there would be nothing left of it.

"Why in the hell would you do that?" he demanded.

"It was foolish, I know," she said. "My mother was sick. I didn't leave the house very much. I was curious. A whim. I don't know."

"And just what exactly did they tell you of my demise?" His voice was noticably hostile.

Oh, how she wished she had kept her mouth shut. His silence was better than his anger. Somehow this was leading to his nightmare — of that she was certain. And he would tell her nothing of that — of that she was also certain. Instead of easing the tension between them, she had exacerbated it.

"Let go of me and I'll tell you," she said.

He let go.

She walked over to a small boulder and sat down. "The letter told me you were sent to Mexico to aid Juarez. And that you were somehow betrayed . . . injured in an ambush. It said you were taken prisoner by the imperialists and later murdered."

He stared at her for a long minute. She didn't know about Merrick. She must have gotten the letter before he'd returned to Washington to resign his commission. He remembered Grant's surprise at seeing him alive. It wasn't until he'd given Grant his report, that the treachery of Ross Merrick had been revealed. Grant had thought Merrick dead too. Stacey had heard Merrick's name for the first time tonight, and only through his nightmare. He felt some of the tension drain out of him.

"Obviously I wasn't murdered," he said.

"Obviously."

"If we've talked enough now, maybe we can go. We're losing daylight."

They hadn't really settled anything, she thought. But his harshness no longer upset her. She was quietly thoughtful as she saddled her horse. She was beginning to piece together the puzzle of how this Joshua Steele differed so radically from the man in the Wilderness of Virginia. He said she didn't know him. But she knew enough to see that this Joshua was a hard, bitter, driven man. He had not been so seven years ago. And the key to his transformation was a man named Merrick.

She shivered, but not from the cold. To reduce a man like Joshua to a trembling nightmare could only mean that whatever Merrick had done to him bordered on the demonic.

The next two days of travel were strained, if uneventful. Joshua was sullen and withdrawn. His pride had been stung by her witnessing his nightmare, and perhaps just a little, by her rejecting his advances.

And though the nightmare did not happen again, she knew that he pushed them harder and faster because of it. She wondered if he had gotten any sleep at all since that night. His haggard features only fueled her suspicions.

Spring Canyon had come into view an hour ago from atop a rutted plateau. A wave of homesickness had swept over her. She was ready to take on the Garth Greevys and Mrs. Eberts again. Joshua's studied indifference even gave her cause to look forward to seeing Martin again.

The town was settled deep in one of the country's numerous canyons, troughed out by glaciers uncounted centuries before. Awesome rock formations dotted the landscape all around them. She had pointed out her uncle's house, but it was scarcely visible at that distance. Steele had not seemed interested anyway. He'd been preoccupied all morning.

"You keep doing that," she said as she watched him check their backtrail yet again. "Now are you finally going to tell me what you see?"

It was the Indian, the Apache from Barnett's gang. But he did not want to tell Stacey.

"It's Barnett, isn't it?" she persisted. "You think he's going to attack this close to town? We're practically there!"

"I've been wondering why they haven't attacked a half dozen times before this," he conceded. "That compadre of theirs, the miner in E'town wounded is the only thing I can think of who would have slowed them down. They probably waited for him to heal—or die."

Stacey shifted wearily in the saddle. Her sorrel plodded listlessly alongside Steele's dun. They had scarcely rested at all. Driven by a need to escape Barnett, and, she perceived, to escape an opportunity for another nightmare.

"Maybe Barnett has given up on us," she said hopefully.

"Not likely," Steele said. "This is personal. I killed his brother." And if anyone knew about that kind of motivation, it was Steele. Barnett would follow him to hell if he had to.

Steele removed his Stetson. Using the red bandana tied around his neck, he mopped a trail of sweat and grime from his face. The daily temperature had risen considerably now that they were out of the mountains.

The dun stumbled on a loose stone. The unexpected motion caused Steele to pull back sharply on the reins. The horse stopped, its head down. Stacey reined her horse to a halt beside him. Joshua was leaning over the pommel, breathing hard. He pressed a hand angrily against his left eye. "Not now!" He swore bitterly.

With a frustrated oath he reined the dun over to an outcropping of rocks and dismounted. He had to grab the pommel to keep from falling. Stacey grabbed her canteen and hurried over to him. He refused her offer to lean on her. Staggering over to a huge boulder, he slid to the ground in front of it, his back enjoying its support after long hours in the saddle. His vision was already foggy.

"Leave me be," he growled at Stacey. But he accepted her canteen. Before she could object, he dumped some of the water over his eye. The warm liquid did nothing to offset the mounting pain. Steele sighed heavily, recorked the canteen, and allowed it to slide to the ground beside him. He tilted his gray Stetson forward over his eyes and leaned back fully against the rock.

"Keep your eyes open," he warned her.

Stacey scrunched down beside him. Her eyes checked the countless boulders all around them. A man could hide an army in these rocks, she mused. Still she kept watch.

"Did you sell your ranch in the Colorado Territory?" she asked, not sure where the question had come from.

A muscle in his jaw worked, and she marvelled at how incredibly easy it was to aggravate him. Was it the question? Or was it just her?

"The ranch is still mine," he said, not moving his hat from over his eyes.

"Do you go back there often?"

"I haven't seen it for ten years."

She gasped. He'd never gone back! He hadn't seen it since before the Wilderness.

"How do you know it's still there? Someone could have usurped it!"

"I trust the people who care for it. I keep in touch by letter occasionally."

She leaned against the rock, her eyes still watchful. She felt almost giddy. This was the first conversation she'd had with him that hadn't sparked an argument, since their reunion in E'town.

"I remember how you spoke of it," she said. "How beautiful it was. Where just before dawn on your mountain lake, the silence is absolute."

He pushed his hat back and looked at her. He'd all but forgotten that. How had she remembered? The pain pressed in on him. He didn't want to think about Colorado. "I hope that uncle of yours is as good a doctor as you claim he is," he said.

"Oh, he is, Joshua. I promise you."

Something jogged in his memory. "Didn't you tell me you wanted to be a doctor once?"

She blushed happily that he had remembered, then sighed. "That's a rather long story, I'm afraid."

"We all get our dreams side-tracked," he said cryptically. He climbed to his feet. "We'd best get out of here."

"Can you ride?"

"I'll have to."

She watched him mount, his horse staggering slightly under his weight. They'd pushed their animals brutally. When Barnett had probably been camped, they had ridden on. She realized another reason for his haste. His eye. He had wanted to reach Spring Canyon before it acted up again. If he couldn't see when Barnett attacked, the outlaw would kill them both.

She climbed on her mare, riding close beside him. The way his hands gripped the saddle horn, the knuckles showing white, he was already well into another attack.

Her eyes scanned the country ahead of her. She was thankful Spring Canyon was so close. In the distance she could see the beginning of the Llano Estacado, the staked plains. Canyons ripped toward it, torn open in ancient cataclysms. The rugged beauty of the country never failed to stir her. She glanced again at Steele.

"Joshua, I know you object to my asking, but how is your eye doing?"

"Not very well," he said. He checked the Winchester in his scabbard. His vision was blurred, but he could still distinguish shapes. "Barnett could be in front of us now," he warned. "Stay alert, Stacey. It might save your life. I'm afraid I may not be too much help if the need arises."

She sensed his irritability at what he perceived as weakness in himself because of his faulty vision.

They topped the final ridge leading to town. "We're skylined here," he said. "We'd better move faster." He nudged the tired horse with his knees. Before the horse had gone another three steps, Steele reined in

194

sharply, rolling out of the saddle. He dragged Stacey from hers.

"Stay down," he hissed, pushing her behind a nearby boulder. He hadn't mistaken the sound. The sharp metallic click of shod hooves on rock.

Jim Cloudmaker cursed under his breath. Half Apache, half Irish he was incensed that he had alerted his quary to his presence. He dismounted and took up a perch behind a huge slab of rock. Steele was of no interest to him. The woman of even less interest. Cloudmaker would merely make certain they stayed put until Barnett arrived.

He pulled a bottle of bocanaro from his saddlebags. He considered briefly that his drinking was the reason his tracking was slipping, the reason that Steele and the woman were now aware of him, and the reason that Steele had spotted him yesterday. He yanked the cork from the bottle. It really didn't matter. Steele was still a dead man.

Cloudmaker checked his own backtrail. He had left one a blind man could follow, which was exactly the kind of trail Barnett needed. Joe Dunston had finally died last night from the slug that miner had pumped into him. Barnett had no reason to be lagging so far behind.

Cloudmaker's black eyes and squat features betrayed the heritage of his father. Only the lightness of his skin gave any evidence that he was not pure Apache. His hatred for his mother's blood never ceased to amaze Barnett, who figured it should be the other way around. But Cloudmaker had never seen it that way.

His father had been a warrior, filled with fierce pride in himself and the land. His mother was a captive white woman, who hated everything Indian, including her own son. She had killed herself when he was only two years old. Cloudmaker swilled down more of the fiery liquid and settled down to wait.

Jake Barnett flailed his downed horse mercilessly. How dare the damned beast collapse under him when he was so close to his prey? Couldn't the stupid animal see the blasted hole in the ground? It wasn't until Tony Pogget and Raul Griego dragged him away from the now dead horse that Barnett could manage some semblance of sanity.

"Take your filthy hands of me," he seethed. The two-inch ragged scar that twisted his lower lip flamed red. His yellow snake eyes spit venom at both Pogget and Griego. They backed off.

Barnett stomped over to the nervously dancing mount on which Ernie Timmons still sat.

"Get down!" Barnett bellowed.

Timmons fear-filled glance went from Barnett to Pogget and Griego. The latter two showed no support. Frank Harvey, who had remained outside of town during both the aborted hold-up and Barnett's break-out, showed no interest either.

"I said get down!" Barnett reached up and hauled the frightened owlhoot from the saddle by his shirt front. Ernie landed ungracefully on his butt in the dirt. Barnett leaped into the vacated saddle without a backward glance.

"Aw, Jake, why'd you have to throw me off like that? I woulda got down. You didn't give me a chance," Ernie whined. He didn't bother to dust off his trail stained clothes, as he struggled to his feet. Timmons' bulky body made his every move seem awkward.

"Mount up behind Griego," Barnett snapped.

Griego, a swarthy Mexican with a full mustache and mean black eyes, had remounted his own piebald. He opened his mouth to protest, but thought better of it and allowed Timmons to heave himself up behind him. The horse snorted at the combined weight of the two men, not liking it in the least.

"That damned animal of mine better not have cost me my chance at Steele," muttered Barnett, as he kicked his new mount in the sides and headed out after Cloudmaker's trail. Unless the breed had cornered Steele, there was no way they would get to him before he reached Spring Canyon. Damn Dunston anyway, Barnett fumed, why couldn't he have died right off?

Jake Barnett was a man of simple rules. Stay out of his way and stay alive. The first man who hadn't done that, a storekeeper who had caught a fourteen-year-old Barnett swiping licorice, had paid the ultimate price. Barnett had beaten the old man to death with his fists. He'd broken a hand doing it, but Barnett to this day still considered it worth it.

He couldn't even guess at how many men he'd killed since then. On his own since he was nine, there'd only been one person in the world he'd ever cared about, and that was his half-brother Jeff.

At the age of sixteen Barnett had gotten word that his father had died. He'd felt no sense of sadness at the news. He'd run away when he was nine partly to keep from killing the old man himself. In a drunken rage his father had beaten his mother to death before his eyes. When Jake attacked him, the older Barnett had nearly beaten his son to death, too, leaving him with a deformed lip as an eternal reminder of his hate.

His father had married again, and when Jake arrived purposely two weeks after the funeral, he'd found a consumptive woman and a towheaded two-year-old named Jeff. The woman had no interest in the boy, and one night three years later, Jake had taken the kid and left, never to return.

Barnett murdered, raped, robbed, and cheated any time the mood struck him, but for Jeff he reserved whatever decency he had in him. As the boy grew he kept him out of his more vicious crimes, allowing him only to participate in robberies and card cheating schemes. And Jeff had worshipped his older brother, as a boy would worship the only human being who had ever cared about him.

Joshua Steele had killed the only person who had ever meant anything at all to Jake Barnett. That Jeff had shot at Steele first did not even enter his thoughts. Steele would pay for what he had done, and pay dearly. His would not be a quick death either, if Jake had his way about it. For killing Jeff, Joshua Steele was a dead man.

Steele fought desperately to focus his good right eye.

"You can't see, can you?" Stacey demanded.

"Things are a bit blurry at the moment," he acknowledged, "but I can still see."

"The pain?"

"Tolerable."

The way he gasped out the word, she surmised that tolerable meant barely tolerable. "Do you have an extra gun?"

"You stay out of this!"

"Stay out of it! I'm in it, Joshua! Up to my neck! Or hadn't you noticed? If they kill you, do you think they're going to let me live to tell about it?"

"Get the rifle out of my scabbard."

Quickly Stacey hurried to the horses. She had tied them out of sight. She gripped the heavy weapon, tugging it free of the saddle boot. The thought of pointing it at another human being sickened her. The only thing that bolstered her resolve was the need to protect Joshua.

The image of Hector Caulfield rose to haunt her. She wondered if she would hesitate today, as she had then. She prayed she wouldn't have to find out. At least she knew more about handling weapons now. Sam had insisted on it. The west was too unsettled yet not to know how to shoot, he'd said. So she'd practiced with tin cans and empty whiskey bottles until she'd become at least reasonably proficient. She hurried back to rejoin Joshua.

"Barnett's probably beating leather to get here," he said. "The Indian will make sure we stay put until he does." He pointed to the boulder about thirty yards to their left. "If I could get over there and get rid of him, we could leave before Barnett puts in an appearance."

He hunched behind the rock ready to follow through on his plan. He took one step. Pain ripped through his eye, doubling him over. Biting back a groan, Steele went to his knees, releasing the Colt and holding his head. Helpless, he could only hope the pain's intensity would subside. If Barnett arrived now, he and Stacey would both be dead.

Barnett reined in as he rounded a bend in the trail. He caught sight of Cloudmaker signalling him to a pile of rocks on his left.

"They're behind that boulder," the Indian told him. "I think the eye pains your brother's killer."

Barnett smiled. He had seen Steele's attack in E'town. If the big man were in that kind of torment again, Barnett was happy. It also meant Steele couldn't see very well. The outlaw leader called Frank Harvey and Tony Pogget over and instructed them to circle around the rocks and come up on Steele from behind.

"He's practically blind, a sitting duck," he assured them.

"What about the girl?" Harvey wanted to know.

"If she shoots at you, shoot back," Barnett shrugged. "Otherwise, we'll save her for later." The suggestive glint in his eyes was not lost on Harvey. The outlaw licked his lips.

"The reinforcements have arrived," Steele said, his voice tight as he fought the pain. "Keep your eyes open, Stacey. You may be our only chance." His voice turned grim. "You're in this because of me. I'm sorry."

"Don't be ridiculous," she snapped, covering her own feelings, as she sensed his genuine regret. "I practically forced you to bring me along. Besides, I owe you one."

"If you're talking about Caulfield, you don't owe . . ."

Behind them someone cocked a pistol. Spinning

quickly, Steele dove sideways and fired a shot strictly by sound. The bullet struck Frank Harvey squarely in the chest. He was dead before he hit the ground.

The speed and deadly accuracy of Steele's shot unnerved Tony Pogget. He slunk back behind a rock and waited for Barnett to make the next move. If that was Steele's shooting half-blind, he'd hate to see him when his eyesight was at its best.

Barnett saw Harvey fall. Furious, he opened fire on Steele's position with his rifle. Rock chips sprayed from the boulder Joshua had settled behind. Some of them caught his right cheek. He wiped at the blood with his fist. He heard Barnett scream at Pogget to shoot. So there was another one behind them. Things were not looking up.

"Give me the rifle," he barked at Stacey. She did so quickly. He raised the Winchester and aimed for the smoke from Barnett'e rifle. He could scarcely make it out. He waited. When Barnett stuck his head up again, Steele fired and narrowly missed Jake's head. He swore in disgust, not accepting his eyesight as an excuse.

Stacey looked around wildly, terrified that one of the outlaws would break through their meager defenses. She thought she saw something move between the two boulders at Steele's back.

Ernie Timmons crept from one boulder to the next. He had seen what happened to Frank Harvey, and he didn't want the same thing to happen to him. He also didn't care to incur the wrath of Jake Barnett. That could be worse than facing Steele. If he could just get above him . . .

"Joshua!" Stacey screamed.

Steele jerked toward the sound. The movement saved his life. Timmons' bullet tore into his back. The force slammed him to the ground. He felt the warm surge of blood trailing down his back. Black rage contorted his features. He lay still.

Stacey stared in horror at Steele's inert body. "You've killed him," she shrieked at the approaching Timmons, unmindful of her own danger. She scrambled toward Steele, tears streaming down her face.

Joshua slowly pulled back the hammer of the forty-four he held against his body. He heard Timmons' approach. And he heard Stacey. Let Timmons get close enough first, he prayed. The outlaw gave Steele's boot a tentative kick. Without warning Steele wheeled and fired.

Timmons fell back in surprised agony. Stacey nearly collapsed in astonishment. She watched the outlaw scurry behind some rocks before Joshua could squeeze off another shot. Brusquely, she wiped away the tears on her cheeks. God forbid, he should see them and let fly another sarcastic remark.

"I'm hit, Jake," Timmons moaned, stumbling back to the outlaw leader. "You gotta help me."

"What about Steele?" Barnett snarled.

"I got him for you, Jake. I hit him good. Please, you gotta help me."

"But he isn't dead!" Barnett hissed. "He had enough left to shoot you, didn't he?"

"He's bleeding bad, Jake. He hasn't got a chance." Such talk only spurred Timmons' own fear. "Jake, you gotta get me to a doctor."

Cloudmaker appeared and pointed down the

winding trail leading to Spring Canyon. A lone rider was coming up fast. From the glint of sunlight off something metallic on his chest, it didn't take much to figure out their approaching company was a lawman.

"Let's get out of here," Pogget hollered.

Heaving Timmons onto Harvey's horse, the group of outlaws took off at a run. Any other time Barnett would not have hesitated to kill the peace officer. But they were too close to town to risk it. Already the shots had obviously been heard there. Other's might ride out to investigate.

Cursing his luck, Barnett took one last look at where he'd last seen Steele. If he was still alive, Barnett would be back. As if in answer to his question, Steele pumped four more shots in Barnett's direction. He was daring the outlaw to ride down on him. But the lawman was too close. Steele's death would have to be postponed. But not for long, Barnett vowed. Not for long.

Steele heard the hoofbeats of the approaching rider and decided Barnett must be answering his challenge.

"Stay down," he hissed at Stacey. She wanted to see to his back, but he pushed her roughly away.

"I'll get the canteen from my horse. I'm going to clean up that wound." Keeping low, she hurried back toward the horses. She spied riders tearing off to the west. At least some of them had given up, she thought.

Steele's back was on fire. He shoved his bandana beneath this shirt to stem the bleeding. His eye still ached a little, but his vision was clearing. As the rider emerged from between two boulders, Steele shouted a command from behind a rock cover.

"Stop or you're dead!"

The startled horseman reined back savagely on his huge claybank. He'd heard the shooting all right, but had seen several riders heading west and thought they had all gone. He regretted his unusual carelessness, wondering if it would now cost him his life.

For the moment it was all he could do to keep his confused and frightened horse from unseating him. When the animal finally came to a trembling standstill, the lawman called out to his hidden assailant.

"I suggest you think about it real carefully before there's any more gunplay, mister."

"Then why don't you just drop yours to the ground. Real easy." Steele peered out cautiously. He didn't recognize this one, but Barnett may have hired an extra hand or two to track him down. He hadn't recognized the dead one either. The others had apparently ridden off, but maybe it was just a ruse to lure him into the open. He hoped Stacey had sense enough to stay with the horses.

"Get off your horse and come this way," Steele said. The lawman walked toward the sound of Steele's voice.

Squinting, Joshua noted the sheriff's badge pinned to the calfskin vest the man wore. Still wary, but feeling some relief, Steele stepped out to face the lawman.

Sheriff Rube Tucker puzzled over the appearance of his dry gulcher. He certainly didn't look like an ordinary highwayman. He looked worse! "You seem to be in pretty sad shape for a robber, mister," Tucker said calmly.

"I'm no thief, sheriff. The name's Joshua Steele.

The men who rode off were trying to kill me, not necessarily the other way around." Steele lowered the rifle.

With a deliberate motion Tucker eased his own six-gun out of its holster and levelled it at the lean, hard looking man in front of him. Steele made no move to protest the sheriff's action. He'd drawn on the law, unintentionally or not, and he'd have to face the consequences.

He was using every effort of will just to remain on his feet. He could feel the warmth still trailing down his back. At least his vision was almost back to normal.

"Mind telling me what this little ruckus here was all about, Steele?" the sheriff asked.

"Just a little misunderstanding. Jake Barnett and his gang threw down on me."

Tucker recognized Barnett's name. The lawman gave Steele a steady, appraising look. Steele didn't move a muscle. Tucker could sense the fierce pride in this man. He decided for the moment he could trust him. A tough, raw-boned man in his middle fifties, the lawman prided himself on his instincts about other men. He'd seldom been wrong in his lifetime. In his line of work accurate judgment about what a man was or wasn't capable of often meant the difference between life and death.

"I think we'd better head into Spring Canyon, Steele."

"Am I going as your prisoner?" Steele inquired without hostility.

"Maybe. There's a dead body over there that needs a little explaining." He indicated Harvey's corpse with a nod of his head. "If I believe your story, then that's all there is to it. If I find out different, you'll be in the hoosegow faster'n free candy goin' at a kids' fair."

Steele met the lawman's steady gaze. Tucker appeared outwardly friendly, but Steele sensed an entrenched caution that doubtless grew from his job.

Joshua stepped from the boulder with the intention of calling Stacey and getting his horse. The rock was supporting him more than he realized. The movement caused ripples of pain to shoot through his back. He collapsed back against the boulder.

Tucker hurried toward him. "You hit, boy? Why in thunder didn't you say something?"

"Joshua!" Stacey screamed, dropping the canteen she carried and rushing toward him.

"Stacey! What in tarnation!" Tucker thundered.

"Rube!" she squealed, "oh, thank heaven! I thought I recognized your voice on my way back, but I decided it was just wishful thinking." She bent over Joshua. "Help me with him."

Steele was nearly out on his feet, but he was conscious enough to again shove Stacey away when she attempted to check his wound. "Leave it."

"Joshua, be reasonable. You're bleeding."

"Your uncle's a doctor, let him take care of it," he hissed.

She took a step backward. "Not you too," she whispered.

His back hurt too much to try to figure out what she meant by that. He only knew that she couldn't see his back.

Tucker helped Steele mount. Stacey swung aboard her mare. The lawman positioned his horse on

Steele's right, so Stacey kept pace on his left. If he started to fall, one of them should be able to catch him.

"You want to explain to me how you got mixed up in this, Stacey," the sheriff probed. "Sam said you were in Denver."

"I was. It's a long story, Rube. Too long to go into now."

He accepted that. She would tell him later. "I don't think Sam's in his office," he went on. "I saw him head out in his buggy real early this morning."

Great, Stacey thought. She'd have to tend to Joshua's back anyway. She glanced at him. His eyes were closed, but she guessed he was still conscious. Probably just concentrating on staying on the horse. So he thought a woman doctor was a contradiction in terms, too. She didn't know when she'd ever felt so miserable.

CHAPTER ELEVEN

They reined the horses to a halt in front of the house. Quickly, Stacey clambered out of the saddle. "You help him inside, Rube. I'll get things ready."

The sheriff dismounted, tied his horse to the hitching post and came under the claybank's head to help Steele dismount.

Joshua sagged heavily against the lawman. "I can manage," he mumbled weakly.

"Sure, boy," Tucker said, keeping his hold on the big man. Steele was nearly out on his feet. The sheriff helped him into Sam Curtis' office, easing him onto the bed.

Stacey stood next to a large chest of drawers, readying some bandages. "Sam's not here," she said pensively to Tucker.

"I barely got him onto the bed, Stacey," Tucker said. "I think he's passed out. Do you know if the bullet's still in him or not?"

"I don't know. He wouldn't let me near him. But I intend to find out."

"Stacey! Stacey!"

Stacey whirled at the desperation in the shrill voice. "Molly, what on earth?"

The saloon girl staggered into Sam's office, her

baby clutched in her arms. "Stacey, please, you've got to help me!"

"What is it? Tell me!" Stacey gripped the girl by the shoulders. Molly's eyes looked sunken, as if she hadn't slept properly for days. Stacey felt the girl's forehead. At least she wasn't feverish. "Hasn't Sam been looking in on you?" she demanded.

"He came by the first few days you were gone," Molly sobbed. "Rance let him in then. After that, he told Sam never to come back."

"Why would Rance Dawson do that?" Stacey asked. She cast a scowling glance at Rube Tucker. Why hadn't the sheriff intervened?

Wincing at the harsh judgment in Stacey's eyes, Tucker defended himself. "I only got back in town yesterday. I've been gone nearly three weeks."

"I'm sorry, Rube," Stacey said quickly. "This is just so unbelievable." She turned to Molly. "Sam just took Rance at his word and didn't come back?" It wasn't possible.

"He tried to," she wailed. "But Rance had me and the baby moved out of my room. He locked us in a shack outside of town. He wouldn't tell nobody where we were."

"He what?" Tucker cut in.

Her sobbing became more uncontrollable. Stacey sensed there was more to the story than the girl was letting on.

"Why did Rance do this to you, Molly?" she asked.

"My baby, my baby, he said I couldn't keep my baby if I didn't do it . . ."

"Didn't do what, Molly?" Stacey pressed. She shot a glance at Steele. He seemed unconscious. She wanted to go to him, but Molly would not be quieted.

The girl held her baby so tightly the infant bagan to wail in protest. Stacey pried the infant from Molly's arms. In spite of Molly's haggard appearance, the baby appeared healthy. Molly had probably been feeding Angel at the expense of her own health.

"Sit down, Molly," Stacey ordered, deciding a firmer tone of voice might work against the girl's hysteria. At the same time Stacey comforted the crying infant by holding her against her shoulder and gently rubbing the child's back.

"Molly, you get control of yourself right now. Angel needs you."

The girl looked up, brushing at her tears. "I'm sorry, Miss Stacey," she said.

"Never mind. I want you to get up to my room and rest." Stacey placed Angel back in Molly's arms. "You rock her to sleep. Feed her if she needs it. I'll be up to see you just as soon as I can. And don't you give Rance Dawson another thought." She led the girl to the stairs. "It's the first door at the top. You make yourself right at home, all right?"

"Thank you, Miss Stacey. Thank you," Molly said, her voice still quivering.

"Go." Stacey gave her a gentle push. "I have to see to another patient right now, then I'll be up."

Molly held her baby close and climbed the stairs.

Stacey hurried back into the office. Joshua hadn't moved. She picked up several bandages and stepped over to the bed. She sat down beside him and tugged his vest open, then undid the buttons of his shirt. The bloody fabric stuck to his right side. Gently she eased it away from his flesh.

Even touching him in this detached, professional manner sent shivers of fire through her. Her hands trembled noticeably.

"It looks like it went clean through, Rube," she said, making an effort to keep her voice even. "It didn't hit anything vital, thank God. I'd guess it's the loss of blood that's sapping his strength more than anything." She pushed the material aside, baring his chest completely. "The bleeding's stopped. It'll need disinfecting, though."

"I've got some water boiling," Tucker said.

She smiled. "Thanks, Rube. You'd make a fine nurse."

"Aw, that's for womenfolk."

"Now don't you start," she flared, then instantly drew rein on her temper. Tucker meant no harm. Heaven knew he'd stood up for her on numerous occasions, when she'd had to cajole reluctant emergency patients into letting her care for them because Sam was out of the office.

She put her hand under Steele's neck, trying to lift him slightly.

"Help me with him, Rube. I want to get this shirt off him."

Tucker stepped forward. "You still haven't told me what you were doing traveling with this hombre, Stacey."

"It's a long story," she said. Briefly she explained how she and Steele met in Elizabethtown, about Barnett, and about John Beal's death.

Tucker looked grim when she finished. "Beal was a good man."

"I know," Stacey said quietly. "Now, are you going

to help me with this shirt?"

"Maybe you'd best leave the room while I get him undressed."

"I've done quite a bit of doctoring in my life, Rube. I know what a man's body looks like." And I certainly know what this man's body looks like, came the unbidden thought.

"Just the same . . ." he stammered.

Stacey could see the color creeping into Tucker's craggy face. She smiled sympathetically, rising to her feet. "I only want the top of him undressed."

Tucker tried to relax. He'd never been very much at ease around women. He stepped toward Joshua.

Steele stirred and opened his eyes.

"Ahh, you're awake. Good," Tucker said. "You can help me get you out of that shirt, so Stacey can take a look at the bullet hole in your back." He extended a hand toward Steele, but was taken aback by the sudden anger that flared in the big man's eyes.

"Where's the doctor?" Steele snapped. His gaze narrowed on Stacey. "If he's not here, I'll wait until he gets back."

"Joshua, your back needs attention now," Stacey said. "I assure you, I'm quite competent, even if you choose to believe otherwise."

Steele measured her with his eyes. She was so lovely. Her green eyes sparkled, her blonde hair falling softly about her shoulders. His breathing quickened in spite of himself. She was quite a picture. With her hands on her slender hips, the material of her shirt drew tighter across her fully rounded breasts. Irritated that she should have this effect on him, he grew even more sullen and defensive.

He already knew she wasn't one to be denied her own way in many things. But then neither was he. He wasn't going to take off his shirt. He couldn't let her see the evidence of those months spent in a Mexican hell-hole.

"I'm not going to take 'no' for an answer, Joshua." Stacey tried to be firm, even though she found his glare unsettling. "I don't know when my uncle will be back, so I have to insist that you let me take a look at that wound. The bullet went through, but it needs to be disinfected and bandaged."

Steele's gaze did not falter. Stubbornly she went on, "I can wait until you pass out again from loss of blood. I can use chloroform on you. Or you can make it easy on both of us and cooperate."

Damn this woman. She didn't know what she was asking, yet Steele suddenly knew she was going to win. He didn't know when the doctor would return and his back did need attention. With Barnett in the vicinity and the real possibility that Ross Merrick could even now be breathing the same air in Spring Canyon, he couldn't afford to be laid up very long.

"I'm only asking you to be reasonable, Joshua."

Grimacing more in annoyance than pain, Steele sat up. Never taking his angry eyes off of her, he shrugged out of his shirt.

Stacey released the breath she'd been holding. Her voice was grateful. "Thank you. Now if you'd just lie on your side . . ."

Steele turned his back to her. He heard her sharp intake of breath. His muscles tightened. His jaw set hard.

"Oh, my God." She said it so softly he thought he

might have imagined it. She stared at the criss-crossed pattern of old and deep scars.

Rube Tucker's mouth opened, then closed. This wasn't the time to ask questions, though he hadn't missed the scarred wrists either. Nothing but shackles could cause wounds like that. Had he been wrong in his assessment of Steele's character? He would wait and see.

"I thought you wanted to clean the wound," Steele said through clenched teeth.

Stacey realized, now that it was too late, that she had embarrassed him deeply. She didn't know what to say to make it up to him. She couldn't move.

"Damnit!" Steele seethed. "Either do it or get out, but don't just stand there gaping at me!"

Stacey moved quickly, too quickly. She nearly spilled the pan of hot water sitting next to the bed. Steele remained on his side, facing away from her. Working efficiently, she cleaned and bandaged the wound, sparing him as much pain as possible. He didn't move, nor did he say another word. When she'd finished, Steele put his shirt back on and lay down, closing his eyes and effectively shutting them both out.

Rube walked out ahead of her. Stacey followed, closing the door behind her. She was surprised to find herself trembling. Who could have done such a thing to him? And why?

"If you don't need me anymore, Stacey. . . ?" Rube began.

"No, no, I don't. Thanks for all your help, Rube." She was still in a state of shock. She hardly noticed when Tucker left the house. Molly! She still had to see to Molly. She took several deep breaths before starting up the stairs. She couldn't let the girl see how upset she was. Molly had enough troubles of her own.

Stacey opened the door to her room and smiled when she saw Molly sitting in the horsehair rocker, singing softly to her sleeping baby.

"Feeling better?" Stacey asked, trying to add a note of cheerfulness to her voice, but not quite succeeding.

Molly nodded.

"Good, because I want to find out what Rance did to you. And don't leave anything out."

Molly's lips began trembling. "I can't tell you that, Miss Stacey."

But Stacey would not be dissuaded. "I want to know why Rance had you and the baby taken to that shack. It doesn't make any sense."

Tears slid down Molly's face. She took a deep breath. "After I had the baby, you told me to rest. Doctor Sam told me to rest. But Rance, he . . . he doesn't make any money that way. He said I was costing him plenty and not giving any back."

Stacey's skin began to crawl.

Molly went on. "One night, about four days ago he came to my room. He said he'd take the baby if . . . if I didn't . . . I love my baby, Miss Stacey. Nobody, nothing is going to take her away from me."

"Molly," Stacey whispered, "are you telling me that Rance . . ."

"Made me go back to work," Molly nodded.

Stacey didn't hear Joshua arrive in the doorway.

"In that shack? All alone?" Stacey said, her voice constricted by revulsion.

"In the same room with my baby, Miss Stacey. He made me! He brought men there. He made me!" Sobs wracked her frail body. "My mother birthed me in a saloon. I grew up in one. And I swore to God that I wouldn't do that to Angel. Not to my little girl! I won't! I won't!"

"Rance made you take men to your bed less than a week after you'd had a baby?" Stacey's voice reflected her horror.

Molly's tears were endless. "I hate him! I hate him! I wanted to kill him, but I didn't have a gun!" She clutched her baby to her, rocking methodically back and forth in the chair.

"You're never going back there, Molly," Stacey said fiercely. "Never."

"But what can I do? Where can I go?" Molly cried. "Stacey, I'm scared. Rance will kill me when he finds out I've run away."

"He won't kill you. He won't come near you. I'll see to that."

Molly stood up, her face chalk-white. "He'd kill you too."

"Rance Dawson only picks on helpless young girls," Stacey said. "I don't qualify."

"I'm just so scared." Stacey grabbed for the infant, as Molly collapsed.

"Can I help?"

Stacey whirled at the sound of Joshua's voice. "You startled me." Her voice grew stern. "What are you doing out of bed?"

Steele scooped Molly into his arms.

"Your back!" Stacey gasped, propping the still sleeping infant onto her shoulder.

"I'm all right."

"Can you carry her down to the office?"

"I'm right behind you."

Stacey swept into the office ahead of him. "Lay her on the bed, please, Joshua. I want to examine her."

Gently, Steele laid the girl down.

"Here," Stacey said, plopping the baby in his arms. "Now wait outside."

Awkwardly, Steele accepted the sleeping bundle. He stepped into the anteroom and sat down.

Stacey examined Molly quickly. She heaved a sigh of relief. Her bleeding was not excessive, given the fact that she'd given birth barely two weeks ago. So far too there was no sign of infection. Stacey pulled a quilt out of a bureau drawer and snuggled it under Molly's chin.

"You're not going back there," she whispered to the unconscious girl. "Ever."

She stepped out of the office to find Joshua sitting in the parlor, Angel still sleeping in his arms. He scowled when she did not come immediately to take the baby from him.

"She seems so content. I'd hate to disturb her." Then she smiled and gathered up the infant. "Thank you for your help." She wanted to say something about his back, but knew the subject was better left closed for now.

"I want my uncle to examine your wound," she told him, not sure why. There was nothing Sam could do for him that she had not already done. "He should be back soon. Why don't you go upstairs and rest in my room. When Molly wakes up, I'll put her in the guest room."

He rose, his face its usual expressionless mask. "All right." His back still smarted. He wanted to be healthy in case he was soon to come face-to-face with the man he intended to murder.

CHAPTER TWELVE

Martin Randolph slammed the ledger book shut in front of him. He couldn't concentrate.

"Blast it! She comes home on horseback with some wounded saddle tramp in tow, and she doesn't even so much as come by to see me!" Randolph had run into Sheriff Rube Tucker and been told of Stacey's unorthodox arrival. "Not only is she doctoring some saddle bum, but she's involved herself with that saloon trollop again as well." His eyelids trembled with suppressed anger.

"I know one thing for certain. That nursing, doctoring business is going to stop the minute she becomes Mrs. Martin Randolph. And I don't care what she says!" He was carrying on this tirade solely for his own benefit, for he was alone in his spacious bank office.

A tentative knock roused him from his black thoughts. "What is it, Wilson?" he snapped.

A small man in a white shirt and string tie peered into Randolph's office and asked in a querulous voice, "Excuse me, Mr. Randolph, sir, have you forgotten you have a four o'clock appointment with Mr. Seaverman?"

"Of course, I haven't forgotten, you idiot!" he

roared, but in truth he had. Stacey had distracted him more than he'd realized. He quickly cleared the ledger from his desk.

"Is he here?"

At the timid nod Randolph said disgustedly, "Well, for heaven's sake, man, show him in!"

Randolph smoothed his brown hair back quickly. Danton Seaverman was a man of great wealth and enormous power in the territory. He wanted very much to make a good impression.

"Mr. Seaverman, please, come in. Sit down, won't you? May I offer you a cigar? Only the finest!" For God's sake, Randolph, he chided himself, don't be so obvious. Relax. Give him the idea you don't really need him.

"I hope your first impression of Spring Canyon has been a favorable one," he continued, feeling his self-confidence returning.

Seaverman nodded. He was a relatively small man, but he comported himself in such a manner that he fairly exuded power. He owned one of the biggest chunks of land in the territory, as well as mining and railroad interests that would make a small country jealous.

"My time is valuable to me, Mr. Randolph," Seaverman said. "If we could get down to business, please." His tone was condescending. He wasn't quite sure, but he had a gut feeling about Randolph. He was a fair man, though, and he intended to hear him out.

Martin Randolph was a rich man, who wanted very much to be richer. And he wanted power, a great deal of power. The New Mexico Territory provided the perfect setting in the 1870s. Little law, less order, and an unparalleled opportunity to invest a relatively small amount of money into the land, while expecting twenty to one hundred times that sum back in profits, gave rise to the precise money-power combination Randolph sought.

He was well aware of the land speculators flocking to the territory. Antiquated Spanish land grants coupled with numerous ambiguous laws concerning their disposition provided ample temptation for bending the law to suit individual avarice. Lawyers, judges, merchants, and politicians joined together to buy up many of the grants. The investors could often persuade a government surveyor to certify a grant at up to twenty times its original size.

The Maxwell Land Grant was a case in point, Randolph knew. Originally a grant of ninety-seven thousand acres, it now laid claim to two million acres, all because the investors knew the right people.

Martin Randolph saw Danton Seaverman as his link to those people—to Elkins and Catron and other members to the Sante Fe ring, a powerful cartel of land grant speculators. He wanted in. Seaverman could make it happen.

"So you want to invest your money with me," Seaverman smiled. He may not like the man, but he liked money. If Randolph had as much as he was suggesting he did, he just might want to do business with him.

"Your investments are virtual sure things, sir. I'm hoping . . . "

"That your eventual fame and fortune will spread

far beyond Spring Canyon," Seaverman said, noting the gleam in Randolph's eyes. "Maybe all the way to the governor's mansion?"

"I was thinking beyond that—to the United States Senate—if we can get statehood pushed through."

Seaverman chuckled. He had to admit Randolph's ambition was a point in his favor. The two men spent the next several hours discussing investment possibilities. Finally Seaverman stood up and extended his hand to Randolph, who clasped it eagerly.

"It's been a most interesting evening, Mr. Randolph," Seaverman said. "But I really do want to start back to Santa Fe quite early in the morning."

"I understand, sir. Could you give me any idea . . ."

"We may well work together one day, Mr. Randolph," Seaverman said, though his voice was noncommittal. He had already done some checking into Randolph's background. The banker had only been in Spring Canyon for three years, but his reputation among the citizenry was unimpeachable. He was currently courting a lovely girl whom he no doubt intended to marry.

But his cursory check was scarcely sufficient. With the amount of money they were talking about, Seaverman intended to delve much deeper into Martin Randolph's past. If anything lay hidden there it was of no particular consequence to Seaverman personally, but it would mean he and his business associates would think twice about engaging in any kind of partnership with the man.

"We'll just have to wait and see what the future holds, Mr. Randolph," Seaverman stated, then showed himself out the door.

After Seaverman left, Randolph pulled a bottle of brandy from his lower desk drawer and poured himself a celebration drink. He couldn't conceive of the cartel turning him down. He hoisted a toast to himself, to power, and to a vast amount of money.

CHAPTER THIRTEEN

It was past nine o'clock when Sam Curtis returned to his office. Stacey hurried over to him.

"What are you doing here, Stace?" he asked, surprise evident in his voice. "The stage doesn't arrive until tomorrow."

"It's good to see you, too," she smiled.

"All right, Stacey, what have you gotten yourself into this time?"

Stacey grimaced good-naturedly. Sam knew her too well. "Come sit down in the parlor and have a cup of coffee," she said, "while I tell you all about it."

Curtis settled back in his favorite chair, sipping a cup of Stacey's over-strong coffee. He couldn't believe what she was telling him. How did she get herself into these things?

Stacey left nothing out, from the malodorous man on the stagecoach to Denver, to the ambush with Steele by Barnett's gang, to Molly's troubles with Rance Dawson.

"So we've got ourselves a couple of houseguests at the moment," she finished, waiting for Sam's reaction.

He shook his head. "I didn't think Dawson was that low. I tried everything to find Molly after she disappeared from the Double Eagle, but he's got those other girls of his scared half to death to open their mouths. That monster ought to be locked up."

"Molly's too scared to press charges, Sam. But I've been thinking about it all day." She paused for a moment. "What would you think of this idea? Molly could live with us until she can find a decent job. I mean she could cook and clean, all those things I scarcely have time for. It would leave me a lot more time to practice medicine."

Sam shrugged. "It sounds fine to me."

"Sam, you are wonderful," she said, coming over to give him an affectionate hug. "Now, if you're not too tired, I'd like you to check on Mr. Steele."

"Something special about the wound?"

"Not really, I just want to be sure."

"Lead me to him."

They headed up the stairs, stopping in at the door to her room. Curtis looked at her. "You put him in your bed?"

"I didn't want him going to the hotel until you had a chance to see him. And you need your bed. You know how your back gets if you use the settee. Molly and the baby are in the guest room. I couldn't leave him in the office, other patients might come in. That left my bed." It all seemed perfectly proper and logical to her.

Stacey knocked quietly, then opened the door. She and Curtis stepped in and walked over to the bed. Curtis' brows knitted together in a frown on first sight of the wounded man. He couldn't help but notice the holstered .44 slung from the bedpost.

Steele was conscious and looking steadily back at him. Neither gaze wavered. Finally Stacey broke the deadlock.

"I'd like Sam to look at the wound, Joshua. Make certain everything's all right." She was unconsciously twisting her hands together, nervous all at once to be standing near him while he was lying in her bed.

Steele's gaze shifted to settle on her face, and he was again irritated to feel a rising attraction. He fought it down. She was a woman, and he hadn't had a woman in a long time. That was all. He turned his eyes back to Curtis.

"Well, let's take a look." Curtis was his professional self.

Steele turned his body so that the doctor could examine the dressing Stacey had applied to his back. Sam lifted it carefully to check how much damage had been done to Steele's insides. He noted the vicious weal scars, but said nothing. He nodded his approval to Stacey. As usual, she had done a fine job.

After Curtis re-tied the bandage, Joshua settled back into the bed. The pain was tolerable, and he found himself anxious to be out of here.

Stacey saw the irritation in Joshua's eyes, and took it to mean that he was remembering this afternoon when she had seen the scars on his back. Her own temper nudged her. She had only been doing what she had to do.

"I think you'll recover," Sam stated, rising from the bed. He gave Steele a half-smile, and extended his hand. "I'm Sam Curtis."

Steele acknowledged the handshake. "I've got something I'd like to ask you, doctor, but . . ." he looked meaningfully at Stacey.

She thrust out her chin defiantly. So he expected her to leave, did he? Well, then leaving was the last thing she would do.

"What is it, Mr. Steele?" Curtis asked.

"Josh."

Sam nodded, reading the discomfort in Steele's eyes. Maybe this was something private, for men only.

"Stacey, would you bring us some coffee, please?" he asked.

Stacey tossed her head in quick anger, her neck arching until she was staring up at the ceiling. She took a deep breath and gazed solemnly at Joshua.

"You're going to ask him about your eye, aren't you?" daring him to deny it. "So why can't I stay? I already know all about it. If I'm ever to be a doctor, I have to examine patients." She sighed and shook her head. "I can see it now. I could open a practice in Denver, but my patients will all be in Santa Fe. I'll write them letters on how to take care of themselves." Fighting a rising frustration, she stormed out of the room, slamming the door in her wake. But before she did, she shot Steele another angry glare.

Curtis turned to Steele. "I apologize for my niece. She can be a little highstrung when it comes to medicine, and the practice thereof. She may not have a diploma, but I'd count her one of the best doctors I've ever known."

"Then why did you suggest she leave?"

"Because I saw that you were uncomfortable, and the patient comes first. She'll calm down." Curtis leaned forward. "Now, what's this about your eye?"

Steele recounted the symptoms to Curtis.

The doctor took Joshua's head in his hands and peered closely at his left eye. "Well, it's nothing obvious, that's for certain. How often does this happen?"

"A couple of times a week maybe. It started five months ago."

"Did you have any kind of head injury at the time?"

"Nothing."

"How long does it last?"

"A few hours usually."

Stacey reentered the room, carrying a tray with a coffee pot and three empty cups. She set it down on the table beside her bed. She was still coldly furious with Joshua and did not look at him.

"Can I pour you a cup, Sam?" she asked.

"No, no, Stacey," he said. "I'm sorry I had you bother. I'm a little more tired than I thought. I couldn't treat a hangnail right now. I'm going to bed." To Steele he said, "First thing in the morning I'll give that eye a thorough examination in my office." He paused, then added, "With Stacey, if that's all right with you?"

Joshua sighed. "It's fine."

Curtis nodded good-night to them both and left the room.

Stacey turned to Joshua. "Are you really going to let me sit in on Sam's examination?" she asked, unable to keep the excitement she felt out of her voice.

"I didn't feel I had that much choice in the matter," Steele muttered.

"I see." Why was he so determined to keep this barrier between them? Part of her wanted to leave the room. Out of his presence at least, he couldn't inflict any more damage to her pride. But part of her derived a sweet pleasure just by being in the same room with him. She would not examine her feelings to discover why this was so. For the moment she was merely content to admit that it was. "Would you like some coffee?" she asked.

Joshua shifted uncomfortably on the bed. It was not a place he would have chosen to be while she was in the room. He sat up, grimacing slightly at the pull on the wound in his back. He was determined not to let her affect him this time. "As a matter of fact," he said, "I would."

Stacey filled one of the cups and handed it to him. "Aren't you going to have any?"

"I didn't want any in the first place, remember," she said. "It was Sam's way of getting me out of the room, while you told him about your eye."

"That really upset you, didn't it?"

"You're damned right it did," she snapped. Then she added more softly, "I'm sorry. You don't know what it's like for me, Joshua. A woman doctor. It's . . ." She sighed. "Never mind."

He put the coffee cup back on the tray. "It is hard for me to think of you as a doctor," he conceded.

"Because I'm a woman."

"Not exactly."

"Then why?"

He stared at her. The heat from those gray eyes seemed to burn into her flesh. She knew she should leave the room at once, but found she couldn't move. He reached out and took her hand, gently pulling her toward him. She sank down next to him on the bed, closing her eyes as he cradled the side of her head in his hand. Ever so slowly he massaged the sensitive cord on the side of her neck.

"Stacey," he murmured, more to himself than to her, "why did I have to meet you again?"

His mouth found and possessed hers. She returned his kisses measure for measure, unable, unwilling to stop herself. Her hands smoothed the silky mat of hair on his chest, caressing his male nipples with the tips of her fingers. She felt more than heard the low groan in his throat.

He entwined his hands in her soft, golden hair. He teased her lips apart with his tongue, sending a tremor of heat through her body. If he had wanted to, he could have taken her. She would not have resisted, so drugged was she by the sweet rapture of his touch. But he seemed to content himself with kissing her, touching her—and for that, later at least, Stacey would be grateful.

At last he set her away from him. His breathing was ragged. His gray eyes smoldered in the lantern light.

"You'd better get some sleep," he said. "It was a long trail ride out there, and I didn't exactly let you get much rest."

She stood up, confused and a little embarrassed all at once. She had not ended their embrace, he did. She astonished herself by realizing she had not wanted it to end, at how effortlessly he could have seduced her. Why did Joshua so easily arouse her, when a man as passionate and attractive as Martin Randolph failed utterly? Perhaps it was a residual adolescent infatuation, she thought. After all, she had once denied this man nothing. Why should he expect it to be any different now. She trembled. She had come dangerously close to being used again. From now on she would have to be on her guard.

"I'll . . . I'll see you in the morning for the eye exam," she whispered. She turned and quickly left the room.

Steele stared into the night, his thoughts remaining on the fair-haired woman downstairs. What made her so different from other women he had known? Try as he might, he could not rid himself of his growing obsession with her. He recalled her reaction to his scarred back, the gentle hands that had cared for his wound. A woman with the desire to be a doctor in a man's world must have an uncommon curiosity, yet she had not questioned the origin of the scars.

Her slender figure, her flashing green eyes, the sense of pure stubbornness about her ensnared his thoughts. Angrily, he shook it off. He had not time for such fantasies. Again he chalked up his body's response to her as a long unappeased hunger, a bittersweet memory of a moment's rapture in the midst of war. He forced her image from his mind, knowing that if he indulged himself further he would awaken long buried needs. Needs that must stay buried until Ross Merrick was under the ground.

Joshua woke in a cold sweat, his hands squeezed tightly together. In a variation of his familiar nightmare, he had actually found Merrick, found him and strangled him. But he didn't die. Merrick never died in his dreams. Hate gnawed at him as a knock on the door broke the morning stillness.

"What is it?" he called gruffly.

Stacey eased the door open. She was carrying a breakfast tray.

"Good morning, Joshua," she beamed cheerfully. Sam was getting everything ready downstairs for Steele's eye exam and since Joshua had agreed to let her assist in the procedure, she was feeling thoroughly happy. She pushed memories of last night out of her mind. She was not even going to let his obvious ill-temper this morning upset her.

She brought the tray over to him, still smiling disarmingly. Steele's scowl deepened. He didn't understand how this woman could arouse his emotions so deeply just by walking into a room. Though famished, he said, "I'm not hungry."

Stacey set the tray on the small table next to the bed. "If you feel like eating a little later, this will keep for awhile." She sat down in the rocking chair.

"Don't you have something to do?" he frowned.

"Not really." Oh, she was feeling impish this morning.

"I'd like to get dressed."

She recognized the broad hint to leave the room, but said simply, "Don't let me stop you."

So that was the way it was going to be. "I sleep in the raw," he emphasized, "when I enjoy the luxury of a real bed."

Her eyes locked on his. Nothing betrayed the little niggling fear that started in the back of her mind. He was lying, of course. Wasn't he? She could see his bare shoulders.

"It's your modesty that will be offended, not mine," he said. He took hold of the bedcovers as if to fling them back.

She stood up. "I don't believe you're naked."

"Want to bet?"

Oh, he thought he was so superior. "Bet what?" she challenged.

"A kiss," he said rashly, wishing it back, but confident she would not take him up on the wager.

She remembered with sudden passion the power of

his kisses. Maybe she wouldn't want to win this bet. "You're on."

"Don't say you weren't warned," he told her, suddenly enjoying himself. Sitting up, he planted his feet on the floor. He had the blanket nestled around his middle.

Stacey swallowed. He was now naked from the waist up, except for the two-inch wide wraparound bandage on his wound. And he was naked from mid-thigh down. She could feel color creeping into her cheeks. She had seen him naked once before, but that was during the throes of passion, the act of a rash, frightened girl. And that was seven years ago. They were two different people now. He'd made that point clear enough. Surely, he was bluffing. He wouldn't.

"You've got five seconds to get out of here, so I can get dressed," he said, "otherwise, you are going to be even more embarrassed than you are now, Eustacia Hamilton."

"Why should I be embarrassed?" she shot back. "I've seen you naked before."

His eyes narrowed. "And you're about to see me so again." He started to shift the blankets.

Stacey wanted desperately to stay, to show him that he couldn't intimidate her like this. But what if her really was stark naked? This wasn't the same as the Wilderness, and they both knew it.

"One," he counted.

"You're bluffing."

"Two."

"You wouldn't dare, even if you are naked."

"Three . . . four."

"No!" She help up a protesting hand.

"Five."

He jerked the blankets back. But in that instant, Stacey conceded defeat. She turned and fled, slamming the door in her wake. Once outside the room, she leaned back against the door, gasping. It was several seconds before she could breathe normally again. What in the world had possessed her to bait him into such a horribly compromising situation? She blushed heatedly, not wanting to admit the mortifying truth. But knowing the truth just the same. She had egged him on because some outrageously shameless part of her had ached to see Joshua Steele naked once again. Only her last-second cowardice had preserved her modesty. She would never have been able to look him in the face again.

She listened to him moving around inside the room. Pulling on his clothes no doubt. Of course, he had been bluffing. Hadn't he? Still trembling just a little, she realized she would never know. She hurried downstairs.

"Joshua should be here any minute," she said to Sam, as she entered the office, hoping her uncle didn't notice the quaver in her voice. "Do you have any clues yet on what might be wrong with his eye?"

"Not a thing. I'm hoping this examination this morning will tell us more."

She turned to see Steele stride into the office. Nothing in his manner betrayed any evidence of his disgraceful behavior in her bedroom. He looked roguishly handsome. He was freshly shaved, except for his dark mustache. His wavy near-black hair, which could be so unruly at times, had been brushed into a semblance of managability. He wore a light blue chambray shirt tucked into darker blue levis, accenting his lean, well-muscled build. On top of the shirt he wore a black leather vest. Her eyes fell to the walnut-handled Colt nestled in the holster on his hip. She wondered suddenly if Jeff Barnett was the only man Joshua had ever had to kill with that gun. Somehow she didn't think so.

She flushed, when she realized she'd been staring. Quickly, she busied herself around the office, readying the things she and Sam would need for Joshua's examination.

"How's the patient this morning?" Sam asked, greeting Steele with a handshake.

"Just fine," he answered. "I'll be getting out of your hair as soon as you're through with the eye."

"That may take a little while," Sam said.

"I don't have much time, doctor. I have a man on my trail, and I'm doing a little tracking of my own."

"You've asked me for help with your eye, and now I'm intending to give it to you."

Steele relented. There was no denying that.

"Have a seat here, please," Stacey requested, indicating a well-worn wood and leather chair.

Joshua sat down. His impression of the doctor's office this morning was more vivid than it had been yesterday afternoon, when Stacey had treated the wound in his back. The strange odors of the place struck him first. Glass carboys filled with various colored liquids and powders were carefully labeled and sat at attention on sturdy mahogany shelves covering the far wall of the room. He noted the names on a few: laudanum, ipecac, Dover's powder, Calomel, paregoric. More small wooden boxes and jars made of porcelain lined the lower shelves. He recognized the language on their labels as Latin.

A skeleton languished sardonically against a needlepoint pillow on the horse-hair settee abutting the wall to his left. The doctor and his niece seemed not averse to a little macabre humor.

"That's Milton," Stacey said, noting Joshua's gaze falling on the skeleton.

"Milton?"

"Umm hmm, we're treating him for malnutrition."

Steele groaned, but Stacey didn't miss the smile tugging at the corners of his mouth. She found it impossible to comprehend how she could feel so much pleasure, just by being in the same room with this man.

Steele settled back in the chair and waited for Curtis to start the examination. He noted several issues of Ewall's Medical Companion and the New England Journal of Medicine stacked on the oak desk in the corner of the room nearest the street. A much-read copy of Lister's "On the Antiseptic Principles in the Practice of Surgery" lay next to the magazines. On the desk also sat the only homey touch in the room, the gilt-framed picture of a rather handsome woman.

One small table held several instruments neatly arranged for future use. It was in this room that Sam Curtis mended the bullet holes, set the broken bones, and treated the varying ailments of any who sought his care. Did Stacey do as much?

"Okay, let's get started, shall we?" Curtis said, stepping in front of the chair in which Steele sat.

The examination took several minutes. Sam had Stacey hold a candle near the eye, as he palpated it with his fingers. Stacey watched the entire proceeding with keen interest. Joshua had the uneasy feeling of being a zoo specimen.

When he finished, Curtis shook his head. Steele fought a stirring of disappointment.

"There's pressure there all right," Curtis said. "I suppose it could be some sort of chronic inflammation. Probably the most telling thing would be if I were to witness one of these attacks of pain that you have."

Sam crossed to the window, slanting a glance back at Steele. "Until that happens I may not be able to help you very much."

Steele grimaced with remembered pain. He didn't relish the idea of having another attack, just so Curtis could examine him during it. "It's not likely to happen again for a few days," he said.

A knock on the door interrupted them.

Stacey glanced up to see Claire Jensen framed in the doorway to the office. She chided herself for the feeling of instant animosity that assailed her.

"Come in, Claire," she said.

"Why, thank you, Stacey," the girl replied, her voice dripping with sweetness. She may have been speaking to Stacey, but her eyes were fastened on Joshua. Stacey couldn't suppress a brief stab of jealousy at the obvious interest in the girl's eyes. Joshua wasn't exactly regarding Claire with indifference himself.

"Is there something we can do for you, Claire?" Stacey asked, forcing the girl to look away from Joshua.

"Oh, it's my stomach again," she sighed. "You know how it is after too many of pa's meals." She giggled girlishly.

Stacey closed her eyes. This really was getting to be too much for her. There was nothing wrong with Claire's stomach this time, or any other time she'd stopped by the office. Stacey could appreciate the girl's need to escape her father's cafe for a few minutes from time to time, but her continual use of physical ailments as an excuse was beginning to wear thin. Her real reason for coming, as always, was the chance to flirt with any unattached male patients who might be in the waiting room. Stacey had no doubt that Claire had heard the town gossip about Joshua's arrival and had immediately invented a stomachache in order to stop by and meet him.

"Do you think you can give me something for it, Doctor Curtis?" Claire asked. "It does hurt so." She rubbed her stomach rhythmically, managing to touch the underside of her full breasts with each circular motion. Her eyes were again on Joshua.

"I think we can fix you up," Sam said. He too had grown tired of Claire's over-frequent complaints, but right now, the look of obvious fire in Stacey's eyes had him chuckling to himself in right good humor. He had never seen that look in Stacey's eyes before. If he hadn't known better, he could have sworn she was ready to claw the girl's eyes out for looking at Josh like that.

Claire stepped toward Sam. "I really do thank you, doctor. Oh, my," she sighed, touching the back of her hand to her forehead, "I do believe I'm going to swoon." Stacey didn't miss Claire's quick backward glance, before she collapsed directly into Joshua's arms.

"Oh, my heavens," she exclaimed, not making any

attempt to extricate herself from Steele's grasp. "I don't know what came over me, sir. I was just suddenly so weak. I am so sorry. Please, forgive me, Mister. . . ?"

"Josh." He smiled at the girl, not seeming to mind supporting her against his chest.

"I'm Claire Jensen," she smiled back at him.

Stacey glared at them both. "If you're really that sick, Claire," she said, speaking slowly, "perhaps we'd better do a complete check up on you. Don't you think so, Sam? I mean Claire might have a bad appendix or something. She might need surgery at least . . ."

"Surgery?" Claire cried, struggling to her feet. "Oh, my heavens, Stacey, don't be silly. It's just a little ol' tummyache, that's all. Why Doctor Curtis would know that in an instant."

"I don't know, Claire," Sam said, deciding to help Stacey out, "you've had these symptoms so often, that it could well be more serious than we thought. Maybe you'd better lie down on the examining table and we'll take a look."

"No, honestly, doctor," Claire said, "it's nothing. I'm sorry to have bothered you. I'll just tell papa you told me to go home and lie down for awhile." Straightening, she started for the door. She turned to smile at Joshua. "It was so nice to meet you, Josh," she said. "I do hope you forgive me for falling into your strong arms like that. I don't know what would've happened if you hadn't been there."

You wouldn't have fainted, Stacey thought sourly.

"Believe me, it was my pleasure," Joshua told her.

"Oh, you must call me Claire," she tittered.

"Claire it is."

"We'll meet again real soon, Josh."

"We just might at that."

Claire sighed happily and walked out of the house.

Stacey stared after her. "I do hope you'll forgive me for falling into your strong arms," she mocked. "Of all the . . ."

"I found her rather sweet," Joshua said.

Curtis chuckled. "Claire's a charmer all right."

Stacey couldn't believe her ears. Men! Were they all blind to Claire's tactics? She might believe Joshua could be taken in by the buxom beauty, but Sam had always had more sense! Curtis laughed again.

"What is so funny, Sam?" Stacey fumed.

He couldn't very well tell her, not in front of Steele. But if looks could do physical harm to a person, Claire wouldn't have been faking her need for a doctor. "It's nothing, Stace," he managed. "Can we get on with this examination?"

There was another knock on the door.

"That will be Martin, I suppose," Stacey groaned, unhappy at this second interruption of Joshua's eye exam.

Sam was pleased to see that his niece didn't seem especially interested in seeing Randolph. He had never particularly liked the dandified banker.

"He's probably furious because I didn't come to see him yesterday," she said, scowling. "And, of course, he'll want to lecture me on tearing about the countryside on horseback with a band of outlaws on my trail." She looked at her uncle, "I don't suppose you'd want to tell him I'm not here, Sam?" She sighed. "Never mind. I shouldn't have said that. I'd better go."

She stepped into the entryway and opened the door. When she saw Martin, she tried not to let the annoyance she felt show in her eyes. He expected her to be available whenever it suited him. Right now she wanted to be with Sam to finish the check-up on Joshua's eye.

"Hello, Martin," she said, her gaze going back to her uncle's office. Sam had a solid hold on Steele's head and was peering intently into his eye once again.

"How about an early lunch, Stacey?" Randolph asked, his voice solicitous. He had decided to forgive her for not coming by his office yesterday. He wanted to be in her good graces. Things could start moving fast with Seaverman, and he wanted to marry Stacey as soon as possible.

Stacey was more than mildly surprised to find him so amenable. She had expected to be the target of one of his domineering little speeches, and she was nonplussed by his charm. She felt her resistance melting. She smiled at him.

"All right, Martin. But could it wait a few minutes? It's just that Sam is examining a patient and I'm interested in his condition."

"Can't you put your doctoring aside long enough to treat a love-starved suitor to your presence for a mere hour?" he teased warmly.

She giggled. "Let me check with Sam. He might still need me for something more with his examination of Mr. Steele."

"Steele?"

"The man who was shot yesterday," she explained.

"Yes, Tucker mentioned it to me, but he didn't give my any names."

"Oh, well, you wouldn't know him anyway. It's Steele. Joshua Steele." Stacey headed back to Sam's office.

A choking bile rose in Randolph's throat. It couldn't be! His mouth twisted. He dared a glance after Stacey. Curtis' patient was profiled to him as the doctor leaned in for a closer inspection of Steele's left eye. It was true! Randolph's hands shook. Had he come here deliberately? Did he know?

Stacey returned. "Sam said it's all right if I go."

Randolph swallowed the raw fear in him. Stacey would not have guessed his inner turmoil.

He doffed his hat to her. "I'm terribly sorry, Stacey." He gave her a peck on the cheek. "I just remembered some bank papers I need to go over for a client who's coming in this afternoon. I hope you'll forgive me."

"Of course, Martin," Stacey assured him, trying not to sound as happy as she felt. "Now I can help Sam with Joshua."

Back in his office Randolph again pulled out the bottle of brandy from his lower desk drawer. It was all he could do to pour some into a glass. He coudln't stop trembling. Steele alive! It wasn't possible. That blasted Frenchman, Captain Brissot, had sworn he would have Steele killed. Damn him! He lied! Brissot had always admired Steele's courage. He hadn't had the guts to carry through with his promise.

Randolph thought about Mexico, about how he had betrayed the man in Sam Curtis' office, the brutality he had subjected him to. He shivered, and he recognized the cause. Cold terror. Steele had sworn to kill him. Was that what Steele was doing in Spring Canyon? Was he looking for him, or was this merely an ungodly coincidence?

The banker fidgeted in his chair. He could leave town for awhile. There was always business that could take him to Santa Fe. But how long could he stay away?

Calm down, you're overreacting, he chided himself. Steele was just here because he had been shot and needed a doctor. He'd probably ride out of town in a day or two. Randolph had worked too long and too hard to establish his identity. He wasn't going to throw it all away. Not if he didn't have to. All he had to do was stay out of sight for a few days.

If Steele was looking to cause trouble, well, there were ways of handling that too. Steele had survived Mexico, but that didn't mean Randolph couldn't correct Brissot's mistake, if it came to that. Maybe he could even reason with Steele, offer him money to be on his way.

He remembered the slaughtered men on Steele's last arms shipment. He remember his own order to murder Rudy Montoya. And he remembered the savage beating he had ordered inflicted on Steele, when the man stubbornly refused to tell him where he could get his hands on more Mexican gold. He had forced the French captain to accede to his command to threaten Steele with castration, and for the first and only time he had seen raw fear in Joshua Steele's eyes. No, there would be no reasoning with Steele. If the two of them met again, one of them would die. Randolph didn't intend for it to be him.

CHAPTER FOURTEEN

Steele left Curtis' house and headed for Sheriff Tucker's office. Before he paid a visit to the Spring Canyon bank president, he wanted to know the man's personal history in this town. And though he would have been hard pressed to admit it, he wanted to know something else. For Spring Canyon's suspected Ross Merrick sported one major difference that set him apart from others he had confronted these past four years. This one could be acquainted with Stacey Hamilton.

It was a small town and he knew the chances were great that she at least knew this bank president. She might even regard him as a friend. And for reasons he would not examine, he had to know *before* he met the man what Stacey's opinion of him was.

The sheriff stood in his office, gingerly adding kindling to his Franklin stove as he fired up a pot of coffee. He offered Steele a cup when it was ready.

"Have a seat," the lawman said, indicating a chair near his desk. Steele sat down. Tucker perched himself on one of the desk's corners. "Glad to see you up and about so soon. You had me a little worried yesterday."

"I appreciate the help," Steele acknowledged, sipping the hot liquid.

"Stacey told me how you got on the wrong side of Jake Barnett," Tucker said. "I was real sorry to hear about John Beal. To be killed over the likes of scum like Barnett . . ."

"He knew the risks," Steele said, setting the coffee cup on the desk. "It was part of the job."

Tucker shot Steele a quick glance.

"I liked him, too," Joshua said quietly.

"Yeah." Tucker sighed. "It comes with the badge, like you said. Which reminds me . . ." He paused, giving Steele the same kind of appraising look he had when he'd first seen him on the trail. His initial impression that Steele was no outlaw stayed with him, but that didn't prevent his next words.

"As a lawman I'm bound to ask you about those scars on your back. Your wrists, too. I'd be willin' to wager you've got the twins to 'em on your ankles." Tucker watched Steele's jaw working. The big man didn't like this one damn bit. Tucker nevertheless went on, "Only one place I know a man gets those kinds of scars—and that's prison."

"You find me on any wanted posters?" Steele grated.

"No," Tucker admitted.

"Until you do, don't ask."

Steele stood up. He paced to the other side of the room and back. He knew if the situation were reversed he would be asking the same questions. But that didn't mean he had to like it. Steele watched the sheriff. Tucker didn't seem fazed by his evasiveness.

In fact, Tucker's voice remained unperturbed even as he said, "I'll be keepin' an eye on you, son. Just don't forget it. One step out of line and your next step will be into one of those cells yonder."

"Fair enough."

Steele wanted to ask about the town's bank president, his latest lead to Ross Merrick. He wondered now if Tucker would oblige him with any kind of information on a man, who was probably held in high esteem in the community. The sheriff had him figured now as an ex-convict at best. He decided on a little mild deceit.

"I may not look like I'm well-heeled, sheriff," Steele said, "but I've got a big spread in the Colorado Territory. I was heading for Spring Canyon even before Barnett got in the way." That much was true enough. "You see, I'm always looking for ways to invest my money. And I've heard the Spring Canyon bank has a president who's a financial wizard of sorts."

"That's God's truth," Tucker said, puffing up with a little community pride. "Martin Randolph is one smart banker.'

"Martin Randolph?" Steele's pulse quickened. The similar initials were not lost on him. "I like to know who I'm dealing with. Can you give me a little background on the man?"

"I don't see the harm," Tucker shrugged. "Martin loves to talk business. Maybe he'd give me a commission if I sent him a big investor.

"He came to town about three years ago from Santa Fe, a born and raised New Mexican. Made a lot of smart moves with the bank's money."

"What's he look like?" Steele put in.

"What's that got to do with banking?"

"In case I run into him on the street. I'll introduce myself."

"Well, lemme see, Martin's maybe five feet ten, a hundred seventy pounds, brownish hair, blue eyes. Nice looking fella." Tucker chuckled. "That's probably why he's lucky enough to have Stacey Hamilton for a fiancee."

"What?" Steele's voice was deceptively soft.

"Well, it ain't exactly official or nothin'. But he's been courtin' her for more'n six months now. They're real sweet on each other. But anyways, you got money to invest, you see Martin Randolph. He'll do right by ya, I guarantee it."

Somehow Steele managed to thank Tucker for his help. He stepped outside. He was in desperate need of fresh air. Like a man sleepwalking, he turned the corner of the jailhouse and wandered into the cul de sac beside it. He sagged onto a wooden crate.

Stacey and Randolph. Stacey and Merrick? Stacey in love with Ross Merrick. Ross Merrick, the living, breathing monster who had reduced Joshua Steele to an animal? Who had made Steele sob in frustration because he ached to die and couldn't?

Stacey touching Ross Merrick. Kissing Ross Merrrick. Maybe even sharing a bed with Ross Merrick.

Joshua felt as though he were going to be violently ill. For the first time in four years of hellish hate he prayed to God that he had not found Merrrick. That Martin Randolph was who he purported to be—gentleman banker and lifelong resident of New Mexico.

He stood up, surprised to notice that he was trembling. He headed back to the street. He spied the word "Hotel" on the two-story, false-front building across the street. He strode over to it. His back ached suddenly, and he realized the need to rest the wound.

He registered at the front desk and accepted the key to a room overlooking the street. The room was sparsely furnished, but Steele gave it little notice. He stretched out on the lumpy mattress. At least he wouldn't be spending another night in the Curtis house.

Part of him wanted to leave the room and confront Martin Randolph immediately. He ached to know, but at the same time, he was afraid to know. It would wait another day. A bank president wasn't going anywhere.

The next morning Stacey watched from Sullivan's Mercantile as Joshua crossed the street and headed toward Jonas' livery. She guessed the wound in his back still ached considerably, but there was no evidence of it in his strong, even strides. Why was he headed for the stables? Surely he hadn't decided to leave town. Not without saying good-bye. Had he already seen Martin and discovered he wasn't the man he sought? She headed toward Jonas'.

Steele had decided to reconnoiter the area immediately surrounding Spring Canyon. He wanted to see if he could get a fix on Jake Barnett's location. And he wanted time to think. He still hadn't worked out Martin Randolph in his head. For the life of him he couldn't figure out why he didn't confront Randolph and get it over with. If he wasn't Merrick, there was no harm done. If he was, he would kill him and be done with it. Then why didn't he do it? Emerald green eyes . . .

Nathan Jonas, an ageless black man who could have been anywhere from forty to seventy, greeted Steele moodily when he strode into the livery.

"You're the man with the dun gelding." It was a statement, not a question.

"I am." Steele had an idea what was coming.

The black man faced him. There was disgust in his voice when he said, "It's been many a year since I seen an animal so poorly used, mister."

Steele shifted in irritation. He could scarcely blame the man, yet there was little he could have done. Nor did it occur to him to offer any excuses.

"Do you have a horse I could use for a few days?" Steele asked curtly, wanting Jonas to drop the subject of the dun.

"Mister, I don't have any piece of horseflesh I could let you have."

Steele felt his anger rising. He fought it down, knowing that Jonas considered his position justified. He doubted that even knowing about Barnett would make any difference to him.

"Nathan, I think I can vouch for this man."

Steele turned sharply to see Stacey standing just inside the livery's entrance.

Jonas looked at her quizzically. "You sticking up for this horse beater, Stacey?"

"If he was a horse beater I wouldn't be sticking up for him. I think you know me better than that, Nathan. Mr. Steele had some pretty strong reasons for riding the horse so hard. The mare I rode in wasn't exactly raring to go to the races. There were men trailing Mr. Steele, one of whom put a bullet in his back." She stopped, embarrassed by how defensive her tone had become.

She twirled a stray wisp of blonde hair nervously, wishing suddenly she hadn't followed him. He was watching her with those unreadable gray eyes.

"I heard about them owlhoots trailing this hombre, Stacey," Nathan said, "but I still don't think that makes what he done to that horse excusable."

Steele cut in. "I'm not offering any excuses, Mr. Jonas. I meant no hard to the animal. You can believe me or not."

Jonas met Steele's gaze. Something about the big man's eyes told Jonas that Steele spoke the truth.

"Okay, Steele, you can have a horse."

"Obliged." He was about to pick up his saddle, when Stacey stepped over to him.

"Are you leaving town?" she asked in a small voice.

"Just for today. I'll be back."

She felt a warm rush of relief, and prayed it wasn't obvious to him. "Where are you going?"

"To look for Barnett."

"By yourself? Joshua, that's insane!"

"Don't you have some doctoring to do or something?"

She clenched her fists in frustration. Why was he always so unpredictable with her? Just when she was thinking they could be friends, after helping with his eye exam yesterday, he had to be his arrogant self again.

It was as if he was dismissing her from his presence. He turned to speak to Nathan. "Which horse do you want me to take?"

"There's a bay in the corral," the hostler said. "I'd appreciate it if you'd rope him yourself, though. I got me a little mare in the back stall that's ready to foal

249

any minute now, and I don't want to leave her alone."

"Sheba's going to foal today, Nathan?" Stacey's green eyes flashed with excitement, Steele's rudeness forgotten. "May I see her?"

"Sure, Missy," Jonas said. "Be real quiet, though, you know how skittish she is."

Stacey moved past Steele without looking at him.

"Oh, thanks for your help, Miss Hamilton," he called to her retreating back. "With the horse, I mean."

She turned to see him give her a mocking smile. Why did he have to be so infuriating? As haughtily as she could manage she turned and stomped to the back of the livery.

Steele grabbed the rope that was hanging in front of a nearby stall and started out the door toward the corral. A shrill cry from Stacey brought him instantly back. He and Jonas arrived at the rear stall at the same time.

"Something's wrong, Nathan!" Stacey cried, looking at the stricken mare. "She's in trouble."

Jonas quickly opened the stall gate and moved in toward his favorite little mare. Expertly he ran his hands along her swollen belly.

Without warning the mare begin to kick and writhe in agony. Nimbly Jonas stepped out of her way, barely avoiding the flailing hooves.

The mare's screams brought quick tears to Stacey's eyes. "Isn't there anything you can do for her?" Her medical skills did not extend to pregnant horses in trouble.

The mare quieted for a moment. Lying on her side, she breathed laboriously. Steele moved in beside her.

He felt the position of her foal, speaking softly to the horse all the while. Rising, he and Nathan exchanged a few words which Stacey could not hear.

Sighing heavily, Joshua turned to Stacey. "It doesn't look too good. The foal's moved to a breech position." He wanted to say something to reassure her, but knew that she would rather have the truth.

"Is she going to die?" Stacey heard herself asking.

"I don't know." Steele put his hand on her shoulder. The gesture, offered as comfort, unexpectedly sent a shaft of desire through him. To cover his feelings he led her over to the forge.

"I want you to stoke up this fire and boil some water. Will you do that?"

"Of course," she said, anxious to be useful.

He forced his attention back to Jonas and the mare, his business of looking for Barnett temporarily forgotten.

For the next three hours, Jonas and Steele put up a grueling battle to help the mare deliver her foal. Several times toward the last, Steele had to bow to the pain in his back and let Nathan do the physical work. At least it hadn't started bleeding again. Stacey had made him stop frequently to make certain of that.

Stacey was struggling with another bucket of water when she heard a shrill whinny, followed by a whoop of joy from Jonas and Steele. She dropped the bucket and raced back to the stall. She giggled with delight to see a splindly-legged foal awkwardly trying to gain its feet. Sheba was busily licking its wet coat.

"Mother and daughter are doing just fine," Nathan beamed. He extended a gnarled hand to Steele, who grasped it firmly.

Stacey clapped her hands like a pleased child. "Oh, she's so beautiful, Nathan."

"I'd say we've done a fair job," Steele pronounced. He was smiling.

It came to Stacey as a shock that it was the first time she had seen him smile since the Wilderness. It softened the hard planes of his face, giving his eyes the pleasant warmth she had committed to memory. So there was still room for gentleness in him.

Jonas beamed. "Looks like you've got yourself a beautiful filly, Stacey."

It was only then that Stacey remembered Nathan had promised her Sheba's foal in return for occasional medical attention to his livestock. "I'm going to call her 'Bashful'," she announced, "since she acted so shy about getting herself born."

To Steele Jonas said, "You can have any horse of mine for as long as you want him. A man who would do what you just did has an understanding for animals I find uncommon. I apologize for earlier."

"Forget it," Steele said. He left the stall, bending down to pick up the rope. There was still plenty of daylight left. Maybe he would get lucky and find Barnett. That would at least solve one of his problems.

As he headed out of the barn, he heard Stacey mentioning to the hostler that she would have to tell Martin Randolph all about the foal at dinner. Her words stirred a rage in him. There couldn't be a God in heaven, if Stacey Hamilton was in love with Ross Merrick.

CHAPTER FIFTEEN

Steele spent a fruitless day and night searching for any trace of Barnett. Being brutally honest, he didn't much care. He just had to be alone for awhile.

He'd broken camp at dawn, nearly two hours ago. He would be back in Spring Canyon by noon. It was time to face the inevitable. It was time to meet Martin Randolph.

It would have been so simple if Stacey hadn't been in Elizabethtown. He would have come to Spring Canyon and sought out the bank president at once. If the man wasn't Merrick, he would have continued his search elsewhere. If he was, he would have killed him.

But there was something he had to do before he met Randolph. He had to talk to Stacey. He had to know from her own lips. He had to know why he suddenly felt betrayed by her too.

Once back in town, he stopped first at Curtis'. The only one home was Molly. Stacey had a luncheon date with Martin Randolph, the girl told him. Steele walked up the street. He decided he could use a drink.

Steele stopped in front of the Gold Eagle saloon. Glancing up the street, he was in time to see a man in a black broadcloth suit greet Stacey at the door of Jensen's Cafe. The man had his back to Steele. He put his arm possessively around Stacey's waist.

Steele resisted the impulse to tear down the street and find out in that instant whether or not the man was Ross Merrick. He had trailed him for years with a soul full of rage and now, this one time, he couldn't yet face knowing. He had to talk to Stacey first. He pushed aside the bat-wing doors and stepped into the saloon.

"Beer," he said to the bartender, tossing a coin on the bar. He took a swallow of the warm liquid, alone with his black thoughts.

Rance Dawson chose the supreme wrong moment to cross paths with Joshua Steele.

"You're the hombre who was shot," Dawson said, sidling up to the bar. His voice was insolent. He was a man used to bullying others into doing his bidding. "You're a patient of Doc Curtis and that snippy little niece of his."

Dawson didn't notice the rigid set to Steele's jaw.

"I want you to give those two do-gooders a little message for me," Dawson smirked. "Tell 'em I'm going to get that little whore of mine back. And that both of them will wish they'd never laid eyes on that bitch."

Steele's gun was in Dawson's face. The hammer clicked back. His voice was death. "If you ever harm, or even think of harming Molly, her baby, Stacey, or Sam, I'll kill you."

Dawson seemed to shrivel up before his eyes. "Hey, I was only kidding, mister. Honest. Can't you take a little joke?"

Steele stepped back and re-holstered his gun. "Remember what I said." He swallowed the remainder of his beer and left the saloon.

Rance Dawson's power over his girls was never quite the same after that.

Outside Steele almost collided with Stacey.

"Joshua, I'm sorry," she said, "I wasn't watching where I was going. I just waved good-bye to Martin. We had lunch at Jensen's." Why was she prattling on like this? And, why had she mentioned Martin?

"I was looking for you," he said.

"In the saloon?" she asked doubtfully.

He gave her a half-smile. "No, there I was looking for a beer." He had to ask her now. Because in the next five minutes he was going to meet Martin Randolph face-to-face.

"You see this Martin fellow a lot," he continued, his voice deceptively casual.

"I suppose," she hedged, studying Joshua's face. It wasn't like him to be so personal with her. His gray eyes were hooded.

"Are you in love with him?"

She gasped, literally shocked to her toes at the bluntness of his question. "I . . . I," she couldn't seem to catch her breath. "I don't see that that's any of your business." Her knees quivered. She unconsciously gripped the support post in front of the saloon.

"You wouldn't have allowed him to court you for six months if you didn't care for him."

How did he know how long Martin had been calling on her? Why would it even interest him? "Joshua, why are you asking me these things?"

"I simply want to know your feelings for the man. Is that so unreasonable? Maybe I'm sizing up the competition."

His voice was so cynical, she knew he was lying. Was he trying to hurt her yet again? She couldn't bear it if he was. She couldn't let him know the power he had to touch her heart.

"The competition has had quite a sizable head start," she said, straightening. He wasn't going to hurt her with his mocking sarcasm this time. She wouldn't give him the chance.

"So you're in love with him?"

"Let's just say Martin and I have reached an understanding," she said, with all the feigned indifference her thudding heart would allow.

She was astonished to see a brief flash of raw pain in his eyes. Then it was gone and he looked colder and more remote than ever.

"You were right, Miss Hamilton," he said softly, "It was none of my business, and I apologize for my ill manners." He turned and headed up the street.

Stacey stared after him, still unable to comprehend what had just happened. Why on earth had she told Joshua that she and Martin had an understanding? Their only understanding was that her interest in him had been on the wane for weeks. Joshua had so bewildered her by his uncharacteristic prying that she had childishly struck back at him. She was terrified that he might otherwise have been able to guess where her true feelings lay, feelings she had yet to fully accept or understand herself.

She couldn't take her eyes off him. His strides were purposeful, ominous. He was heading for the bank.

She had a sudden, compelling urge to race after him—to demand to know why he had spoken to her as he had. Her heart pounded wildly. What was it that was making her feel this way? It came to her in a rush. It was fear. Cold, blind fear. She was terrified. Of what, she couldn't have said. But she knew Joshua was the reason for it.

He'd asked about Martin. Martin! She remembered suddenly the description of a man Joshua had given to John Beal. A description that was so close that even she had thought of Martin. She remembered Joshua's nightmare. And she remembered the scars on his back. Dear God, were all of these things somehow connected? Did Joshua think Martin was this man called Merrick? Merrick, the name of the man she had heard him cry out in the night. The name of the man he intended to kill! With her knees threatening to give way with every step she took, she ran up the street.

Steele had almost reached the bank. He halted abruptly when a man stepped out of the main entrance. From the suit the man wore, Steele recognized him at once as the man who had had lunch with Stacey. Martin Randolph. The man adjusted his hat, glancing up and down the street.

His hair was darker, maybe a few extra pounds of flesh. Yet it was there. Ominous familiarity. Steele unconsciously quickened his pace.

The banker's blue eyes caught Steele's gray ones at the same time Steele's mind made the decision. Panic seized Randolph. Frantically, he scrambled to get back into the bank, somehow regarding it as a refuge.

Steele's heart pounded. At last, at long last his vengeance was at hand. This was not a dream. Ross Merrick would not escape his righteous retribution. Ross Merrick was about to die.

Steele was on top of him before the banker could

bolt away. Randolph half-shrieked in terror. Words formed in his throat, but Steele's hands prevented their escape.

"Merrick. Merrick. Merrick." Steele hissed the name over and over.

For an instant Stacey stopped dead in her tracks, frozen with horror. Joshua was choking Martin! Somehow she forced her legs to move. She raced toward them.

Before she could reach them, Rube Tucker was there. She cried out in alarm as Tucker pointed his gun at Joshua's head.

"Let him go, Josh!" the lawman shouted. Randolph was turning blue. "Let him go!"

Steele remained oblivious to everything but Merrick's neck. His gray eyes burned with hate. Again Tucker shouted his order to stop. Steele's hands squeezed harder. The sheriff's gun barrel came down hard against the back of the big man's head. Steele slumped forward. Tucker reached out and eased him to the boardwalk.

Randolph sucked in air in great gasps. "Sheriff," he croaked, "I want that man in jail immediately."

"I can't believe it. I just can't believe it," Stacey murmured, trembling with shock.

"Some of you men carry him over to the jail," Tucker ordered, indicating Steele's inert form.

Stacey recovered enough to see that Joshua wasn't seriously hurt before she let them take him away.

She straightened, "Martin, are you all right?"

"First you check him, I see," Randolph seethed. "How could you even touch that vermin after what he did?"

"He seemed to think you were someone else, Martin. I heard him saying a name. Merrick." It was the name in Steele's nightmare. She remembered again the description she'd heard him give John Beal. The similarity had struck her then. But surely it was only a coincidental physical resemblance. Joshua had made a mistake. Martin couldn't have done anything to inspire such single-minded hate.

"I've never heard the name," Randolph raged. "I've never seen the man before in my life." Still rubbing his sore throat, the banker coughed spasmodically. Stacey tried to help him, but he pulled away from her. He stalked inside the bank, slamming the door behind him.

"Are you all right, Stacey?" Tucker asked.

She could only nod weakly.

"I've got to lock Josh up, you know that, don't you?"

"Of course, Rube. You go ahead. Really, I'm fine." She just wanted to run home and cry for a week. "I'm fine."

"Oh, Molly, it was so awful," Stacey sobbed. "Joshua was actually going to murder Martin. Murder! Martin didn't have a chance."

The young mother tried awkwardly to comfort Stacey. She was used to the situation being reversed. Stacey always seemed so strong, so self-assured.

"I can't believe Mr. Steele would do such a thing," Molly said. "He seemed so nice. Why when he was here a couple of hours ago . . ."

"Joshua was here? Today?"

"He said he was back from searching for that outlaw. He was looking for you. I don't know, Miss

Stacey, he just seemed so strange."

"In what way?" Stacey demanded. Maybe Joshua had left some clue with Molly about his peculiar behavior, about why he had pressed her about Martin Randolph just before he tried to kill him.

"Well," Molly said, "it was right after I told him you weren't home. That you were having lunch with Mr. Randolph."

"What did he say to that?"

"It wasn't exactly what he said. He just . . . he just looked kinda sick. That's the only word I can think of that comes close. It was his eyes, like he was in pain or something."

Stacey winced. She had seen the same pain. But it didn't make any sense. Why should Joshua care about her relationship with Martin? "I don't understand, Molly. Something has Joshua all twisted up inside. He wasn't like this before."

"Before?"

Stacey hadn't realized what she'd said. She looked into Molly's sympathetic eyes, and for the first time in her life she told another human being about her first, passionate encounter with Joshua Steele.

When Stacey finished, Molly whispered, "It must have been awful for you, when you thought he was dead."

"It was," Stacey admitted.

"You love him, don't you?"

The question startled her. "Of course not," she stammered. "Don't be ridiculous. It was just a . . . a schoolgirl crush, an infatuation." But Stacey could see that Molly was not convinced. She wasn't sure she had convinced herself. "But I do care about him," she conceded. "He's a human being. And I think he's been terribly hurt."

"It was an awful thing he did to Mr. Randolph, but if he is carrying a mountain of hate around with him, he must have convinced himself that Mr. Randolph was the man he was looking for. Poor Mr. Randolph just has the bad luck of looking like somebody else."

Stacey walked over to the mirror on her closet door. Her eyes were puffy from crying. "I was thinking the same thing, Molly."

"Maybe you ought to go to the jail and talk to Mr. Steele?"

Stacey whirled to face the girl. "Oh, Molly, I don't think I could do that."

"He likes you, Miss Stacey. I know he does."

Stacey shook her head, remembering his studied indifference, the coldness of those gray eyes. He might want her physically, as a man will want a woman. But she had seen no real tenderness in him towards her since they had met again in Elizabethtown. "I don't think so, Molly."

"It can't hurt you to talk to him."

Oh, you're wrong there, Molly, Stacey thought. It could hurt. God, it could hurt.

"You could convince him he's wrong about Mr. Randolph," Molly continued. "And maybe you could even convince Mr. Randolph about the mistake. He might let Mr. Steele go free."

Molly's confidence was infectious. Stacey picked up her brush and ran it through her tangled hair, until it shone like the sun. She washed her face to remove the evidence of her tears. Then she whisked off the somewhat drab calico dress she was wearing in favor of her lime green taffeta.

Molly giggled. "You look real pretty, Miss Stacey. Now you go on and talk to Mr. Steele. Don't worry about a thing. If Doctor Sam comes home, me and Angel will get him fed good and proper."

"Oh, Molly," Stacey smiled, hugging the girl, "I'm so glad you decided to stay here. It's like having a sister." She hurried out the door to her room.

Molly experienced the happiest moment of her life. "Miss Stacey thinks of me as a sister, Angel," she cooed to her sleeping infant, lying in the middle of Stacey's bed. "And as a sister, I'd say I have a right to take note when she's fibbing. 'Cause I don't care what she says, sweet Angel, Miss Stacey is in love with Mr. Steele."

Joshua woke on the hard cot of a jail cell. Instantly, he was at the cell door yelling for the sheriff.

"You just pipe down, boy," Tucker called, his voice gruff. "Randolph's got attempted murder charges against you." The lawman stepped into the cell area and eyed his prisoner. "What in the hell got into you anyway?"

For a moment Steele considered telling the lawman, then decided against it. Merrick was his, and no one was going to deny him the pleasure of killing him. He remembered the whip, he remembered Garcia, and he remembered a lot of dead men, dead because of Merrick.

The bell on the office door clanged as Sam Curtis walked into the sheriff's office. He approached Tucker, but his gaze settled on Steele.

"What is this I hear about you attacking Martin Randolph?" he growled.

"Why'd you do it, boy?" Tucker repeated.

"I had my reasons," was Steele's icy response.

Tucker said, "Folks aren't going to take too kindly to your roughing him up."

"I didn't intend to rough him up, sheriff," Steele said evenly. "I intended to kill him."

"Now, Josh, don't you talk that way," the sheriff scolded. "I don't want to be at your hangin'."

Steele knew he wasn't making this very easy for Tucker. The lean ex-federal agent crossed over to the cot in his cell and lay down. He closed his eyes, shutting out further questions by both the doctor and the lawman.

As Tucker and Curtis stepped back into the front office, Stacey came through the door.

She greeted her uncle and the sheriff. "I want to see him, Rube," she said, in a voice that brooked no argument. "Alone."

"I don't think that's a good idea," Sam said.

Her determination didn't waver. Sam knew when he was licked. "You'd better let her back there, Rube. We'll never hear the end of it until you do."

Stacey gave her uncle a rueful look, then stepped back to the cells, closing the door that separated them from Rube's office. Joshua was lying down on the cot in his cell. but he did not look at her.

She stood in front of the cell door. "Why, Joshua?"

A muscle in his jaw worked. He opened his eyes to stare at the ceiling.

She gripped the bars to his cell, pressing her head against them. Her voice shook. "I have to ask. I have to know."

263

"I asked you if you loved him. You implied you're going to marry him." His voice was bitter. "I can't tell you about him, Stacey."

"Joshua, Martin isn't Merrick. He can't be! It's a mistake. Martin just resembles this man Merrick."

Tears stung her eyes, as she turned and fled.

Stacey toyed with her supper. Her uncle chided her to eat more, but she had no appetite.

Sam had examined Martin and pronounced that he would live, though his throat would hurt for a few days. Randolph's anger at Stacey had subsided, but he wanted to retire early. She was alone for the evening.

No matter how she tried to keep her mind from him, her thoughts kept returning to Joshua. The look in his eyes when he'd attacked Martin haunted her.

Listlessly, she cleared away the supper dishes. She knew that prison was one answer. She shuddered, remembering the scars on his back, wondering if prison was where he had acquired them. There was so much she didn't know about Joshua Steele. How could a man she'd known for a sum total of scarcely a week, so effectively turn her life inside out?

She pumped water into the basin, barely cognizant of the dishes she washed. When Martin had had time to calm down, she decided, she would ask him to drop the charges against Joshua. He'd made a mistake, that was all. If she could get Joshua to promise that it wouldn't happen again, maybe Martin would let him go to appease her.

CHAPTER SIXTEEN

Jake Barnett had been in town nearly two hours. Darkness had long since settled over Spring Canyon. Barnett sat in the shadows of a cottonwood tree twenty feet from Sam Curtis' house. Four people had come and gone since his arrival. Probably patients seeking advice or medicine. When the last light in the Curtis house winked out, Barnett waited another full hour before he signalled to Pogget and Griego.

Whispering for them to bring the horses to the rear of the house, Barnett crept toward its back door. It was unlocked. He let himself in. Like a prowling animal, he searched the house until he found the medical man's bedroom.

Barnett put his hand over Sam Curtis' mouth as he pulled back the hammer of his Colt. Curtis started from sleep, but relaxed as he focused on the gun's gray-black barrel in the moonlight filtering through the window.

"You be real quiet and maybe you'll live to see the sun come up," Barnett whispered. "You're coming with me. I got a shot up compadre who needs doctoring. He can't come to you, so you're going to him."

"I'll have to get some things from my office," Curtis said.

"You do that. But be real careful. I'd hate to have to kill that pretty little niece of yours."

Curtis trembled. Under no circumstances could this vermin get his hands on Stacey. He prayed she would sleep soundly. He said the same prayer for Molly and her baby.

"Where are we going?" Curtis asked in a low voice, as he led the way into his office.

"That's for me to know," Barnett hissed. "You just worry about the doctoring."

Curtis stopped at the oak desk. He collected several things and placed them into his medical bag.

Barnett watched from across the room. He kept his gun pointed at Curtis until they were safely out of the house. Outside, Barnett shoved the doctor toward a large, mangy roan. Curtis mounted awkwardly. He rarely rode a horse, much preferring his buggy.

"Give me your hands, doc," Barnett ordered.

Curtis reached down and Barnett quickly lashed a rawhide strip around the physician's hands. Curtis looked at the two men with Barnett—one, a trail-stained sort Curtis hoped he didn't have to ride downwind of, the other a stocky Mexican with a sweeping mustache and malignant black eyes. A huge chaw of tobacco rested in the Mexican's left cheek. With a contemptuous glare Griego let loose with a spew of juice that nearly landed on the right front hoof of Curtis' mount.

The strange quartet moved out at a walk. Once out of town the pace increased to a trot. Curtis bounced painfully on the poorly gaited nag. If the ride took very long, he doubted he would be able to walk when it was over.

For three hours they continued the bone-jarring pace. The only time they slowed down was to trace a path along tedious switchbacks. Narrow openings between boulders occasionally had to be negotiated one rider at a time. They reached the outlaws' encampment just as dawn was breaking.

A rutted gorge surrounded by a huge circle of boulders created a natural hide-out. From any distance the rocks seemed a solid mass, but a small fissure allowed the single file entry. Inside, the whole area encompassed scarcely more than an acre.

Barnett dragged the bound Curtis from his horse and shoved him over to where Ernie Timmons lay under a thin blanket. With a swift motion Barnett pulled a knife and cut Curtis' rawhide bindings.

"Get to doctoring," he said.

Curtis bent down and examined the outlaw's wound in the early morning light. He knew instantly there was no way the man would survive. He considered telling Barnett, but the thought occurred to him that the outlaw's death could well signal his own.

"I'll do what I can for him," Curtis said.

"You'd better." Barnett's tone was ominous.

As the day progressed, Curtis scanned the camp frequently, from his position at Timmons' side. With a sinking feeling, he recognized he had little hope for escape.

Stacey woke up and grimaced at the thought of preparing breakfast. She had told Molly last night to sleep late this morning, saying that she would fix the morning meal. But she found she still had no appetite after the unsettling incidents of the day before.

Joshua's cold blooded attack on Martin Randolph haunted her every moment. He obviously had had no thoughts of escaping after the deed was done. Whoever Merrick was, and whatever he had done, his death meant more to Joshua than his own life.

Steele's later dismissal of her at the jail added to her overall feeling of misery. Go back to your lover, he had said. Did he truly believe Martin was her lover? She frowned. She had contributed directly to his misconception herself by telling him that she and Martin had some sort of romantic understanding.

She shook off her thoughts, chiding herself. Sam didn't deserve to starve just because she was upset. She climbed out of bed and dressed quickly in the morning chill.

She walked over to her uncle's room before going downstairs and was surprised to find it empty. Thinking he may have had an emergency during the night, she checked the night stand where he always left her a note at such times. Nothing.

Downstairs in the kitchen, it was obvious Sam had not been there either. A feeling of undefinable uneasiness touched her. Dismissing it as silly, she started to make breakfast. Sam was a grown man. He could take care of himself. He was probably running a quick errand in town.

The uneasiness persisted. She put the frying pan down and stepped into Sam's office. Nothing seemed out of order. Then she noticed the picture of Aunt Jenny lying face down on Sam's oak desk. To a casual eye it might seem a minor thing, but Sam would never have been so careless. She decided to see the sheriff.

Tucker wasn't nearly as concerned as Stacey had by

now become. She attempted to explain the significance of the picture but Tucker would have none of it.

"He's in trouble, Rube," she protested. "That picture means more to him than anything."

"He probably just strolled off for a walk. It's a beautiful morning."

"Sam is not out taking a walk," she snapped. "And if you won't go looking for him, I guess I'll just have to do it myself." She stomped out of the office, her concern for Sam for once preventing her from dwelling on Joshua.

Tucker watched after her, shaking his head. One damn pig-headed woman, he mused, but he still liked her.

Dressed in a pair of levis and carrying a two day supply of food, Stacey saddled her chestnut mare. She did so as quietly as possible, not wanting to alert Nathan Jonas to her presence. He might ask too many questions. She led the mare back to Sam's house. So Rube Tucker wouldn't listen to her! She'd find Sam herself if she had to search the whole blasted territory.

Behind the house she cast an experienced eye to the ground. She was no novice at picking up a trail. She'd once followed a cougar for three days just to discover its lair. The creature never once became aware of her.

But now the task before her was much more grim. Her uncle was in trouble. The tracks confirmed it. Four horses had been at the house during the night. She recognized her uncle's boot tracks leading up to where he had mounted one of those horses. Sam detested saddle riding; he would have to have been forced. She clucked at the mare, heading into the boulder-strewn canyon country that surrounded the town.

The going was difficult in places, but apparently the riders had seen no reason to disguise their trail, at least not in the beginning. She hadn't yet considered what she would do if she came across their camp. She was too intent on finding them first.

Nearly four hours of slow tracking later, a horse's whinny jerked Stacey's head up. It came from a mountain of boulders just ahead. She stroked the mare's neck, hoping to prevent an answer, but the damage had already been done. Leaping down, she yanked her rifle from its sheath and scurried up a nearby rock. Its pitted surface gave her relatively easy access to the top. She peered over it to see her uncle tending to a prone figure. Two other men peered from places of cover. One of them was Barnett. That left two unaccounted for.

She turned—too late. Raul Griego was nearly on top of her. She kicked out with a fury that sent him sprawling back down the rock. He had expected no trouble in corralling her. The bandy-legged outlaw scrambled to his feet, swearing fiercely in Spanish. Stacey slid to the ground several feet away from him and raced for her horse. Jake Barnett barred her path, his .44 Colt staring at her.

"You'd better not have hurt my uncle," she cried defiantly, determined that they not discover the terror that had her knees turning to jelly.

"Why don't you come over and see, Missy," Barnett crooned, laughing at Griego as the outlaw dragged himself to his feet.

Barnett reached for Stacey's arm, but she jerked it

away. He allowed her to pass in front of him. The outlaw leader pointed out the fissure in the rocks, and Stacey eased her way through it. She hurried directly to her uncle's side.

Curtis was red-faced with anger. "Stacey, what in God's name are you doing here?" His anger scarcely concealed the real fear he had for her among these outlaws.

"Rube wouldn't believe me when I told him you were in trouble," Stacey said defensively. She knew it wasn't much of an excuse. She was a fool. Now she was as much their prisoner as Sam was. She had accomplished nothing. That fact would probably bring a mocking sneer to the face of Joshua Steele, she thought. Then she berated herself for thinking of him at all.

Barnett came over to them. Without warning he grabbed Stacey by the hair, yanking her painfully to her feet. Involuntary tears sprang to her eyes. Refusing to cry, she swore at him instead.

"Get your filthy hands off me, you pig!"

Retaining a solid hold on her hair, he twisted her head back so hard she couldn't move. The fingers of his other hand trailed along her face, easing their way down her body to a full, curving breast. Curtis dove at Barnett, but was clipped by Griego's gun. He staggered on his hands and knees. Looking up, he begged Barnett not to hurt her.

"Well, now," Barnett snarled, "if she's a real good little girl, she won't get hurt. All she has to do is what she's told." His leer was evil itself. Stacey fought to control a sinking despair. She swore inwardly that Barnett would get nothing without a fight.

Barnett made the mistake of loosening his grip on her hair, as he brought his slimy mouth to her lips. Stacey whirled, then threw every ounce of her strength into a punch that connected solidly and unexpectedly with Barnett's stomach. The outlaw doubled over, swearing.

Griego stepped up and slapped Stacey hard across the face. She stumbled backwards. Blood oozed from her lower lip. Her left eye ached.

"No!" Curtis shouted, as Barnett recovered and advanced toward Stacey. "If you hurt her, your friend dies. I swear to God I won't lift a finger to help him, if you lay another hand on her."

Barnett considered this, but the thing that decided him was something else entirely. It came to him that he could use this willful woman for his own purposes. With her uncle as hostage she could scarcely refuse.

"All right, doc, you win," he said. He smiled, but no warmth showed in his yellow eyes.

"Forgive me, Miss Hamilton," he said affectedly. "I don't know what got into me."

"Go to hell!"

"Someday I'm sure, but first I'd like you to do me a small favor."

"They'll build snowmen in Hades first," she spat at him.

"Look, Miss Hamilton," Barnett snarled, "unless you want to see your uncle's brains all over this rock, you'll do as I say."

Stacey's shoulders slumped. "What do you want me to do?"

"I want you to break Joshua Steele out of jail for me."

She couldn't have heard him right. "Why would you want to do that?" she cried. "You tried to kill him."

"Exactly. I tried. That's the problem. With your help this time I'll succeed. You see, you're going to bring him to me."

Stacey's eyes reflected the hopelessness she felt. Joshua would never come with her. Desperately she tried to reason with Barnett, "How could I break a man out of jail?"

"A smart girl like yourself? You'll think of a way."

She would be bringing Joshua to his death. How could she trade one life for another? "He wouldn't come. Why should he?"

"Miss Hamilton, maybe I haven't made this clear enough for you. You convince that son-of-a-bitch to come here tonight, or your uncle won't live to see another sunrise. Now, do you understand?"

Stacey's despair mounted. "But what reason could I give him?"

"Tell him anything you like. Tell him the truth. It doesn't matter to me in the least." He moved closer to her. "You'll stay here until dark, so you might as well make yourself comfortable." He pushed her to her knees beside her uncle.

"Keep an eye on them," Barnett snapped to Griego. The Mexican's tobacco stained teeth spread in an evil smirk, but Barnett's glare warned him that guarding them was all he'd better do.

Stacey watched Barnett stalk away. The outlaw paused beside his wounded gang member, apparently checking to see if Timmons was still alive. After doing that he wandered over to his own blankets and sat

273

down. He yawned widely and lay back. It wasn't long before she heard him snoring.

"I still can't believe that you came out here alone, Stacey," Curtis said, keeping his voice low enough so that Griego could not overhear. "Just what did you hope to accomplish?"

"Obviously not this," Stacey said in self-disgust. "I was going to go back for Rube as soon as I found where they were holding you. Oh, Sam, what am I going to do? How can I ask Joshua to come out here? I'll be asking him to come to his death."

"If Barnett lets you leave here," Curtis hissed, "I want you to promise me that you'll stay the hell out of this! I mean it, Stace. Don't you dare come back here with Rube or Josh or anyone. You just tell Rube where this place is, and let him handle it. Do you understand?"

"I can't tell Rube anything, and you know it, Sam. One whiff of the law and Barnett would kill you." She glanced around her, staring at their prison of rock. "If only there were some way out of here . . ."

"If you're thinking of making a break for it, I won't hear of it. It's too dangerous."

"Sam, we have to try! I can't ask Joshua to come to his death!"

Sam eyed his niece intently. "What is it about Joshua?" he asked. "You seem to care about him a great deal more than a few days' acquaintance would account for."

"Caring has nothing to do with it," she said. "I couldn't ask any man to give up his life!"

"Elizabethtown wasn't your first meeting with Joshua Steele, was it?" he persisted gently.

She squirmed under her uncle's scrutiny. "I don't want to talk about it, Sam. I'm sorry. I just can't."

"All right, Stacey."

She detected a trace of hurt in her uncle's voice. She didn't want him to take her reluctance to speak of Joshua personally. But she knew if she mentioned anything at all about her first encounter with Steele, it would take very little imagination for her uncle to deduce the rest. She didn't want to burden him with that.

"Please, Sam," she said, "can we just concentrate on getting out of here?"

"There isn't any way out of here, Stace. That's what I'm trying to tell you. There's one fissure in the rocks, and that's it."

"We could go over the rocks."

"We wouldn't get far on foot."

She sighed; that was true enough. She looked out on the outlaws' encampment. Barnett was still snoring loudly. Cloudmaker was swilling down a bottle of alcohol. Tony Pogget curried his horse about thirty yards to their right. His back was to them. Griego, who stood barely twelve feet away, had his malignant black eyes riveted on her.

"If we could get Griego over here," Stacey whispered, "maybe we could get his gun."

"I don't want you hurt, Stacey. Just forget about getting away. When Barnett lets you go for Steele tonight, then you'll be safe."

"But you won't be! And neither will Joshua! If I don't bring him back, Barnett will kill you. If I do bring him back, I'm not so naive as to think that he won't just kill us all."

Stacey had only given voice to the thought that had been with Curtis all along. That was why he begged her not to come back with Steele. But he knew her too well. She would come back. "All right, Stacey," he said, "you get him over here, and I'll see what I can do about getting his gun." He hefted a fist-sized rock in his right hand.

Stacey stood up. There was only one way to get Griego over here, and her whole body recoiled at the thought. She imagined Barnett shooting Joshua and managed to overcome her revulsion.

"Raul, is that your name?" she called. "Could you come over here a minute, please?"

Griego looked at her suspiciously. He was no fool, and he wasn't crazy enough to think that the doctor's niece had suddenly decided he was a handsome man. But he had watched the swell of her breasts when Barnett had twisted her arm behind her back. He would love to see what they looked like naked. He glanced over his shoulder. Jake was asleep. Cloudmaker and Pogget would give him no interference. What could the girl do anyway. He had the gun. "What do you want?" he asked.

"I think I twisted my ankle, when Barnett pushed me," Stacey said. "I was wondering if you could help me get my boot off."

"Why can't your uncle do it?"

"He hurt his back when Barnett knocked him down. Please, I don't want it to get swollen inside the boot, then I won't be able to get it off."

Griego approached Curtis and his niece with extreme caution. He knew they were in fear of their lives. That they would try to escape was a real possibility. "Sit on the rock and I'll pull it off," he told Stacey. "You stay where I can see you, doctor."

Stacey sat on a small boulder. She had unbuttoned the first two buttons of her blouse, so now when she bent over to help Griego with the boot he couldn't help but notice the enticing valley between her breasts. The outlaw licked his lips. Stacey suppressed a shudder. If this plan backfired, she would be in desperate danger.

Griego found the cleavage irresistible. He pretended to stumble over a loose stone, catapulting against Stacey. She slid off the rock to the ground, feeling his body crushing down on top of her. She didn't utter a sound.

For a full second the sight of her soft flesh beneath him made Griego forget about Curtis. It was all the time Sam needed. He brought the rock down hard on Griego's skull. The man collapsed forward onto Stacey.

Sam quickly dragged him off of her. Stacey swallowed hard, trying to still the trembling that shook her body. "I don't want to do that again real soon," she whispered.

Curtis picked up Griego's gun. "Now we try for the horses."

They crept from boulder to boulder, inching their way toward Pogget, the closest outlaw. Barnett continued to sleep. Cloudmaker had apparently passed out.

"Drop your gun!" Sam told Pogget, as he came up behind him.

Pogget dropped the currycomb, then unbuckled his gunbelt and let it slide to the ground. "You'll never get away with this."

"We'll just see about that," Curtis said. "Get us two horses saddled. Now. And not a sound out of you."

Pogget did as he was told.

"Keep your eyes on Barnett," Curtis warned Stacey. When the outlaw had finished saddling the two horses, Curtis motioned with the gun that he wanted him to go stand by Barnett. "Now you can wake him up," Curtis said.

Pogget gave his boss a poke in the ribs with his boot. Barnett leaped to his feet, swearing loudly. When he saw what had happened, he swore a string of epithets that had Stacey's ears burning.

"Tie him up," Curits ordered Pogget.

Curtis stepped over to Cloudmaker, who had collapsed beside the wounded Timmons. He nudged the Indian with his foot. He didn't stir. He was out cold. "Tie him up, too," Curtis told Pogget, when the outlaw had finished trussing up Jake.

Cursing, Pogget did so.

Sam handed the gun to Stacey. "I'll tie up Pogget," he said. "Keep the gun pointed at him, so he doesn't get any heroic ideas."

"You're not going to get away with this," Barnett fumed. "I'll track you both. I swear I will."

"I wish we could take them with us and turn them over to the sheriff," Stacey said, as Sam finished binding Pogget's hands behind his back.

"There are too many of 'em, Stace," Curtis said. "We'll have to settle for getting ourselves out of here."

Stacey climbed aboard one of the saddled horses, stuffing the pistol into her belt. "We'll herd these other horses ahead of us."

Curtis was about to put his foot in the stirrup of his mount, when a hand reached out and grabbed his ankle. He had not been paying any attention to Timmons. The outlaw wrenched Sam's foot, sending him sprawling in the dirt.

Stacey made a desperate grab for the revolver, but it was too late. Timmons had his arm around Sam's neck, his gun at his head. "Get off the horse, little lady," he gasped, "or I'll kill him."

Tears stung her eyes. They had been so close, so close. She climbed down from the saddle.

"I'm sorry, Stace," Sam muttered. "I thought he was unconscious."

"So did I," she said quietly.

"Untie Jake," Timmons said.

Stacey could see that the man was barely conscious. If she dared to wait, he would pass out within seconds. But he had a gun to Sam's head. She couldn't take the chance. She untied Barnett.

Jake climbed to his feet and struck her viciously on the chin with his fist. "You try anything like that again, and you're dead," he raged. "Dead! Both of you!" He untied Pogget. "Go wake up Griego," he seethed. "Then both of you watch 'em. If either one of 'em so much as twitches, kill the other one."

Sam helped Stacey to her feet. "The damn bastards!" he said, dabbing at the blood on her lip with a cloth he pulled from his medical bag.

"I'm all right, Sam," she said wearily. Actually, she was far from all right. There was no hope she could escape Barnett now, and that meant she would soon be asking Joshua to ride to his death.

Two hours before sunset Barnett brought her her

horse. "You've got until midnight to have Steele back here. No tricks. You bring anybody else, anybody—or Steele tries anything—your uncle gets the first bullet. Understand?"

Stacey nodded mutely.

Barnett offered his hand to help her mount, a suggestive leer on his face. Angrily Stacey pulled away, mounting by herself.

Chuckling, Barnett swatted her horse on the rump and watched her ride off. A triumphant sneer spread across his face. Steele was his! The damned bitch was too scared to try anything that might endanger her uncle's life.

CHAPTER SEVENTEEN

All the way back to town Stacey worried about what she must do. If only she could tell the sheriff everything, let him handle it. But she knew Tucker would never let Joshua out of jail. Steele was adamant about killing Martin Randolph, and as a lawman Tucker couldn't take that chance. Above everything else, she had to get Sam safely away from those killers. Reluctantly, she resigned herself to the reality of the situation. She was in this alone. Somehow she would have to break Joshua Steele out of jail.

She trembled slightly as she remembered their last meeting. He had been cold, withdrawn. God, what if he refused to come with her? What if he lied to her? He could agree to go along, then hunt down Martin instead. Could she possibly trust her uncle's life to the hellishly bitter man in the Spring Canyon jail?

It had been dark for nearly an hour when she came in sight of the town. She would barely have time to get Steele back to Barnett's camp by the midnight deadline.

Moving like a shadow, she tied her horse at the rear of her uncle's house, and padded softly to Jonas' livery. Nathan was snoring loudly enough to wake the dead. Stacey stood by the livery wall for several seconds, her heart pounding. She said a desperate prayer that the hostler would stay asleep. She had to get another horse for Steele.

She'd made up her mind to ride with him. He wouldn't like it, but he would have to go along with it. If she were with him, he wouldn't dare seek out Randolph instead of helping Sam. She saddled the bay she had seen Steele take from Jonas' the day Sheba had foaled. As quietly as she could, she led the big gelding back to her mare.

She considered taking both horses to the dead end alley behind the jail, but decided it would be impossible to do so undetected. The jail was accessible only by a direct approach. She hurried across the street, rehearsing again in her mind what she would say to Joshua.

She halted, gasping for breath, at the corner of the jailhouse. She was scared to death. Taking deep breaths to keep her courage up, she peered into the cul de sac. Even though the moon had not yet risen, she felt spotlighted. She crept to the first cell window. This was the one she remembered Steele occupied.

Suddenly she was attacked by the thought that Tucker could have arrested someone else. What if Joshua had been moved to another cell? Swallowing hard, she knew it was a chance she would have to take. She only had until midnight.

Steele's cot would be directly beneath the window. She picked up a few pebbles and aimed them one by one through the bars. Nothing happened. *God, where is he?* she wondered in terror.

Steele's keen animal instincts had caught the movements outside the jail. The pebbles only further kindled his wariness. He was not about to stick his face through those bars and possibly get a bullet in it. He rose stealthily. From the left side of the window he peered out. He could see no one. He spied Stacey when she moved away from the building to pick up another stone.

"What the hell are you doing here?" he hissed.

Stacey was so startled by the sound of his voice, that she almost cried out. She waited a few seconds before she replied. Her bruised face was hidden in the shadows.

"I've come to get you out of here," she said, keeping her voice as low as possible.

"What are you talking about? Go home!"

"No! You have to come with me. I can't explain now. But Sam's life depends on it. Please, Joshua." the real anguish in her voice came across to him.

"What do you suggest?" he asked. "That I squeeze through the bars?"

"Stop being sarcastic. I'm going in for Rube. I'll get him to leave. Then I'll find the keys and unlock your cell. We'll go over to Sam's. I have the horses tied there." She hesitated. So much depended on this man. "You have to promise that you'll wait for me. You won't try to just ride off. Please, Sam will die. Promise you'll wait."

"I'll wait.' He frowned. Why should he trust her? She could have Merrick waiting to ambush him. She'd all but admitted she was in love with the son-of-a-bitch. He looked out again, but she was gone. He heard the knock on Tucker's office door.

"Stacey, what on earth . . ." She interrupted Tucker with a wave of her hand.

"Rube, please, they've got Sam. Jake Barnett and his gang! They have him prisoner. I saw them." She was crying.

Steele heard what she said and felt his blood run cold. He knew she wasn't lying.

"Where are they, Stacey?" Tucker demanded. "Why would they do such a thing?"

"One of them is wounded. I trailed them, but there was nothing I could do. And if you attack them, I know they'll kill Sam. You have to go in easy. Please, Rube, he's the only family I have."

Tucker strapped on his six-shooter and pulled a rifle and shotgun from the wall rack. "I'll round up some men. You stay here. When I get back, you can show us the trail."

"Thank you, Rube."

As the sheriff hurried down the street, Stacey wiped the tears brusquely away. They had been genuine, but now she could afford no more of them. She hoped Tucker would understand.

After a quick search, she located the cell keys in the upper right hand drawer of the sheriff's desk. She ran back to Steele's cell, her blonde hair falling loosely across her bruised left eye. She fumbled with the big key in the lock, anxiety riding her hard. At last the door opened.

"I'll follow you," she said to Steele, keeping her face averted. She didn't want to be slowed down answering questions.

"You're not going anywhere."

"Didn't you hear what I said? They'll kill Sam! This is no time to continue our personal hostilities."

He said nothing. She watched him grab up his guns

from Tucker's desk. She had to hurry to keep up with him.

Steele was already half way out the door, peering cautiously up and down the street. Because the sheriff had started to gather a posse, they were forced to take a roundabout way back to the house.

Steele caught up the bay's reins, checked the cinch, and swung into the saddle. "Tell me where they are."

"No!"

"I don't want to have to be watching out for you," Steele snapped, unable to keep the irritation he felt from creeping into his voice. "I'll have enough problems."

"I can take care of myself," Stacey returned hotly. "Besides I intend to make certain that you do go after Sam."

"What the hell does that mean?"

"I mean alone you might decide differently. That maybe Sam doesn't matter. That maybe this would be your perfect opportunity to kill Martin Randolph."

Steele swore softly. Realizing that further argument would be useless, he kneed the bay away from the house. Stacey quickly mounted her mare and took the lead.

Close to two and a half hours later they stopped and dismounted. A good distance still separated them from the outlaws' camp. This time the horses would not give them away.

Steele asked her for the layout of the camp. As accurately as she could she described it to him. Steele had to admire Barnett's ability to camouflage himself. He must have searched within a couple hundreds yards of this place without a clue that Barnett was nearby.

"Won't they be expecting some sort of attack from you?" Stacey asked anxiously. Her fear for Sam's life gripped her like a living thing.

"Probably. But that doesn't mean I can't succeed." He did not look at her when he said, "I promise you that if at any time I think I can't make it, and Sam's life is in danger, I'll toss in my guns."

She wasn't sure why, but she believed him. "Thank you," she managed, but considered it entirely inadequate. The man just told her he would forfeit his life for her uncle's.

Steele felt in his pocket for the makings and fashioned himself a smoke. He smoked rarely, but right now it would taste good. He struck a match on his backside. The light flared on Stacey's face. With an oath he dropped the flaming stick.

"What happened to your face?" Steele's voice was fused with anger.

Not quite knowing who the anger was directed at, she backed away, her hand going to her face. With the worry over her uncle she had forgotten how painfully bruised it was. She touched her swollen cheek gingerly.

"They got a little nasty."

"Barnett did that to you?" Steele's anger deepened.

"Actually he and Griego both took a swing at me," she said, trying to make her voice light, hoping to defuse some of his anger.

"What else did they do?"

"Nothing." She said it too quickly. Her face flushed as she remembered Barnett's pawing hands and foul mouth. She could never tell Joshua about that. It was enough that he had witnessed what Hector Caulfield had done to her in the Wilderness.

"What else did they do?" Steele repeated tightly, unconvinced by her response. This woman meant more to him than he dared to admit, even when he thought of her with Merrick. The thought that Barnett had so much as touched her incensed him to a killing anger.

"Nothing. Really. Please, Joshua, it's Sam who is important here." She could almost feel the fury in him.

"How's your eye?" she asked, deliberately changing the subject.

"No problem since that last day on the trail. Maybe it's cured itself," he said, though he didn't believe it had. Stacey obviously wasn't going to tell him anything further about her bruises. He would have it out with Barnett later.

She watched the tip of his cheroot in silence, until he finished the smoke. She felt safer somehow just being with him. Again the vision of what she had seen in his face when he had attacked Martin rose up to haunt her.

"Well, I guess we'd better see what we can do about getting your uncle away from these killers, Miss Hamilton."

He motioned that she should stay behind him. They circled the boulders and came up on the side opposite the one Stacey had been discovered on that afternoon. Climbing from rock to rock, they edged their way to the top of the highest one.

Stacey flattened herself against it. Joshua stretched out beside her. His every instinct was alert to danger, yet this woman continued to make him acutely aware of her presence. It was nothing she did consciously. Sighing, he raised his head to peer out at Barnett's camp.

"That's Sam and the wounded outlaw," Stacey whispered, pointing to two men lying under blankets near a small camp fire.

As they watched, a solitary figure moved toward the fire. Steele recognized Barnett. The outlaw hunkered down in front of the flames and checked his pocketwatch. 11:45. The woman had fifteen minutes to have Steele back here.

"You stay here," Steele told her. "And don't move. I don't want to shoot you by mistake."

He gripped his Winchester in his right hand and crept over the rock. Like an Apache he dropped down to camp level. Barnett had been stupid enough to stare into the flames. He was night blind for the moment. Steele ignored him. He wanted to get a fix on the others first.

He circled the camp moving to his left like a cougar on the prowl. It wasn't long before he discovered what he thought he might. Raul Griego sat perched expectantly behind the boulder that guarded the fissure entrance-way. Steele didn't hesitate. He brought the butt of his rifle down on the Mexican's head. The man fell as if pole-axed.

Continuing his circular path around the encampment, Steele came upon Tony Pogget sleeping peacefully at his guard position. Steele nudged him with his rifle butt. Pogget was too frightened to move. Steele indicated with a movement of his head that the stocky outlaw should head toward the fire.

At the sound of Steele's approach, Barnett whirled

and grabbed for his rifle lying on the ground near his feet, but his night blindness prevented a quick shot. He saw Pogget's hands in the air and backed off. When the captured outlaw got close enough to him, Barnett nearly broke his jaw with an unexpected right cross.

"Idiot!" he fumed. "Stupid bumbling idiot!"

"Shut up, Jake," Steele said. "Now, where's the Indian?"

"Wouldn't you like to know."

"Either he's out here in five seconds, hands in the air, or you're a dead man, Jake."

Barnett watched the reflected flames of the campfire leap in the eyes of this wolf of a man who faced him.

"Cloudmaker get in here," he roared.

The half-breed glided in like a ghost. Steele's breath caught. Cloudmaker's knife pressed tightly against Stacey's throat. He held her arm twisted painfully behind her back.

"Drop the gun," the half-breed snarled at Steele.

Stacey experienced the bitter taste of despair. If Joshua dropped the rifle, Barnett would kill him. Yet she knew he would do it to save her life. How could she have been so stupid? The Indian moved like a shadow. He was on her before she knew he was there.

Curtis was standing, looking first at Stacey, then at Joshua. He watched the play of emotions on the big man's face. He had come so close to making this work. If Stacey had stayed out of it, it would have worked. But that was history. Steele heaved the rifle near the fire.

The half-breed released his hold on Stacey. She fell

to the ground, sobbing. Barnett grinned malevolently as he stooped for his rifle. "I figured you'd try something," he said. "That's why I had the breed waitin' up the trail a ways."

Barnett turned his attention to Stacey. "I warned you not to try anything, Missy." Stacey glared up at him, brushing at her tears with the back of her hand. "Now I'm afraid I'm just gonna have to kill you and your uncle after all. That is, after I take my time killing Steele here."

The outlaw leader turned to Joshua. "On your knees, gunfighter." Barnett's rifle levelled off two feet from Steele's gut. Steele's jaw tightened.

Tony Pogget had re-acquired his gun and had it aimed at Sam. Griego was still out cold. The Indian sheathed his knife, pulled a bottle of bocanaro from his saddlebags and squatted near the fire, the proceedings no longer of interest to him.

"I said on your knees," Barnett repeated, "or I'll have Pogget put a bullet in the good doctor's pretty little niece."

Stacey stared at the bore of Pogget's rifle, as it settled on her. Inwardly, she trembled, but her eyes betrayed no fear. She ached for Joshua. Barnett would kill him before the night was out, and it would be all her fault.

Steele considered the odds. A sweep of his hand might beat Barnet's finger on the trigger, but Pogget could kill Stacey at the same instant. He couldn't take that chance. He would have to play along, hoping for an opening. He sank to his knees, cold hatred building in him.

Barnett stepped closer, and with the back of his

right hand drove Steele sideways with a sharp blow to the jaw. Stacey winced at the sound.

She had to do something. The outlaws would kill Joshua and Sam, and she would be responsible. She couldn't live with that kind of guilt. If she could distract any of them for even a second, it might give Joshua the time he needed to gain the upper hand. The outlaw holding the rifle on her had his eyes glued to Barnett and Steele. The Indian's only interest was the bottle in his hand. It would have to be now, before the other one woke up.

Stacey sprang forward, forcing Pogget's rifle into the ground and shoving the outlaw sideways with her body. Startled, Barnett jerked around, bringing his rifle to bear on Stacey. Joshua reacted instantly. He launched himself at the wiry outlaw, catching him around the waist and sending him sprawling.

Sam Curtis pounced on Pogget's rifle. "Keep those hands where I can see them," he yelled. He levered a cartridge into the chamber and snapped the same command to the Apache. The Indian offered no resistance.

Barnett and Steele struggled on the ground. Curtis shouted for them to stop, but Steele waved him off. He was going to enjoy this.

"You beat up on women, Barnett. Now let's see what you do when you've got somebody closer to your own size to fight."

The two men scrambled to their feet, circling each other like pit bulls, both looking for an opening. Barnett lunged. Steele brought up a knee and caught the killer squarely in the face. Barnett snarled with rage. He flung himself forward, catching Steele around the middle. They grappled, going to the dirt once again.

"Sam, make them stop!" Stacey cried.

"I don't think Josh wants it stopped," Curtis chuckled, keeping his eye on the fight, as well as Pogget and Cloudmaker. Occasionally he shot a glance at the still unconscious Griego near the rocks.

Steele gained the advantage. Barnett was staggering. Steele landed blow after blow. The outlaw leader swayed drunkenly. Steele brought down a vicious chop to the back of Barnett's head, sending the outlaw to his knees. He tried to get up, but a bone crunching backhand sent him sprawling on his face near the fire.

Joshua stood with his legs spread, breathing hard. His body ached, but he felt good.

Sam came over to him. "Are you all right?"

"Just fine."

"The eye?"

"No problem."

"I want to thank you for what you've done for Stacey and me."

"Forget it. Let's get these buzzards tied up."

Steele dragged the still inert Griego over to the others. Sam kept them all covered, while Joshua put the ropes on them.

Stacey watched in fascination. Joshua continued to confound her. He was a man capable of murderous hatred, as evidenced by his attack on Martin. The barely controlled violence in him was conspicuous even now in his obvious enjoyment of the fight with Barnett. And yet she remembered his gentleness with Nathan's mare, the way he'd held Molly's sleeping baby, and tonight his willingness to sacrifice his own life for her and her uncle. And she remembered unwillingly those rapturous moments spent in his embrace in the Wilderness. She shook her head, conflicting emotions assailing her. It would take a lifetime to truly know a man like Joshua. She blushed, guessing the direction of her thoughts.

Steele and Curtis saddled the outlaws' horse. Stacey waited in front of the fire. She found the flames intoxicating. They warmed her thoughts away from the chilling fear of the preceding hours.

As Joshua fastened the cinch on one of the horses, he paused a moment to study her. She had been through a lot today, but except for the slight bruise on her face, no one would know it to look at her.

His eyes narrowed as his thoughts turned to Ross Merrick. How could she care for that monster from hell? The man couldn't have buried his true character that well. And yet, he admitted, Merrick had fooled him once, too.

Steele boosted the groggy Griego up near his horse. He braced the outlaw against the animal.

"I understand you like to hit women." Steele's voice was as smooth as fine leather.

Griego's flesh crawled. "No, senor . . ."

Without warning Steele delivered a savage blow to the man's mid-section. The outlaw grunted in pain. Steele righted him and slung him up on his horse without another word.

When all four outlaws had been secured to their mounts, Sam Curtis walked over to Ernie Timmons. He knelt down by the wounded outlaw. The man was dead. Curtis motioned to Stacey. Together they gathered enough rocks to quickly cover the body. At last the group was ready to head out.

Stacey led the way toward Spring Canyon. They would take a shorter, more direct route than the one over which they had come. She wanted to get to town as quickly as possible. Rube Tucker would probably like to shoot Joshua on sight, maybe her too, she thought wryly, then ask questions. She wasn't going to let that happen.

The route was treacherous at best. Dropoffs lay hidden in the darkness. She would have to trust her horse. At a point where the trail widened slightly, Steele edged his mount up next to hers.

"Are you sure you can see well enough to lead the way, Miss Hamilton? I'd like to stay behind these varmints, but I don't want you riding over a cliff."

"So we're back to how incapable I am, are we?" she gritted. "I assure you I'm perfectly capable of finding my own way, *Mister* Steele." She was immediately contrite, "I'm sorry, I haven't even thanked you for what you did for us tonight. You saved our lives."

Steele scowled. "You weren't bad yourself. Besides, Barnett was my problem to begin with. You don't owe me any thanks." He held his horse while the outlaws passed in front of him.

Curtis pulled alongside. "I want to thank you again . . ."

Steele cut him off.

Curtis continued. "I suppose Stacey didn't give you much choice about bringing her along."

Joshua laughed with genuine humor. "Now that is an understatement, Sam. She is . . . different." He made certain his voice wasn't loud enough to be heard further ahead.

"That she is, Josh. That she is," Curtis laughed. "I was never so scared in my life this afternoon, when I saw Barnett dragging her into camp. And I was furious, too, that she should have come out here on her own. But it's just like her. She pulled the same thing during the war."

"I know," Steele said quietly.

"You do?"

Steele told Sam of his initial encounter with Miss Eustacia Hamilton, cavalry mounted infantry private—all except the part about making love to her.

"So that's it," Curtis said. "I thought there was more to you two than met the eye. I wonder why she wouldn't tell me about it."

"I doubt if she likes to be reminded of Caulfield."

Curtis nodded. "She probably didn't want to upset me."

More likely, Steele thought grimly, she didn't want Curtis suspecting what happened after Caulfield's attack, when a frightened girl sought comfort in the arms of a man who should have known better.

Curtis was chuckling. "Her father wrote me letters about some of the stunts she pulled that would curl your hair. Ol' Ben was fit to be tied when she showed up in that uniform. But she wouldn't listen to a word he said about going back home, so he caved in and let her stay. All she cared about was being a doctor."

Joshua suddenly regretted not asking her anything about her life since that day in the Wilderness. He'd been too wrapped up in his hate to care. "She told me about wanting to be a doctor," he said, warming to the conversation with Stacey's congenial uncle. "I admit I dismissed it as an adolescent notion she would grow out of once she got back to civilization. I pictured her resuming a life of parties, dances, and lovestruck young men."

Curtis studied Joshua in the faint moonlight. Was there a touch of jealousy on that last note about lovestruck young men? "I'm afraid Stacey's life hasn't been a mad social whirl, Josh."

Steele damned himself for doing it, but he asked anyway. "It's none of my business, I know, but what did happen to that dream of hers to be a doctor?" He remembered telling her that dreams had a way of getting side-tracked. He had been speaking of his own dream to return to his Colorado ranch. What had happened to hers?

Curtis sighed. "She doesn't talk about it much, because she's not much on self-pity. Her mother happened mostly, from what I've been able to piece together. My sister, Beatrice, was a very straight-laced woman. No daughter of hers was going to be a doctor. Stacey defied her mother, and Beatrice had a stroke."

Steele fingered the reins of his horse.

"Stacey blamed herself, of course, though it wasn't her fault. It probably would have happened sooner or later anyway. But her father had been killed just a few months earlier, and she'd wound up blaming herself for that too." Curtis explained about the poor medical procedures that led to Ben Hamilton's death. "Stacey figured if she had been there, Ben wouldn't have died. Instead of going to medical school she sacrificed five years of her life caring for her mother."

Steele was silent. His image of a pampered emerald-eyed vixen on an adventurous lark in a war zone, running home to be courted by dapper, well-heeled young men, had just had a large hole blown in it. But what about Randolph/Merrick? a cynical voice nagged at him. The man was a bank president. Maybe her attraction to him wasn't personal, but monetary. Damn, what difference did it make anyway? Her personal life was none of his concern.

How it happened Stacey could never say for certain, but suddenly her horse seemed to lose its footing in the darkness. She felt herself being catapulted through space. She heard the horse screaming as it fell in front of her. Her last conscious thought was that Joshua would be furious with her, then a jarring impact drove all thoughts from her mind.

Steele heard the horse falling. He was about thirty feet behind her with Curtis and the four outlaws separating them. Thoughts of Merrick vanished. A cold fear such as he had never known came over him. Without caution he spurred his horse around the others. Twice the animal stumbled, but recovered itself. The path was extremely narrow. The high boulders on the left blocked what minimal light there was from the quarter moon.

Steele clambered out of the saddle. By touch he found the break in the rocks where she had gone over.

"Stacey! Stacey, can you hear me? Are you all right? Answer me!"

Silence.

Steele dallied the rope around his saddle horn. Making certain it was secure and that the horse would stand, he started over the precipice. Curtis hovered beside him.

"Josh, do you think there's a chance she's . . ." He couldn't finish.

"Stay by the horse," Steele said through gritted teeth. "I'll let you know the second I get to her."

Painstakingly, Steele made the descent along the face of the cliff. He couldn't hurry for fear of passing her in the darkness. His ears strained the night air, hoping to hear a sound from her telling him that she was still alive. God, let her be alive!

Balancing himself on a rock outthrust, Joshua groped blindly with his hand. His fingers discovered something soft. He probed further.

"Stacey."

She was so still. He found her neck and felt for a pulse. It was fast, but strong. "I found her, Sam. She's alive!"

Barnett wasted no time. "Griego, Pogget, Cloudmaker—let's get the hell out of here," he hissed.

"But our arms are tied, boss," Pogget said.

"You can still knee that nag of yours forward, can't you?" the gang leader fumed. "And hurry up about it. As soon as they find that bitch, Steele will be on our tails again. I don't intend to be here when that happens."

Barnett kicked his horse savagely, forcing the animal to maneuver around Curtis' mount. The doctor was too busy peering over the edge of the cliff to notice. Barnett thought briefly about trampling the medical man, but dismissed the notion because it would alert Steele to their escape.

As the horse moved up the trail, Barnett worked furiously on the ropes that bound his hands. It would take time to free himself. But then Steele and the others would be gone. "We'll still have our time together, Steele," Barnett swore, "and I will kill you."

Joshua touched Stacey's face. It would be best if he could rouse her, find out the extent of her injuries before he tried to move her.

"Stacey, can you hear me?" Gently he ran his hands along her arms, her legs. He tried unsuccessfully to block out the sensual feel of her body. He checked her wrists, her ankles. Nothing seemed to be broken. His heart pounded as he pressed the palms of his hands along her rib cage. He opened her blouse, assuring himself it was a better way to tell if she had any broken ribs.

His hands touched the underside of her breasts. He swallowed hard. God, how he wanted her. He felt the stiffening in his loins. He touched her face, smoothed her hair. He whispered her name over and over.

At last he felt her stir. He heard her sharp intake of breath. She was in pain. She tried to move, but his hand stopped her.

"Don't try to get up." He spoke soothingly. "You've had a bad fall. Do you think there's anything broken?"

It took a few minutes for Stacey to remember what had happened. Slowly and deliberately she moved her arms and legs, while Joshua steadied her in his arms.

"I don't think there's anything broken," she said. "Except maybe my head." She groaned slightly. "How am I going to get out of here?"

"I'm going to put this rope around you and let my horse and your uncle pull you out."

"Thanks a lot," she said. "It takes my uncle *and* a horse to lift me, does it?"

He could sense the humor in her voice and was grateful. Maybe she wasn't too seriously hurt after all. The fall was about twenty feet, but she could have slid part of the way.

He helped her stand up, then took the rope from around his own waist and settled it around hers.

Stacey noticed the open buttons of her blouse. She was grateful for the darkness, so Joshua couldn't see the color rise in her cheeks. Quickly she re-fastened the buttons.

"I was checking your ribs," Joshua offered lamely. It sounded like the excuse it was. It would have been better if he'd said nothing.

"It's all right. I understand," she said quietly.

"Pull her up, Sam," he called.

With agonizing slowness Stacey struggled back up to the trail. The steadying hands of her uncle supported her the last couple of feet.

"Thank God," Sam whispered.

When he got her settled, Curtis lowered the rope back to Joshua. The ex-federal agent climbed further down the precipice. He had heard the painful breathing of Stacey's mare. A shot echoed through the craggy rocks and canyon walls. He scrambled up quickly then, his eyes scanning the trail.

"Where are Barnett and the others?"

"Oh, no," Curtis cried. "I was so worried about Stacey, I didn't even pay any attention to them. They must have gotten past me and took off. Do you think they'll try to ambush us?"

"It'll take them awhile to get themselves untied," Steele said, "But we'd better get off this trail."

"I don't think it's good idea for Stacey to ride," Sam told him. "Couldn't we wait here until dawn?"

"If Barnett does get free, this would be the first place they'd look. Hand her up to me, Sam."

Steele mounted his horse and re-coiled the rope. Sam helped Stacey to her feet and as gently as possible helped her up on Steele's horse. Joshua cradled her against his chest, feeling how tense she was. This couldn't be very comfortable for her.

Only now did some of the tenseness of the past few minutes drain out of him. It brought him up short to realize how frightened he had been when her horse had tumbled over the cliff. When he thought of how close she had come to dying . . .

Stacey felt the shudder that passed through Joshua's body. He was probably furious with her. Her head throbbed miserably, but she was well aware of the fact that the outlaws had escaped because of her. Aware, too, of the rippling muscles in Joshua's arms as he held her against him on his horse. No doubt he'd like to throw me back over the cliff, she thought dejectedly.

They rode back up the trail for a short while, then headed left. About half an hour later they crossed into a tree-shrouded grove near a small stream. Steele dismounted, letting Stacey slide into his arms. Sam had already spread out a blanket. Gently Steele laid her onto it. She was either asleep or unconscious, he didn't know which.

Joshua built a small fire, while Sam tended his niece. Finally after what seemed a long time, the doctor stood up and walked over to the fire. Steele sat facing away from the flames, the Winchester positioned for instant use. If Barnett came back, he would be ready for him.

"She's going to be all right, Josh," Sam said. "Just bruises. Nothing's broken."

A long sigh of relief coursed through Steele's body.

"I'm glad to hear it." He tried to make his voice sound matter-of-fact.

Curtis snorted. "Glad to hear it?"

Steele heard the soft mocking in the doctor's tone, and felt suddenly as though his feeings for Stacey were transparent. He shifted uncomfortably. "Why don't you go sit with her, while I keep watch," he said.

Curtis was sorry if he had embarrassed Steele. "You've been sitting here for an hour already," he said gently. "It'll be dawn in less than two hours. Get some sleep yourself. I'll watch."

Joshua handed Sam the rifle, walked over to his horse and grabbed a blanket. He spread it out on the ground and sat back against a tree. Stacey was less than four feet away from him. He sat quietly, watching the even rise and fall of her breasts as she slept. She must have moved wrong in her sleep, because her eyes suddenly flew open.

"Joshua?" she called out in a frightened voice.

"I'm right here." He shifted his position to touch her shoulder gently.

She seemed to visibly relax. "Are you angry with me?"

"For what?"

"It's because of me that Barnett got away. After you told me to be careful on the trail. I'm so sorry."

"Forget it. It's done. It doesn't matter. There'll be another time for Barnett and me."

"Does there have to be another time? Can't you just let it go?"

"You seem to forget that Barnett is the one who has the grudge against me."

She closed her eyes. He thought she had gone back

to sleep. Her voice came softly to him once again.

"Joshua? Are we going back to town soon?"

"At first light. Get some sleep. You can use it."

"I'm really not sleepy. But you don't have to talk to me. I just like to know that you're there." She closed her eyes again, sighing quietly.

Joshua felt a tightness in his throat. How could this woman ever care for a man like Merrick? Just looking at her against the flickering light from the fire played riot with his senses.

Stacey turned on her side, wincing as she did so from a painful bruise on her hip. She regarded Joshua. He had his eyes closed, but she doubted he was asleep. She wondered idly how he could be comfortable sitting against that tree.

She shivered suddenly against the pre-dawn chill and thought how much warmer it would be if she could lie next to Joshua, and in the same instant she felt her face flush hot with embarrassment. She really was becoming quite shameless, she admonished herself.

Steele shifted his position, stretching out on the ground in front of the tree. He was scarcely a yard away from her. For an unguarded moment he allowed himself the warm feeling of tenderness. Then angry with himself for such weakness, he swore and turned so that he was no longer facing her. He would rest for a couple of hours anyway.

Stacey had been watching covertly as Steele shifted his sleeping position. She misunderstood his quiet oath. No doubt he really was angry with her for getting him into this mess. She tried, but she couldn't get back to sleep. Deciding her uncle could use some company on guard, she climbed painfully to her feet. Steele was instantly alert at the sound.

"You shouldn't be up," he said sharply.

Stacey winced at his anger. "I feel fine. Really. I just ache a lot." She gave him a tentative smile. "I'm sorry all this happened. I didn't want to involve you in our problems." Steele sat up, but said only, "Barnett is in this part of the country because of me." He didn't trust himself to speak further. What little moonlight there was, accented the shine of her pale hair. She was so beautiful. He rammed back the thought. She was Ross Merrick's woman. The night air must be affecting his mind.

Cursing softly, he rose to stand near a cottonwood tree. It was impossible to keep his eyes from turning toward her. God, how he wanted to touch her! The hopelessness of it tore at him. There was too much in his past life that would come between them now. If only Mexico had never happened . . .

His thoughts were interrupted by a sudden savage aching in his left eye. He tried unsuccessfully to stifle a groan. Stacey rushed to his side.

"Sam!"

Her uncle hurried over, carrying the rifle. One look at Steele sent him for his medical bag.

Waves of agony forced Steele to the ground. "Joshua! Joshua! For the love of God!" Stacey cried, kneeling beside him.

"Damn the man!" Curtis swore, returning with his medicines. "He said the eye hurt him. He never said it was like this."

"Sam, this is worse than the attacks I saw," Stacey told him.

"See if you can get him to put his hands down. I want to take a look."

Stacey smoothed Joshua's hair, touched his face, speaking to him, not even thinking of what she said. He gave no indication he was aware of either of them. Several minutes passed and still the pain showed no signs of relenting.

"Sam, do something!" The despair in Stacey's voice tore at Curtis. There was nothing he could do out here.

At last, Steele's features relaxed a little. Stacey continued to talk to him. Comprehension returned to his gray eyes.

"Josh, can you understand me?" asked Sam.

Steele nodded, his head throbbing. He could not make out Sam's face.

"Have you ever . . . ever had a head injury of any kind?" the doctor demanded. "In the war maybe?"

Stacey started, remembering the bullet from Hector Caulfield's gun. Surely that couldn't have anything to do with this. She couldn't bring herself to mention it to Sam. She wondered if Joshua would.

Steele thought back to the blast that had killed six of his companeros in Mexico, compliments of Ross Merrick. Something had slammed into his head. "A cannon shell exploded near me," he told Curtis, his voice tight because of the pain. "I was hit with some shrapnel. But somebody dug it out. Besides that was four years ago."

Sam shook his head. He would have to get Joshua back to town. He wanted to check something in an old medical journal. The symptoms had triggered a memory, but he wanted to be sure.

To Stacey he said, "Keep him quiet. I'll get the horses ready." Remembering her injuries he asked anxiously, "Are you all right to travel?"

"I'm fine, Sam." Her hand continued to stroke Joshua's head which lay cradled in her lap. Curtis hurried to the horses.

"Does he think he knows what it is?" Joshua asked. The pain had lessened, though it was barely tolerable.

"I don't know," she said,. "Oh, Joshua, when Sam mentioned a head injury, I thought . . . I thought of Caulfield. He shot you." She touched the nearly invisible scar above his left temple.

"Don't be ridiculous," Steele said, catching the guilt in her voice. "That was over seven years ago."

"If I'd shot him . . ."

"Stacey—stop it!"

She couldn't stop. "I've thought about that day so often, Joshua. I still don't think I could shoot him. Even now. The difference between pointing a gun and pulling the trigger . . . I just couldn't do it." She trembled. "He could have killed you."

He squeezed her hand. "I told you to forget it."

"No, Joshua, I'll never forget it. Never. But at least Sam sounded hopeful. Maybe a simple operation . . ."

"No."

"What?"

"Your uncle's a good man, Stacey, but I won't have him cutting into my eye. I can't chance being blind."

"But you don't know that would happen."

"And I don't know that it wouldn't."

He sat with his head in one hand, his elbow perched on a raised knee. The pain was nearly gone, but his vision had not cleared.

Stacey put a tentative hand on his shoulder. He turned his head to face her. He knew she was there, but he could not see her. Dawn was approaching, yet the only thing he could distinguish in his foggy world was the fire six feet away. Would this be the scope of his vision from now on? He forced the thought from his mind.

Stacey's hand touched his face. Damn, she was so close. So very close.

Without conscious thought his arm circled her waist, and he drew her to him. She did not resist. His lips found hers. She returned the passion he gave her measure for measure. Her arms flew around his neck. His kisses grew harder, more demanding.

His need for her was a hard force inside of him. He traced the contours of her body with his hands, hesitantly at first, then when she arched against him, more boldly. Her mouth was warm and welcoming beneath his own. Steele's heart pounded. With his right hand he gently caressed her hair. Her whole body shuddered beneath his touch.

He stopped kissing her long enough to glide his fingers ever so softly around the fine lines of her face. It was a way to see her without his eyes. He wanted to take her here and now. And if Curtis hadn't been present, he might have. Maybe he could rid himself of his growing obsession with her by bedding her, having his fill of her body. It was a cruel thought, but he felt cruel when he wondered if she returned Ross Merrick's kisses with the same ardor.

"No," he whispered, denying it fiercely, but wondering just the same. He kissed her again.

Stacey, felt as though she could drown in the

enveloping warmth of his embrace. Why couldn't it always be so between them? She longed for a fulfillment she had known but once. He could be so gentle, so caring. She wanted desperately to believe that his motives were more than simply lust. She searched his face hoping to find something else, some tiny flicker of feeling for her. When she did not, she pulled away.

Steele felt her stiffen, but could detect no reason for it. He took it as rejection and released her. Maybe she had thought of Merrick too. His shoulders straightened, pride taking over.

"I'm sorry," he snapped. "I forgot Merrick had prior possession."

She slapped him. Hard. She leaped to her feet and walked stiffly to stand beside her uncle, who was returning with the horses. Why had she let it happen? Why had she let him hurt her yet again? Would she never learn?

Steele lay back, his thoughts muddled by the growing fear that he might be permanently blind. The added turmoil of these last few minutes with Stacey did nothing to ease his mind. Frustration lay heavily on him. He'd be better off to be done with Spring Canyon. Done with Barnett and Merrick. And gone and done with Stacey Hamilton.

CHAPTER EIGHTEEN

Stacey mounted behind her uncle. She still felt stiff and sore, but riding was better than walking. Joshua was slumped forward in his saddle. She'd watched him grope his way aboard the horse. He could make out only the barest light and was virtually blind. Sam wanted to get him back to the office as quickly as possible. She yearned to comfort him, to apologize for striking him, but his words had stung too deeply.

When they were within sight of Spring Canyon, Sam reined to a halt. Stacey had been pulling Joshua's horse along behind them. The gelding stopped when Sam's horse stopped. The sun had been up for over two hours.

"Do you think Rube is out with a posse looking for us?" Stacey asked.

"There's only one way to find out," her uncle said. "I'll go in first, alone."

"Rube's going to be boiling mad."

"No doubt." Curtis frowned. He had to get the sheriff to let him take Steele to his office. The man needed medical help.

Out of Steele's earshot, Sam asked his niece, "Do you think you could get Randolph to drop the charges against Josh?"

It occurred to her how impossible that might be. Then a thought came to her. "Maybe," was all she would say.

"I'll head in," Sam said. "If Rube is in town, I'll have everything explained to him. If he isn't, we'll take Josh right to the house.

Stacey agreed. She slid off the back of her uncle's horse. Joshua remained mounted. He did not extend a hand for her to mount behind him. She gathered the reins and began walking the horse toward town.

"What in the name of hell?" Rube Tucker roared, when he caught sight of Sam Curtis heading toward his office. "Do you know I been out since ten last night scouring this countryside for you and that niece of yours? She busted my prisoner out of jail. Can you believe that? Why, if my horse hadn't thrown a shoe I'd still be out there!" Tucker's words ran together as he railed at Curtis about everything at once.

"Calm down and I'll tell you all about it, Rube," Curtis finally interrrupted.

"Calm down? Your niece broke loose an attempted murderer!" Tucker watched Curtis' face and couldn't help relaxing a little. "Now I know she's got a feeling for Josh. And I like Stacey a lot, Sam. But she can't be breaking prisoners out of my jail."

Curtis grabbed the sheriff by the arm and aimed him back into his office. When Sam had finished telling Tucker of Barnett's kidnapping and eventual escape, the sheriff's anger had changed to fury. Not at Joshua and Stacey any longer, but at Barnett.

"He put a hand on that girl and he'll hang! By God, he'll hang!"

"They've no doubt gotten each other loose by now," Curtis said through thin lips, still blaming himself for the outlaws' escape. "Maybe you could send some men out to look for them."

"You can bet I'll be doin' that!"

"What about Josh? He's in a bad way, Rube," Curtis continued. "It's that eye of his. I saw it act up for myself. He could scarcely tell you his own name. He's a strong man, Rube, but it had him doubled over. The pain is gone now, but he still can't see clearly yet. I'm hoping it will clear itself up, but I want to take him to my office and do another examination."

Tucker shook his head regretfully. "Randolph was in here just a few mintues ago, screaming to break all hell loose about Steele's escape. You can be sure I didn't mention Stacey's part in it. There'd have been no shutting him up them. I tell you, Sam, I'm beginning to wonder a little about Martin Randolph myself. I've been doing a little digging into his past, and, I shouldn't be telling you this, but there are some things that just don't add up. Right now it's all too circumstantial for any legal action on my part."

Tucker sighed. "Hell, I don't want Josh going back into that cell any more than you do, Sam. I like the man. But legally there's nothing I can do about it. You can bet it'll snow in hell before you could get Randolph to drop the charges against him."

"Stacey's going to talk to him," Sam said. "She and Josh should be on their way in right now."

Tucker and Curtis walked outside the office in time to see Stacey tie Steele's horse to the hitchrail in front of the jail. A crowd was beginning to gather.

Steele gritted his teeth and dismounted. The

thought of being guided around grated on him like a physical pain. But his vision had made no progress. He knew the sun was out, but that was all he knew.

"Are you going to give me any trouble?" the sheriff demanded, making his voice gruff in spite of his sympathy for Steele.

"No," Steele said.

"Come on inside then."

Joshua didn't move. Without being obvious Stacey gently touched his elbow, nudging him in the right direction. He would have been grateful, if he hadn't been so angry.

Inside, the lawman fetched his keys. Stacey let go of Joshua's arm in front of the cell door. He stepped inside. Tucker clanged the key in the lock.

The sheriff's gaze hung on Steele for a moment as Joshua felt his way to the back of the cell, found the cot and laid down. A damn shame, Tucker thought frowning. With a sigh he escorted Stacey back to the front office.

She fidgeted next to her uncle. Joshua had not said a single word to her on the ride into town. He had remained sullen and withdrawn, since their passionate embrace had ended with his insulting remarks.

"Can't you let him go over to Sam's office, Rube?" Stacey pleaded.

"Sam can examine him right here."

"Rube," Stacey couldn't meet his eyes, "Rube, I'm sorry about last night. I just didn't know any other way. Barnett said he would kill Sam."

"It's my fault, Stacey," Tucker conceded. "For not believing you earlier when you said your uncle was in trouble. I should have known better."

Stacey smiled at him, grateful that he wasn't angry. She walked back and looked into the cell, where Joshua still lay stretched out on the cot. Heaven knew he could use the sleep. He'd saved her life and Sam's no matter what he now thought of her personally. She could never repay him for that. But she could try to make it up to him somehow. She would talk to Martin.

"I'm going to head back to the office," Sam told her. "I'll just leave Josh sleep awhile."

"Fine," Stacey said. "I'll be home later. I'm going to have that little talk with Martin."

"Good luck," her uncle called after her, knowing she was going to need it.

"Never! Never would I allow that animal out of jail!"

"Martin, please, at least listen to why I'm asking." Stacey struggled against the urge to slap Martin Randolph right in the mouth. His arrogance grated on her more all the time. How could she convince this pompous ass that Joshua didn't deserve years in prison for a mistake?

"Martin, he saved my life. He saved Sam's life. And as for what happened between you and Joshua, he simply mistook you for someone else. He doesn't deserve prison for that."

"You don't know anything about the man," Randolph seethed. Steele hadn't mistaken him for anyone. He wanted the man locked up. Yet, he thought suddenly, how long would Steele be in prison for attempted murder? A few years at best.

Those years might give him the time to establish a

new identity elsewhere, but he didn't want to leave behind his role as Martin Randolph. He had finally found his niche. He was cultivating everything he needed right here in Spring Canyon, though Danton Seaverman, the territory's financial wizard, had yet to get back to him on any land investment opportunities. But he was certain he would hear from the man any day now.

Besides when Steele got out of prison, he would no doubt return to finish what he had started. Perhaps it would be better to put an end to it now. If he had Steele released, it would further raise his own stature in the community. Forgive and forget. Randolph knew Steele would come for him again, but this time he would be ready.

Steele would never attack him again as he had the first time. It was a flaw in Steele's character; he really wasn't the murdering type. Next time the fool would probably give him an even chance.

It was Randolph's intent to make Steele look like a cold blooded maniac, harassing one of Spring Canyon's finest citizens. The whole town would be against his ex-compatriot. When Randolph killed Steele, everyone in town would believe it was self-defense. Even if it wasn't.

Martin Randolph, vis-a-vis Ross Merrick, continued to listen to Stacey Hamilton's pleas. He had already made up his mind, but he couldn't make it look too easy. He didn't want her getting suspicious. Finally, after she started to cry, he decided it was time.

"Stacey," he said softly, putting his arm around her shoulders, "it's all right. I can understand your debt to the man. It was a mistake on his part, of course, to attack me like that. I'm not this Merrick person. But we can't have him sent away for a mistake. I'll drop the charges."

He kissed her, deeply, insultingly. It was all Stacey could do to keep him from seeing how revolted she was. Her response was as much pretense as she could manage. She had to do it, lest he change his mind about Joshua.

Steele still couldn't believe he was a free man. The sheriff had let him out of his cell just minutes before, but only on the condition that he give his word not to murder Martin Randolph. That was no problem, he'd conceded to himself. He'd be willing to give Merrick an even chance, then he'd kill him. But why had Merrick dropped the charges? Somewhere there had to be a good reason in it for him. The man never did anything unless it was to his own advantage.

Physically, Steele felt much better. Thankfully, too, his eyesight was returning to normal. He wondered if Sam was any closer to knowing what the underlying cause of the problem was. He might head over to Curtis' later. Under no circumstances could he allow an operation, though. Not with Barnett and Merrick both waiting to get him in their gunsights. Besides, he wondered how many doctors were actually qualified to operate on a man's eyes. He liked Sam, but he couldn't take that kind of chance. He shoved through the batwing doors of the Gold Eagle Saloon. For the moment a stiff drink sounded good.

He put his money on the bar and ordered a bottle and a shot glass. Rance Dawson was nowhere to be seen. Steele crooked a smile. The saloon owner had probably seen him come in and dove under a table. He had been a little rougher than necessary on the man. He could have gotten his point across without the gun in Dawson's face. But it had not been one of Steele's better days.

A red-headed woman approached him at the bar. Too much make-up hid what would have been an attractive face, were it not for the hardness in her blue eyes. She had probably been in this business a long time. A smile that didn't quite make it to those eyes greeted him.

"But me a drink?" she queried hopefully.

"Help yourself," he said, pushing the bottle toward her on the bar.

She took in the lean, hard length of him. A good looking one for a change. Business had been slow lately.

"Thanks." She poured each of them a drink.

He looked at the whiskey and then at the woman. Long unheeded hungers edged their way to the surface. He wondered if a night with this woman would end his excessive awareness of Stacey Hamilton.

"What's your name?" he asked.

"Martha." She slid her hand into the crook of his arm. "You can call me Martie." She rubbed her body suggestively along his. "We could go upstairs. It's a lot quieter. More private, if you get my meaning."

"Lead the way," Joshua said. He set his glass back on the bar and allowed her to lead him up the stairs. He wondered suddenly why he felt like a foolish inexperienced boy. This wouldn't be the first time he had partaken of the favors of a prostitute. He grinned inwardly. It might be the first time he'd ever had to pay for the privilege. For some reason he didn't feel very amorous all at once.

Martie opened the door to her sparsely furnished room. Steele stepped inside. She closed the door and hurried over to her bed. She turned toward him and smiled overbrightly, "You are a handsome one." Her eyes narrowed. "Are you going to hurt me?"

Joshua's brows knitted together. "Am I going to what?"

"Oh, it's okay if you are," she said quickly. "But I charge extra."

"Oh, for the love of . . ." He turned to leave.

"No, please, wait . . . I didn't mean to make you mad. Please, I'm sorry. Don't go!"

She pushed the straps of her gown down over her shoulders. "Would you unhook me?" she asked, giving him a tentative smile.

Joshua unfastened the back of her dress. Martie wriggled out of it, letting it lie in a heap on the floor. Her chemise followed. She turned to face him.

His eyes trailed slowly over her body. Her skin was soft in places where it might have been firm, but her breasts were full, her nipples already stiff and erect. Her lips were slightly parted. She gripped his hand and led him to the bed.

She pulled him down beside her. "Touch me," she breathed. "Please, I need to be touched."

She was a woman who made her living by knowing how to please a man. Her hands were all over him, opening buttons, caressing his skin, kissing him, touching him. She tugged off the last of his clothes, eyeing his manhoood with obvious pleasure.

"I knew you'd be a fine one," she sighed.

He looked into Martie's blue eyes and was surprised to find them green. Her red hair had been transformed to the color of the sun. He swore softly.

"What did you say?" Martie asked.

"Nothing." He reached for her, gathering her in his arms, eager for the heat that would fire his loins. He felt himself stiffen. What woman made no difference! He kissed her. Eyes like green fire. He caressed her flesh with his hands until she begged him to take her. Stacey . . . Stacey. Her image was like a curse on him. He could not separate her from the woman lying next to him in this bed. His body would take Martie, but his mind would not.

"Damn it to hell!" he hissed, sitting bolt upright. He swung his legs over the side of the bed and started to pull on his pants.

"What's wrong!" Martie cried. "What is it? What did I do? Please, don't go! Tell me what you want! Please!"

"I'm sorry," he snapped, then added more gently, "I'm sorry."

She scrambled off the bed and came around to kneel in front of him on the floor. "Please. It'll be on the house," she said. "I won't charge you. It doesn't happen very often that I want it any more." Tears glittered in her blue eyes.

With the tips of his fingers he touched her cheek. "I should never have come here. I am sorry." He shrugged into his shirt, then reached into his pants pocket and pulled out more money than was necessary. He pressed it into her hands, then stood up to leave.

"She's one helluva lucky woman," Martie whispered.

Joshua halted at the door. "What did you say?"

"Your woman—I hope she knows how lucky she is."

His jaw clenched. He opened the door and walked out of the room. In the darkness outside of the saloon he lit a cheroot—and cursed himself for a fool.

CHAPTER NINETEEN

Stacey stood in the open doorway gazing at her uncle with an almost motherly fondness. He was the one who was supposed to take care of her when she came out west. His letter had insisted on it, in fact, when she'd written him of her mother's death. But instead it seemed she was the one taking care of him. Not that she minded. She doted on him. His kindness, and most of all, his understanding of her own desires to be a doctor captured her heart immediately. He accepted her, as many men would not. And for that she had been only too happy to cook his meals and clean the house. Now Molly had taken on many of those chores. She smiled, knowing that without Molly and herself, the place would be a shambles and Sam would never taste a home-cooked meal.

Sam had already dug through piles of old medical journals. In each one he flipped to the table of contents. He looked through dozens of back issues of Ewall's and the New England Journal of Medicine. Magazines were scattered everywhere.

"Are you looking for something in particular, Sam?" Stacey asked, coming over to the roll-top desk. Her uncle's absent-mindedness was legend.

"I certainly am, my dear. I could swear there was

an article, I think it was in Lancet, or was it Ewall's
. . ." he mumbled something further but Stacey didn't
catch it. "Really, my dear, I'm beginning to worry
about me." He chuckled. "I had a bookmark in it and
everything. I was so tired last night when I found it, I
thought I'd better wait until this morning to read it."

"A big red bookmark?" Stacey asked.

"That's the one."

Stacey pulled the magazine from the desk's top left
hand drawer. "I knew it was a mistake to attempt any
tidying up in here. I'm sorry."

Curtis smiled. "It's all right, Stacey. I'm just glad
I'm not getting as old as I thought I was a minute
ago."

They both laughed. "What's so important?" Stacey
queried. Her eyes brightened. "It's about Joshua, isn't
it?"

He thumbed to the correct page in the medical
journal and began to read quickly. Finally, Stacey
could stand the suspense no longer.

"Sam, please. What is it?"

"Post-traumatic secondary glaucoma."

"What?"

He repeated it. It sparked a memory in her. She
had read something, she couldn't put her finger on it,
but it had been years ago. Grimly, she wondered if
maybe it was her deep personal involvement in this
case that had caused a medical lapse.

"Joshua?"

"I'm almost certain of it," Sam said.

"What does the article say?" It was easier than trying to probe her memory about the obscure ailment.

"For one thing, it's one of the most excruciatingly

painful tortures known to man. The pain has driven many victims to suicide."

Sam continued reading snatches of the article aloud. "Let's see, it differs from primary or normal glaucoma because the cause is external, rather than an aberration in the body itself. A blow to the eye perhaps, causing a hemorrhage . . ."

Stacey thought again of Hector Caulfield's bullet, but she said, "Do you think it may have been the shrapnel wound Joshua mentioned? But that was so long ago, Sam."

"Certain kinds of secondary glaucoma have a dormancy period that can last as long as ten years before any real symptoms appear."

Stacey hugged her arms tight against her. Ten years. It could have been Caulfield's bullet then, just as easily as the shrapnel wound. She realized she would never know.

Quickly she scanned the article. The symptoms matched exactly. She damned herself for not thinking of it long before now. The magazine was over six years old. "This is really it, isn't it, Sam?"

Curtis walked over to the window of his office and gazed out into the street. "I noticed the pressure in Josh's eye the first time I touched it. I just wasn't certain because he was so close-mouthed about those attacks of his. He made them sound almost insignificant."

"I was there, Sam, for the two previous to this last one. I think they're getting progressively worse—and lasting longer besides. He would never admit it, I'm sure, but I think he's starting to get more than concerned."

Curtis nodded. "I think he's getting damn scared. And well he should be."

"They mention a surgical procedure in the article," Stacey said, unable to keep the hope out of her voice.

"It also said that very few cases respond to surgery, and the cases that do respond—well, no one knows why." He ran a hand impatiently through his gray-white hair. "There's so much we don't know about the human body, Stacey. So much.

"I don't even know if I can do the surgery. Von Graefe's procedure is outlined here, but it's one thing to read about it, and quite another to do it. Von Graefe's been doing it since '57, but even he admits he doesn't know why it works for some patients and not for others."

Stacey sank into the chair by the desk. "Joshua's already given us his opinion on surgery anyway."

Sam grimaced. "I doubt there's any way we could convince him either."

"But the pain he suffers, Sam, how can he prefer that to at least a chance his condition could be relieved? We have to convince him. We have to!"

"I agree. Because without the operation he'll be blind. This procedure is the only chance he has at all. I can't predict when it will happen, but it will happen. And if those attacks are increasing in severity and duration, it could happen anytime now."

Tears pricked her eyes. "A man like Joshua—blind? It would kill him." She set her mouth in a determined line. "He'll have the operation, Sam."

"You know how stubborn he is."

"I can be pretty darn stubborn myself," she announced, rising to her feet, as though her uncle were not already well aware of that trait in his lovely niece. Her emerald eyes sparkled with determination. "I'm going to talk to him. Right now." With that she marched out of the house.

Sam watched her go, and suddenly it occurred to him that this time maybe his sympathies should be with Steele. In a test of pure stubbornness Stacey had few equals.

Steele heard the banging on his hotel room door and wondered for a brief moment if the place was on fire. He caught no other noises to indicate such an emergency. With his guard up, he approached the door.

"Who is it?" he demanded.

"Eustacia Hamilton. Open the door, please."

Steele did so, surprise showing in his gray eyes.

"Eustacia, eh?" he mocked. It wasn't often she used her full name.

"Never mind," she said primly. "I want to have a talk with you, if you have a moment."

"By all means," he said, curiosity overriding the stinging conclusion of their last conversation. "Would you like me to leave the door open? I wouldn't want anyone to suspect the motive of this visit. Unless, of course, the motive is suspect." He cocked an eyebrow at her.

"Shut the door," she flared. "I could not possibly care less what anyone thinks." She was angry, but mostly at herself, for letting this man upset her so. Why couldn't she be in the same room with him without getting weak in the knees? "Well, can I talk to you or not?"

Determined that she would not toy with his senses this time, his voice nevertheless softened towards her when he spoke. "Sit down. Please." He indicated the only chair in the room, a spare looking cane-back with most of the cane missing.

Since the only other place to sit was on the bed, Steele remained standing. Stacey found looking up at him from the chair disconcerting. Yet she couldn't trust herself to stand.

"Would you sit down, too? Please?" she asked, realizing that he would have to sit on the bed opposite her. Well, so what, she thought vehemently, it's only a place to sit!

Steele sensed how uncomfortable she was, and he weighed that against how uncomfortable he was going to be sitting on that bed with her in the room. Damn, he thought, doesn't she know how dangerous this little game of hers is. Abruptly he sat down, his emotions under tight rein.

Stacey squirmed in her chair. She had come storming over here armed with all sorts of logical reasons about why Joshua had to submit to her uncle's surgery. And now every one of them seemed to have fled her mind. All she was conscious of now was the pounding of her heart, and how much she longed for Joshua to simply crush her in those powerful arms of his—to hold her and never let go.

"I had to talk to you," she began haltingly. "It's very important. But I'm not quite sure how to go about it. You have such a nasty temper that I'm hesitant to even broach the subject."

Her assertion mollified him somewhat. Her allusion to his temper, in light of her own, he found quite amusing.

"Please, continue," he said, "I promise not to throw anything."

He was mocking her as always, but at least he had promised to be civil. She spoke rapidly. "Sam believes he's discovered the cause of your eye problem. He thinks it's definitely connected to that shrapnel wound you had several years ago. Or maybe," she said grimly, "to Caulfield's bullet." She hurried on before he could interrupt, "Some cases can be cured by an operation, Joshua, and Sam and I both think you should have that operation." She sat back, waiting for the explosion.

Instead Steele merely said, "I will not discuss it with you."

"Why not?" she demanded, her temper flaring at his apparent disinterest.

"It's really none of your business, Miss Hamilton. If that's all you came to say, I have things to attend to."

Stacey rose, fury adding heightened color to her cheeks. God, she was beautiful, he thought. He couldn't suppress a grin, which she misunderstood.

"Do you have to look at me like that?" she snapped.

"Like what?"

"Like a wolf at a lamb!"

His laughter filled the room.

"I don't find anything particularly funny," she said. Why did he have to be so infuriating? She was doing her best to be professional about this.

"Oh, Stacey," he said, continuing to laugh with genuine warmth, "of all the animals on this planet I might have likened you to, a lamb would not have been one of them."

"And why not?"

Still chuckling he said, "Because, my dear, a lamb is a defenseless, shy, innocent creature, and you are most certainly none of those things!"

Her throat constricted. Hot tears stung her eyes. "You of all men would know that, wouldn't you?" she cried.

The laughter in his eyes died. "What the hell are you talking about?" He stood up and gripped her arms. "I asked you a question." His gray eyes were dark as night. He glowered down at her, until her lower lip trembled. She tried mightily, but she couldn't hold back the tears a second longer.

"Oh, for God's sake," he snapped, thrusting her away from him. "I would have thought that little female trick beneath you, Miss Hamilton.

She sank back into the chair, sobbing softly. "I'm sorry. I didn't mean to."

Joshua threw up his arms in exasperation. It wasn't like her to be so capitulating. "All right, I apologize," he said. "You are a lamb."

"No, I'm not."

"Okay, you're not." He pulled her roughly to her feet. "You're a woman, and a very lovely one at that."

She refused to meet his eyes, until he tilted her chin back and forced her to look at him.

"Why did that upset you so?" he asked softly.

Her cheeks burned with embarrassment. Obviously he had not meant it the way she had at first thought he did. But how could she tell him . . .

"Why does it bother you that I can't think of you as an innocent little lamb?" His eyes were warm, caressing.

"It doesn't matter."

"It does."

"I . . . I, please, Joshua . . ."

"Tell me."

"I just thought . . . I mean . . . I thought you were making some sort of snide reference . . ."

His eyes narrowed.

"You talked about the lamb being innocent . . . I mean . . ." She wanted to pull away from him and run from the room, but his grip only tightened.

"You thought I was referring to your virginity?" he asked, his voice very quiet.

"I'm sorry. You weren't. I know that now. I . . . I'm sorry. Oh, God, Joshua, let go of me." She struggled against him, terrified to meet his eyes.

"Do you really think so little of me?" His voice was expressionless.

"Of course not! I mean . . . oh, Joshua, I don't know what I mean. I came over here to ask you about the surgery . . ."

She was in his arms, his mouth crushing hers. He kissed her with a fierce anger at first, that gradually subsided as she molded herself against him.

No! she thought wildly. This can't happen. Not again. But even as she thought it, she was surrendering to the slow, torturous movements of his hands. She did not protest when he lifted her into his arms and carried her to the bed.

"It's been so long, Stacey. Too long." As he undressed her, it was as though he paused to worship each tiny fraction of her body. He memorized every line, every curve—kissing, caressing, teasing, touching, knowing. For the briefest instant Ross Merrick rose in his thoughts, and he wondered if she had surrendered to him as completely as she was doing now. But he banished the thought. Nothing was going to spoil this moment, not for either of them.

She writhed beneath him, whimpering with longing. She wanted him so badly, that not having him was like a physical torment she could no longer endure.

"Joshua, please . . ."

"Hush, green eyes," he whispered, "why deny what we both want?" He spread his length on top of her.

She felt the soft mat of his chest hair brush against the tips of her nipples. The hard heat of him nuzzled against her thigh. "I want you, Joshua," she moaned. "God forgive me, I do."

"Then God forgive us both," he said, as he eased her legs apart with his knee.

She gasped with the sheer joy of it when he entered her. She was past stopping him. He was past being stopped. She met each thrust with a quivering sigh, faster, faster, until they were both swallowed by a shattering release.

For a long time she lay next to him, her palm resting against his chest. She loved to feel the beat of his heart, to know he was here with her, passionate and alive. A single tear rolled down her cheek.

He brushed it away with the tip of his finger. "What's that for?"

"I don't know."

"Another rash act by a foolish young girl?" He couldn't keep a trace of anger out of his voice.

"No!" she said fiercely, starting to jerk away from him. But his hand gripped her wrist and held her fast. "How dare you?" she choked.

"How dare I?" he mocked. "It takes two people for what just happened in this bed, Stacey."

"Do you enjoy making a fool of me?"

He let go of her wrist. "You'd better go."

She didn't turn to look at him, but she knew he watched her as she dressed. It only added to her sense of humiliation. How had this happened? Why had she let it? And how had something so joyous turned out so badly? She threw the door open and ran from the room. She heard him call to her, but she didn't stop running until she reached home.

Sam Curtis knocked on the door to his niece's bedroom. It had been more than two hours since she'd come flying in without a word, ran up the stairs, and slammed the door to her room. Even Molly hadn't been able to get her to come out. Curtis knew the reason without asking. Steele. But now she'd missed supper, and he decided it had gone far enough. He knocked again.

"Go away, Sam. Please."

"Eustacia, open this door."

She did as she was told. He could see that she had been crying.

"Oh, Sam, I just don't understand him at all!" she said. "All I wanted to do was tell him about the operation, and somehow . . . somehow . . ." She stopped. She couldn't possibly tell Sam what had happened in Joshua's room. "He wouldn't even let me explain the procedure," she finished.

"You shouldn't take it so personally, Stace," Sam chided. "I'm sure he would've told me the same thing."

How could she help but take it personally? Joshua had made love to her for the second time in her life. And she had responded as wantonly, as recklessly as she had the first time. What was her excuse now? She was no longer a frightened adolescent. She was a grown woman. But she didn't want to hurt Sam. She couldn't let him know the true reason she was so upset.

"He's a very unreasonable man, Sam," she said. "He wouldn't listen when I tried to tell him he could be blind." She sighed. "Maybe it's just that I'm a woman."

"I doubt that very much," Sam said. "I'm more inclined to think that he just doesn't want to hurt my feelings."

Stacey looked incredulous.

"I mean it. I don't think he believes I can handle the operation. Frankly, I'm not exactly positive myself. I've never done it, heaven knows. And, after all, I am just a country doctor."

Her mouth twisted as she tried to prevent a smile from forming. She didn't want to be humored out of her black mood. But at last she gave in to it and laughed.

"Oh, Sam, why haven't you told him you had a huge practice in Boston before you came west for Aunt Jenny's health?"

Sam chuckled. "Partly because I'm not sure that's what's scaring him off. We'll just have to give him a little more time. Between the two of us, we'll wear him down to a point where he'll have the operation just to be rid of us."

Stacey stood up and gave her uncle an affectionate

hug. "I love you," she said. "You're the best uncle a girl ever had."

She knew she had embarrassed him, but he was tickled, too.

"So," he asked, "are you going to the dance tonight, or are you going to stay in your room and feel sorry for yourself?"

Stacey gasped. She'd nearly forgotten it was Saturday. "I'd better start getting ready."

Curtis left her alone. A thought occurred to him. He decided to pay a visit to Joshua Steele.

CHAPTER TWENTY

Steele toed the dirt in front of him. Why he'd let Sam talk him into coming to this dance, he couldn't now understand. Stacey would no doubt be furious to see him here. He shouldn't have made love to her this afternoon, at least not have allowed it to end as it had. He hadn't had to be so rough on her about the surgery either. It was never in his mind to hurt her, yet somehow he always did.

"I don't understand where she could be, Josh," Sam frowned, as he again looked up the street. They were both standing in front of Jonas' livery, the doors of which had been gaily decorated for the evening's festivities.

"Maybe she saw me and went back home," Steele said.

Sam grinned. Joshua and his niece liked each other in spite of their repeated attempts to sabotage their relationship. Tonight he had taken it upon himself to help matters along a little bit. Joshua was an infinitely better choice than that puffed up popinjay, Martin Randolph, though Sam admitted to certain reservations about Joshua, too.

"She never misses a dance," Sam went on. "She loves them. She can be so demanding of herself

333

sometimes, studying, giving her time to people. But dancing, it's like it transforms her. She has such a fine time. It's infectious. Even Randolph can be halfway tolerable."

At the mention of the banker's name, Sam watched Steele's face darken. "Now don't go getting moody on me," he said. "Ah, here she comes."

Stacey spotted her uncle at the same time he saw her. She waved a greeting. Joshua stood in the shadows of the barn door. When she caught sight of him her heart began to race madly. She tried to be angry with him, but found it impossible. How handsome he looked in his dark blue broadcloth jacket, light blue shirt and string tie.

She blushed happily. She hadn't expected to see Joshua at the dance. Had he come to see her? Her blonde hair cascaded to her shoulders, the canary silk dress she wore accenting her figure to perfection. The scooped neckline allowed for just the right touch of decolletage.

Steele's pulse quickened. Their eyes met, and for a moment all of their past animosities vanished. The sound of a rapidly approaching horse shattered the illusion.

Randolph dismounted hurriedly and swung an arm possessively around Stacey's waist before she could verbally acknowledge Joshua's presence. Under Steele's watchful glare, Randolph guided her into the center of the barn, where he quickly joined in the dancing.

It took every ounce of will Steele possessed to keep the promise he had made to Rube Tucker and not rip the life out of that breathing monster.

Curtis read Steele's inner turmoil and ushered him

away from the dancing over to a table lined with food and punch. The doctor suddenly wished the sheriff had not had to go to the county seat. He sensed this night would not end without violence.

Bill Rainey, a local rancher, called a good dance. Stacey was loving every minute of it. She and Martin whirled to the music. She had seen Joshua's face when Martin arrived, but she refused to let the temperamental gunman spoil her evening.

Randolph was in a jovial mood, and Stacey relaxed. He displayed no jealousy toward any of the other men in town, graciously allowing several of them to cut in while he and Stacey danced. Stacey was popular with both the men and the women of Spring Canyon. Even the usual gossip mill about her medical activities had ground to a halt lately.

Wives did not get jealous when she danced with their husbands. And in turn they thought she was quite generous in allowing them to dance with her dashing fiance, or so they thought of Martin Randolph.

Sam ladled a cup of punch for both himself and Joshua. Joshua made a face at its sweetness and put the unfinished cup back on the table. A thought occurred to him. He picked up a fresh glass and filled it with the fruity liquid. He started across the floor of the barn.

"Oh, Josh," Claire Jensen beamed, coming up to him, "how nice to see you again."

"It's nice to see you, too, Claire," Joshua said, his eyes moving past her to seek out Stacey.

"I haven't seen you dancing yet."

"No, not yet."

"Perhaps I could get you started."

Steele looked at the girl, then at Stacey, who was smiling warmly at some remark Martin Randolph had made to her. His eyes narrowed, his free hand involuntarily balling into a fist.

"Is something wrong?" Claire asked.

Steele forced his eyes away from Stacey. "Nothing's wrong, Claire. And I'd be honored to dance with you." He set the punch on the table. He pulled the girl into his arms as the music started up again.

"Are you really a gunfighter?" Claire asked with a trace of awe in her voice.

"No," Steele replied. Randolph and Stacey were dancing again. Steele nearly missed a step, when Randolph pulled her possessively against him.

Claire continued to rattle on, not noticing the tenseness in her dancing partner. "It's just that I've never danced with a gunfighter before. My father, bless him, would have a pure fit, if he saw me dancing with you." She wrinkled her nose. "To be truthful papa has a pure fit if he sees me dancing with most anybody. Except Mr. Randolph. Mr. Randolph's a banker, you know. For some reason papa doesn't mind me dancing with a banker." She giggled at her little joke. "You attacked Mr. Randolph, didn't you, Josh?" she prodded suddenly. "Why would you do such a thing?"

Steele grimaced. The girl was a nuisance. He hoped the dance would end soon.

"Why do you keep looking at Stacey?" Claire demanded petulantly. "Don't think I don't see you looking at her. That's one thing I certainly don't understand about Mr. Randolph. How any man can want to mary a woman who wants to be a doctor . . . I mean really. Touching diseased people and everything. Can you imagine?"

She deliberately pressed herself closer to Joshua. Her fingers caressed the back of his neck. She didn't seem to notice the exasperated look in his eyes, as she whispered in his ear, "Why, did you know that Stacey actually took a bullet out of Sean O'Brien? He's a local ranchhand. And that bullet was in his lower stomach, and I do mean lower. Doctor Sam wasn't even there. Isn't that simply scandalous?"

"Would you rather O'Brien had died?" Steele asked tightly.

"Of course not!" Claire said, "but I mean she could have waited for her uncle, or something. Don't you see what I'm saying? It was indecent, her seeing Sean like that!"

The music stopped. Steele immediately released his hold on Claire. She grabbed his arm. "They'll be playing another song in a minute."

"You'll have to excuse me, Miss Jensen," Steele said. "I'm afraid the next dance is already taken."

He removed her hand from his arm and stepped over to the refreshment table.

"Did you survive?" Sam chuckled, coming up to stand beside him.

"Barely," Steele snorted. "Does she ever shut up?"

"Not that I've ever heard." They both laughed. Curtis noticed Steele's eyes scanning the barn's interior. He smiled. "She's over by the band talking to Bill Rainey."

Joshua followed the direction of Curtis' nod and frowned ruefully when he saw Stacey. "And how did you know it was your niece I was looking for?"

"A lucky guess."

Steele grinned and picked up a fresh glass of punch. He was glad to note that Randolph was nowhere in sight.

Stacey, who had been surreptitiously seeking out Joshua, gasped in surprise when she heard his voice behind her. Smiling, she accepted the proffered punch.

"I saw you dancing with Claire," she said, remembering the pang of jealousy that had shot through her. But she had no claims on Joshua, in spite of their obvious physical attraction to one another, and she wasn't about to let him guess that she cared one whit who he danced with. "Did you enjoy yourself?"

"My ears may not stop ringing for a week," he said dryly.

She had to laugh at that. "Claire does run on a bit sometimes."

"A bit."

"Are you saving your next dance for her?"

"Actually I told her the next dance was taken." He held out his arm. "Is it?"

She hooked her arm in his. "Maybe."

He led her to a quiet corner of the barn. "First, I'd like to apologize for this afternoon.

Misunderstanding, Stacey's green eyes sparkled with instant fury. "Do you always apologize to a woman after you make love to her? Or is it just me?"

"I wasn't apologizing for that," he snapped, struggling to keep his voice low. "I was talking about not discussing the surgery with you."

Their eyes locked for long seconds, neither willing to back down. Finally, Stacey let out the breath she'd been holding. "I'm sorry," she said, though there was little contriteness in her voice.

"Why do all of our conversations end up like this?"

"You noticed that, too," she sighed. "All right, Joshua, I accept your apology about the operation. Maybe I'm the one who should apologize to you. I had no right to press you into something you obviously don't want. It doesn't make any sense, but . . ." She stopped herself. "I'm sorry, there I go again. It's just that . . ." Exasperated, she finished simply, "I'm sorry."

Joshua smiled. "We're a strange pair, Stacey."

She smiled back. "I can't argue with that."

The band struck up another tune. Joshua bowed at the waist, "Would you honor me with this dance, Miss Hamilton?"

She curtsied demurely, "I'd be delighted, Mr. Steele."

Randolph had been talking to Mrs. VanderPrice, a woman whose husband could be as influential with his eventual political bid as Danton Seaverman. He did not notice Steele talking with Stacey. When the dancing started again, he looked for her. He wanted to be seen dancing with her several times tonight, lest people forget she was his woman.

Anger washed over him, as he turned to see Stacey on the dance floor securely wrapped in the embrace of Joshua Steele. His blue eyes twitched menacingly, as he watched her smile up at Steele with the doe eyes of a lovesick schoolgirl. Steele's gaze at her was anything but platonic. What would the town think of his woman consorting with a man who had tried to murder him? To avoid an embarrassing confrontation, he would wait for the dance to end, then he would put a stop to her disgraceful behavior once and for all.

Stacey felt as if she were floating. Just the touch of Joshua's hand in hers made her whole body tingle. She prayed it wasn't obvious to him. Why did everything have to happen in extremes with this man? Either she was rapturously happy or desperately miserable. The happy moments were those rare times when she had managed to burrow past the hard, cold exterior he presented to the world to reach the gentler side of him he'd all but buried. Yet when she did touch that part of him, he reacted almost like a wounded animal, instinctively protecting his own savage bitterness. She suspected it was a gesture of self-defense. His hatred for this man Merrick had driven him so hard, for so long, that to abandon it now would mean admitting he had wasted irretrievable years of his life.

"Stacey?"

She started at the insistent tone of Joshua's voice, then realized he must have spoken her name several times before she heard it. "I'm sorry," she said, "did you say something, Joshua?"

He sighed. "You seemed a million miles away for a moment there. Aren't you enjoying the dance?"

She was surprised that he almost sounded hurt. "I'm enjoying the dance very much," she said. "I was just daydreaming a little, I guess." Her heart pounded as she met his gaze. His gray eyes were dark with desire. She felt her body's quivering response and knew it had not gone unnoticed by him.

When the dance ended, he put his hand in hers and led her outside the barn.

"It's a lovely night," she said, suddenly nervous. She looked up at the star-studded sky.

"Um hmm, lovely," he agreed. He was not looking at the sky. He put his arm around her waist and drew her to him.

She wanted to resist, her heart telling her there was no future in this for her. Not as long as he held to his vengeful purpose. But he was holding her against him, and she was lost to the sweet warmth of his body touching hers.

When had it happened? she wondered. When had she fallen completely and irrevocably in love with him? It was the only explanation for such illogical behavior. He had hurt her time and time again, and yet when he held her, kissed her, touched her like this, she was in a paradise of their own making. This was the Joshua Steele she loved. The one he fought so hard to bury. And as long as he did that, she knew he would never be free to care for her. No matter how much it hurt her now, it would hurt her more later. She would have to put an end to what little relationship they had and soon, before it left her without even a memory to cherish.

But not just yet, she thought slowly, languidly, not just yet. His mouth covered hers, the searing sweetness of his lips driving all other thought from her brain.

Joshua kissed her long and deeply, his mouth alternately tender and savage. Try as he might to put her from his mind, his body would not be swayed. He felt the spreading tightness in his loins.

"Take your filthy hands off her, gunslinger."

Randolph's voice was low and menacing. He stood about two feet behind Steele. Though he hadn't meant to be overheard, something about the tone of his voice caused several other voices near them to be stilled. Their stillness in turn led to a general stillness throughout the barn.

Randolph decided to use the town's attention to his own advantage. This would be a defense of his honor. Steele had dared to kiss Stacey, the woman the town acknowledged as Randolph's future wife. He grinned slyly. This might be his chance to get rid of Steele once and for all.

Stacey trembled at the look on Joshua's face as his boundless hatred for the man edged its way to the surface. This was the part of him he nurtured with such care, the part of him that frightened her because she sensed what he did not—the power it had to destroy him.

He pushed her abruptly away from him. He had promised Rube Tucker not to harm Randolph, but now he was being challenged directly. She knew he would not let the challenge go unanswered. The sheriff could not blame Joshua if Martin provoked the encounter. A malevolent smile formed on Steele's lips, his eyes mirroring the depths of his barely controlled rage. He turned his back to Stacey. Fists clenched he advanced toward Randolph.

"I'm going to tear you apart, Steele," Randolph said.

"You can try," Steele returned softly. His body was tense with excitement. He was going to enjoy this. His muscles ached for the fight to begin.

Stacey overheard several of the people from the

barn murmuring in disgust over the whole incident. She noted her name being liberally sprinkled in their conversations. No doubt they sided with Martin. She shouldn't have accepted Joshua's invitation to dance. But she had wanted it so much. These people were supposed to be her friends! She shook her head sadly and followed the crowd to the middle of the street.

The townsmen had formed a ring about the two soon-to-be combatants. At least Martin hadn't challenged Steele's gun, Stacey thought gratefully. Martin was as strong as an ox, but he was no gunman. Joshua had the edge in height of maybe four or five inches, but Martin might have an advantage because of Steele's recent gunshot wound. And his eye. Stacey gasped. Oh, god, what if Joshua should receive a blow to the head? He had been lucky in his fight with Barnett.

Forgetting all sense of decorum she raced out to the center of the ring of men. Steele and Randolph were squaring off to begin the battle. Both had removed their jackets and rolled up their shirtsleeves. Stacey stared at Joshua's scarred wrists, almost feeling the pain that had put them there. She forced her eyes away. She looked at Martin. His face was pinched and nervous. Joshua's was hard and implacable. He looked almost too calm.

"Stacey, get out of here," Randolph muttered. "This is none of your affair.

"Yes, Miss Hamilton, please get out of the way. Your friend is anxious to get started." Joshua watched her face. He couldn't decide whose side she was on.

Stacey stepped up to him. "Joshua, please, don't do this. Martin is just angry. Let it be."

She couldn't mention the eye to him for fear Martin would overhear. It struck her then that she wasn't surprised that Martin would use such information without conscience, that if he knew Steele's weakness he would attack it like a lobo wolf after a stricken elk.

"Please, Joshua."

Steele took her words to mean that she feared for Merrick's safety. He stiffened, but said nothing.

Stacey turned to Randolph. "Martin, please, it was just a dance. It isn't worth brawling over. Just take me home."

"Get out of the way, Stacey," Randolph growled. "It wasn't just a dance. You think I didn't see what was going on between you two *after* the dance? You throw yourself at this . . . this trash, and you expect me to accept it gracefully? You're my woman, and I won't have it!"

Stacey blushed furiously. She felt hot tears well up in her eyes, but she fought them back. She shocked herself by her sudden urge to hit Martin herself. "Don't you dare call me your woman, Martin," she snapped. "I am the property of no one!"

"Let's get this over with," Steele broke in, his fury further kindled by Merrick's attack on Stacey's character.

Sam Curtis stepped inside the ring of spectators and gently pulled his niece to one side. She whispered urgently to him, "Sam, if Martin hits Joshua in the head, couldn't it injure his eye further?"

"Not necessarily. It would have to be a direct blow, and I think Josh is too cagey for that."

Stacey wasn't convinced. She wanted to run home and forget this was even happening, but she found she couldn't take her eyes off the two men.

Merrick was circling warily, looking for an opening. He didn't doubt his own strength, but he knew Steele would be driven by overwhelming hatred. Yet that could make him careless.

Steele refused to make the first move. He kept baiting Merrick by feinting a move one way then the other. Merrick was getting frustrated.

"Damn you!" he roared. "Do you want this fight or not?"

Finally Merrick proved overanxious and plunged in to land the first blow. Steele moved to his left and avoided it, countering with a savage right uppercut that connected solidly with Merrick's head. The punch scarcely fazed the wiry banker. Shaking his head, he drove at Steele with a body pounding blow to the mid-section. Steele, shielding his head, was forced to back off a couple of paces. He attempted a right cross that missed, but recovered quickly and slammed in with a left that caught the oncoming Merrick squarely in the gut.

Merrick staggered, the wind momentarily knocked out of him. His anger mounted, but his wariness increased as well. Steele was a worthy adversary as always. Parrying his blows, Randolph danced around waiting for Steele to let his guard down. What was it he had heard Stacey say once about Steele's eye? Was something wrong with it? Merrick was about to find out.

Accepting the punishing blows from Steele's fists, Merrick forged closer to the big man. Scarcely measuring his punches, he rallied everything behind trying to get to Steele's head.

Stacey saw Martin's change in tactics and knew instinctively what he was trying to do. Steele sensed his enemy's ruthless mission at the same time. He redoubled his efforts to put an end to the fight with one telling blow. But Merrick would not be denied. Ducking his head with unexpected suddenness he plowed his body into Steele sending the big man reeling on his back in the dirt. Merrick landed on top of him, set himself, and with chopping blows tried to cut his way past Steele's protective arms.

Steele, temporarily stunned, merely tried to survive Merrick's onslaught long enough to get out from under him. Drawing on a reserve of sheer will, he slugged a tremendous right at the attacking Merrick. The blow did not connect solidly but it was enough to shove the banker off Steele's body.

Merrick scrambled to his feet, but he was not quite quick enough. Steele was already up. He landed a solid left to Merrick's chin as the banker struggled to rise. The blow sent Merrick to his hands and knees in the dirt. His fingers closed around the sandy soil. Staggering unsteadily, he waited as Steele moved in for another punch. With the swiftness of a snake Merrick heaved the dirt directly in Steele's face.

Steele reacted instinctively. His arm shot up to repel the flying sand. Some of it caught in his eyes. He blinked violently at the harsh stinging, raking his fingers across his eyes in a swift attempt to clear them.

Randolph roared in, striking a hard right to Steele's left temple before Steele could get out of his way. Steele reeled back. He sought to focus on the banker, but his vision refused to clear. A hazy figure approached him. Steele swung wildly and missed.

Stacey darted forward, but was restrained by her uncle. "Martin will kill him, Sam! Joshua can't see!"

Seeing Steele's temporary helplessness, Merrick closed in with a savage knee to the groin. Steele couldn't stifle a groan of agony. Even with the pain he still managed to hook his arms around Merrrick, as the traitor tried to back away after delivering the vicious punishment. Steele, reacting with animal instinct, judged where Merrick's head should be and delivered a brutal right and a left. Merrick went to his knees.

"I'm going to kill you, Merrick," Steele seethed between clenched teeth, his vision clearing.

Merrick looked into the eyes of his own death. His hand darted to his boot. When he brought it back up he was clutching a wicked looking knife. He heard the jeers of the crowd. He was behaving like a coward. So what, he thought, he'd rather be a live coward.

Steele's sides heaved from exertion. His eyes still burned, his head ached. Now he had the knife to contend with.

Merrick lunged forward. Steele hooked his right leg around the traitor, sending him sprawling backward. Reacting in one fluid motion, he kicked the knife from Merrick's fingers. Merrick twisted his legs, seeking to bring Steele to the ground with him. Joshua avoided the maneuver, but the split second gave Merrick a chance to gain his feet.

Steele blocked Merrick's next blow with his left arm and connected with his own savage right. Merrick slumped foward, tried feebly to rise, then collapsed. Steele's hand closed around the knife on the ground. He brought his hand around in a sweeping arc, shoving the knife against Merrick's throat.

"No!" Stacey screamed.

Steele stared at her, not understanding.

"No," she said again, so softly that if he had not been looking at her he would not have heard it. His hatred for Merrick pushed hard, but the look in Stacey's eyes stopped him as nothing else could. He released the knife, stood up and walked into the night. Curtis followed him.

The crowd parted as Steele, leaning lightly on Sam, made his way up the street. Behind them Merrick groggily returned to consciousness. A couple of men helped him to his feet, but most of those who had cheered so loudly just minutes before, now ignored him.

Steele glanced back once looking for Stacey. He did not see her. He could no longer see Merrick either. She was probably helping him home. His eyes were bitter, his face grim as he allowed Curtis to lead him.

"I'd better get you back to the office," Curtis was saying. "You could use a little bandaging here and there."

"Just take me to my hotel room," Steele said. Sam could tell by the tone of Joshua's voice that the man would brook no arguments on the subject.

Curtis got him up the hotel steps. Steele dug out the key to his room and opened the door. He was feeling more unsteady that he thought he should. He sat down on the chair next to the bed. Curtis poured water in a basin, picked up a clean towel, and carried them over to him. He set them on the table between the bed and the chair.

Several minutes passed as the doctor worked on the

cuts and bruises on Steele's face. None of them seemed significant. They would be gone in a couple of days. Still he noticed how quiet Steele had become.

"Are you all right, Josh?"

"I'll be fine. Just tired." Steele couldn't dismiss his mounting uneasiness. Curtis' face was already an indistinct blur. He couldn't afford an attack now, not when Merrick might be gunning for him because of the humiliation he'd just suffered at Steele's hands.

"It's the eye, isn't it?" Curtis wasn't really asking, he was telling.

"No, it's all right. But Joshua knew that it wasn't. The pain did not creep up on him. It struck like a Texas twister. He grabbed the side of his head and staggered out of the chair. He collapsed almost immediately. Sam reached for him.

"Josh, can you stand?" he shouted. The doctor knew he could not manage the big man by himself.

Joshua struggled to his feet. Curtis got under one of his arms.

"I'm going to get you to the office." Sam wasn't sure how much of what he said got through to Steele. The man was in agony.

Joshua said nothing. His full concentration focused on staying on his feet. He allowed Curtis to guide him from the room.

Stacey watched her uncle help Joshua from the scene of the fight. She wanted to rush after them and help, but decided that Steele probably wouldn't want to see her right now. He was too busy nursing his hatred for Martin.

She watched Randolph struggle to his feet a few

yards to her left. She wondered suddenly what she had ever seen in the man. The cold-blooded way he had attacked Joshua with the knife sickened her. Bowing to her medical instincts, she stepped over to see if he needed any help.

"Are you all right, Martin?" she asked.

"What would you care?" he seethed, brushing the dirt from his clothing.

"I was asking on a purely professional basis," she said.

Randolph glared at her. The music had begun again, and the townspeople for the most part had returned to their dancing. "What do you see in him, Stacey?" he demanded.

She ignored the question. Her relationship with Joshua was certainly none of Martin's business. "If you come by the office," she told him. "I'll take care of those cuts on your face."

"I can manage."

"Whatever you say." She turned away from him, ready to head home. She stopped when she heard Claire calling her name.

"Oh, my, wasn't it just awful, Stacey?" Claire gasped, hurrying up to her. "But kind of romantic too."

"What in the name of heaven are you talking about, Claire?" Stacey had no patience left tonight.

"Having two men fight over you like that," the girl said dreamily.

Stacey grimaced. "They weren't fighting over me, Claire," she said. "I was just the excuse." Stacey didn't bother to explain to the girl that Joshua would have used any reason to fight Martin.

"Is Martin . . . Mr. Randolph all right?" Claire asked.

"You'll have to ask him." Stacey pointed to Randolph's solitary figure. He was heading up the street toward the bank. She shook her head when Claire raced up the street after him.

"Mr. Randolph, are you all right? Can I help you?" she heard the girl ask anxiously. Stacey frowned as she watched Martin put his arm around the girl's shoulders. Martin had no use for Claire. He didn't even like her. Claire was going to have one hard lesson to learn one day.

Stacey gave herself a wry smile. Was she going to have a hard lesson to learn one day herself—at the hands of one Joshua Steele? She took a deep breath, unable to account for the sudden uneasiness that touched her. She quickened her pace as she headed for home.

CHAPTER TWENTY-ONE

"Help me get him to bed!"

Stacey gasped in horror as her uncle led Joshua into the house. It was all Sam could do to support him. Joshua's breathing was ragged and uneven as he fought the pain in his eye. He didn't seem aware of her.

Quickly she ducked under Joshua's other arm and helped Sam get him up the stairs. Hurrying ahead, she turned back the covers of her bed. Joshua bit back an agonized groan as Sam eased him onto the mattress.

Stacey placed her hand on Joshua's forehead and was alarmed to discover it hot and dry. She helped her uncle undress him, grimacing again at the sight of the mass of scar tissue that criss-crossed his back. Her uncle shooed her out of the room when he started to take off Steele's pants. Joshua had yet to say a word. As Stacey stood outside of her room listening to him hurt, she felt as if the pain ripped through her own body.

"God, help him please!" She stifled back a sob and ran downstairs, unable to bear the sounds another second.

A few minutes later her uncle joined her in his office. He sat down heavily at the oak desk.

"You're going to operate, aren't you, Sam?" she asked, standing next to him.

"Yes," His face was grim.

"Has he agreed?" She already knew the answer from her uncle's face. In spite of his agony, Joshua was still refusing his only chance for help.

"I want you to talk to him," Curtis said.

Stacey did not reply.

Sam looked directly at her. "Convince him, Stace. It's his only chance. I know he didn't listen before, but I think if he listens to anyone, he'll listen to you. Without the operation he's blind anyway. I can't say when, but it will happen. And the pain will still be there. With the operation he may still end up blind and in pain, but with Von Graefe's method there is that chance of complete success."

Stacey's mind reeled with reasons why she should be the last person to talk with Joshua. Sam read her uncertainty.

"Once he's blind, no operation can help him. His sight will be gone forever."

"He'll have the operation, Sam." Stacey's voice was low, but determined. She looked up the stairs for a long minute. If Joshua said no, she would give him enough laudanum to make him pass out and then she would tell Sam he'd said yes.

But even as she thought it, she knew she could never do it. She had to convince him. She climbed the stairs and opened the door to her room. Her heart lurched at what she saw. Joshua Steele, a strong, powerful man, lay on her bed breathing in choking gasps. His hands clutched the sides of the bed, his features contorted in the painful throes of his personal hell. He was not aware of her, though she had crossed the room to stand beside the bed.

"Joshua?" Her voice was tentative. She feared breaking his concentration against the pain, lest it would somehow overwhelm him.

With great effort Joshua opened his eyes to look at her. He could scarcely tell where she was standing. The whole room was blurred and indistinct. He hadn't thought the human body capable of feeling such pain. All he wanted to do was scream.

"It'll pass," he rasped through gritted teeth. He didn't like her seeing him like this. "Just let me lie here for awhile, and I'll be all right."

"How many hours will it last this time? Or days? Why do you do this to yourself?"

"Sam sent you up here, didn't he? Well, it won't work. I admit the pain is making me a bit more open-minded about the surgery at the moment, but I can't risk being blind. I'd be a dead man. In more ways than one. Anyway," his voice grew harsh, "what are you even doing here? I thought you'd be with Merrick." He sucked in a deep breath, as another rush of pain shot through him. "I was a fool not to kill him when I had the chance. I won't make that mistake again."

"Nothing is worth murder, Joshua. Nothing."

"You might not say that if you knew . . ." he gasped.

"Knew what?" she cried. "Tell me!"

He shook his head, his jaws clenched against the pain. "Never. Never. Not you. I could never tell . . ."

A new spasm of pain convulsed him. "Sweet Jesus!" He tore the wooden slats from the side of the bed in

354

mindless agony. Turning over he tried to bury the pain in the mattress. Nothing worked. A frustrated sob escaped his throat. An inner fury raged over his helplessness. He covered his head with his hands, pressing savagely against the offending eye.

Stacey hurried over to the dressing table and poured a dose of laudanum. She had to shout to get through to him, to get him to take it. It had no effect.

Suddenly Joshua leaped out of the bed, clad only in his underwear. He crashed into the far wall his hands wrapped around his head. He sank to his knees, his jaws locked together to keep from screaming.

Sam Curtis burst into the room. He forced more laudanum down Joshua's throat.

"Get the chloroform!" he shouted at his niece.

Stacey raced downstairs, nearly tripping over her dress. She hurried to the medicine shelves, snatching up the chloroform and a cloth. She raced back up the stairs to find Joshua still doubled over in agony.

"Hurry, Stace," Curtis said, his voice shaking.

Averting her head she sprinkled some of the sweet smelling liquid onto the cloth and pressed it over Joshua's resisting face. His tortured breathing forced him to take in the anesthetic in great deep breaths. In less than a minute he sagged limply against Sam. It took their combined strength to get him back into the bed.

"Sam, I can't bear this," Stacey sobbed. "He hurts so much." She carefully tucked the blankets under Joshua's chin.

"That's why we're operating. Right now."

"Sam, you can't. He never agreed."

She watched the indecision play across her uncle's

face. She wanted Joshua to have the surgery more than anyone, but suddenly she knew how important it was that Joshua want the surgery himself.

"He'd never forgive us, Sam. Not even if it was successful. I don't think I could live with that."

Curtis regarded his niece thoughtfully. He admitted a grudging admiration for Joshua, but the idea of his niece being in love with him was still unsettling. He knew there had been an attraction, but until this moment he hadn't realized how deeply it went, at least on Stacey's part.

"We'll wait until he wakes up then," Sam said softly. "We'll give the ethical way one more try." He shook his head in wonder at the unconscious Steele. How a man could endure such pain, yet be so apparently afraid of an operation was beyond him.

In the morning Joshua was still visibly shaken by his ordeal of the night before. His face reflected the pain he had been through. Stacey brought in his breakfast tray and set it on the night table. She wanted to speak with him before he ate.

"I don't imagaine you've ever had an attack quite as bad as yesterday's, have you?" she prompted.

"No." His reply was quiet and thoughtful. He did not look at her.

She moved closer to the bed, her heart pounding. She prayed he wouldn't resurrect the subject of Martin Randolph. She had to convince him to have the surgery. Nothing else mattered. Nothing. She sat down next to him and took his hand in hers. He did not pull away. Stacey made a great pretense of examining his fingers as she spoke.

"Would you be willing to at least talk about the

operation now, Joshua?"

He sighed heavily. "I guess I'd better."

Stacey continued to allay her own nervousness by toying with Steele's fingers. She held first one then another, until she'd gone over each of them several times. Joshua suppressed a smile, but not the pleasant feeling her touch gave him.

"First, I'd like to tell you why I think you've avoided the surgery so far," she said.

"Feel free."

"I think you're afraid."

Joshua's hand clenched, then relaxed, but he said nothing.

Stacey continued. "Not the kind of fear that makes you a coward. Heaven knows, you're not that." She blushed, and hurried on, "but I think you've seen what some doctors have done to their patients. The cure is worse than the disease. And you've decided that the pain and blurred vision are preferable to a bad operation.

"Well, you won't get a bad operation from Sam. He's one of the finest surgeons in the country. As good as my father was, and he was the best." Her eyes shone with pride.

"Is your father the only reason you wanted to be a doctor?"

She frowned. "You're changing the subject."

"Maybe. But I really would like to know what makes a woman want to be a doctor."

Stacey studied him closely for several seconds, wondering if he was mocking her again. She decided that he was not.

"What makes anyone want to be a doctor?" she

shrugged. "I was steeped in it from infancy, driving my father to distraction with questions. But the day I truly decided to become a doctor happened seven years ago in an Albany hospital. I was working as a volunteer, when one of the patients started hemorrhaging. He had a terrible wound in his leg. Dozens of wounded soldiers had arrived that day and all of the doctors were busy elsewhere. I knew what to do for the boy, so I did it. I saved his life. And at that moment I knew that being a doctor was the one thing I wanted to do with my own life." She smiled ruefully. "Even though the doctors at Albany all but had me thrown in jail for touching one of their patients. I sometimes think they would rather he had died, than have him saved by a woman."

Joshua regarded her intently. "I still sometimes picture you in that private's uniform, green eyes," he said. His free hand reached out and toyed with a stray wisp of her hair. "You know, you never struck me as a welcher."

She started. "Now what on earth are you talking about?"

"A few days ago, in this very room, you bet me a kiss that I wasn't naked in this bed."

She felt her heart pounding in her chest. "You weren't naked," she stammered.

"Are you sure about that?" he teased.

"Joshua, please." She realized she wanted him to make love to her again, but she couldn't bear the pain that always came afterwards.

The hand that had been holding his was now imprisoned by his strong fingers. She tried to rise, but he held her fast.

"You're not going to pay off your debt?"

"Listen, Mr. Steele," she said, trying to sound firm, "I came up here to discuss your having surgery, not to pay off some ridiculous wager, you all but forced on me."

"Am I forcing you, Stacey?" His gray eyes darkened with desire. He pulled her close, his arms crushing her against him. "Oh, God, Stacey," he whispered, his lips claiming hers, as his hunger for her threatened to consume him.

She tried to keep her feet on the floor, but the position twisted her waist awkwardly. She pulled her legs onto the bed, making no effort to resist his passionate embrace. Her fingers traced a bold path along his bare arms, curling possessively in the fine mat of dark hair on his chest. She felt him tense, felt his heart thudding against her palm.

This time it was her tongue which demanded entry into his mouth. She pressed herself against him, molding her body to his. She wanted an end to the tormenting ache that was spreading through her body. When his fingers tugged at the buttons of her dress, she shifted to allow him easier access to them. She longed for the searing heat of his mouth on her breasts. Impulsively, she gripped his hand, caressing the two-inch band-like scar around his wrist. She kissed it softly.

Steele didn't move for several seconds. He stared at her with eyes that burned and an aching need that tore at his heart. Again his damnable hate nudged him. No, not this time! Ross Merrick would not rise up between them this time.

"I want you, Stacey. I have to have you. I need to

have you." His voice was thick with passion.

That he at last admitted any kind of need for her at all sent a shiver of pure joy through her heart. His mouth teased her unrestrained breasts. She surrendered herself utterly to his expert touch. As always, in the sweet rapture of his embrace, she was unable, unwilling to remember her resolve to end this one-sided love affair.

She heard the noise, but it took her passion-drugged mind several seconds to identify it. Someone was knocking on the door to her room.

"What is it?" she somehow managed to call out, her voice shaking with frustration.

"Doctor Sam would like to see Mr. Steele in the office, Miss Stacey," Molly said through the closed door.

Stacey caught the nervous pitch to Molly's voice. The girl was embarrassed. Evidently the sound of Stacey's voice had been enough for her to surmise what was going on inside the bedroom. Stacey pulled herself upright. "Tell Sam he'll be right down, Molly," she said.

"I will."

Stacey heard the girl's retreating footsteps. She looked at Joshua, strangely not nearly as embarrassed as she thought she might be. His eyes still betrayed the passion he felt. "I'm sorry," she whispered.

"Not nearly as sorry as I am," he said dryly, "but I definitely take back what I said earlier."

"What's that?"

"You are not a welcher."

She smiled and leaned over to kiss him lightly on the cheek. "Paid in full," she announced.

"Maybe," he drawled.

"The operation?"

"So that was what this was all about, eh?"

She started to get angry, then caught the teasing glint in his eyes. "Will you have the surgery, Joshua?" She was deadly serious.

He took a deep breath and nodded. "Tell Sam he can have my head in his hands."

A warm smile brightened her lovely face. "You won't be sorry, Joshua. I'll go down and tell him while you get dressed." She hurried from the room.

For a long minute she stood at the top of the stairs thinking about what had just happened between Joshua and herself. It was the first time they had ever exchanged a moment's tenderness without recriminations afterward. He had been almost boyishly playful with her, and she could scarcely believe the joyous warmth she felt just being near him.

Still, he had said nothing that would let her believe that he wanted anything more than a physical relationship with her. She closed her eyes. As much as she longed to share even that much of his life, she knew it wasn't enough. He deliberately shut her out of everything else—his feelings, his dreams, even his hate for the man Merrick. She loved him, but he didn't love her. If their relationship continued as it was, she could only be crushingly hurt. It had to end. Her mind made up, she walked down the stairs. She would tell him after the surgery.

Curtis was sitting at his desk when Steele stepped into the doctor's office. The gray haired physician seemed heavily engrossed in some sort of magazine article.

"Sam?"

Curtis nearly jumped out of his chair.

Steele gave him a wry grin. "Sorry."

"It's all right. I was just going over the technique for your operation." Curtis laid his spectacles on the magazine and looked gravely at Joshua. "I'm glad you decided to go ahead with it."

Steele shrugged fatalistically. "Just what are you proposing to do to me anyway?"

"It's called an iridectomy. Von Graefe first used the procedure in '57." Curtis drew a hurried diagram on a sheet of paper. "I'll make an incision, kind of like a triangle, at the top of the eyeball."

Steele winced visibly, but said nothing.

"To be perfectly honest with you, it works in some cases, but not all. And when it does work, nobody knows why. At least not yet."

"That sounds encouraging." Joshua couldn't keep the edge out of his voice.

"It's the only chance you have," Curtis replied quietly. "It either relieves the pressure, or it doesn't. If it doesn't work, well, hopefully you're no worse off than before. Except that eventually you will be blind."

Steele took a deep breath. He looked at Sam for a long moment, considering the amount of trust he would be putting into those hands of his. He walked to the office door and put his hand on the knob. Without turning he said, "Will tomorrow morning be all right?"

"Fine." Curtis sensed the turmoil going on inside the man.

Steele walked out of the office.

It was nearly ten p.m. when Stacey closed the

medical journal in front of her. She had the procedure she and Sam would use on Joshua in the morning committed to memory, backwards and forwards. Anxiously, she stared at the street outside. Sam should have been home by now. She wanted him to get plenty of sleep tonight. Joshua's surgery would be very delicate, very precise. If anything went wrong . . .

The door to the office slammed open. Stacey stared at her uncle's pain streaked face. "Sam, my God, what is it?" Then she noticed he was holding his right hand in his left. "Oh, no! Oh, no! Not your hand. Sam, what happened?"

"Is Josh awake?" Sam gritted.

"No, he's asleep upstairs. Sam, please, tell me . . ." He uncovered the injured hand for his niece. "Oh, my God," she whispered, staring at what she immediately recognized as two broken fingers, maybe three. "Joshua's surgery?"

"I can't possibly do it now," Sam muttered, fierce disappointment evident in his voice. "That damnable Garth Greevy. He was drunk, fell off his horse and broke his arm. I was in the process of setting it when he sent me flying across the room. Landed square on my hand."

He shook his head in self-contempt. "I should never have listened to that old fool. He refused the laudanum, saying it was for old women. He could take the pain." Sam laughed mirthlessly. "The second I touched his arm, he lit into me. What in heaven's name am I going to tell Josh?"

Stacey's voice trembled. "It could take weeks before that heals enough for the kind of surgery he needs."

"I know."

Stacey busied herself, gathering bandages and splints. "Sam, I don't know if he could bear another attack like the one he had yesterday. I don't know if I could."

"There could be several more attacks before I could operate, any one of which could blind him permanently."

"Sam, what are we going to do?" she half-sobbed, as she mechanically tended to her uncle's injury.

He sucked in a sharp breath, his face paling, when she snapped the two broken digits back into place. "I wish you would tell a person, when you're going to do that," he grimaced.

"Sorry." She splinted the fingers.

"I was thinking about this long and hard on the way back here," Sam said slowly.

Something about the tone of his voice made Stacey pause before tying off the bandage she had wrapped around his hand. She looked into his brown eyes and read his thoughts.

"Sam," she gasped. "I couldn't!"

"Yes, you could, Stacey, and you know it," Sam said. "You're as skilled a surgeon as I am. Your father wrote me many times during the war, praising your ability to the heavens. And I've seen your work here with my own eyes."

"When I've been able to find a willing patient or two," she put in. "But Sam we're talking about Joshua's *eye*. I've never done anything like that!"

"Neither have I, Stacey. All either of us has to go on is the procedure outlined in the journal."

"Sam, I just couldn't."

"Because of the eye—or because it's Joshua."

She didn't answer. She stepped over to the window and peered into the darkness. Finally, she said, "He would never agree to it."

"We wouldn't tell him."

She whirled to face him. "What did you say?"

"Stacey, this operation is his only chance. You know that. And he's agreed to have it."

"He's agreed for you to do it, not me."

"The subject never came up," Sam persisted.

"Sam, please, you don't know what you're asking."

Sam Curtis did something he'd never done with his niece before in his life. He lost his temper. "Dammit, Stacey. How many times have you railed at me about how no one will give you a chance to prove what a fine doctor you are? You complain, and rightly so, about their blind ignorance, but now you have the perfect opportunity to prove to all of them, once and for all, that you're a damned fine doctor, woman and all! Yet you back away from it!"

"This is not the same thing, Sam," she pleaded.

"It is!" he shouted, then lowered his voice lest he awaken Steele. "It is the same. You're a doctor, period. And you have a patient upstairs who will be blind if you don't help him."

"What if I blind him? What if I make a mistake?"

Sam walked over to his niece. He gripped her shoulders, his eyes boring into hers. "You are now the only chance he has of saving his vision."

The tears glimmering in her eyes came tumbling out. She leaned against Sam's shoulder. "I'm so frightened. Sam, this whole conversation is pointless anyway. Joshua may agree in principle to a woman's right to be a doctor, but it was all he could do to trust you to do the surgery. He would never allow me to do it."

"Like I said, he would never have to know."

"Sam, your hand is rather obviously out of commission. There is no way he wouldn't know."

Sam looked at her eagerly. "That's what I've been trying to tell you. I've got it all worked out. You get him ready for surgery in the morning, and I'll come in at the last minute with a surgical towel draped over my hand. You'll put him under, and he'll never know the difference."

"He'll see it when he wakes up!"

Sam shrugged. "We'll tell him it happened while he was unconscious."

Stacey sagged against the window. "We'll never pull this off, Sam. Never." She thought about the tenuous thread of trust that she and Joshua had somehow managed to weave this morning. A deception of this magnitude could destroy that trust forever. If he ever found out . . .

But Sam would not be dissuaded. "We have to pull it off, Stacey. Or Joshua is a blind man."

The next morning Steele watched with morbid curiosity as Stacey got things ready for his surgery. She set several instruments on the small tray next to the operating table. He had been lying there trying to relax for more than ten minutes. The problem was he had no trouble at all seeing just how nervous Stacey was, and that did little to reassure him. Maybe he should call this whole thing off. He remembered Sam's warning that he would be blind without the surgery and said nothing.

Stacey had been right about his being afraid. Not

that he would have told her so. But the idea of anyone cutting into his eye unnerved him. He had seen doctors, or at least men who called themselves doctors, commit acts of mayhem on the bodies of living men that under any other circumstances would have gotten them hanged.

She eased a cloth over his hair to keep it out of the way. He warmed to the feel of her hands on him, even under such professional circumstances. She used whiskey to disinfect the area around his left eye. The smell of the liquor made him strangely nauseated. He was surprised to find that his shoulders ached, until he realized how tensely he was holding himself.

"Where's Sam?" he asked suddenly.

Stacey jumped. "What?" She dropped several bandages onto the floor. Cursing, she picked them up and threw them into a hamper. She pulled clean bandages from a bureau drawer.

"I asked you where Sam is," said Steele, starting to sit up.

"Lie down," she snapped. "He'll be here in a minute. He had a late call last night. He's just sleeping a little later than usual."

Steele lay back. "You don't seem to have too much confidence in this whole thing."

"That's not true," she said, then sighed, "I'm sorry, Joshua. This technique is new to us. But I'm sure everything will be fine."

She poured a small amount of chloroform onto a clean cloth. "I'm going to put you out now."

"Before Sam gets here?"

"I told you, he's coming."

A hint of suspicion came into his gray eyes. He was

about to push the cloth away when the door opened.

"Good morning all," Sam called cheerfully. "Sorry, I'm late." He was carrying a large white towel draped over his right hand. He walked purposefully over to the operating table. "You look ready, Josh," he said. He stepped behind the table and plopped the towel near the clean bandages. He kept his injured hand next to the table, below Steele's eye level. "Shall we proceed?"

Stacey sprinkled more chloroform onto the cloth and stood at the head of the operating table. With her free hand she couldn't resist a reassuring squeeze to Joshua's shoulder. He arched his head back to peer at her. He managed a weak grin, but she didn't miss the fear in his gray eyes.

"Let's get this damned thing over with," he said, taking a deep breath. His body began to feel lighter, as if he were floating. He breathed again and thought he heard himself say, "It'll be a cinch." Sleep claimed him.

Sam exchanged places with Stacey, taking up the chloroform. Stacey washed her hands and arms vigorously, then Sam poured whiskey over them. She picked up the sterile scalpel. The trembling that had been in her hands all morning disappeared.

"I'm going to do it, Sam," she said fiercely. "And he's going to be just fine."

The surgery went even better than she could have hoped. With Sam's assistance they followed the procedure exactly. Joshua's eye seemed to be a textbook example of the traumatic glaucoma von Graefe described. The ultimate test, of course, would be time, but for now she was confident.

She patted another quilt around Joshua's shoulders. She hadn't left his side for a minute. His left eye was lightly bandaged.

Joshua shifted in his sleep. He moaned softly. "I think he's coming around, Sam," she said. "Get your hand out of his sight."

Steele's first conscious thought was how strange it was that he couldn't seem to open his eyes. There was a dull ache on the left side of his head, but he couldn't remember how it got there. He reached up with his left hand, probing gently at the gauzy cotton.

"Josh?" Sam Curtis' voice penetrated the fog in his brain.

"Sam, are you there?"

"Right here, Josh. You just lie still. The surgery went very well."

Surgery. Of course. Now he remembered. Fine, Sam said. Then why couldn't he see? He tried to sit up. A pair of hands pushed him gently back down.

"Sam?"

"It's all right, Joshua," Stacey assured him. "We just want you to lie here for a little while longer. We'll get you up to bed in a couple of hours."

He relaxed a little. "When will you take the bandage off?"

"In about a week or so," Sam said, "but you're not to do anything even remotely strenuous for at least two months. No lifting, no nothing. Understand?"

Steele grunted an acknowledgement. Concentrating he forced his right eye open. The room swam into focus. He smiled. He could still see. Stacey patted his shoulder. "Try to get some sleep."

He closed his eyes and was asleep almost at once.

He stayed asleep for over four hours. After she and Sam finished lunch, Stacey stopped in the office to check on their patient. He was awake, but groggy. Stacey piled the blankets to one side.

"I want you to take it real easy," she cautioned. "I'll help you up to my bed."

"Now that sounds mighty tempting, Miss Hamilton," he drawled.

"Never mind."

He staggered slightly when he eased himself off the operating table, but recovered enough to let her help him up the stairs. "Where's Sam?"

"He had an emergency," she lied.

She opened the door to her room.

"I have just got to stop using your bed, ma'am," he moaned sleepily, as she helped him into it and pulled the blankets over him.

"You get some rest," Stacey said shortly, but she was amused.

Joshua was asleep as soon as his head hit the pillow. The trip up the stairs had worn him out. Stacey smiled at him. Maybe if he were like this more often—complacent. No, she thought, she liked the wilder moments too. His fierce pride, his incredible stubbornness, it all added up to make him who he was.

Joshua slept nearly fourteen hours, not waking until the next morning. He felt a bit muddled from too much sleep, but was otherwise alert. Looking around the room, he frowned when he didn't see his clothes. He sat up, letting his body adjust gradually to a more vertical position. He spied his pants on Stacey's dressing table, but there was no sign of his shirt.

He didn't relish the idea of wandering about the house half-dressed, especially when it meant parading his maimed back. He yanked on his pants and boots, then opened the bedroom door to see if anyone was about. He heard muffled voices coming from Curtis' office. Stacey would know where his shirt was. He headed down the steps. His head hurt, but the pain was only a dull throbbing sensation. He was beginning to feel confident about the surgery.

He was about to knock on the office door, when something about the tone of the voices brought him up short. As he listened his heart began to pound, anger stirring in him.

"Sam, I don't ever want him to know," Stacey was saying.

"But, Stace, you did such a fine job, I don't think he would object to the fact that you did the surgery." Sam's voice.

"It's not the surgery, Sam. It's the lie, and you know it. Joshua would never . . ."

Steele pushed the slightly ajar door all the way open. Startled, Stacey and Sam turned to see him framed in the doorway. He didn't speak. His mouth was set in a grim line.

"Joshua . . ." Stacey's face reflected her misery.

Sam stepped toward him. "Now don't you go blaming her, Josh. It was all my idea. As you can see by my hand here," he raised the bandage, "I couldn't very well go through with it." Curtis started to explain about the accident, but Joshua cut him off.

He crossed the room, halting directly in front of Stacey. His unbandaged eye flashed with bitter accusation. *"You* cut into my eye? You?"

"You did agree to the surgery," she said weakly, wishing she were anywhere else.

"Don't twist what I agreed to, woman," he hissed.

"Josh, I told you it was *my* idea," Sam cut in.

"You had no right, Stacey," Steele shouted, ignoring Curtis completely. "No right in hell to touch me, and you know it. My God, you're not even a doctor! You're a woman—with no medical degree, no license to practice medicine, nothing! Just the consummate gall to put a knife to my eye! My eye, for God's sake!"

If he had struck her, he could not have hurt her more. Her eyes glittered with unshed tears. Somewhere in her heart, she realized, she had nurtured the faint hope that he would understand what she had done. She had heard the words so many times, for so many years, but never had they hurt so much. Something snapped inside her. Instead of sobbing contritely, she slammed a hand against his bare chest in righteous fury, pushing him out of her way. Then she turned and faced him.

"No, Mr. Steele," she charged. "I am not a doctor. I don't have any blessed diploma. Never mind that half the *doctors* in the west got their diplomas by writing their names on a sheepskin and putting "doctor" in front of it. All I did was read medical texts and journals until my eyes ached. All I did was pester my father and my uncle with questions until they were ready to strangle me.

"And then there's the small matter of working night and day for months beside my father in a stinking hospital in a stinking war." Her eyes blazed at Joshua, tears falling freely as she spoke. He did not interrupt.

"I amputated arms and legs, I dug out bullets and shrapnel, I've sewed men's guts back together. I've treated cholera, consumption, and dysentery. I've set broken bones and delivered babies. But I am certainly not a doctor," she sobbed. "I'm not even a very good woman. I can't embroider worth a damn, and I'm only a tolerable cook. And God forbid, I hate gossip!"

She stopped, astonished herself at the vehemence of her words. She waited for Joshua to say something, anything, and when he did not, she ran from the room.

"You didn't quite deserve all that," Sam said quietly to Joshua, after she'd gone.

"You're wrong there, Sam," Steele said. "In spite of past rhetoric, my main objection to finding out she did the surgery wasn't her lack of a degree, it was because she's a woman." He rubbed a hand across the back of his neck, his voice hardening in self-disgust. "No, that's not true, not *a* woman, but Stacey herself. If it had been another woman doctor, someone you might have recommended, I wouldn't have any objections at all.

"But Stacey . . ." he sighed. "I kept seeing her as a young girl on a lark in the Wilderness. I didn't give her credit for being serious. Not even when the evidence was all around me." His half-smile was self-mocking, "I guess I just think she's too pretty to be a doctor."

"She's a doctor, Josh," Sam said. "She could pass any test those medical colleges could throw at her."

Steele started to say something, but was interrupted when a young boy burst into the room. "Doctor Sam, you gotta come quick. My ma's having her baby."

Curtis smiled at the tow-headed youngster. "take it easy, Peter. I'll be right with you." He picked up his medical bag. To Joshua he said, "Are you all right?"

Steele only nodded. "I think I'll just sit here for a few minutes." He ran a hand up a bare arm. "You wouldn't know where my shirt is, would you?"

"Stacey washed 'em," he said, brown eyes twinkling. "Woman's work, you know."

Steele scowled.

"They're sitting on the operating table. She was going to bring them up to you, when I started arguing with her. I was so proud of her about your surgery." Curtis put a restraining hand on the youngster, who was anxiously tugging on the doctor's coatsleeve. "I'll level with you, Josh. I think she did a better job than I could have. She's younger. She has a steadier hand and keener eyes."

Steele shrugged into a shirt. "I'll talk to her, Sam."

Curtis smiled and allowed the youngster to drag him from the room.

Stacey sat in Molly's room, trying to regain her composure.

"You just go ahead and cry your heart out, Miss Stacey," Molly urged, hugging her shoulders. Between sobs Molly had managed to piece together what happened downstairs. She gave a derogatory snort. "Men have to be the most worthless creatures God ever invented," she announced. "I mean even He thought so."

Stacey stopped sniffling long enough to cast a puzzled glance at Molly.

"Well, figure it out," Molly said. "If men were so

374

all-fired perfect, why'd God turn right around and make a woman?"

Stacey giggled hysterically, half-laughing, half-crying. "Oh, Molly, that's priceless. I guess I'd never thought of it quite that way before." She reached into her pocket for a hanky and blew her nose. "Thank you for being so sweet." She rose to her feet. "I think it's time I stopped concerning myself with Mr. Steele's distorted opinions about my medical competence, and went back about my business being the best doctor I know how to be."

"Good for you, Miss Stacey," Molly declared. "I'll bring Angel down and keep you company for awhile, if that's all right."

"That sounds wonderful," Stacey agreed, watching the young mother cross the room to gather her sleeping infant from the crib. An anguished scream from Molly sent Stacey racing to the child's bedside.

"Stacey! Stacey, something's wrong with her," Molly cried. "She's dead! She's dead, isn't she?" Molly was shaking the limp child, but getting no response.

Stacey scooped the infant out of her mother's arms. "Let me see her!" she commanded, breaking through Molly's hysteria. She laid Angel on Molly's bed and threw off the infant's blankets and clothing. Angel was burning up with fever. "Was she all right when you put her down for her nap?"

"She was a little fussy," Molly sobbed, looking guilt-stricken, "but she didn't have a fever. I swear! Oh, Miss Stacey, is my baby going to die?"

"Of course not," Stacey snapped, but she wondered. The baby was already badly dehydrated. She turned to Molly. "I want you to make her bottles of sugar water, like I've shown you before." Molly's stricken eyes didn't seem to comprehend what Stacey was saying. "Now, Molly," Stacey shouted. "Do it now! Angel needs you to do this for her!"

"I'll do it, Miss Stacey," she sobbed. "I'll do it!"

"I'm taking her down to the office. Bring the water there."

Steele rose to his feet, when Stacey rushed into the office carrying Angel. "Where's Sam?" she demanded.

"An emergency. Can I help?"

She stared at him for a long minute. "Yes," she said finally. "I need a lot of cool, wet towels. We have to get her fever down as quickly as possible."

He did as she asked. And, in fact, she accepted his help frequently during the next several hours. Molly brought in the water Stacey had requested, but was too upset to do anything but cry helplessly, begging God to spare her child.

Stacey forced water down the baby's throat. She folded wet towels around her tiny, fevered body, cring at the piteous wails the infant emitted. She carried her, soothed her, her own clothes made soaking wet by the constant exchanging of the towels.

When exhaustion began to tell, Joshua took the baby from her, repeating the procedure she had taught him. He bathed Angel in cool water, carried her, fed her water, even sang to her in a soft, pleasant baritone.

Stacey had nodded off to sleep on the settee, but woke to the sounds of Joshua's singing. His back was to her, as he sat in one of the office chairs. Angel seemed to be sleeping peacefully on his shoulder. Stacey recognized the lullaby as one her father had sung to her as a child. Tears stung her eyes, which she wiped brusquely away. How could she care so fiercely for a man who continued to bring her nothing but hurt? She climbed wearily to her feet, walked over to Joshua and put her hand on the sleeping baby's forehead. Her eyes widened with joy. The fever was gone!

"Molly! Molly!" Stacey cried, rushing over to shake the young mother, who had passed out on the floor from sheer emotional exhaustion. "Molly, Angel's going to be all right!" she cried.

Molly struggled to open her red-rimmed, swollen eyes. "Are you sure, Miss Stacey?" she said, in a voice that shook with near despair.

"I'm sure," Stacey said. "These things can come and go so quickly in babies, it's miraculous. The things you have to watch out for are the fever and the dehydration. Take care of those, and nature takes care of the rest most of the time, and certainly in Angel's case."

"Oh, Miss Stacey, thank you, thank you forever!" Molly flung her arms around Stacey's neck.

Within two hours Angel was greedily sucking at Molly's breast, blissfully unaware of the turmoil she had caused.

"You get some sleep, Molly," Stacey told her, as she closed the door to the girl's room. She frowned, when she thought of returning to the office and cleaning up the avalanche of towels down there. She didn't relish facing Joshua again, now that the crisis with the baby had passed. The few minutes sleep she'd managed to snatch did little to offset her staggering fatigue. The last forty-eight hours had left her emotionally and physically exhausted. She had no energy left for word games with Joshua. If he so much as looked at her wrong, she wouldn't be responsible!

Steele was picking up the last of the towels, when she stepped into the room. "You shouldn't be doing all of that bending over," she said, more sharply than she meant to.

"I'm all right," he said.

"You're not all right," she retorted. "You had surgery yesterday morning. Very delicate, precise surgery. And as your doctor, I am telling you not to be bending over, not to be lifting things. Do you understand?"

"Yes, ma'am." He watched her carry several armloads of towels out of the room. When she'd finished, she picked up a mop and began to sop up some of the excess water on the floor. "Maybe I should have said: 'Yes, doctor,' " he murmured, coming up to stand beside her.

She poked at his feet with the mop, forcing him to back off a couple of steps.

"You wield a vicious mop, doctor."

"Go ahead and make light of it," she hissed. "How could you possibly understand?"

"Understand what, Stacey? Tell me. I truly would like to understand."

She dropped the mop and stomped over to her uncle's desk. Yanking open the third drawer she pulled out a small book. Steele couldn't see the title. The book fell open on a page that was obviously much read.

"This is what!" she said. "Listen to this. Just keep your mouth shut and listen. It's about Harriet K. Hunt."

"I'm afraid I don't know the lady."

She glared at him. He decided to listen.

"Harriet Hunt tried to get into Harvard Medical School in 1850," Stacey told him, her voice charged with anger. "She'd already been practicing medicine for fifteen years without a diploma. Well, the male student body protested her admission. I quote:

"Resolved, that no woman of true delicacy would be willing in the presence of men to listen to the discussion of the subjects that necessarily come under consideration of the student of medicine.

"Resolved, that we object to having the company of any female forced upon us, who is disposed to unsex herself, and to sacrifice her modesty by appearing with men in the medical lecture room."

Her voice trembled. "Unsex herself! Because she wanted to be a doctor. Can you imagine?"

Steele stepped over to her and settled his hands on her shoulders. "No," he said softly. "I can't imagine that at all."

She tilted her head back to look at him. Her voice quivered. "I just want you to understand why it hurt so much when you said what you did. Joshua, there is no reason why a woman can't be a doctor. Women were doctors in ancient Greece and Rome." She shook her head. "I'm sorry, I don't mean to take it all out on you. I'm just tired."

He placed the palms of his hands on either side of her neck. "It's all right. I deserved it. And I do apologize for what I said about your doing the surgery." He gave her a rueful smile. "It's not so much that I care one way or the other about women being doctors. It's just that I hadn't thought of you as one. I have a tendency to think about you in other ways." He lowered his mouth to hers.

She pushed him away, but he pulled her back. "Joshua, please — your eye. No strain whatsoever." She thought of the promise she had made to herself to put an end to their lovemaking, but felt her resolve dissipating in the enveloping ecstasy of his touch. God, why did she have to love this man?

His mouth teased her throat, her chin, her lips. His hands explored the curving softness of her body. "Believe me, Stacey," he said huskily, "this is no strain . . . whatsoever."

She melted against him, unable to resist the intoxicating effect of his mouth, his hands, his voice. She wrapped her arms around him, feeling the pressure of his desire against her body. "No, we shouldn't," she breathed, even as she allowed him to lead her upstairs to her room. She knew she was lost.

Inside on her bed, she insisted that he lie still. It was she who undressed him. Then she undressed herself — slowly, sensually, revelling in the feel of his eyes upon her. She eased herself onto the bed and settled her body onto his. She heard him gasp, heard his throaty groan of pleasure.

Rhythmically she moved her hips, leaning forward until the tips of her breasts brushed against his chest. His fingers kneaded the soft flesh, teasing the nipples to stiff erection. Faster and faster she rocked, until she felt the long, shuddering sigh that coursed through him. Blissfully she nestled against his chest and fell asleep.

He let her sleep for nearly an hour. He stroked her hair, wondering for the thousandth time why he'd let things come this far between them. He didn't want to hurt her. Yet every time he came near her, his passion would get the better of him. He admitted it wasn't simply her body he desired, though each time he made love to her, his hunger for her did not diminish but it increased. It was more than that. He found himself craving her warmth, her zest for life and the living. She could find a child-like delight in things most people took for granted. Her desire, her need to be a doctor hadn't detracted from her womanhood, but enhanced it.

She stirred slightly in her sleep, instinctively snuggling closer to him. He closed his eyes, fighting the tightness in his throat. Damn, if only Merrick . . . But just thinking of the name changed him. His eyes clouded. He shook her gently. "We'd better re-arrange our sleeping quarters," he whispered against her ear, "before Sam comes back, or Molly and her baby wake up."

Stacey came awake quickly. "You shouldn't have let me sleep at all," she said sharply. "Sam could've come home at any time."

"Are you ashamed of what happened?"

She looked at him. His eyes were not mocking her. He was waiting for her answer. "No, not ashamed," she said at last. "It's a little too late for that."

"Then what?" He touched her cheek with the back of hand. Damn Merrick to hell for coming between them!

"Confused would be a good word, I think."

"I don't understand."

"No, Joshua, I'm the one who doesn't understand." She stood up and buttoned her blouse. It had to be said. She had to end it. She loved him too much to go on like this. "You've shut me out of your life time and time again, until we get to this part." She made a sweeping gesture with her hand, indicating the bed. "And I can't bear it any longer. You know," she said softly, "there's a word for a woman whose only hold on a man is sex."

He bolted out of the bed, gripping her wrists savagely. "Don't ever say thah again! Don't ever compare yourself . . ."

"To a whore?" she finished for him. "Why not? It fits, doesn't it? It's the only part of your life that includes me."

"Dammit, Stacey!" he hissed. "Why are you doing this? What's wrong with what we have? I find you a highly desirable woman. Don't try to tell me that you didn't find just as much pleasure in this bed as I did."

"No, I won't try to tell you that," she said. She could scarcely deny it any more, not even to herself. The rapture of his touch overwhelmed her more sensible nature. "I'm just telling you that it's not enough. Not for me."

He tried to pull her close, but she pushed him away. She crossed over to the door of her room, her back to him.

"What do you want from me, Stacey?"

She swallowed hard. "I want you to promise me that this will never happen again."

He straightened, his jaw working. "If that's what you want . . ."

"It's what I want." She gripped the doorknob so tightly her hand hurt.

His voice came to her, very soft. "It'll never happen again, Stacey. You have my word."

Without looking back she left the room.

Sam returned a few minutes later to discover Stacey and Joshua putting the finishing touches on cleaning up the office. The tension between them was palpable. The only words they exchanged were perfunctory. "What in the world happened here?" Sam demanded.

Quickly Stacey told him about Molly's baby. "What about your emergency?" she asked.

Curtis chuckled. "Mrs. Anderson's eighth boy child made his appearance two hours before I got to the ranch. As experienced as that woman is, I don't know why Abe made his eldest come and get me."

Stacey giggled. "Maybe she was hoping you could make it be a girl."

"She claims she going to keep doing it until she gets it right!"

"I don't know about you, Sam," she said, "but with all the excitement around here, we didn't have any supper. I'm suddenly ravenous. How about if I cook us something?" To Steele her voice was icily polite, "Do you want something, Joshua?"

His eyes caught and held hers. "Yes, Stacey, I definitely want something."

She blushed at his meaning and hurried toward the kitchen.

Ross Merrick sat in his office. It was well past midnight, when he finally reached his decision. With Steele on the loose, he could never feel safe. He'd heard about Steele's eye operation and knew the man was at least partially incapacitated. Tonight he could change partial to total with one well-aimed bullet.

A bullet would serve a dual purpose. It would kill Steele, and it would end forever Stacey Hamilton's foolish infatuation with the tall gunfighter.

Merrick cleaned the Remington Army revolver with meticulous care. Its octagonal steel barrel glinted in the light of the kerosene lamp. He rarely used a weapon of any kind anymore. He would have to hope for a cripple shot.

He hefted the gun, getting the feel of it against his palm. It was late; Steele might be asleep. But there was also the small chance he was awake, maybe standing in front of a lighted window. He would make his first try tonight. If he had to, he would go back tomorrow. He sighted down the steel blue barrel and imagined his target to be Joshua Steele's head.

CHAPTER TWENTY-TWO

Curtis eyed Joshua standing ill-at-ease in the kitchen doorway. "Come on in," he said. "Sit down. Stacey's set a place for you." His gaze became more critical. "Are you sure you're feeling all right? You've been up half the night."

"I feel fine," Joshua replied, watching Stacey bustle about the kitchen, her every movement a deliberate act of ignoring him.

"The food's ready, Sam," she announced.

Curtis cast his eyes heavenward and indicated to Joshua that it was all right if he sat down too. During the meal Stacey spoke only to Sam. When Barnett's name came up, Steele interjected a question. Stacey's response was to have Sam assure "Mr. Steele" that she was no longer speaking to him.

Simultaneously angry and miserable, Steele excused himself and walked toward the back door. He felt for the makings and stepped into the cool night air, hoping to clear his thoughts. He heard Sam Curtis' footsteps behind him.

"Beautiful night," Sam said.

"Uh huh," Steele agreed.

"Josh," Curtis started, then stopped. Steele said nothing. Curtis tried again, "I see you and Stacey haven't exactly come to a meeting of the minds."

"Not exactly, no."

"I still say she did a fine job on your eye."

"I think so, too," he said quietly. "Except for some pain from the surgery itself, I haven't had any discomfort at all. I'm already convinced the attacks are over. I should never have put if off as long as I did. If I lose my sight, it could be because I delayed so long, couldn't it?"

"Maybe," Curtis agreed. "But don't think that way. I think you'll be fine, as long as you take it easy for a couple of months. Stacey couldn't put stitches in your eye, medical science hasn't come that far yet, so any heavy exertion could cause a hemorrhage, and that would blind you—permanently."

Steele nodded his understanding. "I tried to apologize to her, but I don't think she was listening." He couldn't tell Curtis that it was no longer a question of Stacey's doing the surgery that fueled the hostility between them. It was a mutual physical attraction that neither seemed to want, yet both continued to feel.

"I think she's more hurt than angry," Sam said. "She's a sensitive, compassionate woman, who happens to be a doctor. Most men, most women can't understand that. It's unseemly, even immoral, they say. In spite of my best efforts, she still frequently gets a rough time from patients here in Spring Canyon." Curtis paused, considering his words carefully. "I think the part that hurt her most was that she had somehow decided that you were different, that you did understand her needs."

Steele straightened. She had told him as much. He

took a long drag on the cheroot, then stubbed it out on the post on which his hand rested.

"I'd give anything not to have said it, but maybe it's for the best."

It was a cryptic comment, that Curtis was going to ask Joshua to explain, but Stacey chose that moment to join them on the porch. Sam immediately made a to-do about having some papers to work on in his office. He excused himself and went inside.

"Good evening," Joshua said, without turning to face her. He felt damned awkward all at once.

"Good evening," Stacey said.

At least she had spoken to him, he thought dryly.

The silence stretched to several minutes. She knew how uncomfortable he must be. His head probably hurt. She was suddenly ashamed of herself for making him stand out here like this. She admitted she had been doing it deliberately.

Steele could stand the silence no longer. He cleared his throat. "Stacey . . . I . . ."

"I don't want to hear any more apologies," she interrupted defensively. "I performed the best surgery possible, and I wish just as much as you do that what happened tonight hadn't happened."

His jaw clenched. She wasn't making this any easier. He ran his finger along the wooden support post under the porch overhang. He uttered a short oath when he snagged a splinter for his efforts.

He was digging at it with his other hand hoping to dislodge it, when Stacey reached over and took hold of his injured finger.

"Stand under the lantern over here, so I can take a look." She kept her tone professional. He followed her

387

obediently to the other side of the porch. She poked at the finger, mumbling something under her breath about grown men.

"Just stand there a minute, while I run in the house and get a needle."

Steele remained where he was, poking ineffectually at the finger until Stacey returned.

"Now hold still," she said. She shook her head, amazed that he could live with the pain in his eye, yet make such a fuss over a tiny splinter.

"Ouch!" Joshua yanked his hand free. "I didn't think you'd be doing an amputation."

"I didn't even get it out yet," Stacey retorted, grabbing his hand back. "Honestly!"

She studied his hand in the lantern light, knowing it would be a lot easier if they went inside. She could barely see. She did not suggest that to Joshua, however, because in spite of everything she liked being out here alone with him.

She inserted the needle under the tiny piece of wood. It came away reluctantly. "There. I don't think it will be fatal after all." She didn't let go of his hand.

He used his other hand to tip her chin upward, until he was looking directly into those green eyes. "Now, if you'll listen to me for one minute without losing that blasted temper of yours, I would like to thank you, *Doctor* Hamilton, for removing the splinter—and for saving my sight and my sanity."

She gave him a quivering smile. "Thank you, Joshua. You don't know what that means to me."

He remembered the promise he had made to her. But she looked so beautiful standing there. He'd promised not to make love to her, but he hadn't said anything about kissing her. Damn, would he never rid himself of his desire for this woman?

His arms encircled her. He crushed her against him. His hunger pressed him to be almost savage, as his lips claimed hers. "Stacey, Stacey," he murmured, "I'd never deliberately hurt you. Never."

She molded her body against him, drowning in the sweet, tormenting sensations only he could arouse in her. She returned his kiss openly, wantonly. "Oh, Joshua, love me," she pleaded, as he bent to kiss her throat, her hair. No! This couldn't happen again! She had promised herself that it would never happen again.

His hands found her breasts, kneading the pliant flesh, feeling her nipples harden with desire under the thin material of her dress.

"I want you. God help me, I want you so much," he whispered hoarsely. He buried his hands in her hair, his mouth plundering hers once again.

Stacey thought she would die from the exquisite torture of his touch. Why did they both fight it so? Why did he seem to almost hate himself for wanting her?

He tore at the buttons of her dress, shoving the material roughly aside. His breathing tortured, his need for her drove all other thoughts from his mind. For the first time in four years he did not think of Ross Merrick.

He tugged at the string at the top of her chemise, pulling the laces aside and freeing her breasts to his seeking hands. Her naked flesh burned into his palms. He tore his mouth from her lips and buried his head in the softness of her body. His mouth closed over her right breast, his tongue teasing the nipple to full erection.

She bit back a scream of pleasure, remembering at the last instant where she was. "Joshua, please," she sobbed, "why do we torment each other so?"

Her stopped. For long seconds he held himself perfectly still, his head resting against the pillows of her breasts. He dragged himself away from her, pinching her chemise awkwardly together and buttoning her dress. "I'm sorry, Stacey," he rasped, "I made you a promise. I guess, for a minute there, I thought you might have changed your mind."

"Why must it be this way between us?" she cried. She chouldn't bring herself to pull away from him. Her lips brushed his.

"Stacey, for the love of heaven," he groaned, setting her away from him. "Don't push me any farther. I won't be responsible."

"But Joshua. . .?"

"What do you want me to do?" he snapped, frustration riding him hard. "Rip your clothes from your body and take you here on your uncle's porch?"

"No, of course not," she whispered, trying to understand how he could be so ardent one minute, so angry the next.

"You told me you never wanted me to make love to you again. Is this your way of getting back at me—to entice and bedevil me with your body, a body I can no longer have? I gave you my word, Stacey. What more do you want of me? I'm not made of stone."

"I . . . I'm sorry. I . . . I guess I'd better go inside."

He reached down and brutally hauled her to her feet. "Yes, Stacey," he said, "please do go inside. I . . ." He shoved her violently to the right, off the porch and into the dirt. He scrambled to avoid landing on top of her. A bullet, its report echoing in the night, slammed into the wall of the porch directly behind the spot where they had just been standing.

His body curled protectively over hers. He felt her trembling. "Joshua . . ."

He put his hand over her mouth. Someone was running away from the house.

Sam Curtis appeared in the doorway with a loaded shotgun. "What the hell's going on out here?"

"Whoever it was is gone," said Steele. He heard the hammers click back into place as Curtis awkwardly uncocked the weapon with his left hand.

Sam came over and helped them both to their feet. "Get back into the house. Both of you."

Stacey's knees were shaking so badly she didn't think she could make it to a chair. Anxiously, Sam examined Joshua's eye. He sighed with relief. No damage seemed to have been done by the fall.

While the eye was uncovered, Steele noted that he could distinguish light and dark, but little else. He wondered if it would always be so.

"Joshua, how did you know anyone was there?" Stacey asked, taking deep breaths to calm her shattered nerves.

"I thought I heard a gun being cocked. I didn't want to take any chances. I hope I didn't hurt you."

"No, no, not at all. Thank you."

"I doubt you were in any danger," he went on. "I was the target, but then I don't know how good a shot Merrick is any more."

"Merrick! You mean Martin Randolph, of course," Stacey cried, leaping to her feet. "Why couldn't it have been Barnett?"

"I don't think Barnett would come into town again. Too chancey for him. But Merrick lives here."

"How dare you? I'm tired of your accusing Martin of things you can't prove."

Steele stood up, facing her. "Don't say any more. You don't know what you're talking about. Martin Randolph *is* Ross Merrick. That knowledge alone makes me a dead man as far as he's concerned. But what he did to me makes him a dead man."

"Just what did this Merrick person do to you that would require such maniacal hate?" she demanded, sick to death of his relentless lust for vengeance. "You're alive, aren't you? He didn't kill you. Did he put those scars on your back? Is that enough to spend the rest of your life hating?"

"Don't say any more, Stacey," he said, his voice strangely quiet. "Don't say another word about Ross Merrick."

She whirled to face her uncle. "Sam, Mr. Steele will have to leave here at once."

Curtis started to object, but Steele interrupted. "It's all right, Sam. I have overstayed my welcome."

"Don't flatter yourself," Stacey snapped. To Sam she said, "Someone tried to kill him just now, probably Barnett." She hurried on to prevent any disagreement from Joshua. "He can't stay here. It's too dangerous. And he can't fight until the eye heals. He makes too tempting a target, obviously. So we . . . I will have to get him out of town for awhile."

"You're not taking me anywhere," Steele grated. "I'll go alone."

"She's making sense, Josh," Curtis said, "You are a sitting duck here. And I can't leave my patients.

Stacey knows this country very well. She could find you a safe place to hide out for several weeks if necessary. And like I told you, you can't do anything strenuous. That includes something as seemingly innocuous as saddling a horse."

Joshua grimaced with unbridled annoyance. The idea of being escorted to safety by Stacey Hamilton went against everything in him. He would be no protection to her if Barnett or Merrick should discover their whereabouts.

"I can't take the responsibility, Sam. If someone should see us on the trail . . ."

"I can shoot as well as any man," Stacey said.

"Tin cans, maybe, but not human beings," Steele said softly.

She stiffened, remembering Hector Caulfield. Joshua had spoken without rancor, but in his own way he was telling her that having her along as protection, was like having no protection at all.

"I'm taking you out of here, Joshua," she said.

Steele sighed. He had little choice in the matter. Staying here would mean jeopardizing more lives than his own. And Sam had made it abundantly clear that he couldn't fend for himself on the trail yet. He would have to hole up for a time, whether he liked it or not. He looked at Stacey. "When do we leave?"

She let out the breath she didn't realize she'd been holding. "I'll get things ready right now," she said. "We'd best leave before it's light." She added with a strange quality he couldn't read, "Just in case it was Martin."

CHAPTER TWENTY-THREE

Behind her uncle's house Stacey tied off the reins of two horses. She yanked on the halter of a third, bringing it nearer the house so that she could load up the pack animal with provisions. She decided to bring enough to last for six weeks. Sam stood guard making certain the ambusher didn't return.

Steele still had hard reservations about going. "Whoever it was won't attack at the house again," he argued.

"I disagree," said Sam. "The minute I left on a call, you and Stacey would be vulnerable, not to mention Molly and the baby. Besides, if they can't find you, they can't shoot you."

Joshua knew Sam was right. He just didn't want the responsibility of Stacey's life; not when he couldn't protect her properly. But there was no convincing either of them.

Joshua and Stacey walked out to the horses. He noted the smaller bay mare for her and a buckskin gelding for him. He mounted and waited for Stacey to say her good-byes to her uncle.

She pulled Sam nearer to the house, out of Steele's earshot. "I'll be staying with him, Sam. If he doesn't throw me out, that is."

Curtis started to object, but Stacey cut him off. "He can't defend himself, Sam, and you know it. Any jarring impact on that eye, any strain at all, and it could hemorrhage. The operation will have been for nothing, and he'll be blind. You know it, and I know it. Molly will see to it that you get fed properly," she said, giving him a half-smile, "and that the house doesn't crumble."

Curtis looked long and hard at his niece. He loved her like a daughter. He had a father's fears for her now. Six weeks alone with Steele. He knew the implications, but she was a grown woman. She knew her own mind. And Curtis thought, he knew Joshua. The man would never force himself on a woman. He wanted to say so much to her, but no words came to him except, "You take good care of yourself, hear?"

"I hear." She kissed him lightly on the cheek, then walked back to the horses. She climbed aboard her mare, giving Joshua a covert glance. He didn't look too pleased. This had to be taking a toll on that damnable pride of his.

The horses stayed at a walk even after they left town. A faster gait could be harmful to Joshua's healing eye. Stacey's rifle lay across her pommel, ready for instant use. Steele glared balefully at the weapon, but said nothing. He may not be able to see all that well, but he'd be damned if this woman would outshoot him if anything happened.

When they had left Spring Canyon a good distance behind, Stacey turned the horses onto a seldom used deer trail. She kept the pace slow but steady for the next several hours. She paused to watch the sun peek up in the distance. The multi-colored layers the light brought out in the ragged canyon walls never failed to fascinate her. Steele stopped his horse beside hers.

"There's a smaller canyon up ahead," she said. "It's a box canyon, so no one can come in, hopefully, without our knowing about it. There's a cave at the bottom of it. That's where you'll stay. I'll wipe out as much of our trail as I can later."

Dozens of tedious switchbacks later, they arrived on the canyon floor. Steele surveyed the flat surface. A nameless pool of water fed by an underground spring spread out not too far from them. Clumps of juniper and blue grama dotted the landscape. He stared at the cave entrance and shuddered involuntarily at the unbidden memory of a Mexican hell-hole. He shook it off.

Stacey left almost immediately to obliterate their trail. When she returned he watched as she unsaddled first his horse, then hers. When she finished, she started on the pack horse. He grimaced. He knew he couldn't help her. According to Curtis any kind of lifting at all could ruin the surgery and leave him blind. This dependency on someone else was probably harder to take than the surgery itself. As he watched her busy herself setting up the camp, a disturbing thought came to him.

"You're not planning on staying here, are you?" His voice had an unreadable tone to it.

"Of course not," she lied. She was suddenly embarrassed. She had been going to stay, but somehow when he put it into words it didn't seem right.

"I'll just get you settled here today and head back. I'll stop out from time to time."

"That wouldn't be a very good idea," Joshua said. "You can get here once undetected. But if you started making a habit of it, someone is liable to get curious."

Stacey had to agree with that. "But I can't leave you here alone for six weeks."

"And why not?" He was angry again.

"For one thing you could be shot dead and I wouldn't even know about it until I came back."

"If I was dead, it wouldn't much matter when you found out about it,"

"You do enjoy being insufferable, don't you?"

Steele cocked his head, grinning. Yes, he was enjoying this.

"Well, I'm hungry," Stacey announced suddenly. "I'll make us some breakfast and try to think this thing out." She gathered wood for the fire, pulling a match out of her pants pocket to get it started.

Joshua sat down, leaning against the wall of the cave. He closed his right eye, listening to her clanking pots and pans together. Soon he smelled the frying bacon and hot cakes. He could get used to having her around. She knew how to take care of herself.

"Coffee?" Stacey asked, interrupting his thoughts. He nodded. She poured him a cup and handed it to him. The hot liquid warmed his insides against the dawn chill. When the food was ready, she brought his plate over to him. They ate in silence. After she'd finished, she came over to sit beside him.

"I've decided to stay," she said.

"No." His voice had a finality to it that made her bristle with defiance.

"There's really not much you can do about it," she continued.

Steele stood up, exasperated. "You'll do as I say and go back to town, dammit! If Barnett or Merrick find me here . . . I can't allow you to face that kind of danger."

"I'm staying, Joshua," she said, her voice very quiet. "There is no way I could tolerate being in town wondering whether you were dead or alive out here."

He watched her rise and walk toward the horses. He threw down his coffee cup in disgust. She was right, there was nothing he could do about her staying, short of taking her back to town by force. That would defeat the purpose of their coming out here in secrecy. But he was damned if he was going to like the arrangement one bit!

He stalked down the canyon floor for several hundred feet. When he found a suitable place, he sat down, pulled his hat down over his forehead and tried to go to sleep. Later, when she called him to lunch, he stayed put. He could smell the food cooking, but he ignored it, much to his stomach's dismay. His mind was in turmoil. He had resigned himself to her staying, in that he would fight off Barnett or Merrick with his bare hands if he had to. But he could not resign himself to spending six weeks alone with Stacey Hamilton and not making love to her again. He had made her a promise. Yet he wanted her with a hunger so deep it frightened him. His deep respect for her warned him that nothing had changed. His goal was unaltered. The one reason he couldn't allow her into his life was that he still intended to kill Ross Merrick, though sometimes now he had to consciously force himself to think of Merrick. Stacey even had the power to affect his hate. Grimly, he decided he was about to spend the longest six weeks of his life.

When time for supper came and went and still Joshua made no effort to rejoin her, Stacey piled a plate full of food and took it to him. At her approaching footsteps he started, reaching at his hip for a gun that wasn't there.

"It's me," she said.

To himself he made a mental note to strap on the weapon. Even half-blind having it with him would give him some comfort.

"I thought you might be hungry." She handed him the food.

"Thanks." The silence between them dragged out. Stacey headed back to the camp.

She cleaned up the supper dishes. Sitting back against the wall of the cave, she considered her situation. She admitted she had dreamed of an opportunity like this, to be alone with Joshua. But this was not how it was supposed to be in her dream.

Her mind wandered. She imagined herself lying in her blankets, the night folded around her. Then Joshua would come to her. He would be gentle as always, but he would be all man. And this time there would be no apologies, no regrets afterwards. Her body flushed warmly. She heard his footsteps. He tossed his supper tin by the fire. She kept her eyes averted, terrified he would be able to read the shameful thoughts in her mind. She had forced him to make a promise, and she knew he would keep his word.

Her dream did not come true that night. They lay down in blankets several feet apart. Exhausted, Stacey's troubled thoughts did not keep her awake long.

Her deep, even breathing came to Joshua. He swore angrily, her nearness allowing him no peace. He grabbed up his blankets and stomped to the mouth of the cave. It was colder away from the fire, but at least he could no longer hear her breathing. He fell into a fitful sleep, but now his dreams were only half Garcia, the other half belonged to emerald green eyes.

Four more days passed in which they exchanged no more than a half dozen words. A tenseness grew between them that was palpable. The fifth morning Stacey could stand it no longer.

"You could at least be polite," she snapped.

"Me?" he cried in mock outrage. "You're the one who has managed to raise the silent treatment to an art form."

"Oh, you're impossible. I don't even know why I bother."

"I've certainly never asked you to!"

"That is it!" she raged. "I'm leaving!" At the look of triumph in his unbandaged eye, she said, "Oh, no, I'm not leaving the canyon. I'm just leaving this particular part of it. You're not going to win this one, Joshua Steele. And don't bother to wait up for me. I'll be back when I damn well feel like it!"

She stomped away from the cave. She walked for hours without regard to her surroundings. Even the primeval beauty of the canyon floor could not stir her from her brooding thoughts. She pondered what her life had become. Was this what love was like?

She remembered her parents with a sweet pain. They had been so obviously in love. Her father doted on his spoiled, sheltered wife, not seeming to mind her unbending rules of propriety. At the same time,

Beatrice Hamilton had looked the other way when her husband had taught their daughter how to play poker, how to fish, and how to climb trees. Perhaps it was her indulgence to him, because Stacey had not been a boy. Stacey accepted the fact that her mother regretted never giving her husband a son. But she knew in her heart that her father had never regretted having Stacey as his daughter.

Holding to a path along the canyon wall, she recalled the night she left her father during the war, the last time she was ever to see him.

"Oh, Pa, you know mother is just overreacting as always," Stacey had stormed at him. "Do I have to go?"

"She's your mother, and she needs you."

"And I'm her daughter, right? Daughters should be with their mothers! If I were your son, you'd want me to stay with you!" She was fighting tears.

"If you were my son," Ben Hamilton said, "and your mother needed you, I would want you to go to her. But if you were my son, you would be a soldier—killing or being killed in this senseless violence—and I wouldn't have the power to send you home.

"Eustacia, your compassion for others is a priceless gift I could never have found in a dozen sons. You say that women aren't free. And you're right. You'll fight prejudice all your life if you become a doctor. But men aren't free either."

He put his hands on her shoulders. "You didn't know that, did you? You think men own the world. But we have our shackles, too. We can't love as a woman can, or feel as a woman can. Men can't cry,

Stacey. We don't know how. I suppose my father knocked it out of me, as I would have knocked it out of my sons.

"I thank God I never had those sons. Look at this madness, Stacey. A man should be able to cry when he looks at all of this death."

The pain in his voice tore at her heart.

"Stacey, there is no other child in the world I could have loved as much, or been as proud of, as I am of you."

She sobbed against him. "I love you, papa."

"Then you go on caring, Stacey. Be a doctor. Show the whole damned medical profession how to care."

She hugged him again. She never wanted to let go, and neither did he. It was if they both knew that they would never see each other again.

Stacey sighed, forcing away the poignant memories. "I wonder if Joshua knows how to cry, papa," she whispered, thinking of the savage bitterness that twisted his heart.

She was surprised to feel her own face wet with tears. She wiped them brusquely away. "No more tears for you, Joshua," she vowed, then added ruefully, "at least not today."

Glancing behind her, she decided that she must have walked nearly ten miles deeper into the canyon. There was no sign of the cave. She had rounded a bend in the ancient lake bottom.

Feeling suddenly reckless and wanting to shake off her excess emotional energy, she trotted over to a huge, pitted slab of rock, that jutted away from the canyon wall. The slab came away from the wall at a steep angle and rose nearly sixteen feet in the air.

She put her hands in the fist-sized holes in the front of the rock. She would climb up this side, then shimmy down the side that formed a cleft between the rock and the canyon wall.

When she reached the top of the slab, she was delighted to discover a foot-wide shelf on top. Panting from exertion, she sat down, letting her feet dangle over the side. The physical activity had had its desired effect. She felt calmer, more content. She took the time to simply breathe in the spectacular beauty of the canyon.

Stacey hadn't realized how long she'd sat there in the stillness, until she noticed the sun beginning to disappear over the far western lip of the canyon.

"I suppose I'd better get back," she muttered aloud. "Not that he would be worried or anything. He'll just want me to fix him something to eat." She smiled. "Well, Stacey, at least you haven't lost your sense of humor."

She would follow her original plan and descend on the opposite side of the rock. At the top of the slab the space between it and the canyon wall was a good five feet, but it tapered inward rather sharply all the way down, until the slab met the wall about four feet from the canyon floor.

"This should be a lot easier than the climb up," she mused. "I could practically slide down."

Lying on her stomach, she eased herself down the sloping rock. Handholds were easy to spot, but in the shadows and because the rock was between her and the setting sun, footholds could be found by feel alone. Securing her left foot on a small ledge, she swung her right foot free to search for the next toehold. Without warning the ledge gave way. Her body bounced and scraped the remaining six feet to where the rock and wall met.

"Now that wasn't at all graceful," she grimaced, brushing off the front of her blouse. When she tried to move, her left foot didn't follow. She looked down and to her horror discovered that her foot had slipped into a small opening at the base of the slanted rock, between it and the sheer canyon wall.

Hunching down awkwardly in the narrow space, she trailed her fingers along her leg, trying to reach her ankle. It didn't hurt at least. She tugged at the trapped appendage.

"Get out of there," she grumbled to her foot. She struggled for another ten minutes. If anything, the foot was more firmly trapped than ever. "I don't believe this is happening."

Joshua! The thought of him finding her like this renewed her efforts to free herself. "First, it's a runaway horse," she groaned, "then flying bullets, then falling off a cliff . . . Oh, but this is the worst. I'd never live this one down. I can just hear him. 'Of all the dumb females.'"

You could always scream, she told herself. In the box canyon her voice would travel a long distance, especially if he were already looking for her. But she wouldn't scream. She yanked at her foot until she could feel the blood oozing from her ankle inside her boot.

"No, no, no!" she sobbed in frustration, leaning back against the slab. "Calm yourself, Eustacia," she snapped. "This isn't doing you any good at all." She lay back, her free foot propped against the rock wall.

She lay that way for several minutes, forcing herself to relax. Relax. Unbelievably, she fell asleep.

When she woke she was shivering violently. She looked up, the rim of the canyon blocked her view of the sky, but the darkness was total. She listened. Surely, Joshua would be calling to her, searching for her. Then she remembered her parting words to him, that she would be back when she damn well felt like it. It wouldn't be unreasonable for him to assume that she would spend at least one night out here alone, sulking.

Sulking was about the right word for it, she chided herself. Of all the childish stunts! Joshua knew she was perfectly capable of taking care of herself. She looked down ruefully at the trapped foot she couldn't even see in the darkness. "See what a good job I do?" You could always scream, a little voice niggled her. "The hell I will," she said fiercely. "It'll snow in this canyon before I scream for that insufferable man to help me out of here."

A coyote howled somewhere up the canyon. She peered into the blackness. Were those fluffy, white flakes falling out there? She sighed and leaned back. "I will not scream," she repeated. "I will not." She wiggled her foot. The cold would reduce the swelling and she could just pluck it free in the morning. She hoped. She had herself half-convinced when the coyote howled again. Closer this time.

"Oh, this just keeps getting better and better," she said, "It'd serve that man right to find me all chewed up in the morning. I wouldn't be in this mess, if he wasn't so pigheaded."

She laughed giddily. She was trapped in the rocks in

a bone-numbing cold with a coyote closing in on her, yet she refused to call for help that would almost certainly come. And she was calling *him* pigheaded?

"Oh, Joshua," she sighed. "I do love you so much. Why do you shut me out? Tell me what hurts you and I'll make it better. I promise. Whatever Ross Merrick did to you, I can undo. Just let me into your life, please?"

Tears stung her face, but she hardly felt them. Her body burned again with a fire that only Joshua could ignite. He had only been thinking of her safety when he wanted her to leave the canyon. The open vulnerability he created in her heart had made her lash out at him to keep from being hurt any more deeply than she already had been.

It wasn't his fault that she loved him utterly, without reservation, without regard to future consequences. He hadn't asked for her love. She had given it of her own free will.

"Oh, God, Joshua, it hurts so much to love you. Couldn't you love me just a little?"

Her head jerked. Something growled to her right. Her fingers scrambled into her pocket. Trembling, she struck the match twice before it flared. The coyote's translucent eyes were visible in the dancing light. His paws were hooked over the crack where the slab pulled away from the wall of rock. He growled again. Stacey threw the match at him. The coyote backed down.

"I don't really want you to find me all chewed up, Joshua," she said fervently, her heart thundering in her chest.

The coyote had its nose in the fissure again, sniffing the air. She could almost feel the hair rise on the animal's back. "I taste terrible," she said, trying to sound calm. "Honestly. You'll have indigestion for a week."

She thought about screaming now, but feared it would only make the beast more anxious to attack her. He must be awfully hungry or sick to even consider attacking a human being. He could probably smell the blood on her ankle. She pulled out another match, ready to light it if she sensed the coyote come closer.

"Joshua, help me," she whispered.

The coyote grew bolder. She could hear its hind feet scratching at the rock, seeking a purchase from which to leap into the opening. She could feel the heat of its body. If she reached out, he could bite her hand. That was how close he was. She held her breath. The coyote snarled and sprang into the fissure.

Toward dusk Steele paced in front of the cave. "Blast that woman," he seethed. "It should be no concern of mine, if she wants to spend the night freezing on the canyon floor."

He admitted grudgingly to himself that she could, of course, build a fire. But she was probably too stubborn, thinking he would see the flames when he came to drag her back to the cave, where he could keep an eye on her. Why should he look for her at all? It was her choice to leave. He hadn't forced her.

Couldn't she understand how dangerous it was for her here? He was certain it had been Merrick who had taken the shot at him at Sam's. Even now the man could be on their trail. And there was still the matter to be settled with Barnett. All around him, his enemies put her life in jeopardy. If anything happened to her because of him . . .

If anything happened to her at all! God, how he ached to tell her he loved her. But how could he love her, as she deserved to be loved, when he still deliberately nurtured his hatred for Ross Merrick?

As the sun set he built himself a fire and cooked a meager meal. Once he thought he heard a sound and turned toward it. He smiled a warm welcome before he realized he was doing it. But it had only been the wind knocking an empty can loose near their cache of supplies.

He bit off a curse. He wasn't about to go traipsing off after her. Wouldn't that give her already inflated ego a boost to catch him searching for her, while she lounged in front of a roaring campfire?

"Let her play her little games," he muttered. "I'm not the patsy she thinks I am." Joshua spread his blankets and lay down. An hour passed. During that time he imagined her drowned in the stream, dead of a broken neck at the bottom of some cliff, devoured by a mountain lion, and murdered by Barnett.

"Damn it to hell!" he spat, flinging off his blankets. His unbandaged eye dark with rage, he quickly saddled his horse, ignoring her warning not to. He fashioned a torch from the firewood, mounted, and rode into the night. He travelled in the direction she had headed this morning, knowing there was no way he could trail her in the dark. All he could do was ride along the canyon wall and hope for the best.

Several miles disappeared under the horse's easy loping stride. More than once, he'd reined the animal around and started back to camp, deciding he was making a total jackass of himself. She had probably been hiding in the rocks near the cave all along, just waiting for him to leave. She might even be asleep by his campfire right now, after having laughed herself silly first, watching him ride off into the dead of night looking for her.

He held up the firebrand. It was rapidly burning itself out. At best it spread light barely thirty feet ahead of him in the near pitch blackness of the canyon floor. He pulled the horse to a stop. This was ludicrous. He was searching for a woman who didn't want to be found. No campfire winked at him on the trail ahead. She couldn't have gotten any farther than this.

"Enjoy yourself, Miss Hamilton," he muttered, offering her a mocking salute with the torch. He was about to toss the firebrand on the ground in disgust and head back to camp at a gallop, when he heard the sound. A low guttural sound. A coyote growling. It was close. Very close. A coyote wouldn't threaten a man on horseback. The animal snarled again. He heard a scream.

"Stacey!" He slammed his heels viciously into the horse's sides. Startled, the animal sprang forward at a run. The sound came from a jutting slab of rock ahead. When he reached the rock, he leaped from the animal's back, gun drawn.

Stacey lit the match. The light flared on bared teeth. She screamed, imagining them tearing into her throat, imagining too, in her desperate terror, that she heard Joshua calling her name. The tiny fire seemed to startle the beast for just an instant. He was now fully inside the crevice with her, growling menacingly at the sputtering match.

She gripped the match in her right hand, groping in her pocket with her left. Nothing. This was her last match. The flame died.

Instinctively she covered her head with her hands, waiting for the agonizing feel of her flesh being torn from her body. A gun sounded. A single bullet that racketed like a fusillade in the tiny fissure. The coyote yelped in fear, scrambling backwards, falling awkwardly out of the crack. He tore off into the night.

She stared with unbelieving eyes at the sight on her left. Joshua stood there, a torch in his left hand, a gun aimed skyward in his right. His shirt was unbuttoned, his hair disheveled, his unbandaged eye openly revealing raw fear. Fear, she realized wonderingly, for her.

His voice was shaking when he said, "Are you all right?"

She couldn't speak. She could only nod weakly.

He anchored the torch in the crack. "I'll go around to the other side." As he walked around the slab of rock, he trembled with the knowledge of how many times he had turned back, how close he had come to not looking for her at all. But he was coldly furious by the time he hoisted himself into the crevice beside her.

Stacey had had time to realize she was safe now too. And when she read the anger in his face, she said tightly, "If I hear one word about how incapable I am of taking care of myself, I will not be responsible for my actions."

"You're already not responsible," he gritted.

She swung at him, but he saw it coming and easily

avoided the blow.

"You want to ruin all of your fine surgical work?" he mocked.

Her eyes widened in horror at what she had almost done. Even with his bandage, her anger had made her forget about the delicacy of his eye's condition. "I'm sorry," she whispered. Her voice trembled, everything that had happened in the past twenty-four hours seemed to crash in on her. "I'm sorry. I'm so sorry," she sobbed brokenly.

"You missed, remember?" he said gently, somehow managing in their cramped quarters to wrap his arm around her shoulders and draw her close.

"You're the only person I've ever tried to hit in my life," she whimpered.

"And you succeeded once," he reminded her.

"You deserved that one."

"Yes, I did," he agreed. "I never mean to hurt you, Stacey, but somehow I always do."

She looked at him, the love she felt naked in her eyes. He was being so warm, so considerate. He pressed his lips on hers and she was lost. They clung together, sharing deep, passionate kisses, each revelling in the need of the other.

Finally, he pulled away from her. "This is ridiculous," he said. "Your foot is still stuck in this rock. If I got carried away, you wouldn't even be able to run."

"I wouldn't run, Joshua."

"Don't," he warned, and as she started to say something, he repeated, "Just don't." He shifted away from her. "Let's see what we can do with this foot."

"I suppose you could chop it off."

"You're the doctor, not me."

She smiled at the matter-of-fact way he said it.

"I've got some lard in my saddlebags," he said, "though why I threw them on my horse, I'll never know. Maybe if we grease your foot . . ." He climbed out of the crevice.

A half hour later her foot was a smelly mess, but was free. Joshua pulled off her boot and grimaced at the blood on her ankle. "Were you trying to twist it off?"

"It'll be all right. It's just scraped a bit and a little swollen." She rubbed it gingerly, accepting the cloth he gave her to wipe off the grease.

"You feel up to riding back?" he asked.

"I'm fine," she assured him, though she accepted his help getting to her feet. He gave her a boost up on the horse, then climbed on behind her. He deliberately avoided putting his arm around her waist, as he gigged the horse into a trot.

Her voice had an unaccustomed timidity to it when she spoke to him the next morning. "I should check the bandage today. Maybe take it off. Would you like me to do it now?"

He shrugged, finishing his coffee. "If you like."

"Come back into the cave. I don't want you straining the eye at this stage."

He stood up and followed her. About twenty feet into the cave she paused. "This is all right, I guess," she said. "Not too bright, not too dark."

Joshua sat down, his back leaning against the rock wall. His heart pounded.

"I know you're tempted," she said. "Heaven knows I would be, but please don't open that eye right away.

412

Let me do it for you."

Aware that her knowledge of such things was greater than his, he reluctantly agreed. A few minutes later the bandage was off.

"Now close your good eye, and open the one we did the surgery on. Then tell me what you see, but don't look toward the mouth of the cave." Her voice reflected her tension.

He did as she asked. Interminable seconds ticked by, when he could only distinguish a vague light. Gradually the eye adjusted to the brightness, after days of black. He opened the other eye.

"Well!" she demanded anxiously. "What do you see?"

He smiled, his eyes alive with warmth. "I see the most beautiful emerald green eyes God ever created."

"The eye's all right?" she pressed. "You're sure?"

"The eye is fine. And you are a fine surgeon, doctor."

She visibly relaxed, sinking next to him against the wall. "Thank God." She shifted to look at him. "This doesn't change anything about your being able to do any heavy lifting, that sort of thing, you know. The eye could still hemorrhage, though every day that passes makes the chances of that happening more remote."

He picked up her hand and pressed her palm to his lips. "I owe you my life," he whispered.

"Joshua," she chided, "I operated on your eye. I didn't save your life. If you want to talk about saving lives, my heavens, I'd hate to think how many times I owe you mine. Between runaway horses and hungry coyotes . . ."

He leaned over and kissed her, effectively silencing her. When he pulled away, he said again, "I owe you my life, woman. In more ways than one." He sighed and climbed to his feet. He couldn't guarantee his behavior if he continued to sit with her like this. "I feel like a walk." He reached down a hand, "Join me?"

Shyly she took his hand, as he helped her to her feet. He did not release her hand, but held on as they walked into the sunlight.

They walked along the canyon floor for several minutes in companionable silence. Stacey couldn't believe how good she could feel just having her hand linked in his. When they reached a spire of rock, Joshua guided her into its shade. He put his hands on her shoulders, gazing down at her. His eyes searched hers for long seconds. He seemed to be making a decision. She waited.

Finally, in a quiet voice, never taking his eyes from hers, he said, "I'm not much on talking about myself, but it's become important to me that you know why I lead the life I do."

"You don't owe me any explanations, Joshua," she protested.

He pressed his fingers against her lips. "I want you to know." He sat down against the rock and beckoned her to join him. They sat for long minutes just watching white clouds scud across a sky of perfect blue. She thought maybe he had changed his mind, but then the words came, in a voice so soft she had to strain to hear them.

"It all started, believe it or not, the day I met you in the Wilderness. Those orders sending me to Washington for 'secret skullduggery'." He gave a short laugh and leaned his head back, looking at the sky again. "In Washington I was introduced to Colonel Ross Merrick. He and I were to travel to Mexico to aid Benito Juarez in his fight against the French and Maximilian. The letter you received from the War Department about 'my death' told you that much."

"Why were you and Merrick singled out?" she heard herself asking. "I mean you had your command in the war."

"We both got along in French and Spanish, as well as English."

Stacey's eyes widened. She couldn't imagine this rugged looking man speaking a language as genteel as French.

"I plead guilty to a rather privileged upbringing," he said. "My father was a wealthy man. At least part of my schooling was in Paris. In our home in Philadelphia we had a maid who spoke only Spanish. She spoiled me thoroughly, adding to my incentive to speak her language." He paused. "But that isn't what I want to talk to you about."

"You want to tell me why you have to kill Ross Merrick," she said softly.

"Yes."

She laid her head against his chest, her arms circling him. "Tell me."

He stroked her hair with his hand as he spoke. "In Mexico Merrick and I ran guns and gold for Juarez. Merrick did his job well enough for nearly three years, but more and more the gold was getting to him. I got suspicious when three shipments in a row were attacked, no matter how much secrecy I attached to the plans. So on what turned out to be my last shipment, I laid a trap for him.

"There were no guns and no gold. But what I didn't know was that there was an imperialist infiltrator among the juaristas. When Merrick and the French attacked, we were overpowered from within. And when Merrick found out he'd been tricked, he was furious. To teach me a lesson he ordered one of his men to murder a friend of mine. They shot him in the head. And since Merrick wasn't much on witnesses, he had the six caballeros who survived the attack lined up in front of a cannon and blown to bits."

Stacey stiffened in horror, but he did not stop.

"Part of the shrapnel caught me in the side of the head. When I woke up I was in a Mexican lead mine, a prisoner of war."

"Why did Merrick let you live? It seems you would be his most dangerous witness of all." She spoke against the roughness of his shirt, her arms still securely wrapped around him.

"Merrick seemed to think that I possessed knowledge of more gold shipments. I was privy to more of that information than he was."

"You wouldn't tell him."

"I wouldn't have told him my name," he said, his voice congested with hate.

"He whipped you?"

"He had me whipped. Merrick would never have dirtied his hands to do it himself."

"To leave scars like that," she said, her voice shaking, "you would have had to be whipped repeatedly." She heard his heartbeat quicken, felt his body tense.

"When they finally tired of it," he said, each word

an effort, "they chained me, like some sort of beast. My body was twisted, so I could scarcely move. They put me in a hole, like a box, and they locked the door. My hands were chained behind me. I was naked. I was covered with sores from the beatings. And there were rats, so many rats. A hundred and twelve, as a matter of fact." He remembered his running total.

"After someone finally dragged me out of there, following Maximilian's defeat, it took me four months—four months—to get over it. No, that's not true. It was four months before I could sit on a horse without falling off, but I've never gotten over it. Never." He looked at her face and was surprised to find it wet with tears. "I shouldn't have told you. I'm sorry."

"No!" She said it with astonishing vehemence. "I'm glad you did. I could never understand what had changed you so, from the man I met in the Wilderness to the man I met in Elizabethtown. Now, I understand."

He wrapped his arms around her, holding her as tightly as she held him. He could never tell her that Merrick had threatened to castrate him. But he had told her enough. He still hated Merrick. He still wanted him dead. But sitting here, holding this woman in his arms, the when of Merrick's death no longer seemed important.

Stacey ached with the pain he had suffered. She longed to heal him of the bitterness he still suffered. They had reached a new stage in their relationship. He was learning to trust her, to let her into this very private part of his life. They lay in each other's arms for a long time. And for each of them for the

417

moment, it was enough.

Dusk was settling in the canyon when they finally headed back toward the cave.

"Maybe I'd better go back to town," she said.

He scowled. "Why?"

Her emotions roiled inside her. She knew as a woman knows that if she stayed this night, she would let him make love to her. One word from her and she could release him from his promise. She wanted it. And she sensed that he wanted it as well. But would they both be letting an emotional tide sweep them into something they would regret later? Did he love her? Did she love him?

The only question she could answer was the last. Yes, she did love Joshua, with a fierce passion that consumed her. And it frightened her more than a little. It made her vulnerable to a new kind of pain, a new kind of hurt. If he left her, rejected her, she didn't think she could bear it. If she let him make love to her again tonight, she would never be able to leave him. Tears stung her eyes. She was a romantic fool. Joshua Steele lived for his revenge against Ross Merrick. He wouldn't tolerate the interference she might cause in his pursuit of that goal.

"I asked you why you wanted to go," he repeated, moving closer to her.

How could she possibly tell him that the reason she had to leave was because she wanted him to make love to her? After she had all but forced him to make the promise that it would never happen again.

As if he could sense her thoughts, Joshua said, "If you're worried about the continued propriety of this arrangement, because of what was said out there, I can assure you that I will continue to be a perfect gentleman. I made you a promise, Stacey, and I will keep my word."

He damned himself for saying it. Keeping that blasted promise was the last thing he wanted to do. He wanted her so badly it hurt. But if it would ease her mind about staying, he would hold himself to it. Being alone with her in this canyon was becoming the most peaceful, contented time he had ever known.

"I wasn't worried about your being a gentleman, Joshua," Stacey said quietly. "I know you would never force your attentions on me. I don't even know that you would want to any more, if I were willing . . ." She stopped, feeling a hot flush of shame. It was a stupid thing to say. She was baiting him.

"Don't be coy with me!" he snapped. "It's not like you. You know damn well I want you."

This conversation was taking a dangerous turn. The need was strong in him. Maybe she should go back to town, if she was going to talk like that. He stood riveted to the ground as she moved toward him. She stopped directly in front of him, looking up at his strong, square jaw. She put her hands against his chest. He straightened, holding his arms locked at his sides. He had made a promise. Why was she doing this? She couldn't be so naive as to be unaware of her effect on him.

When she spoke her voice was scarcely more than a whisper. "I'm sorry. That was an awful thing to say. I'm just so confused, Joshua. It's not that I'm afraid you won't continue to honor your promise. It's that, if I stay, I'm afraid I'll ask you to break it."

She stood on her toes and kissed him lightly on the

mouth. She started to back away, but his arms encircled her like a vise. He crushed her to him. His kisses were fevered, the passion he'd held in check spilling over like a bursting dam. Over and over he whispered her name, his hands losing themselves in her golden hair.

Joshua knew he should stop it before it went any further. It could end in nothing but hurt for her. Her hands touched his face, his hair. Her arms surrounded him, holding him fiercely against her. He was alive to the softness of her, the yielding. And he knew he would not stop, no matter what the cost. Her eyes told him she wanted the same thing. Holding her hand, he led her into the cave.

Inside, he embraced her again. He kissed her hungrily, revelling in the taste of her, the sweetness.

"This can't happen," he rasped. "Tell me to stop and I will. Please, Stacey, I don't want to hurt you again."

"You can only hurt me by shutting me out, Joshua," she said. "Take me. Love me. I need you to love me."

He undressed her slowly, his fingers caressing every part of her until she whimpered with longing. He pulled off his own clothes, sucking in his breath when her fingers gently fondled his manhood. His pleasure-sated groan sent shock waves of delight through Stacey.

She wanted to please him, to love him as she never had before—completely, utterly, with no thoughts of what tomorrow might bring. Even if he did not feel the same, he did want her. And for now she would content herself with that. She teased him, toyed with him, caressed him, until he shuddered with the need for release.

· "I love you, Joshua," she whispered, as he drove himself inside her. "God help me, I love you so much."

His mouth closed over hers, his need for her bordering on madness. "Stacey, Stacey," he groaned, "tell me you want it. Tell me it's all right."

"Oh, yes, Joshua. Yes!" she cried. "Take me. Love me." She wrapped her legs around him, holding him to her, as she matched his movements with her own. Together they rode the crest to a soul-shattering release.

For long minutes afterward she lay contentedly nestled in his arms. Briefly, the fear that he might apologize for breaking his word disturbed the serenity of the moment. But she dismissed the thought. He had wanted it as much as she did. She didn't waste time wishing that he loved her, she simply marvelled in her own acknowledgement that she loved him—totally and without reservation.

She trailed a slender finger down his chest and lower. She touched him gently and smiled when he growled with pleasure.

"It truly is a medical marvel," she said.

"Yes, doctor," he grimaced good-humoredly.

"It's fascinating how it works. I could study it for hours. That is, if you don't mind?"

He roared with laughter. "Oh, God, Stacey, any time you wish, believe me."

She snuggled closer. "I think a thorough examination is in order here."

His eyes closed, a groan escaped his lips.

"So fascinating . . ." she giggled.

He turned toward her. "Witch," he whispered, then he possessed her again.

421

CHAPTER TWENTY-FOUR

Ross Merrick sat in his bank office and fumed. He still didn't know how he could have missed Steele from that distance. Even half-blind the man had the senses of a wolf. The thought of his spending night after night in Curtis' house with Stacey infuriated him even more. It was disgraceful.

Now Steele and Stacey had disappeared. Curtis wouldn't tell him a thing, and neither would that little slut, Molly. But Merrick guessed that Stacey had taken Steele into the canyons to hide until he had healed completely. Curtis was evasive about whether or not Steele was able to see. Merrick assumed it was because the doctor just didn't know. Cursing, Merrick hoped Steele would be blind for life. It would end looking over his shoulder.

It came to him that even that wouldn't be enough. Steele and Stacey were alone together, a fact that made Merrick's blood run hot. He would find them, and they would both die. He'd been made a fool of in front of the entire town. His dreams were finished here. Some of the people had even begun suspecting that Steele may not be all wrong about their banker's past life. Merrick knew one of those most suspicious was Rube Tucker.

Danton Seaverman had cursorily dismissed him in any future investment plans, saying his partners didn't need any unsavory publicity. Steele's reappearance in Merrick's life had proved to be a stroke of extreme ill-fortune. But Merrick intended to remedy that very soon.

A knock on the door brought a forced smile to his lips. "Come in, Claire," he called, rising to his feet.

The buxom young waitress opened the door and gave Randolph a tentative smile. "You wanted to see me, Mr. uh, Martin?" Claire was astonished that her father had allowed her to leave the cafe in the middle of the day. She could only guess that he regarded Randolph as potential husband material for her. If so, it would be the first time Isaiah Jensen had encouraged one of her suitors. The fact that Martin Randolph was a bank president, where most of the men previously interested in her had been ranch hands, probably had a good deal to do with it.

"I'd like you to do me a favor, Claire," Merrick was saying.

"Me? What could I possibly do for you, Martin?"

"I want you to go over to Doctor Curtis' house and find out what you can about where Steele and Stacey have gone."

Claire frowned. "Why don't you ask Dr. Curtis yourself, Martin?"

Merrick's jaw clenched, but he kept the smile on his face. "Because Sam knows about the animosity between Mr. Steele and myself. He wouldn't tell me anything."

Claire surprised herself by saying, "Then maybe you shouldn't know where he is."

Merrick came around the desk and put his arms around Claire's shoulders. "The man wants to kill me, Claire. Surely you can see why I want to know where he is?"

"Yes," she said slowly, "I guess so."

"Then you'll find out for me, won't you?"

"All right, Martin." She leaned forward to kiss him. He started to jerk back, then allowed her to kiss his cheek.

"That's a good girl," he said, and ushered her out of the room.

An hour later Claire returned. Merrick greeted her warmly. "Well, did you find out anything?"

"She's taken him into the canyons, Martin. Dr. Sam says Mr. Steele's eye could bleed or something, if he's not real careful. If that happens, he'd go blind." Claire squirmed in her chair, feeling like a tattle-tale all at once. Martin Randolph might be a bank president, but he certainly was being pretty sneaky about all this. She wasn't sure she should tell him any more.

"Why did Stacey stay with him?" Merrick couldn't quite keep the edge out of his voice.

"I think I'd better go, Martin," she said. "I don't think this is right."

He took her hand in his. "I can't tell you how much I appreciate this, Claire. Please, what do you know about Stacey's part in this?"

"She . . . she's staying with him because he can't do anything that might cause the eye to bleed." Claire backed toward the door. "Really, Martin, I've got to get back to the cafe."

"Fine," he said, "you go right ahead, Claire." He all

but shoved her toward the door.

"Where are you going?"

"To bring Stacey home, of course."

"But I thought . . . well, I thought, since you asked me . . ."

"You thought wrong, Claire. Now why don't you go back and wait on tables, where you belong."

"You're a horrid man," she cried, "I should have known it the minute my father liked you!" Fighting back tears, she ran from the room.

Merrick headed for the livery. There he rented a horse and began his search. For days he turned up nothing. Stacey had hidden her trail well. Then one day he turned up the tracks of four horses. The signs were very fresh. Perhaps the riders had seen the pair he sought. He decided to follow them awhile.

An hour later he halted abruptly at a terse command from a nearby mass of rock. "Hold it right there, mister!" the voice called.

Merrick turned slowly. Jake Barnett. Merrick recognized him immediately from all the talk around town. Rube Tucker had had no luck in ferreting out the gang of killers, and had recently called off the search for them. A slow smile spread across Merrick's features. This could work out very nicely.

"My name is Martin Randolph," Merrick said, "I understand we have a mutual enemy—Joshua Steele."

"Get off that horse," Barnett snarled.

Merrick obliged him.

"What about Steele?" Barnett demanded.

"I'm looking for him, too," Merrick went on. "Same purpose. I want him dead. Maybe we could help each other."

"I don't take in outsiders."

"Suit yourself," Merrick shrugged.

Barnett considered the nattily dressed dandy. He scarcely looked like a man on the trail. "Do you know where Steele is?"

"He's in these canyons somewhere, recuperating from an eye operation," Merrick added the lie; "He's blind."

A smile crossed Barnett's pinched features. "Blind?"

Merrick nodded.

"Then what's he doing in the canyons?"

"Keeping out of my gunsights mostly," Merrick said. He explained his abortive attempt to ambush Steele.

"He's alone . . . and blind?" Barnett sounded doubtful.

"The doctor's niece is with him."

"Aaah!" Barnett sneered.

Merrick stiffened. "It's not like that!"

"Oh, of course not," Barnett demurred. He just might need this slicker's help. "Tell you what. We'll both go on a little hunting expedition. Whoever finds him first, gets him."

"Suits me fine." Merrick didn't care who killed Steele, just as long as he was dead. He didn't take the time to be concerned about what Barnett might do to Stacey should the outlaw find them first.

With that Barnett let Merrick be on his way. He watched thoughtfully after the slicked-up popinjay. There went a man it would not do to underestimate. Barnett was crafty enough to recognize cold-blooded ruthlessness when he saw it, maybe because it was like looking in a mirror. He hoped, though, that Merrick

426

would not be the one to find Steele. Barnett wanted that pleasure all to himself.

Steele blind, Barnett relished the thought. Never would he enjoy killing a man quite so much.

CHAPTER TWENTY-FIVE

Steele woke from a peaceful sleep. The whip, Garcia, Merrick—all had vanished from his dreams. Three weeks of shared ecstasy with Stacey had driven them from his nights forever. He lay still for a moment, wondering what it had been that disturbed him. He cocked his ear toward the cave entrance. The only sound he heard was the deep, even breathing of the woman sleeping beside him.

He inhaled the soft, sweet scent of her hair and kissed her lightly. She did not stir.

A scraping noise sounded outside the cave. He recognized it now as the noise that had awakened him. Someone was out there. He eased his right arm out from under the blanket that covered them both, reaching for the revolver above his head.

Light flooded the cave, light from a hand-held torch. The firebrand was tossed violently aside as soon as its bearer caught sight of the cave's occupants.

Joshua grabbed for the Colt and rolled away from Stacey all in one motion, pointing the gun at the advancing figure. Stacey woke with a start.

"I've got my gun pointing right at her, Steele." The voice was low and menacing, and unmistakably Merrick's. Joshua could hit him with one, maybe two shots, before Merrick could turn the gun on him. But Merrick might follow through on his threat against Stacey. That chance he couldn't take. He lowered the Colt, cocking his ear toward Merrick. The banker studied his hated enemy closely, trying to decide something.

"Martin, what is this?" Stacey cried in confusion.

"Just stay right where you are, Stacey," Merrick said, "and you won't get hurt. My business is with Steele."

"But, Martin, why are you doing this?"

"He tried to kill me, remember?"

"But that was all a mistake," she cried. Or was it? She remembered what the man named Merrick had done to Joshua. Could Martin be that man? The hatred sparking in his blue eyes sent shivers along her spine.

Joshua hadn't moved. He was on his knees about three feet from Stacey. Without his gun he considered the hopelessness of the situation. Merrick would kill him, of that he had no doubt. But what of Stacey? She would be a witness.

"All right, both of you, get up real easy," Merrick said. "I want you outside where it's light."

Joshua stood up, reaching out a groping hand for Stacey. She grasped the hand, as he helped her to her feet. Stacey's mind reeled. Joshua was trying to convince Martin he was blind!

Merrick's eyes narrowed with rage as he noticed the cave's sleeping arrangements for the first time. "My, my, isn't that cozy now? The same blanket!"

Stacey could feel the blood rushing to her face, but she faced him defiantly.

"I didn't think you were the sort who would be whoring with a gunfighter, Miss Hamilton," Merrick snarled, "especially when all I ever got was a stingy kiss or two." To Steele he said, "After you killed that Mexican sergeant, I should have gelded you myself."

Stacey gasped. Even against the gun, Steele lunged at Merrick, fury making him reckless. At the last instant Merrick leaped out of his way, bringing his gun down hard against the side of Steele's head. Joshua went to his hands and knees. Stacey was beside him instantly.

"Joshua, are you all right?" She was terrified the blow had affected his eye.

Steele rubbed the side of his head. A knot was rising, but the skin wasn't broken. Stacey helped him to his feet, as Merrick shoved them both toward the mouth of the cave. Outside, the trio stood beneath the morning sun.

"You are this Ross Merrick Joshua hates so much, aren't you, Martin?" Stacey challenged.

"I suppose it doesn't matter any more if you know, my dear," Merrick conceded.

Stacey felt her blood run cold. He was going to kill them. "Martin, please, you don't have to do this. Joshua can't hurt you now. Look at him. He's blind."

Merrick gazed questioningly at Steele. He remembered the gun pointing at him in the cave, and the lunge Steele had just made at him. Both moves could have been accomplished strictly by sound. The big man's gray eyes did seem blank and lifeless. Merrick chuckled. His lie to Barnett hadn't been a lie after all.

"Tsk, tsk," Martin said, "it is such a shame that shot I took at your uncle's house missed. You could

430

have been spared, my dear."

"Merrick, let her go," Steele said. "She can't do you any harm. It'll be your word against hers. You're a prominent man in Spring Canyon. They'll just think she's mistaken."

"My 'prominence' has taken a nosedive lately," Merrick said. "Thanks in large measure to you, my old friend. No, I can't take the chance." He seemed genuinely sorry when he looked at Stacey. She returned his look with open hatred.

Merrick thumbed back the hammer of his gun, pointing it at Steele.

"No, Martin," Stacey cried, leaping in front of the weapon. "Please, I beg you!" Tears streamed down her face.

"Stacey, don't . . ." Steele reached out, as if feeling for her in front of him. He didn't want her begging for his life, not to this murderous bastard. His heart ached that she should be hurt because of him. He had to be ready for any opening Merrick left him.

"Oh, come now, Josh boy, let her talk," Merrick said. "This very proper young lady, who would scarcely allow me to take her to lunch at times, had just spent a month being your whore. I would like to hear what she has to say. Well, whore?" His hand snaked out. He slapped her hard. Stacey stumbled backward and fell heavily.

Steele, still groggy from Merrick's first blow, lunged forward, propelled by maniacal rage. It made him careless. Merrick's gun butt caught him with a crushing blow. He hit the ground hard and did not get up.

Merrick aimed the barrel of the gun at Steele's

head, ready to end his pursuit forever. Stacey clawed her way to her feet.

"Please, Martin, don't! I'll do anything you say. Anything, I swear!" she sobbed. "Please, don't kill him."

The gun didn't waver, but neither did he shoot. His gaze lifted to her face. "Go on," he said.

"I'll go away with you, Martin," she promised, seizing on the smallest shred of hope. "You could start a new life. I swear I'd never say a word about your past." Never in her life had she known such terror. She would say—do—anything to keep Joshua alive.

Merrick uncocked the gun and walked over to her. "Let me get this straight. You'll do anything I say."

"My hand to God, Martin. Just let him live!"

In truth Merrick didn't like the idea of leaving Steele alive, but if he put a bullet in his head now Stacey would be lost to him. He would have to kill her, too. And that was something, that, at least for now, he did not want to do. He considered the unconscious Steele. The man was blind, virtually harmless, besides, he thought sardonically, there was always Barnett.

"Well, my dear," Merrick said, "I think you've saved his life after all. Of course, it will be a little difficult adjusting to the fact that you've been sleeping with him, but in time I may be able to overlook it." He smiled maliciously. "Let's get out of here."

Merrick made certain not a scrap of food, nor a weapon of any kind, remained before they left. Stacey gave one last imploring look at Steele's inert form before Merrick headed them out of the canyon.

The air was cool when Steele regained

432

consciousness. He shook his head, trying to clear it, unable to believe that he was still alive. With a nameless fear clutching at him, he glanced around searching for Stacey. Everything was dark. He tried to focus. The second blow to his head could have damaged the eye.

He pressed against his throbbing temples. Something seemed to be happening. The dim outline of a juniper clump came into view. Damn, why was everything so dark? He looked at the sky. Swiftly moving clouds scudded past a shining ball. The full moon appeared. Steele blew out the breath he'd been holding. Everything was dark because it was night. He'd been out all day.

That meant Merrick had at least a fourteen hour head start on him. And where was Stacey? She must have gone with him, but why? His jaw clenched. This time there would be no escape for Merrick. This time the traitorous vermin would die. If he harmed Stacey . . . he couldn't finish the thought. But why had he taken her and left him alive?

Steele lurched unsteadily to his feet. There was little he could do without a horse to trail them. He would have to get to town. Why had Merrick left him alive? The thought nagged at him. It just didn't make sense. He started walking. By the time he got a horse Merrick would have more than a day's lead.

CHAPTER TWENTY-SIX

Stacey had to force herself to stay calm. If at all possible she had to get Martin . . . Merrick to trust her. Only then could she help herself or Joshua. They had ridden steadily for several hours. Strangely, Merrick wasn't heading away from Spring Canyon. He was heading on a course parallel to it. When they reached a large outcropping of boulders, he reined the horses to a halt.

"Barnett!" Merrick called. "Barnett, it's Martin Randolph. You in there?"

Stacey felt a cold fear stir in her heart. What did Merrick want with Barnett?

Raul Griego walked toward them holding a pistol. "Come ahead, senor, senorita." The swarthy Mexican stared at Stacey with a wary lust.

"Hold her horse for me," Merrick said. He dismounted and walked toward Barnett.

Stacey suddenly realized what Merrick was doing. He was telling Jake where to find Joshua. Joshua wouldn't have a chance. He had no weapon, he was hurt, and there were four of them. Joshua could even be blind!

Within minutes Merrick and Stacey were on the trail again. "You sent Barnett after Joshua, didn't you?" she shouted. "Answer me!" His silence answered for him. "Damn you! You promised."

He slapped her hard, almost knocking her from the saddle. "I only promised that *I* wouldn't kill him. I can't be held accountable for what an outlaw like Barnett does, can I?"

Stacey fought back tears. She now understood the depth of Joshua's hatred for this man for she felt it herself.

"Are you reneging on your promise?" he asked with a sneer, levelling his gun at her, "or can we continue?"

Stacey began to sob hysterically. "I'm sorry, Martin. I'm sorry. Please, don't shoot me. I'll keep my word to you."

"That's better," Merrick smiled. He turned and headed their horses toward Spring Canyon. He didn't see the tears stop, or the hate-filled look that bored into his back.

CHAPTER TWENTY-SEVEN

Barnett kicked his horse's flanks savagely. Steele was within his grasp now. Helpless. Blind. He was going to enjoy this. Barnett headed for the canyon with the directions supplied by Randolph. He arrived just after dawn.

He swore a string of obscenities when Steele was nowhere to be found, then ordered Cloudmaker to pick up the trail of his brother's killer. The half-breed dismounted and began to cast about. Before long he told Barnett Steele was headed back to Spring Canyon on foot.

"Damn!" Barnett shouted, "he can't be blind. Randolph lied." He spurred his horse forward. "It doesn't matter. We'll still get him before he makes town."

Steele heard the horses long before he saw them. He ducked behind a spire of rocks and watched Barnett come into view. He grimaced. How could he hope to battle four outlaws, when he didn't even have a gun?

"He has not gone beyond here," Cloudmaker asserted to Barnett, scanning the ground in front of him.

"Then he's in these rocks somewhere," Barnett said, "probably looking right at us." He swung a look around at the rock strewn landscape. "Steele, give it up! You haven't got a chance."

Steele eased himself further back into the mountain of boulders. If Barnett split up his men, maybe he could get to one of them and get a gun.

Almost immediately Barnett signalled for Pogget and Griego to fan out in different directions. Watching furtively, Steele kept his eye on Pogget, figuring him as the easier target of the two. Without a sound Steele snaked his way toward the stocky outlaw.

Pogget's heart wasn't in this at all. He feared the tall gunman. His gun hand trembled as he edged his way up the rocks.

"Drop it, or I'll blow your brains out," Steele commanded. Pogget didn't pause for an instant to wonder whether or not Steele was telling the truth. He dropped the Navy revolver as though it had turned to molten lead.

"Don't shoot, please," he begged, not daring to turn around. "I don't mean you no harm."

Steele stooped to pick up the weapon, then deftly clubbed Pogget over the head with it. He dragged the body out of sight. Using the outlaw's suspenders, he tied him up snugly. With a swift tug he yanked off Pogget's gunbelt, loaded with extra ammunition.

He peered carefully over the rock in front of him, getting the feel of the heavy Navy Colt. He couldn't see any of the others. He doubted Cloudmaker was too seriously involved. If Steele could get to Barnett, he could end it once and for all. The others would leave. Time was too important to him right now. He had to put an end to Barnett's grudge fight. Merrick was putting more distance between them all the time. And

Merrick had Stacey.

Griego caught sight of the big gringo and fired three quick shots. The bullets chipped away at the boulder Steele used for cover. Steele couldn't get a clear return shot. He held his fire.

"Give it up, Steele," Barnett called.

Joshua got a fix on Barnett's location and began snaking his way between the rocks. He picked up a small stone and heaved it ahead of him. Barnett whirled and fired in the direction of the sound.

"Freeze, Jake!" Steele called. He had a clear shot at Barnett's back. Barnett stood perfectly still.

"Drop the gun, or I'll split your spine," Steele warned.

"You don't fool me, Steele," Barnett sneered. "Randolph would never have left you a weapon."

"Don't bet your life on it, Jake."

"You killed my brother, Steele."

"He was trying to kill me."

The rationale meant nothing to Barnett. He spun suddenly, throwing his body to one side. He was surprised to see the gun buck in Steele's hand. He felt a sharp, burning sensation in his side, but scrambled behind a boulder before Steele could shoot again. Steele dove out of sight.

"I'm hit," Barnett called. "Pogget, Griego, Cloudmaker, he's over here!"

Steele heard the scraping of boots across the rocks. He guessed Griego was moving up again to help Barnett. Steele would be caught in a crossfire. He pumped several shots at Barnett, sending splinters of rock into the gang leader's face. Swearing, Barnett retaliated until his gun was empty. Steele heard the gun click on an empty chamber.

Barnett rushed to reload, the wound in his side slowing him down. Steele moved in.

Griego stepped into the open, his gun at the ready, confidence surging through him. He would pay the gringo back for the night Steele had beat him. But Griego was in too much of a hurry to repay his debt. Steele heard the bullet whip by his head. He dove and fired. Griego's eyes registered surprise as the bullet slammed into his chest, then his eyes registered nothing at all as he sank to the ground dead.

Barnett snapped the loaded cylinder back into place. He knew Griego was dead, and he wasn't stupid enough to expect support from the breed: Pogget must be dead, too. Damn! Steele had to die. The man had cost Barnett far too much. His brother, his gang, everything.

"Steele!" Barnett screamed, the pain in his side firing his hate. "Steele, you're a dead man. You hear me?" The wound continued to bleed, making his movements sluggish, dulling his thoughts. He couldn't die yet, he had to take Steele with him.

"I'm here, Jake." Steele's voice was soft.

Barnett attempted to spin around, but his muscles would no longer respond to the commands of his brain. It took him a full half minute to shift his body enough to see that Steele was just six feet away from him. His hated enemy stood with his gun at his side. All Barnett had to do was aim and fire. But his arm was dead weight. The gun seemed to weigh a ton in itself. His hate was as strong and real as ever. To have Steele so close and not be able to destroy him was the ultimate defeat for Barnett.

"I'll kill you, you bastard." Barnett's voice faded more with each word.

Steele kept a cautious eye on the outlaw leader, but he knew that the threats were empty ones. Steele caught the feel of Barnett's bitter frustration, to have fought so hard for so long, only to have it end in defeat, in death. He thought of his own pursuit of Merrick.

Using the last ounce of will he possessed Jake Barnett lifted the heavy Colt with both hands. The gun waved unsteadily. Sweat broke out on his forehead. Using both thumbs he cocked the hammer. Steele made no attempt either to get out of the way, or to bring his own gun to bear.

"Kill you," Barnett rasped. "Kill." The color had gone out of his world, everything around him, including Steele was a pallid shade of gray. What was left of his mind knew that his finger rested on the trigger of his gun. All he had to do was squeeze it and Steele would be dead. Squeeze it. Squeeze. His body turned to lead. His arms sagged. The gun hit the dirt in front of him. Steele had won. He tried to look at him one more time. Even that was denied him. Barnett slumped to the dirt, his vengeance forever thwarted.

Steele's eyes were on the Apache, who stood above him in the rocks. Cloudmaker's gun was in its holster.

"You can bury them," Steele said. "Pogget's tied in those rocks. I don't expect to see either of you again." Steele holstered his borrowed pistol. "I trust no one will object if I take Barnett's horse."

The Indian shook his dark head, his black eyes regarding Steele with grudging admiration. He turned

440

his back carelessly and walked toward the trussed up Pogget.

Steele picked up Barnett's rifle, as well as Griego's weapons and ammunition, then he mounted Barnett's bay. The horse seemed sound. Heading back the way he had come, he wondered how long it would take him to track Merrick this time.

Merrick pulled up on the horses. They had been pushing them hard now for nearly a week. He glanced at Stacey, who immediately took on a submissive look.

"There's a town not far from here," he said. "You've been there. Elizabethtown. There's bound to be a preacher there. We'll get married right away. That will remove any residual temptation," he leered. "A wife can't testify against her husband."

Stacey's face turned chalk-white. She didn't dare speak. All she could do was nod meekly. Merrick had not allowed her a moment's rest. She was a strong woman, but he was doing everything he could to break her will. She refused to make it easy for him. She had to stay strong for Joshua.

At the thought of him, her heart lurched. She didn't even know if he was still alive. Barnett could have killed him. Merrick's blow might have blinded him. Any number of things could prevent his pursuit. But she couldn't allow herself to think that way. She had to believe that Joshua would rescue her from Merrick. She couldn't take much more of this, if she believed that Joshua would never come.

They rode into Elizabethtown, and Stacey's heart sank. She didn't see a single familiar face. Population turnover in a mining town was part of the natural

441

order of things. With John Beal dead, there would be no refuge for her here. Her bedraggled appearance attracted a few curious stares, but no one would ask questions. It was none of their business.

Merrick tied off their horses in front of the Miner's Inn. Stacey refused his offer of assistance, even though it was all she could do to stay on her feet as they entered the lobby. He stayed behind her, carrying his saddlebags draped over his right arm.

"My fiancee has had quite an ordeal," he said to the young clerk behind the desk. "She was captured by a gunman, and I had to shoot it out with him." The lies rolled easily off his tongue. "I'd appreciate it, if you would have a hot bath drawn for her."

The clerk hastily ordered an old man to start fetching the hot water. With a little more familiarity than was necessary, he took hold of Stacey's arm and helped her up the stairs.

Merrick called up after him. "Please arrange for a woman to come in and stay with her immediately. I don't want her left alone." He gave the clerk a conspiratorial look that suggested she might try to harm herself.

The clerk nodded in quick agreement. "I'll send for someone right away."

Merrick was confident Stacey would stay put for the moment. He hurried out to find a preacher, keeping a tight grip on his saddlebags. He wanted to be out of the territory as quickly as possible. No doubt the good citizens of Spring Canyon already had Rube Tucker on his trail. He'd made a rather large, and distinctly illegal, withdrawal from the bank on his last trip into town. He grimaced when he thought again of all

Steele had cost him. At least he had solved that problem once and for all.

The hot water felt soothing, intoxicating. Stacey opened her eyes to see a middle-aged woman with the look of life in a saloon, fussing over her like a mother hen.

"My name is Mavis Haynes, honey. I'm gonna take real good care of you."

The woman rattled off a dozen questions, but Stacey answered none of them. Mavis clucked sympathetically. The poor little thing must be in shock.

Merrick returned a short while later, carrying a bulky package. He handed it to Mavis and left the room.

"Your young man has brought you a gift," Mavis cooed. Seeing Stacey make no move to open it, Mavis took it upon herself to rip open the package. A garishly styled gown tumbled out. A whore's dress was Stacey's unbidden thought.

"Oooh," Mavis sighed, "this must be your weddin' dress, dear. It's lovely. Let's get it on you, shall we?"

The thought of being married to Merrick sent a shock wave of revulsion through her. Stacey had to fight the urge to vomit. She offered no resistance, however, when Mavis fitted the gown over her head. This had to be a nightmare. She would wake up soon, safe and warm in the cave with Joshua. He would be holding her, loving her. Suddenly she was crying, sobbing heart-wrenching sounds.

"Joshua!" she screamed.

"My lands, dear," Mavis cooed, "what is it? What's wrong?"

443

"I can't marry that vermin," she cried. "Please, Mavis, you've got to help me!"

"Now what are you talking about, honey?" Mavis chirped. "Oh, I know, you're just a little scairt, that's all. Now don't you worry your pretty little head, the weddin' night's not nearly what it's cracked up to be."

"No!" Stacey shrieked. "You don't understand! This man has kidnapped me. He's threatened to kill the man I love, unless I do what he says."

Mavis regarded Stacey with open suspicion. "You mean that nice Mr. Merrick? Why, I never met a finer gentleman." Mavis seemed to get an inspiration. "Oh, I know what it is," she said, nodding to herself at her insight. "Mr. Merrick mentioned that you were held captive by a gang of outlaws. They did something to you, didn't they, dear? Come on now, you can tell Mavis."

"Ross Merrick is the man who kidnapped me," Stacey said again. "Please, Mavis, before it's too late. You've got to help me get out of here!"

Mavis looked like she was beginning to believe her. Stacey pressed on. "Please, you must help me get away."

"But he'll be back any minute. And if he's really threatened this other man, unless you go along with him, isn't it dangerous for you to run away?"

Stacey's throat constricted. "I don't think the other man will be coming, Mavis. I don't think he can."

"You poor thing."

Stacey eyed the open window. "Where does that lead?"

"To the balcony, then to the ground. But, honey, it's quite a jump . . . "

Stacey hurried over to the window. She saw several men walking along the boardwalk on the street opposite. They all looked like miners or gamblers. Merrick was nowhere in sight. She put one leg over the sill, then climbed out.

"Now you be careful," Mavis said. "I still don't know if I should be letting you do this."

"Believe me, Mavis," Stacey said, "you should."

She edged her way over to the balcony railing. Mavis was right. It was quite a drop. Maybe twenty feet, but she would have to chance it. She didn't dare try the stairs.

Stacey balanced herself on the railing, praying no one would notice her. Or if they did, that they would pay no attention. She would be jumping into an alley. Maybe she really could get away with this. She thought of Joshua and a pang of indescribable pain shot through her. God, let him still be alive! she prayed. Let him be all right!

She heard Merrick's voice inside the hotel room. He was swearing at Mavis, demanding to know where Stacey had gone. It was now or never. Stacey leaped to the ground. She felt the bone-jarring twisting of her right ankle, but she didn't let it stop her. She limped painfully down the alley, clawing her way past trash and overturned crates and even a passed-out drunk. A horse was hitch-tied to a piece of wood protruding from the side of the hotel. The animal probably belonged to the drunk.

Stacey's whole being recoiled at the thought of stealing the man's horse, but her life depended on it. She climbed aboard the animal, her foot still aching fiercely. Merrick might already be out of the hotel by now. She didn't dare return to the street. She kneed the horse down the alley. When she passed the end of the hotel building, Merrick jumped out and grabbed the reins of her horse.

Startled, Stacey leaped off the animal's back, crying out when she landed on her badly sprained ankle. Tears of agony streamed down her face, as she hobbled toward the street. If she could just get there, maybe someone would help her.

Merrick grabbed her by the hair and slammed her against the side of the building. "I persuaded Mavis to tell me how you'd gotten out of the hotel, my dear," he grinned, his eyes mocking her. He dragged her to her feet. "Now let's hurry, shall we? We don't want to be late for our own wedding."

He shoved her ahead of him. "And don't think about asking for help, Eustacia. One word and I'll kill you—and the person you tell." He chuckled. The sound had a sick quality to it that made Stacey's skin crawl. "You're about to become my wife. Mrs. Ross Merrick, though when we leave here you will go by the name Mrs. Daniel Reynolds. Do you understand?"

A shudder went through her. She hugged her arms tight against her, even as she forced herself to let him help her walk. The ankle no longer supported her at all.

"You will cooperate won't you, my dear?" Merrick smiled.

"Yes, Martin."

He slapped her. "What did you say?"

"Yes . . . Ross." She rubbed the side of her cheek. Damn him! If she ever got her hands on a gun. . . .

She looked submissively at him, as he led her up the street.

Mavis Haynes didn't say a word during the ceremony. Merrick had told her to be a witness and to keep her mouth shut. She felt sorry for the little blonde lady, but not sorry enough to risk her own life. The small party stood in a shack that temporarily doubled as E-town's only church.

The preacher was a prospector in town to collect supplies. He rarely officiated at anything even remotely religious since being struck by gold fever three years before. A hard-looking man in his fifties, he looked first at Merrick, then at Stacey. He frowned. The girl looked scared out of her wits.

"Do you have any family here, Miss?" he asked.

"No one," Merrick replied for her.

"Why don't I just talk to the little lady for a couple of minutes. She seems terribly shy . . ." The old man looked tough, but he had a genuine soft spot when it came to womenfolk.

"Just read the words. Now." Something about Merrick's tone convinced the parson that it would be useless to argue.

The ceremony was brief. Later Stacey didn't even remember saying "I do." But she must have. She looked down at the small gold band on her finger. She was Ross Merrick's wife! Dear God, why had she done it? If Joshua was coming, he would have caught up with them long before now. He had to be dead. But even if he wasn't, even if he had somehow survived Barnett, she had promised herself to Merrick in exchange for his life. If he found her now, found her as Merrick's wife, he would never forgive her. A bleakness settled over her such as she had never known.

Within minutes they were mounted again, heading north. Stacey had no idea what Merrick's ultimate destination was. She could only play for time, and pray Joshua could follow the meager trail they left behind.

Two hours after dusk Merrick called a halt for the night. Stacey made no complaints about getting their supper. She was starving. Both of them ate hungrily. Merrick said nothing, but she felt his eyes on her several times. After she had cleaned up the dishes, she sat staring into the flames, grateful for their warmth. As always her thoughts turned to Joshua. What was he doing now? Was he worried about her? Did he think of the moments they had spent in paradise together, as she did? She felt tears sting her eyes. The thought would not go away. Joshua was dead.

Merrick stamped out his pipe and strode over to sit beside her. She stiffened. His arm trailed around her waist. She bolted. She swung her hand hard, feeling it collide with his face. He grabbed her wrists as she struggled to break free.

"What the hell do you think you're doing, wife?" he demanded.

The full import he placed on the word "wife" struck home to her. Her knees buckled in abject terror.

"Martin, you wouldn't?" she pleaded, unable to get used to his new name.

"Wouldn't I! You're my wife now, Stacey. And you're damn well going to act like one." His hands

448

explored her body, cruelly digging into her breasts. "What's the matter, am I not as accomplished a lover as our mutual friend?" He chuckled malevolently. "You know it's only by the compliments of a gutless French captain that you even had the pleasure."

"Joshua told me what you did to him," she sobbed, still unable to break his grip on her wrist.

"I'll bet he left out the best part. Did he tell you I wanted to have your stallion gelded?"

Stacey recoiled in utter revulsion. She remembered Merrick's cryptic comment in the cave, and how it had caused Joshua to attack him so recklessly.

"No wonder he hates you so much," she cried hysterically. "If I had a gun, I'd shoot you myself!"

He slapped her. She screamed, pounding at him with her fists, clawing, kicking. He backhanded her across the face. She stumbled and fell hard. She tried struggling to her feet, but he lunged at her again, driving his body against hers. He forced her to the ground, his full weight on top of her. She kept screaming, trying to get at his eyes, biting, scratching. He tore at her clothes, until she lay naked beneath him. Her terror was mindless now.

He held her pinioned beneath him. She felt his fist dig into her stomach, as he unfastened his pants. He shoved them down past his hips. Stacey screamed until her voice was gone, expecting him to violate her at any second. But it didn't happen. He swore violently, and she felt his flaccid manhood against her thigh.

She jerked a hand free and put all of her strength behind a vicious blow to the side of his head. She felt his blood on her hand, felt his body tremble with rage. Then he rained blow after blow on her until finally everything was blessed darkness.

When she woke the next morning, every muscle in her body screamed with pain. She couldn't move without hurting. Even so, she had won one tiny victory. She knew he had not had his way with her. She had not been raped. But she was still naked, and she felt his cold eyes on her. She looked at him and shuddered at the malevolence she saw in those eyes.

"Don't bother to get dressed," he said, his voice as ugly as his soul. "I like you just the way you are."

She tried to close her ears to the degradation of his leering cackle. He came over to sit beside her. Apparently he was still impotent, for he did not rape her, but she had to endure the sickening violation of his hands and mouth before unconsciousness claimed her again. Just before she sank into oblivion she thought of Joshua finding her now, like this. She wished she were dead.

CHAPTER TWENTY-EIGHT

Steele rode into Elizabethtown. He'd travelled more than a week already, scarcely stopping for more than a few hours each night. Twice he'd lost their trail and had to double back, losing precious hours. After that, he forced himself to stop at night. He couldn't let them get any further ahead of him. He wasn't even sure they had been in E'town. He could only hope they had had to pick up supplies.

He gave descriptions of the pair at several local saloons. When he received only hostile stares in response, he pulled out his gun and asked again. No one had seen them. He decided to make the Miner's Inn his next stop.

"Looking for a couple of friends of mine," Steele said, eyeing the clerk. "A man and a woman travelling together." He told the man what they looked like. "Maybe they passed through here four or five days ago."

The clerk hesitated. Steele's temper broke. He was tired, hot, hungry, and scared. His bitterest enemy had kidnapped a woman who meant more to him than he dared admit. In the blink of an eye he had his .44 shoved against the nose of the now terrified clerk.

The boy began babbling about two people fitting the description Steele had given him. They were at the hotel for only a few hours four days ago. He hadn't heard any names. They stayed just long enough for the lady to have a bath and for them to get married.

Joshua's face contorted. He didn't realize he was choking the boy, until he noticed the blue cast to the kid's face. He threw the boy to the floor behind the desk. He heard him choking in air as he stormed out of the hotel lobby. He did not look back.

Married! Why would Stacey marry that son-of-a-bitch? She had a horse, she could have tried to escape. She could have sought help here in E'town. But she had done neither. Why?

A killing anger such as he had never known took hold of him. They were married. He thought of the nights they had already spent together. Nights when he had been terrified that Merrick might have raped her, killed her. Instead she had married him. She was Merrick's wife! She was sharing his blankets willingly, kissing him, touching him, surrendering herself as she had done. . . . Something seemed to stick in his throat. All this time he had been driving himself like a maniac, nearly insane at the thought of what Merrick could be doing to her by force.

He stomped back into the hotel. The clerk tried to bolt, but Steele corraled him. He forced his temper to settle at a point where he could think rationally again.

"Boy, you listen real good," he said. "Did they say anything . . . anything at all about where they were going?"

The boy shook from head to foot. "Nothin',

mister." Then something clicked, "Well, I don't know if it's worth nothin' to ya, but I seen 'em headin' north out of town. I can't say they kept goin' that way, though."

Steele stalked back to his horse. North. It was a slim lead at best. But it was all he had. His thoughts kept turning to Stacey. Had she just been toying with him all along? Setting him up to keep him from going after Merrick? She had had an understanding with Martin Randolph. Hadn't she told him that herself? Merrick had money. He could establish a fancy medical practice for her in some big city back east. Maybe she even loved him. What else could he think? She had married Ross Merrick! The man Steele had sworn to send to hell personally.

He would find Merrick. He would find them both, if it took the rest of his days. And when he found them, he would make her watch as he killed her husband. Then he would . . . he shook his head. His mind refused to think farther than that.

Steele spent nearly two hours searching for the preacher the clerk had said performed the ceremony for Merrick and Stacey, but he was nowhere to be found. He was a prospector, someone told him, probably out working his claim. Steele couldn't take any more time to look for him. Nor could he find the saloon woman, who had apparently been a witness.

They were still a full four days ahead of him. Four days. She had been his wife for four days . . . and nights. He spurred his horse recklessly, heading north.

Merrick was getting tired of beating her every night.

453

Stacey seemed more and more listless, even though he'd generously allowed her to get dressed today. Perhaps he had done some kind of internal damage. He decided it didn't matter all that much. She wasn't worth the effort. With his money he could find many willing females. She was only slowing him down.

He stared down at her unconscious form. His gun was in his hand. She'd been out for three hours now. She had screamed every time he touched her. His eyes darkened as he remembered that she had been repulsed by his kisses even before she had ever heard of Ross Merrick.

It was an irony not lost on him that she should love his bitterest enemy. She should have been his, would have been his, if Steele had died in that lead mine. But Brissot had backed out at the last moment, saying it was one thing for Merrick to make his despicable threat, quite another to allow it to be carried out. Steele was a man, a worthy adversary and a courageous soldier, Brissot said. By inference Merrick was a coward.

He pulled the hammer back on the pistol, nestling it against her golden hair. He imagined pulling the trigger, watching her body jerk and die. It was too bad in a way that Steele was dead. He would've enjoyed the big man's reaction to what he had done to Stacey. For long minutes his finger twitched against the trigger. It would be so easy, so easy. And it was no less than she deserved.

In the end, out of some sense of loss over what might have been, he found he couldn't pull the trigger. Damn Steele! Even dead he managed to interfere with his life. He uncocked the weapon and

454

slammed it back into the holster on his hip.

Stacey did not stir as Merrick gathered their supplies and horses and headed out. He gave her one last look. He almost regretted what he had done to her. But she had dared fall in love with Joshua Steele. He kneed the horse forward, pulling hers along behind. The winds were blowing in from the north. She would probably freeze to death tonight.

CHAPTER TWENTY-NINE

Steele had been making up for lost time. He was closer to them now than he had been since the day he'd started after them. This morning he had found a camp that was less than a day old. They were making terrible time. Steele puzzled on that. Whatever the reason, he was glad of it. Tomorrow, or the next day, he would catch up with them.

It was two hours past dusk when he forced himself to make camp for the night. This close he didn't want to take a chance on passing their trail in the dark. Merrick might spook and head in another direction.

Steele built a small fire. The nights were getting cold. He made himself some coffee and drank it down. He didn't feel much like eating, but he chewed on some beef jerky anyway. He would need his strength for Merrick.

His stomach churned as he thought of their spending another night together. Did Stacey respond to Merrick's embrace with the same passion he had aroused in her? Did she murmur his name? Did she tell him she needed him, wanted him—loved him? Damn them both! Over and over he thought about what he would do to Stacey when he caught up with them. He imagined his hands closing around her slender throat. He dreamed of it and woke in a cold sweat. No! Dreaming of her had kept him sane in

Mexico. Making love to her had healed him of his tortured nightmares. He could never hurt her. Why? Why had she done this? Had she loved Merrick all along? Pretending to love him only to save the bastard's life? If it wasn't true, why had she married him? There were no answers to his tormented questions. Angrily he rolled over and tried to get back to sleep.

A strange sound caught his attention. He cocked an ear toward it. Nothing. He had just about decided it must have been the wind, when it came again. A moaning sound, like an animal in pain. He threw off the blankets, his gun at the ready. He waited for the sound. This time he got a fix on it. He moved beyond a small clump of trees. The moon was obliterated by clouds, making it nearly impossible to see. His vision still wasn't perfect anyway, though it improved with each passing day.

Steele froze next to a giant cottonwood and listened again. For long minutes he heard only the ordinary sounds of the night. Then it came again. It was a moan all right, but not from any animal except a human animal. Someone was hurt. He advanced cautiously, his every sense alert to danger. He caught sight of a deeper darkness against the dark of the ground. A body?

A sudden tightness seized him. God, no. He ran, dropping to his knees beside it. He felt it. The softness of it. His fingers traced over it. They found her face. It was strangely sticky, not the proportions he remembered at all. He touched his fingers to his mouth. Blood.

He jammed his gun back into his holster. He had to get her back to the fire. She was so cold. Gently, he lifted her. A groan of agony greeted him.

"Stacey, Stacey, it's Joshua. It's all right. I'm here."
He talked to her, saying anything that came into his
head, as he hurried back to the fire.

With great tenderness he laid her on his blankets.
He covered her quickly. He threw more wood on the
fire, watching it blaze up. Then he eased her closer to
it, so he could take a look. Hot tears stung his eyes. He
couldn't hold back the choking sobs that racked him,
when he saw what Merrick had done to her face. Both
of her eyes were blackened and swollen shut. Her lips
were cracked and bruised.

"Damn him! Damn him to hell!" Blindly, Joshua
staggered for his canteen. He wet his bandana and
dabbed carefully at her cuts and bruises. Over and
over he called her name, but she did not hear him.

With a sudden gasp her hands clutched at her
stomach. He laid her blouse open. Her whole torso
was a mass of bruises. Doing the best he knew how, he
bandaged her wounds. She started shivering. He eased
himself under the blankets next to her, warming her
with his own body. He held her as closely as he could
without hurting her further. He kissed her hair, her
swollen eyes. She cried when it hurt so badly she
couldn't bear it. He didn't wipe away the tears that
scalded his own cheeks. Over and over he murmured,
"Forgive me."

In the morning he kept the fire burning. She was
still cold and had yet to regain consciousness. He
eased some water down her throat. Throughout the
day he never left her side. He cursed himself for a fool
time and again. How could he ever have believed she
married Merrick of her own free will? In fevered
delirium she screamed Joshua's name over and over,

begging him to help her, crying when she thought he would never understand or forgive her.

"I did it for you, Joshua," she cried. "I did it for you. I couldn't let him kill you."

He thought she might be conscious, but she wasn't even aware what she was saying. A new surge of pain would grip her and she would scream in agony.

He didn't think he could stand another day of seeing her hurt like this. He raged inwardly at Merrick, who was getting farther and farther away. If his hatred for Merrick had been irrational because of what Merrick had done to him personally, it was magnified a thousandfold now for what he had done to Stacey.

Finally, on the third day her fever broke. "Joshua?" she called.

At first he thought she was still delirious. Then he read the comprehension in her green eyes. "I'm here," he said, picking up her hand.

"Your eye?" she gasped.

"It's fine, doctor."

The tears started then. Her sobs were soft and controlled. He let her cry. He smoothed her hair, sitting close to her.

"Martin . . . Merrick . . . he . . ."

"Don't think about it."

"But he . . ."

"I know."

"Do you hate me?"

"I could never hate you." Gently, with regard to her still slightly swollen lips, he kissed her.

Her arms flew around his neck. She cried again. "He was so horrible. He wanted me to . . . to . . . but I wouldn't. He took off my clothes . . ." Her sobs came harder.

He held her against him. "Don't think of it."

"He tried to rape me," she whimpered, "but he couldn't. He was impotent. That only made him madder. He hit me, he hit me, he hit me!" She couldn't stop crying. "And then he wouldn't let me get dressed. He made me . . . he made me ride the horse naked. He made me lie down at night, and he would look at me. And he touched me, and he . . . he . . . oh, God, Joshua, I want to die!"

He remembered what Merrick had done to him and that he too had prayed to die. Something hardened inside him. He removed her arms from around his neck. "You won't die, Stacey," he said, "I won't let you." He paused, then asked, "Did Merrick say anything at all about where he was headed?"

"Nothing."

"If he gets to a railhead, it could take me years to find him again," he muttered, almost to himself.

She stared at his eyes. They were as cold and hard as the day she had seen him in Elizabethtown. She was suddenly frightened. "Let him go, Joshua," she whispered.

He shot her a look of angry surprise. "You can say that, after what he did to you?"

She cringed at the harshness of his voice. More tears fell.

"I asked you a question, Stacey," he said, straightening to his full length. "Are you telling me you want Merrick to go free?"

She had a vague impression of gentle hands and soothing, caressing words, while she had been gripped by the fever. Looking at him now, she wondered if it had been a dream. "No," she choked, "not free. But

460

let the law catch him this time, please, Joshua. You've already let him destroy four years of your life. How many more are you willing to throw away on a man like Merrick?"

"As many as it takes," he grated. Turning his back to her, he walked over to the fire. Pouring himself a cup of coffee, he said, "I'll take you as far as the next town. You can catch a stage home. I'll be going after Merrick."

"I'm going with you," she said.

"You're in no condition for the kind of travelling I'm going to be doing."

"And what am I supposed to do?" she asked, her voice quivering. "Sit home and wait for you — for how ever many weeks or months of *years* it takes you to catch up with him this time?"

"No, Stacey," he said, not looking at her. "I don't expect you to wait. I don't want you to wait for me."

Her heart was in her throat. "Are you saying you aren't coming back?

He looked at her, his eyes unreadable. "I won't be back, Stacey."

For a full minute she couldn't breathe. His rejection would have been devastating no matter when it came, but for it to come now after all she had been through was an almost physical agony. "You do hate me," she sobbed brokenly. "After what Merrick did . . . after what he did . . ." Her crying bordered on hysteria.

Steele cursed himself for an idiot. He should have waited until she was stronger before he said anything. But he knew if he didn't catch Merrick in the next few days, it could literally take years to find him again. He couldn't allow her to waste her life waiting for something that could never be.

"Stacey," he said fiercely, "this has nothing to do with you." He strode over to her and bent to pick up her hand, but she jerked it away.

Later she would decide that her shattered nerves had ripped away the last vestiges of her pride. She didn't care what she was saying, all she could think about was that she was losing Joshua, and she couldn't bear it. "I love you, Joshua," she cried. "You must know that I love you. How can you tell me you won't be coming back? Doesn't what we had mean anything to you? What were you doing?" she shrieked, "relieving your male frustrations on a willing female?"

"Stacey! Stop it!" he snapped, kneeling beside her and gripping her shoulders. "I care about you. You have to know that. But . . ."

"But . . . but!" she raged, "with you there's always a but, and we both know what that but is—Ross Merrick! Your hating him is more important than loving me. Isn't it! Damn you, isn't it?" She climbed painfully to her feet, yanking her arm away when he tried to restrain her. They stood facing each other.

"I'm going to find him, and I'm going to kill him. For what he did to me, and for what he did to you."

"No!" she spat at him, "don't you dare tell me you're going to murder a man because of me! Don't you dare! If you fit me into your rationale for murder, then at least have the decency to be honest about why, Joshua. It's because Merrick trespassed on what you regarded as your property?! It's none of me. It's all you! You're sick, Joshua. You're just as sick as Merrick in your own way. Look what you've let him do to you. All you can do is hate."

She stopped, astonished by the violent emotions that fired her words. She drew in a deep breath, trying to steady her nerves.

"This isn't getting us anywhere," he said softly, turning to set about breaking camp. "Can you ride?" he asked, after he'd saddled the horse.

"I'll ride." He extended his hand to help her mount, but she ignored it. Gritting her teeth against the pain, she climbed into the saddle.

Steele's only comment all day came at mid-afternoon, when he stopped to check the remains of Merrick's latest camp. "He stayed here two days. He must think he's safe now, that there's no one following him."

Stacey said nothing. Her ribs ached, her head throbbed. It was all she could do to keep from falling off the horse. Yet the pain that hurt the most was not physical. After weeks of intimacy in mind and body, she and Joshua were now further apart than if they had never met.

When they made camp that night, Joshua handed her two of his three blankets. "One blanket won't keep you warm," she said stiffly.

For just an instant she caught a glimpse of naked desire in his eyes, as he must have thought of the added warmth sharing their bodies would bring. But she turned abruptly, feigning indifference, and lay down as near to the fire as possible.

She woke just after midnight, shivering violently. The fire had gone out. With fingers that were numb from the cold, she tried to get the fire started again. The tenseness of her muscles because of the shivering only added to the pain of her still bruised body. It took several tries before she could get the wood to catch. Joshua was curled under his blanket four feet to her left. How could he possibly be warm?

Stacey stumbled over a branch as she gathered more

wood to add to the fire. Steele woke with a muttered oath.

"Why the hell didn't you wake me?" he growled. "You must be freezing." Quickly he got the fire blazing again. When he finished, he turned to her and said, "Come over here." His voice was stern.

"I will not," she said.

Glowering fiercely, he stood up and tromped over to her. He grabbed up all three blankets, settling them around both of their shoulders. He pulled her resisting body against his. "Don't tell me you'd rather freeze to death than have me touch you," he hissed.

"Maybe," she snapped back. She tried to stay awake, to not allow the enveloping warmth of his body to seep into her being. But her exhausted state would not allow her that luxury. Within minutes she slumped against him, fast asleep.

He kissed the top of her head, gently cradling her against him. In time he, too, slept.

The next day they made a few more miles. Stacey was feeling better physically, though the pain in her heart had not lessened. Since they scarcely spoke to one another, she spent a lot of time thinking. She remembered the nights in the cave when Joshua had made love to her. She was positive he had not thought of Merrick during that time. And now, in a way, it was her fault that he was once again committed to this insane vengeance. If she had only succeeded in escaping Merrick, got his gun, anything. Merrick's treatment of her had re-fired Joshua's banked rage.

She wanted to talk to him, ask him again not to leave her behind, but he was more aloof than ever. It was as if he sensed the kill was near, and he would allow no distractions. When they came upon a small town in the Colorado Territory, she knew what he was going to do.

"Merrick was here yesterday," he told her, unable to keep the exhilaration out of his voice. He squeezed some paper currency into her resisting hand. He had rented her a hotel room, and now he was about to ride out of her life forever. "This should be plenty to get you back to Spring Canyon," he was saying. "If you need more you can wire Sam. This town's too small for a regular stage run, but there'll be one through in a couple of days."

"Fine," she said, tossing the money on the bed.

He pressed a pistol in her hand. "You'll be alone. I'd feel better if you had this."

"Fine."

"Stacey," he began, then stopped. He wanted nothing more than to take her in his arms, to pledge his undying love for her, to heal the pain he had caused her, but Merrick stood between them. As long as Merrick lived, he would be there. He would hurt her now to leave her, but in the long run it would be for the best. He couldn't ask her to wait, he couldn't even ask her to understand.

She crossed the room and sat down on the bed. Her green eyes, which had once sparkled with life, now reflected only a studied weariness. "Good-bye, Joshua," she said in a lifeless voice that cut through him like a knife. "I can't tell you that I wish you luck in your hunt, because I don't."

"Stacey, I never meant to hurt you," he said, his voice pleading with her not to hate him. "It's just that Merrick . . ."

"Don't tell me again what he did to you, Joshua," she interrupted. "What he did to you is nothing compared to what you've done to yourself." Her voice was still strangely expressionless. "Please, just leave."

He held his arms rigidly at his sides. "Good-bye, Stacey." He turned and left the room.

She stared at the closed door for long minutes after he'd gone. Then the tears came. And she thought they would never stop.

CHAPTER THIRTY

It had taken him two days, but Joshua could feel it now in the tenseness of his body. Merrick was just hours away, maybe minutes. He itched to have it done with forever. Nothing could prevent this final confrontation. The man he had hated for years, the man who had whipped him, brutalized him to a point where he was scarcely more than an animal, the man who had beaten and abused the woman he now admitted he loved, would soon be in his gunsights. Ross Merrick would be dead.

"Stacey, I'm sorry," he muttered aloud. "If it could have been any other way . . ." He hoped she would forget him, find a good man and get married, have children. Then he suddenly realized what a liar he was. He didn't want her to ever forget him, because he would never forget her. He loved her, loved her with an aching hunger that would never be satisfied, no matter how many times he made love to her. Even his ranch near the Rockies would be empty without her. Maybe he would go back. Maybe she could forgive him. No—she could never forgive murder.

He came on the remains of a campsite. He felt the ashes. Less than four hours old. The shoeprints of the horse matched those of the animal Merrick had purchased in town. Only half broke, the hostler said, but Merrick had wanted a fresh horse, and the gelding had been all he'd had.

He did not stop to eat. The urge to kill was making him reckless. Over and over the image of Merrick and what he had done to Stacey played in his mind. He yanked the horse to a stop, chiding himself. After so many years of patience he couldn't afford to get careless now.

His eyes scanned the immediate area. More canyon country, filled with sheer drop-offs and countless places a man could hide. He pulled the makings from his shirt pocket, rolled and lit the cheroot. He took a deep drag, then kneed the horse forward. A shot echoed around him. Steele poured out of the saddle, diving for a nearby rock.

The bullet kicked up dirt behind him. If he hadn't moved when he did . . . Damn, in spite of himself, his rage had made him careless. It wouldn't happen again.

"Never could face me man-to-man, could you Merrick?" Steele called out, his voice deadly calm.

Merrick sat in the cover of the rocks and fired rapidly three more times. He was scared, scared to death. Steele was alive! The man was unkillable! If the ex-agent got his hands on him now, Merrick knew he was a dead man. He knew it as he had never known anything. He could pump bullet after bullet into Steele, but if there was still a pulse of life left in the man, Merrick would be dead.

Terrified, he fired again, trying to get Steele to panic, to run to another hiding place. He knew even as he tried it, that he would fail. Steele would never panic, never break. Just as he'd never broken under the imperialist whip. Merrick understood with a sickening certainty that he himself would have babbled any information asked of him after the first stroke. Merrick had long ago accepted the fact that he was no man at all. It made his hate for Steele all the more maniacal.

Merrick pumped more lead at the rock Steele had taken refuge behind. Was he still there? A panicked thought struck him. What if Steele had moved? What if somehow Steele had gotten behind him, was even now sneaking up on him.

Merrick whirled and fired. There was no one there.

"I found Stacey, Merrick." Again Steele's voice betrayed no emotion.

Merrick's eyes ripped from rock to rock, trying to deduce where Steele's voice was coming from. "She fell! She fell!" he screamed. "Her horse threw her. I tried to save her, but I couldn't."

"She wasn't dead, Merrick."

Agonized panic washed over him. He knew! Steele knew what he had done to Stacey! Why had he tried to ambush him? When he had seen who it was, why hadn't he spurred his horse into a gallop and fled?

He could still do it, he thought wildly. His horse was just over there, just six feet away. Yes, he'd make a run for it. Where was Steele's horse? First he would shoot it. He couldn't see Steele's gelding anywhere. Where was the horse? Where was Steele?

Fear spurred him like a raging beast. He bolted for his horse. His mind could think of only one thing—escape. The man's strange actions frightened the half-broke animal. It danced nervously away from him. Bullets kicked up dirt around the gelding's legs. The horse reared in terror. Merrick grabbed at the reins with both hands, dropping his rifle as he did so. The gun slid part way down the slope. The terrified animal raced ahead of it, breaking Merrick's grip on the reins. In panic Merrick chased after the horse for several yards, then he realized what he had done. Steele had deliberately spooked the animal to draw him into the open.

Wild-eyed, he looked around him. Nothing moved. Yet Merrick knew at this very instant he was in Steele's gunsights. He bent over to vomit.

"Don't shoot, Steele. Please! Don't shoot me," Merrick begged. "That horse has a lot of money in those saddlebags. We could make a deal."

A bullet kicked up dirt at his feet. Steele wasn't even trying.

"Steele, please!" Merrick's voice was a shriek of terror. "I'll do anything you say! Anything!"

Steele stepped out from behind a boulder. Merrick turned. He was staring into the face of his own death. Steele held his rifle carelessly. It wasn't even aimed at Merrick. But his eyes! Those damned wolf eyes of his!

"I should have gelded you myself," Merrick cursed.

"It won't work, Merrick," Steele drawled. "You're not going to goad me into anything reckless. Not just yet."

Merrick trembled. "Damn it! What do you want, Steele? Go ahead! Shoot! Get it over with!"

"It's been four years, Merrick. Surely you don't expect me to just end it with a single bullet. I have to savor the moment."

"Damn you! Damn you!" Merrick screeched, remembering with abject terror the tortures he had ordered inflicted on this tall man. He couldn't tolerate the thought of such agony for himself. If Steele was going to kill him, he wanted it over now. "Did she tell you how much she liked my hands on her body?"

A bullet tore through Merrick's left leg. He screamed in agony, falling to the ground. The pain somehow renewed his will to live. He tried to crawl to the nearby rocks. A bullet spit dirt in his path. Steele's movements remained deceptively casual, as he stepped closer to Merrick.

"Give me a chance," Merrick begged. "For Godsakes give me a chance!"

"Like you gave Stacey?" Steele snarled. "Like you gave Rudy Montoya, or the six juaristas you put in front of that cannon? Like you gave me?" A new thought came to him, "Where's the marriage license?"

"In my saddlebags. I'll tear it up. It doesn't matter anyway," Merrick babbled. "She fainted during the ceremony. I forged her signature. I forced the preacher and the witness to sign. Stacey never went through with it."

That fact somehow relieved Steele's mind a little. He would write Stacey a letter. She would be very happy to hear that she had never in fact been Mrs. Ross Merrick.

Steele now stood less than two feet away from the crawling traitor. Merrick rolled over onto his stomach, still holding his bleeding leg. His eyes were begging Steele.

Joshua levered another cartridge into the Winchester, pointing it at Merrick's head. Everything in him clawed at his insides, commanding him to squeeze the trigger, to end the life of this snake who had cost him so much. Cost him Stacey.

Merrick sobbed for mercy, the mercy the man wasn't capable of feeling for others. Steele thumbed back the hammer on the rifle. Merrick heard the click. He crawled closer to Steele, his eyes wet with tears.

"Please, Joshua, I beg you."

Steele touched the gun barrel to Merrick's head. The man shrieked in horror, closing his eyes, and unaccountably holding his ears. Sweat broke out on Steele's forehead. His jaw worked. His finger tightened on the trigger. His whole field of vision was reduced to Merrick's head at the end of his rifle barrel. Four years. The finger tensed. Four long years. He wanted this monster dead. And now it was going to happen. Just squeeze the trigger. Squeeze it. He fired the gun.

Stacey paced the confines of her small hotel room. Joshua had been gone for three hours. She had cried until she had no tears left. Her heart ached with grief. It was as though Joshua had died. And it came to her that it was for the third time. She had thought him dead when the letter came from the War Department four years ago. She had thought him dead when Merrick told Barnett where to find him. And now, though he lived, she would never see him again. And it was the same as if he had died.

"No!" she screamed aloud. "Not again, damn you!" She stared with unseeing eyes out the window of the room. What had given Joshua Steele the consummate arrogance to assume that he would kill Merrick? Merrick wasn't stupid. It just might end up the other way around.

"Damn you, Joshua!" she raged in the stillness of her room. "You have no right to do this to me! No right to make me love you! No right to leave me behind! I hate you! Do you hear me, Joshua Steele? I hate your damn guts!"

She slammed a gloved fist into the mirror of the room's wretched-looking vanity. The already cracked glass shattered into fragments. She stomped on several of the larger pieces which had fallen to the floor. "Is it seven years bad luck for each piece I break?" she screamed. "Because it won't work! Nothing worse can ever happen to me, Joshua." She laughed hysterically. "Oh, God, Joshua, you're destroying us both."

If Joshua murdered Merrick, he might feel self-righteously avenged for a week, a month, even longer. But the day would come when he would realize that Merrick had won after all. That Merrick had brought him down that final rung to the level of the beast. That he and Merrick were interchangeable save for motive. One money. The other revenge.

"No, Joshua, I won't let you throw away what we have. I won't let you kill Merrick. If you kill him, you kill us. That's why you aren't coming back, isn't it? Well, hear this Mr. Steele, you are coming back!" Her voice grew soft. "You are."

She wiped away the last of her tears. "That's quite enough, Eustacia," she scolded. "You've got some serious tracking to do." She stuffed the pistol Joshua had left her into her belt. Then she picked up the money he had meant to be used for a stagecoach ticket. Determination in her every step, she hurried to the livery. There she bought her own mare, which had been left behind by Merrick.

Checking the ground leading out of town, she quickly recognized the print of Joshua's horse. She mounted the mare and nudged her into a ground-eating trot.

Apparently breaking the mirror hadn't done too much damage to her fortunes after all. The next morning she spied Joshua breaking camp. She kept a reasonable distance after that, not wanting to confront him until he'd actually found Merrick. If she went to him now, he would just send her back to town, or try to. She would wait.

All the next day she stayed just far enough behind him so that she did not lose him. She was surprised that she could so easily elude his detection. Evidently his hatred for Merrick was making him oblivious to all but the tracks of Merrick's horse. She waited until Joshua had ridden on, then she checked Merrick's latest camp herself. Merrick had been there only hours before. Her throat felt dry. Her heart pounded. She prayed that Joshua's thirst for vengeance didn't get him killed. Mounting the mare, she kept to a steady pace, half a mile behind Steele.

She heard the shots before she saw the battle. Kicking the horse into a run, she rode as close as she could without being seen. Dismounting, she tied the horse to a nearby tree. Terrified at what she might see, she nevertheless scrambled to the top of a pile of rocks and peered over. She gripped the big .44 in both hands.

Merrick and Joshua were exchanging bullets almost directly beneath her. Merrick was higher up the slope. He seemed to panic. She watched as his horse spooked and ran. Joshua moved away from the shelter of the rocks, his rifle hanging carelessly at his side. His back was to her. She wanted to scream at him, to beg him not to shoot, but the words caught in her throat.

She scurried down the rocks. Moving quietly, she took up a position about twenty yards behind Steele. Neither man noticed her. Steele was too intent on Merrick. Merrick was too intent on staying alive.

Suddenly Merrick said something Stacey couldn't hear. Joshua pumped a bullet into his leg. She almost screamed, but at the last second managed to swallow it. She padded closer. Merrick was begging for his life now, his sobs made her cringe.

Stacey watched with horrified fascination as Joshua settled his rifle against Merrick's head. Merrick was so frightened he couldn't even crawl away. He only sobbed louder. She could almost feel the tension in Joshua. He was waging a war with himself. She wanted to call out to him, but knew suddenly that as much as she ached for him not to kill Merrick, it had to be his decision alone. If she asked him to stop, he would, but it would hang between them for the rest of their lives.

Her heart pounding, she could only stare. She was close enough to hear the hammer click back on the rifle, close enough to see the sweat on the back of Joshua's neck, the corded muscles of his back that were tense with strain.

The gun fired. Stacey screamed.

At the last instant Joshua had jerked the gun and fired into the ground beside Merrick's head. He whirled at the sound of Stacey's scream, astonished to see her standing there. "Are you satisfied?" he shouted. "Do you see what you've done to me, woman?"

She stared at him. His voice was trembling with rage. And it was directed at her.

"For four years I've slept, ate, and dreamed of killing this bastard. Nothing else mattered. Nothing. And then I had to meet you again." In frustrated fury he turned and kicked the grovelling Merrick squarely in the head, knocking him out. He heaved the gun on the ground in disgust.

"And now you can't commit murder," she whispered.

Her eyes remained on Joshua. His back was to her, as he strode over to his horse. Neither of them saw Merrick open his eyes. He lay still, staring at the gun six inches from his right hand.

Stacey didn't move. Joshua fingered the trailing reins of his horse, but did not turn to face her. He spoke in a voice just loud enough for her to hear. "A man never fought so hard for so long in a losing cause, Stacey. I didn't want to love you. God knows, I didn't want to. Because I knew that loving you would bring me face to face with what I had become. And I wouldn't much like what I saw."

Stacey's heart thudded wildly. Was Joshua truly telling her he loved her? Loved her!

Merrick's fingers trembled. He would go for the gun and destroy Steele with one well-aimed bullet. All he had to do was reach for it. Now, while Steele's back was still to him. Now! With one swift motion he gripped the weapon and brought it to bear on Steele's back.

Out of the corner of her eye, Stacey caught the movement. "Joshua!" she screamed.

Steele dove sideways, but there was nowhere to hide. He had no gun.

Without conscious thought Stacey brought her gun up. As Merrick fired at Joshua, she fired at Merrick. He gaped at her in shocked surprise, aware of her presence the split second before he died.

To Stacey it all seemed to happen in slow motion. The bullet slammed into Merrick's chest, jerking him back, then he pitched forward face down in the dirt. Several seconds passed before the full import of what she had done registered on her mind. Then she screamed.

"No! No, no, no!" She raced toward Merrick. Flinging him on his back, she tore his shirt open, staring at the gaping wound in his chest. She ripped at his shirt in a futile attempt to make a bandage to cover the blood.

Steele reached Merrick's body at the same time. "He's dead, Stacey," he said, reaching down and gripping her shoulders. "He's dead."

"No," she screamed over and over. "He can't be dead. I'm a doctor. I don't kill people. No! I came to stop you from killing him, not to kill him myself!"

Her hands were covered with blood as she sought to treat the wound in Merrick's lifeless chest. Joshua had to forcibly drag her away from the body. She beat against his chest with her fists. "Damn you! Damn you! You've made me a murderer!" She fought to be free of him, but he wouldn't let go. He held on until she stopped struggling, then he wrapped his arms around her.

Stacey was inconsolable. One minute her life had been heaven. Joshua had not murdered Merrick. And he was telling her that it was because he loved her. Loved her! And the next minute she had taken a man's life. She cried herself into an exhausted sleep, nestled in Steele's protective arms.

When she'd been asleep for several minutes, Joshua shifted her gently to the ground beside him. He rose and walked toward Merrick. He felt no elation looking down at the body of the man he had ached to kill for so long. He felt only a numbing sickness that Stacey

476

had been drawn into his miasma of hate. Her life was dedicated to saving lives. He had dedicated the last four years to ending one. He scraped out a shallow grave and rolled the body into it, wishing to heaven that the bullet hadn't killed Merrick.

Once during the night, he woke to find her lying quietly beside him, her eyes open, but unseeing. With the tips of his fingers he traced the outline of her face. The bruises were all but gone. He kissed her lips, caressed her hair, but she did not respond. He held her closer.

The next morning Joshua kept a blanket wrapped around her, as he settled her on his horse. He mounted Merrick's gelding. Stacey stared straight ahead, saying nothing, seemingly aware of nothing. Her clothes were stained with Merrick's dried blood. Joshua had tried to undress her during the night, but she had started screaming, so he had stopped. He would try again later.

Toward noon they came upon a narrow, tumbling stream. Joshua shifted in his saddle to face her. He had been leading her horse all morning. "I want you to take a bath, Stacey," he said, speaking slowly and carefully, trying to gauge how much of what he said registered on her mind. Gently he eased her off of the horse and into his arms. She did not object this time when he undressed her. He forced himself to be impersonal, detached. She was so lovely. Yanking off his boots, he carried her out to mid-stream and set her down in the shallow water. He waded back to shore and set about washing her clothes.

The coldness of the water seemed to shock some sensibility back into her. She moved a little, turning to see Joshua washing her shirt in the stream. It was then that she looked down and noticed for the first time that she was naked. She ducked into the water until it reached her neck.

"Why did you take my clothes off?" she asked him, her voice a shade bewildered.

Joshua looked up, surprised to hear her speak. "They were filthy," he said simply, though his heart was pounding.

"I killed him, didn't I?" she whispered, the events of the preceding day washing over her.

"He would have killed me."

Tears rimmed her eyes. "I'm a doctor. I killed a human being."

"You killed a man who would have shot me in the back, and if you hadn't shot him then, he would have killed you too."

Her hands moved to massage her arms against the chill water. She considered what he said. In her mind she knew he was right. But her heart was harder to convince. She held his steady gaze.

"He would have killed me," he repeated.

"I know," she murmured finally.

Joshua finished washing out her clothes and hung them on a nearby branch to dry. He hunkered down on the shore, regarding her thoughtfully. "Did I ever tell you, you're beautiful when you bathe?" His voice was husky.

Her skin began to tingle with warmth in spite of the chilly temperature of the water. She remembered how he had accidentally intruded on her bath in Elizabethtown. It seemed like a lifetime ago. This was the first time he had ever referred to it. "That really was horrid of you," she said quietly.

"Yes, it was."

She was surprised by the sincerity in his voice. "Then why did you do it?"

"Because I couldn't take my eyes off you, Stacey. Then—or now." He stood, his eyes locked on hers. Quickly he shed his clothes.

Stacey stood up. The water that had covered her to her neck, now reached only to her waist. She did not hide her breasts from his hungry stare.

"Why did you wait so long to tell me you loved me, Joshua?" she probed softly. "Why didn't you even want to love me?"

He waded into the water, stopping in front of her. His eyes caressed her as surely as if they were his hands. "I was dead," he said quietly. "After what Merrick had done to me, I was still breathing, but I was dead. For four years I had no life but hate. And then there you were—dodging bullets in Elizabethtown, and those emerald eyes that had haunted my dreams started to haunt my days as well.

"It was a hopeless fight." He reached out to gently caress her soft, pliant breasts with his palms. Even in the coldness of the water, his body was fevered, and he was more than ready to take her. "Piece by piece you healed me, Stacey. Your love made me feel again, made me care. It was like being reborn."

He scooped her into his arms and carried her to the grassy shore. He lay beside her, gliding his hands along her already responding body.

"I want you to stay in Colorado with me, Stacey," he said, "I want to share my life with you." He nuzzled his mouth against her throat. "My ranch isn't far from here. We can make love beside my mountain lake." His hand stroked her belly. "We'll have beautiful babies, and you can doctor to your heart's content on the local Indians, cowhands, and prospectors." His fingertips were featherlight against her flesh.

"Be my wife, Stacey. I don't just love you. I worship you. You don't know the power you have over me. Not killing Merrick was just a tiny sample." He kissed her long and deeply. "Love me, Stacey. I need you to love me. You're my life."

Her love had healed his hate. Now his love healed her despair. "Forever, Joshua," she promised, arching toward him, as each transported the other to paradise.